Veterans of

Book nine of the Veteran (

By: William Ke

CW00431774

Visit the author's website **http://www.williamkelso.co.uk/**

William Kelso is also the author of:

The Shield of Rome

The Fortune of Carthage

Devotio: The House of Mus

Caledonia - Book One of the Veteran of Rome series

Hibernia - Book Two of the Veteran of Rome series

Britannia – Book Three of the Veteran of Rome series

Hyperborea – Book Four of the Veteran of Rome series

Germania – Book Five of the Veteran of Rome series

The Dacian War – Book Six of the Veteran of Rome series

Armenia Capta – Book Seven of the Veteran of Rome series

Rome and the Conquest of Mesopotamia – Book Eight of the Veteran of Rome series

Published in 2018 by KelsoBooks Ltd. Copyright © William Kelso. First Edition

The author has asserted their moral right under the Copyright, Designs and Patents Act, 1988, to be identified as the author of this work.

A CIP catalogue record for this title is available from the British Library.

To the enduring friendship between the United Kingdom and the Kingdom of the Netherlands

ABOUT ME

Hello, my name is William Kelso. I was born in the Netherlands to British parents. My interest in history and in particular military history started at a very young age when I was lucky enough to hear my grandfather describing his experiences of serving in the RAF in North Africa and Italy during World War 2. Recently my family has discovered that one of my Scottish/Northern Irish ancestors fought under Wellington at the Battle of Waterloo in 1815.

I love writing and bringing to life the ancient world of Rome, Carthage and the Germanic and Celtic tribes. It's my thing. My aim is to write 100 books in my lifetime. After graduation, I worked for 22 years in financial publishing and event management in the city of London as a salesman for some big conference organizers, trying to weave my stories in the evenings after dinner and in weekends. Working in the heart of the original Roman city of Londinium I spent many years walking its streets and visiting the places, the names of which still commemorate the 2,000-year-old ancient Roman capital of Britannia, London Wall, Watling Street, London Bridge and Walbrook. The city of London if you know where to look has many fascinating historical corners. So, since the 2nd March 2017 I have taken the plunge and become a full-time writer. Stories as a form of entertainment are as old as cave man and telling them is what I want to do.

My books are all about ancient Rome, especially the early to mid-republic as this was the age of true Roman greatness. My books include, The Shield of Rome, The Fortune of Carthage, Devotio: The House of Mus and the nine books of the Veteran of Rome series - Caledonia (1), Hibernia (2), Britannia (3), Hyperborea (4), Germania (5), The Dacian War (6), Armenia Capta (7), Rome and the Conquest of Mesopotamia (8) and Veterans of Rome (9). So, go on. Give them a go.

In my spare time, I help my brother, who is also a Winston Churchill impersonator, run his battlefield tours company which takes people around the battlefields of Arnhem, Dunkirk, Agincourt, Normandy, the Rhine crossing and Monte Cassino. I live in London with my wife and support the "Help for Heroes" charity and a tiger in India.

Please visit my website http://www.williamkelso.co.uk/ and have a look at my historical video blog!

Feel free to write to me with any feedback on my books. Email: william@kelsoevents.co.uk

Veterans of Rome

Book nine of the Veteran of Rome series

Chapter One – Garrison Commander

The City of Seleucia, province of Mesopotamia, late summer 116 AD

The narrow, dusty, mud-brick coloured city-street was packed and teeming with people going about their daily business. It was noon and, in the blue, cloudless sky, the relentless sun beat down on the populace, smothering the city in a blanket of stifling, airless heat. The locals however seemed not to notice the heat, the dust, that got everywhere, or the clouds of annoying flies. Nor did they seem bothered by the smell of rotting piles of garbage in the alleys and the stench of raw sewage coming from the nearby canal. It was always like that. More noticeable were the cheerful advertising cries of the vendors, operating out of their shops or their small push-carts. They filled the street, competing for attention with barking dogs, the mooing of the great horned water buffalo, the rattle of wagon wheels and shrill, excited children's voices.

It was just another day in the vast, complicated metropolis over which he had been appointed the Roman military commander Fergus thought, as he led the small band of Roman soldiers down the street. In the fierce sunlight, the legionaries' body armour, shields, equipment and weapons gleamed and jangled. The crunch of the hobnailed army boots on the paving stones sounded menacing and alien. In the street ahead, the people lowered their gazes, as they caught sight of the approaching Romans and quickly stepped aside. In their shops the voices of the shopkeepers seemed to falter. Fergus, clad in his fine tribune's cloak and wearing a plumed helmet over his short red hair, ignored the furtive glances and the occasional hiss as he pushed on down the street towards the temple of Mithras. His tanned, handsome face remained stoic and expressionless. As commander of the thousand strong Roman city garrison, in this city of six-hundred thousand people, he was in ultimate charge of everything that went on. He had quickly learned that it was a difficult and thankless job. It was a grave responsibility that made him feel much older than thirty. Most of his time had been taken up trying to sort out and reconcile the various competing political, ethnic, economic and religious factions that inhabited Seleucia. Then he had to deal with the interests of the rich versus the poor; the tensions between different religious and ethnic factions; problems with the food supply and trade as well as disputes over water resources and land boundaries. On top of that he had been tasked with implementing Roman law in a city where no one spoke Latin and where no one was used to Roman legal concepts. But the hardest task of all, and yet the most important, was how to effectively tax the locals without causing them to riot. That was indeed a delicate balance. He'd had absolutely no advice or training in how to run the affairs of such a huge, complicated cosmopolitan city. The best he could do was try to apply common sense and a certain amount of diplomacy and charm. But the emperor Trajan was counting on him to do a good job and his career prospects hinged on how he handled this command.

Up ahead along the crowded street, Fergus caught sight of the temple of Mithras. The large mud-brick building looked inconspicuous, but Fergus had been there before. Hiding his irritation, he continued down the street. He was a busy man, with a shed-load of administrative work stacking up back at HQ. He really had better things to do than be out here today. The priests of Mithras had better have a good argument for forcing him to come all the way out here to meet them.

Close to the entrance, a girl of around eleven or twelve was sitting in her usual spot, pressed up against the temple wall, with a small terracotta bowl placed on the ground before her. She was begging.

"Dio," Fergus said sharply, glancing at the old centurion who was accompanying the eight-man Roman close-protection squad, "let's try and keep this brief. You and the men will remain outside the temple. The translator and I will be the only ones to go inside. I don't want the priests to get nervous. You know how these Parthians feel about us going into their temples."

"Isn't that the whole point Sir," Dio said in a sour voice as the old veteran officer cast about him. "A people should know when they are conquered. I am getting tired of respecting their feelings and customs. This city has more mood swings than a company's worth of women. The men are growing frustrated Sir. They were trained to fight. Not this shit."

"Just do it," Fergus said wearily, as he turned to the little beggar girl sitting close to the temple entrance.

The girl had seen him and, as she recognised him, her eyes seemed to light up. As the eight-man legionary squad came to a halt at the temple doors, Fergus broke away from his escort and strode up to the girl and looked down at her. Bravely she looked back up at him. For a moment the two of them said nothing. Then solemnly Fergus bent down and placed a single silver coin in the girl's bowl. The girl's eyes widened, and she blushed as she saw the colour of the metal. Fergus sighed. For as long as he could remember the girl had been sitting begging in the same spot. On his many journeys out into the central market and business district, he had never failed to give her a coin, for the girl reminded him of his eldest daughter Briana. The likeness between the two girls was truly remarkable. It had been nine months since he had last seen Galena and his girls.

"Sir, the priests," Dio called out impatiently.

Fergus gave the girl a wink. Then he turned away and strode up the temple steps towards the doors leading into the building. As he did, the Greek translator hastily appeared at his side. The Greek seemed nervous.

Inside the dark, stiflingly hot building Fergus was greeted by a silent, tense looking priest. Reaching up to undo his plumed helmet, Fergus tucked it under his arm, wiped the sweat and dust from his forehead, and followed the servant of Mithras down a flight of stairs and into the dark subterranean world. Burning oil lamps lit up the staircase and the thick scent of incense hung in the air. As he reached the bottom of the stairs, Fergus was confronted by three solemn and silent men with their arms folded across their chests. The priests were barring his way. Fergus paused to allow his eyes to adjust to the darkness. The priests were waiting for him in a long rectangular room that was completely empty but through a doorway, close by, he caught sight of a stone statue of a man killing a bull. The mysteries of Mithras were just that – mysteries and had been of no concern to him until the Parthian priests had refused to allow some of his soldiers to be initiated into the cult. That refusal had forced him to come to speak with them – using precious time that he could ill-afford.

The three stubborn-looking Parthians were watching him carefully. They didn't seem intimidated by his presence. For a moment Fergus studied their faces. He and all the Romans in the city garrison were fully aware that the locals didn't want them here. Rome was viewed as a foreign occupying force. The simmering hostility and resentment from the populace had been limited to passive resistance, small acts of disobedience, mutterings in the street and the odd stone thrown at his troops. But now the temple of Mithras had refused his soldiers permission to join the cult and that was unacceptable. With a little respectful nod, Fergus addressed the three Parthians with a greeting in their own language. The few words in the Parthian language which he'd picked up, were only enough for the most basic of greetings, but as he had learned, it was the best way in which to get the discussion with the locals off to a good start.

"Tell them," Fergus said as he turned to his translator, "that I fully respect their right to choose who may be initiated into the seven grades of the Mithras mysteries but that I cannot accept having my soldiers excluded, just because they are Romans. Tell them that this is unacceptable. Religion should be open to all."

Quickly the Greek translated, but across from him the three Parthians seemed unmoved. At last, one of them spoke in reply.

"He says Sir," the Greek stammered, "that you are correct. They have the right to refuse to initiate men into the mysteries. So, they don't know what wrong they have done."

"They have refused all the requests of my troops," Fergus said sharply "They have refused to accept a single Roman into the mysteries. That is unacceptable. I am here to see that the temple changes its ways."

As one of the Parthians replied, the Greek hastily translated.

"He says that they have broken no laws," the translator said, speaking quickly. "He says the fact that no Romans were initiated is because the men were not of the right character. They are not true believers. That's all."

Fergus took a deep breath as he fixed his eyes on the three priests.

"Mithras accepts Romans in other places, why not here?" Fergus shot back.

"They say they cannot speak on behalf of other temples," the Greek translated as one of the Parthian priests spoke up. "But here in Seleucia none of the Romans who have come forth have been suitable."

Fergus grunted in frustration. He was losing the argument. He could not leave the temple without a result to show his men, but equally he could not force the priests to allow his men to join the cult. Turning his eyes to the floor he remained silent for a long moment.

"Tell them," Fergus said at last, as he turned to the Greek translator, "that if they allow some of my men to be initiated into the mysteries, that I shall consider providing the temple and its priests with a tax break."

As the Greek translated his words, Fergus studied the Parthians carefully. Most issues and problems in this city, he had found, could be solved by using money. But that created its own problems, for Trajan and the Roman High Command expected the flow of money to be coming out of the city and not going into it. As the Greek fell silent the airless room too, fell silent. The Parthians seemed to be considering his offer in silence. Then one of them spoke up, his dark eyes gleaming in the light from the burning oil lamps.

"He says it doesn't matter anymore," the Greek translated and as he did, the translator frowned. "He says that you should not have come here."

Across from Fergus the three priests of Mithras had turned and were filing out of the room through another doorway. Confused, Fergus called them back, but the Parthians didn't heed his call.

"What the fuck was that all about?" Fergus hissed, as he rounded on the Greek. "What did they mean, "it doesn't matter anymore?"

"I don't know Sir," the translator stammered. "It's very odd behaviour indeed. Shall I ask them to come back into the room?"

For a moment Fergus hesitated. Then he shook his head in disgust and turned towards the staircase.

"No, I think I have had enough for today," he growled. "We have wasted enough time already. Let's get back."

***

Fergus blinked and squinted as he emerged into the fierce and bright sunlight. Outside in the street, Dio and the eight legionaries were standing around looking bored. As Fergus reappeared Dio came towards him.

"Sir," the veteran growled as he fixed Fergus with an inquisitive look.

Fergus shook his head and frowned.

"Odd," he murmured, "I thought I had made them a good offer, but it was as if they suddenly lost interest. I can't explain it. A fucking waste of time."

It was Dio's turn to frown.

"What did they say Sir?" Dio pressed.

"That it doesn't matter anymore and that I shouldn't have come here," Fergus replied, as he turned to gaze around at the people in the street. Amongst the throng of locals going about their business, no one however seemed to be paying the Romans any attention.

Then before Fergus could say anything else, he suddenly felt a small hand clasp hold of his arm. Surprised he turned and looked down to see the beggar girl holding onto him. The girl was looking up at him with her large brown eyes. She seemed completely unafraid, dwarfed as she was by the big burly and heavily-armed Roman soldiers standing around her. For a long moment none of the Romans spoke or made a move as they stared at the girl holding onto their commander's arm. Sensing that Dio was about to raise his voice and chase the girl away, Fergus quickly pre-empted him.

"It's all right boys," Fergus said sharply as he gazed down at the little girl. "It's all right. Ask her what she wants?"

The girl was gazing up at him, staring in fascination at Fergus's red hair. At Fergus's side the Greek hastily spoke but the girl did not answer. And as she continued to gaze at his hair Fergus suddenly understood. The girl must have never seen red hair before.

The Greek repeated his question and this time the girl answered and as she did, she started to walk away, still clutching Fergus's arm and trying to pull Fergus with her.

"She says that you are in danger Sir," the translator stammered. "She says that you should come with her."

"Danger," Fergus blurted out, as he refused to move.

At his side the girl tugged at his arm again and spoke out once more in her childish voice, oblivious to her surroundings and who was listening.

"Yes," the Greek hissed. "She says people are going to try to hurt you. She says you are her friend. She will help you."

"What the fuck," Dio hissed, his eyes widening in alarm. "What is she talking about?"

"Ask her who is going to try to hurt me," Fergus said sharply, as he kept his eyes on the girl tugging at his arm

In response the girl replied with a single word and as she did, she looked up at Fergus, silently imploring him to follow her.

"Everyone," the Greek translator gasped.

For a stunned moment none of the Romans was capable of speaking. Then a grim look appeared on Dio's face.

"If she is speaking the truth, she is talking about an uprising Sir," the centurion hissed with sudden urgency. "A fucking uprising. We should get back to the garrison right now. Even if it's a false alarm."

Fergus was staring in growing shock and alarm at the girl clutching his arm. He had not seen this coming. Hastily he turned to look around at the people in the street, but all seemed normal and peaceful. Around him however he noticed a sudden tension had spread amongst his escort. They were ten Romans alone in the middle of a vast and hostile city.

Behind them the doors to the temple suddenly slammed shut and from inside the building Fergus heard what sounded like a cross bar being placed into position. The temple was bolting its doors. Quickly Fergus turned to look down at the girl as he tried to decide on what to do.

"How does she know that everyone is going to hurt me?" he snapped.

As the translator listened to the girl's reply his face turned ashen. "She says," the Greek stammered, "that she heard her uncle talking about it with her mother. But you are her friend. She wants to help you. She says you should come with her. You can hide in her mother's house."

Softly Fergus swore to himself. He had to get back to the relative safety of garrison HQ, but some instinct was warning him from taking the direct path. As he stared at the closed temple doors, his face suddenly darkened.

"Those fucking priests lured us out here for this purpose," Fergus hissed with sudden insight, as he tried to keep calm. "The rebels know we are here. Vulnerable, out in the open and far from our men. That must be their plan. It's nearly a mile back to the camp. But we will never make it. If the girl is speaking the truth, then they are going to try and take us on our way back. The roads leading across the canals will be watched. What better way to start an uprising than by capturing or killing the Roman garrison commander."

"So, what do we do?" Dio snapped, as he too turned to look around him with growing alarm.

Quickly Fergus turned to look down at the girl.

"We will go with her and hide up until it's dark," Fergus said decisively. "Then tonight under the cover of darkness we shall try and make our way back to our camp."

"You want to go with this girl" Dio exclaimed in disbelief. "You are going to trust her. For all we know she could be part of this whole fucking plot."

"We need to get off the streets," Fergus snapped.

"We need to warn the garrison of this uprising Sir," Dio retorted.

But Fergus shook his head. "No," he said firmly. "They lured us out here. They know we are here. We will never get back to the garrison, not now. I have put contingency plans in place for just such an eventuality. Britannicus is in command whilst I am away from HQ. He has standing orders in case of an uprising. He knows what to do. He can handle it."

The girl tugged again at Fergus's arm and this time he allowed her to lead him towards an alley that ran alongside the temple walls. Behind him Dio, the Greek translator and the anxious legionaries quickly followed.

Away from the busy and noisy main street, Fergus found himself in a maze of narrow, rubbish-strewn alleys and single-storey mud-brick buildings. There was no one about, and the only sign of life was a stray dog sniffing around in the rubbish. As the girl vanished through the dark doorway and into one of the nondescript buildings, Fergus hesitated. Behind him he heard Dio drawing his gladius from its sheath. Doing the same he took a deep breath and stepped through the entrance and into the building. In the gloom it took his eyes a moment to adjust. The building consisted of just a single room. A couple of straw sleeping mattresses lay on the floor and in the corner were a few small cooking pots and amphorae. A flight of stairs led up to the roof. Behind him Dio and the men from his close protection escort piled into the room, weapons drawn and boots scraping on the earthen floor. As they did so a muffled female voice cried out in fright and alarm. In the gloom Fergus caught sight of the girl standing beside an older woman. The older woman had her hand pressed to her mouth and was gazing at the Romans in absolute horror.

"Secure the building," Dio snarled at the legionaries. "You two," the centurion said, pointing at two of the soldiers, "barricade that door and you, get up onto the roof. Warn us if you see trouble approaching but don't let people see you. The rest of you stay out of sight and keep quiet. We're going to be here for a while."

"What's going on Sir?" one of the legionaries asked in an anxious voice.

"Fuck knows," Dio growled as he took up position beside the doorway.

As the soldiers rushed to their positions, Fergus replaced his sword in its sheath and turned to the two women. The little girl was looking up at him, her expression suddenly anxious. Her mother was huddled in a corner, shaking.

"Tell them that they have nothing to fear," Fergus said sharply. "But I can't let them leave the house. We will be staying until its dark. And ask her when she is expecting her man to come home?"

The older woman's voice came out as a whisper.

"She says he is not here. He has gone east to fight," the Greek said hastily.

Fergus muttered something to himself. Then he turned to study the little girl who was standing holding her mother's hand.

"Tell her that she has a very brave daughter," Fergus said at last.

***

It was growing late when one of the Roman lookouts on the roof called out a soft warning. Quickly Fergus scrambled to his feet and headed up the stairs. In the dark, hot and stuffy room below, the silent legionaries sat and crouched along the walls waiting for darkness. As he carefully slithered out onto the flat roof, Fergus could see and hear the growing tumult. The Roman legionary, lying flat on his stomach, did not need to point out what was happening. To the west, in the direction of the former governor's palace where the Roman garrison had made its HQ, numerous columns of black smoke were rising into the blue sky and a growing human din was becoming audible. For a moment Fergus lay on his stomach and stared at the spectacle. The fires and noise could mean only one thing. An uprising had indeed taken place. The girl had been speaking the truth. Behind him he heard someone creeping up the stairs and a moment later Dio came crawling towards him. The centurion swore softly as he caught sight of the columns of smoke.

"We will try and make our way back when its fully dark," Fergus murmured.

"You are counting on there still being a Roman garrison left," Dio said quietly, as he gazed at the columns of smoke.

"There is an emergency contingency plan," Fergus said carefully. "Our defences are strong. The palace is protected on three sides by a canal and backs up against the city walls. In an emergency the plan is to set fire to the canals. Hopefully that is what those columns of smoke are about." Fergus paused as he studied the scene. "Each bridge across the canals is fortified and guarded by our men," he continued. "Britannicus has standing orders to hold those bridges at all costs. He will carry out his orders. He will hold fast."

"You have a lot of confidence in that young tribune," Dio growled unhappily.

Fergus did not reply as he gazed at the columns of black smoke. The shock of realising that he had an uprising on his hands had not yet faded. Having seen enough, he turned and crawled back to the stairs. In the dark, hot room below, Fergus paused to wipe the sweat and dust from his face. The girl and her mother were now sitting in a corner on one of the sleeping mattresses, tensely watching his every move. Moving towards them Fergus crouched, reached for his fine, plumed tribune's helmet and beckoned for the translator to join him.

"Tell her," he said in a stern, serious voice as he fixed his gaze on the older woman, "that we shall be leaving soon and that I shall not forget her hospitality. After we have gone she should get herself and her daughter out of Seleucia whilst she still can and stay away. We may be on the backfoot today, but Rome will never forgive this uprising. When our vengeance comes it will be overwhelming, merciless and brutal. People are going to die, many, many people and the city is likely to be burned to the ground."

Then Fergus turned to the girl and solemnly handed her his helmet. "Tell her that I will be back one day to collect this," he said.

Chapter Two - Flight or Fight

Night had come and, in the darkness, to the west in the direction of the governor's palace and the Roman HQ, Fergus could make out the reddish glow of numerous fires. Along the alley wall the small band of Romans crouched in the gloom. The men were clutching their large oval shields and throwing spears. Around them the night was calm but disturbed by the occasional scream and shriek. Fergus pressed up against the wall as he strained to listen. In the maze of mud-brick buildings and alleys nothing moved, and a balmy night breeze was bringing some welcome refreshment to the stale air. During the hours they'd spent hiding in the house, the lookout up on the roof had reported gangs of armed men roaming the streets. The gangs seemed to be searching for people who had collaborated with the Roman garrison. They were settling scores. At one point they had appeared very close. The rebels had forced their way into a nearby house, had dragged out a man and executed him there and then in the street. The killing had laid to rest any doubts about the seriousness of the situation. Calmly Fergus turned to look at the men crouching in a line behind him. The shock of having an uprising on his hands had been replaced by a cold, primitive determination to survive. And anger too. For the city seemed to have rejected all his efforts to maintain a reasonably just rule. This uprising was a personal slap in the face. Fergus bit his lip. He had no way of knowing whether the Roman garrison was still in control of the governor's palace or had been massacred by the rebels. But he had no choice but to trust that Britannicus had held those crucial bridges. There was no other way out. All the city gates would by now be in the hands of the rebels and he couldn't hide here forever.

"Let's go," Fergus whispered, as he left his position and started forwards along the alley. Closely behind him Dio and the others hastened after him, trying to remain as silent as possible. At the end of the alley Fergus paused. He had no idea how to get through this massive maze of mud-brick buildings and alleys. To his left and right he could see nothing in the darkness. The only thing guiding him was the distant reddish glow of the fires that seemed to line the banks of the canal.

Turning right he began to carefully move on down the dark alley. In the night all seemed peaceful and quiet but, as he reached the end of the passage Fergus nearly tripped over the body of a man lying in the dirt. Pausing beside the corpse, Fergus steadied his breathing and strained to listen. Somewhere close by a dog had started to bark. It was followed by a woman's high-pitched scream. Ahead in the gloom the crossroads seemed to split into four separate alleys. Which one to take? It was impossible to know which one would lead them to the canal. Hissing a quick command to the men behind him, he darted across the intersection and into one of the alleys. The sound of his hobnailed boots on the gravel sounded horribly loud. As he cautiously advanced down the passage with Corbulo's old gladius gleaming in his hand he suddenly sensed movement up ahead. A man was urinating onto a pile of stinking rubbish. He had his back turned to the Romans and was softly singing to himself as if drunk. Fergus came to an abrupt halt. If the man turned around and came towards him there was no way he would not spot them. Behind him Fergus sensed his men pressed up against the alley wall, waiting to move on. Quickly switching his sword into his left-hand, Fergus strode towards the man, grasped hold of his hair and slammed the man's forehead into the wall knocking him out. As the Romans surged forwards up the passageway, Fergus lowered the unconscious man into the pile of rubbish and quickly turned to listen but in the darkness, all remained peaceful.

The maze of alleys, buildings and passageways seemed to go on forever but steadily the reddish glow of the fires drew nearer. The buildings and homes too seemed to be growing grander the nearer to the former governor's palace they got. Pausing along an alley to listen and gain his bearings, Fergus suddenly tasted the distinctive smell of burning petroleum and as he did he blushed with sudden hope. Setting the canals on fire with petroleum was part of his emergency contingency plan. Had Britannicus managed to carry it out?

"Do you smell that boys," Fergus hissed, as he turned to the men crouching behind him in the darkness. "They have set fire to the canal. Our men must still be in control of the palace. Not far now."

"How the fuck are we going to get across a burning canal Sir?" a voice whispered in the darkness.

Fergus did not reply as he turned to peer down the passageway. He hadn't worked that out yet. Cautiously he started moving again and just as he did, a shout rent the darkness. Instinctively Fergus stopped and waited. The shout came again. It was a man's voice. Coming towards him down the alley was a figure holding a burning torch. Fergus stiffened. There was nowhere to hide. The man would be upon them within seconds. Grimly Fergus waited for the inevitable discovery. The stranger clutching his flaming torch seemed oblivious to their presence, but as he finally caught sight of Fergus, he came to an abrupt, surprised halt. For a moment no one moved or said a word. In the flickering and hissing torch light the man was staring at Fergus. He looked old, around fifty. Then awkwardly but calmly the man turned around and began to retrace his steps, still without having made a noise. Hastily Fergus followed him, but as he reached the end of the passage the man had vanished into the darkness.

"Shit," Fergus whispered as he waited for the inevitable cry of alarm, but as the silence lengthened none came. Quietly calling out to his men Fergus dashed across the street and crouched in the doorway of a shop. To his right the street seemed to lead into the main city thoroughfare. Cautiously Fergus started towards it, keeping to the side of the road as his men followed one by one. As he reached the corner and caught sight of the wide, colonnaded and paved highway that ran from one end of the city walls to the other, he knelt on one knee. Seleucia was a Hellenistic city and the wide, colonnaded street reminded him of the one in Antioch. Burning torches had been placed in iron holders along the stone columns, bathing the street in a flickering light. Shadows loomed and faded in the firelight. Fergus swore softly as he saw the gang of armed men and women lounging about under the stone columns that held up the roof of the covered walkway. Close by, two figures were dangling lifelessly from the roof. They had been strung up and hanged. The gang seemed to be celebrating for they sounded boisterous and drunk. In the gloom Fergus managed to count fifteen of them before he gave up.

Behind him he sensed his men crouching in a line along the wall. Carefully he turned to survey the wide city street. They were close to the canal for he could see and smell the petroleum fires just beyond the buildings opposite him. The canal could not be more than a hundred yards away. But to get there they would need to cross the main highway and the gang of rebels was blocking the way. Softly Fergus swore again, as his eyes darted from one end of the street to the other. Out in the wide street there was no cover. They would be sitting ducks. As he pondered what to do the night was suddenly rent by a trumpet. Fergus's eyes widened, and he felt his cheeks blushing with sudden elation. The noise had come from the direction of the palace where the Roman garrison was billeted. As he gazed in that direction, the trumpet rang out again and as it did, Fergus recognised the military signal. The trumpet was sounding recall. Britannicus or whoever was in command was sending a signal. He was letting any Roman beyond the canal know that the palace was still in Roman hands. He was calling them back. Behind him he sensed his men stir in anticipation. They too had understood the trumpet call.

Suddenly he felt someone gently tap him on his shoulder.

"Sir, if the canals are on fire," Dio whispered in the darkness, "then our only chance is to get across the bridges. The main bridge across the canal is straight ahead of us just beyond those buildings across the street."

Fergus nodded. "We can't swim across anyway, not in our armour," he whispered. "But the bridges will be barricaded and guarded by our men. We will have to warn and convince them that we are friendlies, or they will slaughter us."

"You may go first Sir. We will follow you," Dio whispered as his grim little smile was lost in the darkness.

Fergus turned his attention back to the group of rebels lounging about under the covered walkway. For a long moment he studied them. Then he turned his head towards Dio who was crouching behind him.

"We go straight across the street at a run," Fergus whispered. "Into that alley over there. If the rebels pursue us we will turn and kill them in that passageway. Warn the men."

In the darkness Fergus could hear Dio whispering to the men behind him. Slowly Fergus rose to his feet. The grip of his gladius, short sword was wet with sweat and suddenly he felt thirsty. Behind him he sensed his men readying themselves for the dash across the wide street.

"Go," he hissed and without waiting for an answer Fergus shot across the wide paved thoroughfare. His hobnailed boots clattered on the paving stones as he headed for the dark and narrow alley entrance. He'd nearly made it across the street, when startled cries of alarm rose from the group of rebels. Darting into the alley, Fergus heard the cries of alarm turn to squeals of outrage. Behind him Dio and the others, clutching their large shields and spears, came racing across the street towards him. As they stormed into the dark, narrow and confined passage, Fergus stopped and whirled round. The alley he was in was just wide enough for two men to pass each other.

"Form up, four ranks of two," he roared. "Front rank, kneel. Second rank shields up."

Instinctively the legionaries obeyed, abruptly turning around to face the direction from which they had just come. Hastily the last two men into the alley dropped down to crouch behind their shields, forming a solid barrier, their spears pointing outwards, whilst their comrades behind them raised their shields to cover them. It was not a moment too soon, for with savage, confident yells and shouts the rebels came charging into the alley in hot pursuit. But in the confined space and lacking any armour or shields of their own the foremost pursuers ran straight into the spear points of the eight legionaries blocking the passage. The result was a sickening slaughter, as pushed on from behind and with no possibility of escape, the foremost men were impaled on the Roman spears. Screams and shrieks rent the dark alley. Despite the pressure the solid Roman wall did not budge.

"Legionaries drive them back," Fergus roared.

With a defiant cry of their own the eight men packed into the narrow passageway began to slowly inch forwards, one foot at a time, driving the enemy back with their shields, whilst maintaining their tight formation. Using their spears to stab and jab at the enemy, the men behind the front rank cried out to each other as if they were participating in a well-practised exercise. Within seconds of the order the rebels broke, turning and fleeing in panic down the alley and back towards the main thoroughfare. The bodies of the slain and the wounded filled the passageway, partially blocking it.

"Let's go. Follow me," Fergus yelled, as the enemy fled. Turning in the opposite direction to the one down which the rebels had retreated, he started down the alley at a run. The clatter of hobnailed boots followed him down the passage. Amongst the buildings and streets around him the city seemed suddenly to have come alive with panicked and wild, confused shouts and screams. The rebels knew where they were now. It would not be long before they attacked again. As he burst out of the alley Fergus nearly slipped on the smooth paving stones. Through a passageway across the street he caught sight of flames leaping up into the night sky. Dashing across the street he stormed into the alley with his men close behind. He could hear them cursing and gasping for breath. Tripping over an obstruction in the dark Fergus went crashing painfully to the ground. Scrambling to his feet he leapt forwards and stumbled onwards until he came to the end of the passage. Raising his fist in the air he silently commanded the men behind him to a halt. Hastily he poked his head around the corner and quickly surveyed the scene. Across the street the canal was ablaze, a roaring wall of petroleum-soaked fire. Shouts rang out along the street running along the canal, but he could not see anyone. Corpses, overturned wagons, dead animals and discarded shields and weapons lay littered about across the road. Hastily Fergus pulled his head back into cover. His chest was heaving from exertion. In the darkness, above the roar of the flames, he could hear his men panting and gasping for breath.

Exhaling Fergus poked his head around the corner for a second time. Amongst the debris and the blasts of heat coming from the canal he caught sight of the bridge leading to the ex-governor's palace. The bridge was perhaps fifty yards away along the street. It was nine or ten yards wide, but it was completely blocked and barricaded by overturned wagons, debris, corpses and large stone blocks placed there before the uprising. Amongst the barricades he could see no sign of movement or the presence of Roman troops. But they had to be there, watching. Quickly Fergus withdrew into cover and turned to the men pressed up against the wall behind him.

"The bridge is blocked by debris," he called out. "But we should be able to climb over it if the defenders let us. We go on my command. Don't stop running until you are across."

Taking a deep breath Fergus poked his head around the corner for a third time.

"Roman soldiers," he screamed at the top of his lungs. "Roman soldiers. We are coming across the bridge. For fucks sake don't shoot. Roman soldiers! We're coming across now."

"Let's go, go, go," Fergus roared as he turned to the men behind him. Then without hesitating he was away, sprinting down the street towards the bridge. As he ran something smacked into the paving stones close by before bouncing away. A moment later a pebble struck his chest armour bouncing away and nearly sending him crashing to the ground. Behind him Dio and the others were racing down the street towards the bridge. The legionaries had discarded their cumbersome shields and were screaming at the top of their voices. Staggering on towards the bridge Fergus grimaced in pain. He had just reached the first barricade when two men came charging towards him clutching knives. They were shouting. With a savage triumphant cry one of them tackled Fergus and the two of them went crashing and tumbling to the ground in a wild, chaotic tangle of arms and legs. Fergus shouted in pain as the sharp blade of a knife sliced into his left arm, but fear lent him desperate strength. Furiously he grappled with his assailant, but his left arm would not work. Suddenly and violently the man's head jerked backwards and Dio appeared and half decapitated the man. As he staggered to his feet, Fergus caught sight of the second attacker frantically being stabbed to death by two legionaries. The other soldiers were already scrambling and climbing over the barricades that blocked the bridge. There was no time to acknowledge Dio.

"Roman soldiers, Roman soldiers, we're coming across the bridge. Don't shoot," Fergus roared as he turned, stumbled and started to clamber over a large square stone block. The pain in his left arm was growing worse. The whole arm hung limply at his side. He gasped as he slithered over the obstruction. Rolling onto the ground his head struck something hard and sticky blood started to seep down his cheek. With a savage determined grunt he heaved himself onto his feet and launched himself at a wagon that had been turned onto its side. Close by, the roar of the flaming petroleum in the canal was blasting with him heat and smoke. Around him he could hear his men shouting in frantic voices. It was every man for himself now. As he squeezed past the wagon, in the eerie reddish fire-light, he was suddenly confronted by men in armour, clutching spears and shields. They were legionaries and they seemed ready to stab him.

"Roman soldiers," Fergus yelled frantically as he stumbled over a rock and went crashing to the ground.

Chapter Three - "We're in a Shit Load of Trouble"

The Roman officers looked grim and anxious. Some of them showed signs of having sustained battle-wounds, their body-armour stained by blood, grime and dust. They were standing in the room that acted as the garrison's command post, gazing silently at Fergus. Outside, through the open doors, in the direction of the mansion's swimming pool the balmy night was far advanced. Dawn was not far off.

"Thank fuck you are back Sir," Britannicus said as he gripped Fergus's shoulder and grinned with relief. "We thought you were dead. We're in a shit load of trouble. The rebels have us besieged within this palace complex. We're completely cut off. They have us pinned down in the palace with our backs against the city walls. All routes in and out are barred. If the whole city has risen, then the rebels outnumber us six-hundred to one. It's a complete-shambles, Sir."

Fergus nodded as he stood in the middle of the room. A fresh bandage had been wrapped around his forehead and his left arm was in a sling. He looked exhausted, but this was no time for rest.

"Talk to me," he said quickly as he turned his gaze to the mosaic floor.

"The first sign of trouble Sir," Britannicus said hastily, "came when the rebels tried to storm the bridges. We had no warning, but the men were alert Sir and we fought them off. I then implemented our contingency plan and set the canal alight. We have plenty of petroleum supplies. The enemy tried a second time to storm the bridges, but we drove them back. Since then it has been quiet. We are in control of the canal line, the bridges and the section of the wall directly behind us but that's it. I am rotating the companies every two hours."

"Morale, casualties, strength reports," Fergus snapped.

"Morale is good Sir," Britannicus replied. "That's about the only thing that is holding up. We lost twenty-three men holding the bridges, eleven of them dead. Two more are expected to die from their wounds tonight. Excluding yourself and Dio's party we had two other patrols out in the city together with four squads guarding the city gates, plus one squad on its way to relieve their comrades at the southern gate. There were also a few men out in the city for private reasons. We have not seen or heard from any of them. You are the only ones to have made it back. We must presume that the men are lost Sir."

Britannicus paused.

"Current garrison strength is eight hundred and twenty-nine legionaries fit for duty, sixty-eight wounded and sick," he said in a quieter voice." Fortunately, the company of Balearic slingers who joined us a few days ago had not yet left for Hatra when the uprising broke out. I have posted them to the canal line. There may be only eighty of them, but they are some of the finest slingers that I have ever seen Sir."

Fergus grunted as he remembered the pebble that had struck his body armour during the mad dash to the bridge.

"What is the state of our supplies? Has there been any contact or news from the garrison across the river in Ctesiphon? Do we know how wide-spread this uprising is?" Fergus growled.

The young tribune sighed.

"We have enough food to withstand a lengthy siege Sir," he said. "It is our water supply that is the problem. With the rebels in control of the city and the countryside outside our only major source of water has become that swimming pool out there. I have started to ration water but even so, we calculate we have three or four days at the most before supplies run out."

Britannicus sighed again. He too looked exhausted. "Regards the garrison in Ctesiphon. We have had no contact. News from beyond the walls is very limited. The rebels control the countryside and the river. They are preventing anyone from getting through. Gangs of them are roaming at will. It's fucking anarchy out there. But it seems that Ctesiphon has not risen in rebellion. The city seems peaceful. We have had this confirmed by Parthian civilians. Maybe they are waiting to see the outcome here in Seleucia before declaring their hand. Or else the presence of Trajan scares them into obedience. It's hard to say Sir. However, the Roman garrison have made no attempt to come to our aid."

"They lack the man-power to come to our aid," Fergus snapped. "Don't expect any help from Ctesiphon. They will have their own problems to deal with."

"Sir, there is also another explanation," Britannicus said quickly. "All through the day we have had Parthian refugees slipping across the bridges. They are fleeing the rebels Sir. Most have collaborated with us. They are terrified. They are seeking protection with us. I am holding them in the women's quarters under guard." Britannicus paused. "They brought some interesting news with them. It seems Sir, that Prince Sanatruces has finally managed to raise an army in the east and is marching on Ctesiphon to liberate the city. Maybe that is why the city is biding its time. Maybe this uprising has been co-ordinated with Prince Sanatruces' advance."

"Prince Sanatruces," Fergus exclaimed with sudden interest. "Are you sure?"

Britannicus shrugged. "That's what the Parthian civilians told me. There is no way of knowing whether they are speaking the truth."

Softly Fergus swore to himself. How come no one had warned him about this. If true, it would be bad news. A monumental intelligence failure. Until now the Parthians had made no attempt to take to the field and confront Rome in a pitched battle. But that seemed to be changing.

Forcing the thoughts from his mind he turned to look around at the grim and anxious officers standing around him. They were looking to him to lead them out of this mess. They were looking to him to save them. They were hoping that he had a plan, a way out.

"Good work," Fergus said at last with a grateful nod. "Well done all of you."

"What are we going to do Sir?" Britannicus asked quickly. "What's the plan?"

Fergus lowered his head so that his officers would not see the sudden indecision in his eyes. Trajan had instructed him to garrison Seleucia. His job was to hold the city for Rome. If he now abandoned Seleucia how would the emperor react? Without orders allowing him to abandon his position, he could be accused of a dereliction of his duty; a decision that could easily land him at a court-martial. But holding the city was clearly becoming impossible.

"Our position is desperate Sir," Dio suddenly exclaimed as if sensing Fergus's dilemma. "There would be no shame in abandoning the city."

"I agree," Britannicus said. "There is no fucking way we can regain control of the city. Not with our limited man-power. The rebels massively outnumber us. And we are going to run out of drinking water within three or four days."

Fergus bit his lip. It was decision time.

"All right," he said at last, making up his mind and looking around at his officers. "We're not going to sit here and await our fate. If the reports of Prince Sanatruces marching on Ctesiphon are true, then Trajan is going to need every trained soldier he can muster. Our first task will be to defeat Sanatruces before he can recapture Ctesiphon. After that we can return to reduce Seleucia and stamp out this rebellion. So, the plan is to break out, find and join the emperor. The last report of Trajan's movements that I received had the emperor camped on the banks of the Euphrates, at Babylon, around fifty miles to the south of here."

"How many men does Trajan have with him Sir?" a centurion asked.

But Fergus shrugged. "I don't know. But probably not enough to face Sanatruces in a pitched battle. The emperor's strategy was to garrison all captured cities with strong garrisons. The army is spread out across the length and breadth of Mesopotamia. It's a big fucking province. It will take time for Trajan to recall his men and form a proper field army that can meet Sanatruces in the field. The Parthians seem to have caught us by surprise. Trajan will need us."

"How are we going to break out Sir?" another centurion asked. "The enemy control all the city gates and we are hemmed in here. The nearest city gate is half a mile away through dense urban terrain. Those fuckers out there will ambush us as soon as we cross the canal."

"We are not going to fight our way out," Fergus said sharply. "We're going to go over the wall under the cover of darkness. We are slipping away during the night. The men are going to have to construct ladders. Once we are outside the city we head west until we reach the Euphrates. From there we head south towards Babylon and we take our wounded with us. No one gets left behind."

"It's risky Sir," Britannicus said with a little shake of his head. "Such a plan will mean leaving the bridges unguarded. If the rebels guess what we are up to, there will be no one to hold them back if they storm our line. Our men could get caught between the enemy and the city wall. And the wounded will slow us down Sir. And what if the Parthian horse archers catch us out in the open. We have no cavalry in which to drive them off and limited numbers of slingers. If they catch us in the open those horse archers will be able to pick us off at leisure. It will be a fucking massacre just like what happened to Crassus at Carrhae."

Angrily Fergus rounded on his deputy and the anger in his voice took all by surprise.

"What would you have me do," Fergus shouted as he stared at Britannicus. "This is the situation we are in. It's a fucking mess I know, but this is the best plan that I can think of. The plan will work. It's got to work. So, let's make it work. Years ago, my father and grandfather managed to extricate a whole battle-group from Tara on the island of Hibernia right under the noses of the enemy. We're going to do it again. And we are leaving no one behind. That's a fucking order. Now see to it that preparations are made. We go over the wall tomorrow night."

Chapter Four – Over the Wall

The canal was still on fire. A roaring wall of thick, black smoke was pouring and billowing into the sky and drifting away across the huge city. Beside the canal a few men were pouring fresh petroleum into the water to keep the flames burning. Fergus paused to gaze at them. His forehead was wrapped in a fresh bandage and his left arm was still in a sling. The army doctor had told him that the wound was serious, but that it would eventually heal unless he was unlucky, and it got infected. In the meantime, the arm was useless, but he still had his right hand, the doctor had added.

Through the thick smoke it was difficult to see the other side of the canal. But now and then he heard a scream or shout coming from the city. It was late in the afternoon and Seleucia seemed peaceful. There had been no attempt to renew the assault on the palace. Calmly Fergus, accompanied by Dio, turned and started to make his way along the canal. The legionaries and slingers, grouped together in their company and squad formations, were resting and waiting amongst the fine palace gardens and neat lawns, immediately behind the canal. Clad in their full body armour and helmets, and clutching their shields and spears, the men looked tense and few seemed in the mood to talk. Nodding greetings to familiar faces and little words of encouragement to others, Fergus moved on down amongst his men, inspecting their readiness and equipment. It was all he could do to try and raise morale.

As he reached the end of the canal, Fergus paused to look up at the mighty city walls. A company of legionaries had occupied the battlements, protecting the palace from an assault along the walls and securing the garrison's line of retreat. In the fierce afternoon heat the sun glinted off the soldier's armour and shields. And just behind the palace buildings he could see three long ladders leaning against the walls. For a moment Fergus remained silent. Then he turned his attention back to the wall of smoke and flames, wondering as he did, what had become of the beggar girl who had saved his life. In all-likelihood he would never find out.

"Do you have a family? Is there someone waiting for you back home?" Fergus asked as he turned to glance at Dio.

The veteran officer shook his head.

"I am an orphan Sir," Dio replied. "No family. The army is my life Sir. Always has been. I have been in for twenty-eight years. Started my career during Domitian's Dacian war as an ordinary soldier. They offered me retirement and a nice pension a few years ago. But I told them to fuck off and leave me alone. When you reach my age Sir, you realise that there is no time or point in trying to become something else. I don't want to leave the army. I don't want to retire, ever. I am going to hang on until I die."

"No woman or wife waiting for you back home?" Fergus said, as he turned to gaze at the smoke.

"Nope, at least none who won't charge me money." Dio paused. "I have a dog Sir," he said at last. "She is being looked after by friends in Zeugma right now. I found her abandoned on the streets one day and took her in. Suppose the bitch and I are both orphans. We have that in common. She and the army are enough for me."

Fergus nodded, his eyes suddenly looking troubled.

"I have five daughters and a wife," he said. "Haven't seen them in nine months. They are living in a villa on the banks of the Euphrates just outside Zeugma. And it just occurred to me," he said with a sigh, "that if this uprising is wider than just Seleucia; they could be in trouble. I am not there to protect them. Knowing that they are safe gives me the strength to continue. But if the kingdom of Osrhoene too has risen in rebellion, they will be right in the front line."

"You can't think like that Sir," Dio said quickly.

At his side Fergus nodded. The centurion was right. His men were looking to him to lead them out of this mess. That was his job, his first responsibility. He could not afford to focus on anything else.

For a moment the two officers were silent, as lost in thought, they gazed towards the wall of smoke and flames.

"Your father, Marcus," Dio said at last. "they say that he's an important man. A senator back in Rome. The rumour going around is that Trajan listens to him. Is that true?"

Fergus sighed. "I have not heard from my father in nearly two years," he said in a weary voice. "I don't know whether he is alive or dead. Letters have not been getting through. It's a fucking mess."

***

Outside, through the double doors, leading out into the gardens, the light had faded, and darkness was setting in. Britannicus, Dio and their fellow officers crowded around the table gazing at the crudely drawn map and listening to Fergus, as he gave them a final briefing on the withdrawal plan.

"When H hour comes," Fergus said in a grave voice, "we start withdrawing the guard companies one by one from the canal line. It is vital that the enemy do not realise that we are leaving. We will bring in the furthermost companies first. The last to leave their positions will be the men holding the main bridge. Once the evacuation is under way, you will withdraw your men to the wall at this spot here," he said, tapping the map with his finger. "We have three ladders on this side of the wall and three more will be lowered over the other side. The ninth company will go over the wall first. Their task is to secure the ground for the rest of us. Once again it is vital that the enemy do not get wind of what is going on. So, we need to be quiet. Make sure that your men know this. Tell them that anyone who endangers his comrades will be severely punished." Fergus paused, to let that sink in.

"Each man is to take only those vital things which he can carry," Fergus continued, as he turned to look around at his officers. "If all goes well, we should have the whole garrison over the wall within an hour or two. Now once we are beyond the wall, we will have no transport or horses to carry supplies. Each man should therefore have on him grain rations for two weeks and water for at-least a full day. We can replenish our water supplies from the Royal river and the Euphrates. And any man abandoning or losing his equipment will face a court-martial when we get out of this mess. Make sure all are made aware of this. The wounded and sick and those who can't walk will have to be carried out on stretchers to the Royal river. Each company will be responsible for looking after its own wounded. They are their comrades after all. Once we reach the Royal river we will start to follow the canal westwards towards the junction with the Euphrates. After that we head south towards Babylon." Fergus paused. "Any night time operation is always going to be extra difficult, so it will be incumbent on all us, Roman army officers, to see that nothing goes wrong. I expect that all of you will give your best when we leave here. One fuck-up could be the end of us. Speed and silence are going to be vital. I want to put a good distance between us and Seleucia before dawn. Britannicus, you will lead the advance guard. Your job will be to find a route for us to follow. Dio and I will bring up the main column." Fergus paused again. "All right, is that clear? Questions?"

Around the table no one spoke. Then at last Britannicus cleared his throat. The young aristocratic tribune glanced at Fergus, seemingly unperturbed by the public tongue lashing he'd received the night before.

"It's a good plan Sir," Britannicus said in a confident voice. "But what are we going to do with the Parthian civilians who are hiding with us here in the palace? They have put their trust in us Sir. Many have been very helpful. If we leave them behind, the rebels are going to slaughter them."

Fergus gazed at Britannicus. The uprising and his part in holding the palace and keeping the garrison intact seemed to have changed the young tribune. The success seemed to have gone to his head. There was a new cockiness about Britannicus, a mood to challenge that seemed to border on insolence. It felt as if Britannicus knew better. But his deputy and protégé was barely a shade over twenty; a young officer from Londinium, who owed his position to his family's status in society. His military experience was strictly limited.

"We cannot take them with us," Fergus said. "Our wounded are already going to slow us down. I shall inform the Parthians myself that we are going. We shall leave the ladders in place. Once we are gone they will have to make good their own escape. That is the best we can do for them."

"Sir," Britannicus said quickly. "We could get them to help with carrying the wounded. The able-bodied men will be willing to help."

"No," Fergus replied sharply, "Like I said, each company will be responsible for their own wounded. Those are my orders. I don't want a horde of civilians accompanying us. They will consume valuable supplies and slow us down even further. They are not trained to march like we are. Now, all of you, see to it that your men are ready and that all preparations have been made. H hour draws near."

As the O group broke up, Fergus glanced quickly in Britannicus's direction. His protégé had the potential to become a very good officer but he also needed putting back in his box. But now was not the right time.

***

The glow of the fires raging in the canal was eerily reflected in the still waters of the half-full swimming pool. In the night sky the moon and the fantastic array of twinkling stars was half obscured by smoke. In the last hour the wind direction had changed and now some of the filthy, choking smoke was wafting across the palace grounds. In the city beyond the canal all however seemed peaceful. Accompanied by his small military staff, Fergus hastened past the pool and on towards the tall and massive city walls at the back of the former governor's mansion. A white bandage was wrapped around his forehead and his left arm was still in a sling. The fortifications loomed over the palace, hemming it into a protective embrace. In the faint light he could just about make out the companies of Roman legionaries mustering amongst the gardens and lawns. The hushed voices of their officers and the roar of the flames was the only noise. As Fergus reached the first of the wooden ladders, Dio quickly appeared out of the gloom.

"We're ready," the centurion said quietly. "The ninth company have already gone over the wall. They are in position. There is nothing moving out there, Sir."

"Good," Fergus replied coolly. "Start calling in the companies. We go now. Give the order."

As Dio hastened away, Fergus heard him hissing his orders. Calmly Fergus turned to look up at the top of the massive walls and, as he did, he raised his right hand to touch the Celtic amulet that hung around his neck. Galena, his wife had given it to him years ago when he'd first departed for the German frontier. The finely woven iron amulet, she had told him, possessed powerful magic. It would protect him, keep him safe and bring him home. He was going to need that magic tonight he thought grimly. At his side, his cornicen trumpeter had strapped his long, brass tubula to his back and padded the instrument with cloth to ensure it didn't make a noise when banging on his body armour. Standing stiffly behind him, as if on parade, the standard bearer of the First Cohort of the Fourth Scythica Legion was holding up the proud vexillation standard.

Fergus looked on as the first of the Roman heavy infantry companies appeared out of the gloom. The soldiers, many of whom had blackened their faces and armour with dirt and crude oil, were led by their centurion, with their optio clutching his distinctive wooden staffs bringing up the rear. The legionaries looked weighed down by their body armour, helmets, shields, spears and marching packs. As the men reached the ladders they formed an orderly queue and one by one they started to climb.

"Move, move," a centurion hissed in the darkness. "Quickly now. Keep moving. Keep moving for fucks sake and not a sound, boys. I don't want to hear as much as a fucking fart from any of you."

After most of the company had vanished over the wall and into the darkness, Fergus looked on as the legionaries started to carry, push and drag their wounded up the ladder. The effort was painstakingly slow. The noise of straining, softly cursing men and the occasional cry, shriek and moan rent the night.

"Hurry. Keep them moving. Keep the pace going," Fergus called out softly to the centurion in charge of the ladders. Then quickly and followed by his staff he turned and hastened off in the direction of the swimming pool. It was time to break the news to the multitude of Parthian civilians who had sought shelter in the palace that the garrison was leaving.

***

Fergus stood in the garden of the palace silently gazing in the direction of the city. In the darkness the fires dominated the night. He looked sombre and unhappy. Seleucia had been his. He had been entrusted with control of the city and now he had failed to maintain the peace. The city had rejected everything he had tried to accomplish. All his efforts had been in vain and now he was about to beat an undignified, humiliating retreat; stealing away like a thief in the night. Knowing that he'd been defeated was a bitter pill to acknowledge.

"Sir," a soft voice called out from the darkness behind him. It was Dio. "The last of the companies are over the wall. It's time to go Sir."

Fergus nodded and giving Seleucia a final weary glance, he turned and followed by his staff he started out for the city wall. At the ladders a centurion and a squad of legionaries were waiting for him. The officer saluted as he recognised Fergus.

"Sir, the whole garrison are over the wall. We are the last to leave," the centurion growled impatiently.

Without saying a word, Fergus started to climb up the ladder using his right hand to steady himself. As he reached the top and scrambled up onto the battlements he was met by another squad from the rear guard. The eight silent legionaries were kneeling on one knee, their shields and spears facing the darkness. Swiftly moving across the wall, Fergus peered out across the darkened landscape beyond the city. There was not much to see. So far so good Fergus thought grimly. On the soft, balmy night breeze he could taste the smell of smoke and half a mile to the north beyond the city walls, the moonlight revealed the pale, still and gleaming waters of the Royal river.

As he made it to the ground beyond the walls, Fergus was suddenly conscious of the hundreds upon hundreds of heavily armed Romans crouching and waiting around him in the darkness. In the distance a dog was barking but along the wall not a man made a sound.

"Sir," a centurion said in a hushed, urgent voice as he appeared out of the darkness from where he'd been waiting. "We're ready to go. Britannicus and the advance guard have already made it to the canal. They have managed to take possession of two civilian barges. Britannicus says we could use the boats to transport our wounded? He wants to know what he should do Sir?"

Fergus glanced at the officer and for a moment he considered the idea.

"Tell Britannicus to use the boats and get our wounded onto them," Fergus said sharply. "And the centurions are to light their torches. Let's get going. The men are to be silent and to move as fast as they can. We need to put some distance between us and the city before dawn."

As his orders were hastily conveyed, Fergus heard Dio and the rear-guard clambering down the ladders towards him. The darkness had suddenly come alive with the noise of iron clinking against iron, curses, soft urgent voices and the unmistakeable sound of hundreds of men rising to their feet. A few moments later several torches burst into flames and began to move out in the direction of the canal. Calmly Fergus accompanied by his staff tacked onto the end of one of the heavy infantry companies and started to follow the men across the muddy irrigated fields towards the canal. The squelch of hundreds of army boots in the mud sounded horribly loud but the countryside around them remained peaceful. There was no sign of the rebels who controlled the city. Fergus bit his lip. Each centurion and Optio had been issued with a burning torch. They were supposed to lead their men to the canal and the legionaries were to follow them. But in the darkness, it was inevitable that some confusion would arise, and as he made his way across the fields, Fergus could hear the Optio's and Decanii cursing and softly calling out to their men. The neatly ordered columns he had envisioned had quickly descended into a semi-chaotic stream of men, separated from their officers and units. If the enemy were to attack at this very moment, effective movement and control of individual units would be impossible. It would be pretty much every man for himself. Tensely Fergus opened his mouth as he silently said a prayer to Erebus, the Greek god of darkness and son of Chaos. Hastily he followed his first prayer with a second to the goddess Fortuna for, as with everything, he needed lady luck and good fortune to be on his side. His legionaries were counting on him to lead them out of this mess. That was his job. They trusted him. He had to show them that he knew what he was doing. The confidence of a general and the respect for their leader were of vital importance in any military operation.

Reaching the canal bank, Fergus hastily called out into the darkness and a few moments later he heard Britannicus answer. The young tribune was standing at the edge of the still water, clutching a burning torch and grinning from ear to ear. Close by, the stifled cries and moans of the wounded rang out in the darkness, as their comrades hastened to load them onto the two river barges.

"Piece of luck Sir," Britannicus said softly, gesturing at the boats. "We found them drawn up along the bank. No sign of their owners apart from a solitary boy and his dog. Unfortunately, both ran away when they heard us coming."

Fergus nodded and glanced quickly at the boats. In the moonlight all he could see was the outline of their dark hulls.

"Take your men west along the canal and find us a route," Fergus said calmly. "But stay close to the canal. We will need the water to drink and it will protect our flank. Keep up a fair pace but do not exhaust your men, understood?"

"I can do that Sir," Britannicus said in a confident voice.

***

As dawn broke the morning light found the Roman column strung out along the southern bank of the Royal river. Tiredly Fergus rubbed his chin and turned to look back at the legionaries coming on behind him. How far had they come? Five, ten miles? It was difficult to say with any certainty but the men, heavily laden down as they were with their weapons, shields and equipment, were moving as fast as they could. Fergus grunted. There was no point in reprimanding anyone. The column was doing the best it could. It was already a miracle that they had managed to slip out of Seleucia unchallenged by the rebels. Out on the still waters of the Royal river, teams of sweating, straining legionaries clutching thick ropes were hauling the barges down the canal. The boats were completely packed with the wounded and a few rowers were doing what they could do to help, but there was no doubt that the wounded and the boats were slowing the column down. Fergus paused and stepped aside as the columns of weary Roman legionaries filed past. Anxiously he turned to gaze back across the patchwork of green irrigated fields and clumps of palm and date trees. The few villagers they'd encountered had swiftly moved out of the Roman's way but there had been no hostility from the locals, just a strange curiosity. As the men came plodding past him Fergus waited until he caught sight of Dio. The centurion was bringing up the rear-guard, cajoling the stragglers to keep moving with verbal threats and his vine staff. But some of the men were clearly exhausted and not well. A few were being helped along by their comrades.

"We leave no one behind Sir," Dio cried out trying to sound cheerful as he caught sight of Fergus. "Giving up now means betraying one's comrades trust. All of us are going to get out of here. Isn't that right Sir?"

"That's right," Fergus cried out, masking the concern in his voice.

"Come on. Move. Keep moving," Dio roared, as he rounded on the stragglers coming along the high canal dyke. "You are not staying here. Not whilst I am still in charge. You can rest when you are dead. But you are not going to die today. Think that this is hard? I fought in Domitian's Dacian war before most of you were even born. That was a proper war, a proper fight. Compared to that war this is nothing more than a pleasant march to the river and back. So, don't any of you think about quitting on me. Don't you fucking dare."

Fergus remained silent as Dio came up to him and turned to gaze at the stragglers.

"There is no place on the barges for any of them," Dio said quietly. "We need to find some more boats Sir. Some of these boys are not going to last much longer and I would really hate to leave them behind to be mugged and murdered by the locals. I've got a bad feeling about these villagers. They are just waiting for a chance to steal from the dead and dying. Carrion birds Sir, the lot of them."

Fergus sighed. Dio may be right but they had seen no more boats.

"Keep them moving as best as you can," Fergus said, giving Dio an encouraging pat on the shoulder. "I am going to call a halt at noon. We will rest for an hour and replenish our water supplies. Maybe we can use the time to build some rafts to tow behind the boats we have got."

Dio nodded.

"That may work but it will slow us down even more," he said wearily.

***

Fergus was standing atop the high earthen dyke that lined the bank of the canal, supervising the construction of the crude rafts, when a sudden a cry caught his attention. Across the flat expanse of neat, irrigated fields below him, hundreds of legionaries were sitting around resting and eating. But it was not his men that had caught his attention. Frantically racing towards him upon a horse was a solitary Roman soldier. As the legionary caught sight of the vexillation standard of the Fourth Legion he veered sharply towards it. Fergus's expression darkened as the lone horseman came galloping towards him. Where the hell had the man managed to get a horse from?

"What's the matter man?" Fergus shouted.

"Sir," the man yelled, his face streaked with sweat and mud. "Parthian cavalry. Enemy horsemen. They are closing in on us fast. I saw them. Hundreds and hundreds of them."

Chapter Five – Fight for Survival

Fergus stood on the earthen dyke and looked on as, in the muddy irrigated fields, the legionaries rushed to form up in their formations. The shouts and cries of the Roman officers were harsh and urgent. At Fergus's side his cornicen, trumpeter, blew again on his trumpet ordering the men to prepare to receive cavalry. From the corner of his eye Fergus noticed Britannicus running towards him.

"Sir, what's the plan?" the young tribune cried.

"We form up here with our backs against the canal," Fergus snapped, as he gazed in the direction from which the enemy were about to appear. "We stand our ground. The men will stay in their formations."

"Sir," Britannicus gasped, as he came to a halt beside Fergus.

Fergus didn't look at his subordinate. His gaze was firmly fixed on the fields to the east.

"We stand our ground," Fergus hissed. "We have no cavalry. We can't outrun these Parthians. So, we stay here until I have seen what we are up against. The men will stand their ground."

Hastily Britannicus nodded and for a moment he looked lost.

"You men," Fergus bellowed as he turned his attention to the soldiers who had been busy constructing the rafts but were about to rush back to their units. "Stay where you are and keep working on those rafts. Nothing has changed. We are going to need those rafts. Quickly now. Get to work."

Obediently the legionaries returned to their labour. In the muddy fields, at the base of the earthen dyke, the Roman heavy infantry companies had managed to form a four-rank deep line. The Roman position stretched away along the canal with the dyke immediately to their rear. Their flanks were protected by two companies who had taken up positions on the dyke itself. Amongst the crops, the front rank of legionaries was down on one knee and were holding their large shields in front of them, forming a solid and continuous wooden protective wall. The spear points of their throwing pila were pointing outwards, their butts wedged firmly into the ground. Amongst the front ranks the company centurions, easily identifiable by their magnificent plumed helmets, stood amongst their men.

"Form up your slingers along the dyke," Fergus roared at the auxiliary officer in command of the eighty Balearic lightly armed slingers. "Have them lie down on the ground. I don't want the enemy to know who they are just yet. Quick about it."

"Britannicus," Fergus snapped, as he quickly turned to the tribune. "Have the men on the boats bring their craft into the shore and keep them there. The dyke should give them some protection from arrows. And keep those men working on those rafts. We are going to need those fucking rafts."

"Sir look!" the vexillation standard bearer suddenly cried out, pointing to the east. Hastily Fergus turned and peered in the direction in which the man was pointing. And there surging towards him, across the green open fields, were a mass of horsemen. The Parthians looked like they were in a hurry.

"We hold our positions. Not one step backwards," Fergus roared.

No one answered. Every Roman eye was fixed on the approaching enemy cavalry. As the Parthian horsemen caught sight of the Romans they didn't hesitate nor did their pace slow. Instead their foremost riders started to bunch together and form a single fast-moving column. They were heading straight towards the Roman position. The riders looked like they knew what they were doing. Clumps of mud were thrown into the air as the horsemen thundered across the fields, tearing up the crops, and as they did, Fergus suddenly heard their triumphant cries and yells. Amongst the enemy ranks he could make out no banners or standards giving away the presence of a leader or general. The Parthians seemed to be lacking body armour, shields and helmets and they seemed rather rag-tag; more a locally raised militia than long standing professional soldiers. But there were hundreds of them and they seemed confident.

Stoically and silently the Roman legionaries stood their ground as they awaited the assault. However, when the Parthian column was less than fifty yards from the Roman positions their lead horsemen suddenly changed course. Sweeping and racing along down the front of the Roman lines a hail of arrows came whining and thudding into the densely packed Romans. Here and there a man cried out as he was struck. The hail of arrows did not slacken as the Parthian horsemen went charging along the front of the Roman positions.

"Fucking hell," Fergus swore, throwing himself to the ground as several arrows went whining over his head.

Amongst the Roman lines, cries and shouts rose as the officers struggled to maintain order and keep their men in position. Close by, a Roman was struck nearly instantaneously by two arrows and went staggering backwards off the dyke and into the canal behind it, vanishing into the water with a loud splash.

"Give the order for defensive testudo," Fergus bellowed, turning to his cornicen as he pressed himself into the dirt. Bravely the trumpeter scrambled up onto his knees and a few moments later his trumpet rang out. Over Fergus's head the arrows continued to zip and whine through the air. Grimly Fergus lifted his head to see what was going on. The Parthian column was still racing along the front of his men and subjecting them to a merciless barrage. Forcing himself to watch, Fergus saw that amongst the enemy horsemen there was no sign of infantry or heavily armoured cataphracts, shock cavalry. The enemy force seemed solely composed of light, fast moving and highly mobile horse archers.

"Keep working on those rafts," Fergus roared as he turned and saw that the party of legionaries working on the boats had taken shelter behind the dyke. Where the hell was Britannicus? He was supposed to be supervising those men. But there was no time to look for him.

At the base of the dyke the Roman officers were screaming at their men and, as Fergus turned his attention to them the second and third ranks began to raise their shields in a protective embrace forming a densely packed testudo. Grimly Fergus bit his lip as he lay stretched out in the dirt. The testudo would provide some protection from the Parthian arrows, but the enemy had him pinned down.

Out in the fields the Parthian column had completed its first pass and were wheeling around for a second attack. Along the top of the dyke a legionary, half bent over, came rushing up to Fergus and handed him a large infantry shield. Gratefully Fergus grasped hold of the legionary shield and swiftly scrambled to his feet. In the canal, the two civilian barges packed with the wounded and sick had sought shelter immediately behind the dyke. Several legionaries were standing up to their waists in the water holding the two boats in place and straining to fix them together with thick ropes.

Close by lying down on the ground, was the auxiliary officer in command of the eighty slingers.

"On my command," Fergus yelled at the officer, "have your men stand up and shoot those fucking horsemen. I don't care if you think the range is extreme. I don't care if you hit them or not. Just discourage them from attacking us."

As the officer turned to scream his orders along the levee, Fergus caught sight of Britannicus. The tribune was down at the water's edge with the work party, furiously assembling the rudimentary rafts.

"Sir, here they come again," the standard bearer yelled, as he went down on one knee still holding up the vexillation banner. Fergus turned. Out in the fields, some four hundred paces away, the Parthian horsemen were surging forwards once more. Their fierce, savage yells and cries carried across the open ground.

"Now centurion," Fergus shouted turning to the auxiliary officer. "Have your men stand up and shoot at the enemy. Drive them off."

He had barely finished speaking before the officer relayed the order to his men in his native Hispanic language. As one, the slingers, small dark-haired men, clad solely in simple sleeveless white tunics and leather body armour leapt to their feet. In their hands they clutched their slings, whirling them above their heads, faster and faster. Then with a little flick of their wrists they released and their stone or lead bullets when zipping away across the fields.

"Reload," the auxiliary officer roared. "Swing. Release."

Out in the fields a few Parthian horsemen and their mounts went crashing to the ground. But the distance was at the extreme range and the volley did not halt the Parthian charge. On they came, thundering towards the Roman line in a well-practised and expertly carried out manoeuvre. As a second volley of stones and lead bullets slammed into their ranks, more riders went down in a horrible, screaming tangle of horse and man, but it was not enough.

"Down," Fergus roared as he braced himself for the approaching assault. "Get your slingers down now. And stay down until I say so."

If he lost his slingers now, that would be a disaster. They were the only unit he had, capable of fighting back against the enemy. There was however no need to tell the slingers. Hastily they dropped to the ground, face down in the dirt. Exposed, high up on the dyke, Fergus and the slingers made a fine target for the Parthian bowmen. As the foremost Parthian riders swerved and started to race down the Roman front, some fifty yards from the legionaries, Fergus lowered his head, crouched behind his shield and braced himself. Close by, the standard bearer flung himself flat onto the ground. A moment later something thudded violently into the shield and over his head another arrow went whining across the canal.

"Shit," Fergus swore again as he heard a man shriek in pain.

Another arrow struck the earth close by with a thud. Then another went whining just over the top of his shield. Risking a quick peek to his left and right, Fergus saw that everyone up on the dyke was lying flat on the ground or had taken shelter at the water's edge. Down at the base of the levee, facing the Parthians, the densely packed ranks of legionaries, fixed in their immobile testudo formation, could do nothing but take the aerial pounding.

"Fuck," Fergus hissed as he quickly raised his head to gaze at the enemy. The last of the Parthians were wheeling away as they prepared to come around for a third assault. They may be just a militia, but the enemy knew exactly what they were doing. They had pinned down the whole of his force. There was no way he could continue his march with such a threat menacing his flank. The Parthians would pick off his men if they broke their testudo. And all the enemy now had to do was to wait for infantry re-enforcements or heavy cataphracts, capable of attacking and breaking into the tightly-packed legionary formations. Or else they could simply wait until hunger and thirst eventually did the job for them. Tensely Fergus turned to gaze at the legionaries. They could not stay here. He had to do something.

"Keep shooting at those horsemen," Fergus yelled at the auxiliary officer. "When they come around again - get down. Show them that every attack is going to cost them." Then resolutely Fergus stood up and yelled at Britannicus. A Parthian arrow was sticking from his shield and close by, two more were protruding from the soft earth. At his side, the standard bearer and cornicen hastily scrambled to their feet. They looked shocked by the ferocity of the attack.

As Britannicus came scrambling up the steep embankment, Fergus hastened towards him.

"Sir," Britannicus gasped, his face covered in sweat and mud.

"Get those wounded across the Royal river and into cover behind the dyke on the other side," Fergus snapped. "Then come back to this side of the canal with the empty boats and rafts. We're going to retreat across the canal. One company at a time – just like we did when we went over the wall. It's your job to get the men across. Ferry them across on the boats. Once we are on the other side the levee will protect us from those horse archers. We can't stay here. We need to keep moving."

Britannicus blinked rapidly as he considered the plan.

"We have not yet finished constructing the rafts and what about the Parthians?" he said quickly. "What if they manage to swim their horses across the canal? We will be back where we started."

But Fergus shook his head. "No," he retorted. "Do what you can with the rafts. Improvise. The waters of the canal are deep. The only cavalry who can swim their horses across open water are the Batavian regiments. I should know. My father served in one. Those Parthians may eventually get across the canal, but they are not going to fucking swim across. Now go. Get it done."

As Britannicus slithered away down the dyke towards the water, Fergus quickly turned and crouched behind his shield. He had no idea what the Parthian horsemen were capable of, but the decision to retreat had been made and there was nothing else he could do now but pray that it worked. In the fields to the south the Parthian horsemen were galloping towards him again. Along the top of the levee the soft noise of the slingers, whirling their slings above their heads, was nearly drowned out by the thud of hundreds of hooves. Tensely Fergus looked on as the aerial duel between his slingers and the Parthian horse archers quickly reached its climax with the lightly armoured slingers flinging themselves to the ground.

***

Grimly Fergus watched, as another company of heavily armed and laden legionaries came hastily clambering across the makeshift and improvised bridge that spanned the width of the Royal river. It was late in the afternoon and the retreat across the canal was taking longer than he had anticipated. But Britannicus and his men had proved their worth by some brilliant engineering. Instead of ferrying the troops across the water, the young tribune had managed to create a bridge across the canal by lining up the two barges nose to tail. He had lashed them together with ropes and had filled in the gaps with the tree trunks destined for the rafts. It was not a pretty construction, but the rudimentary bridge was doing its job.

As the legionaries made it across the canal the soldiers surged up the steep embankment, some clambering on all fours. In the middle of the Royal river, a solitary half-submerged raft, nothing more than tree trunks tied together by ropes, was being hauled across the water by a party of legionaries. Onboard the dangerously overloaded raft, their comrades, recently wounded and still clutching their shields, packs and weapons could only look on in silence, as they slowly drew closer to the bank.

Quickly Fergus turned his attention back to the two remaining companies of heavy infantry under Dio's command who remained on the opposite shore. The hundred and fifty or so men of the rear-guard still packed together in their dense testudo formations had taken up defensive positions atop of the dyke. Their rows of shields and spear points gleamed in the fierce sunlight. They had been there for hours without moving. In the muddy corpse-strewn fields beyond, the Parthian cavalry were arrayed in a long line. The horsemen had come to a halt and seemed to be watching the retreat from a safe distance. For the last hour they had made no serious attempt to disrupt the evacuation.

"They haven't contested our withdrawal?" Britannicus said with a frown, as he crouched beside Fergus and gazed at the tense stand-off across the canal. "I wonder why? Maybe they know something we don't. Shall I call in Dio and his men Sir?"

Fergus did not reply as he glanced up and down the high dyke. The slingers were standing in a line, ready to provide cover for the final stage of the withdrawal.

"All right, order Dio and his men to retreat across the bridge," Fergus said at last. "Once they are across, burn the bridge and the rafts. We can't use them, not with the Parthians in control of one side of the canal. Make sure that nothing is left that can be useful to the enemy."

"Sir," Britannicus said with a quick nod. But instead of turning away the tribune hesitated.

"And our wounded and sick Sir?"

"We will have to carry them like we originally intended. Each company looks after its own men," Fergus replied. "From here we follow the canal westwards. You will take the vanguard like before. We need to keep moving. If the Parthians pin us down, we are finished."

***

The night was alive with the tramp of army boots, the jangle of metallic equipment, coughs and the occasional shriek and shout. In the dark skies the stars twinkled, too many to count and in their faint light, Fergus could make out the endless fields and crops that stretched away into the darkness. Wearily Fergus kept on walking, following the column of men in front of him. His face was covered in mud and dirt and fine sand seemed to have gotten into every orifice. The balmy night air provided no refreshment and his lips were cracked and bone dry. There had been no further sign of the Parthian cavalry which had earlier pinned them down against the canal. For a few hours the Parthian horsemen had followed the Roman force, keeping to their side of the canal, but come the darkness they had vanished from view.

Finding their direction in the darkness had not been hard for all they had to do was follow the Royal river; the sliver of still water that was just about visible in the celestial light. All day and now for most of the night he'd kept his men walking westwards, pausing only now and then to rest. The need to carry their wounded with them had slowed the column down. In some of the small villages, which they passed the legionaries had forcibly taken carts and horses from the inhabitants, but most of their wounded were still being carried by their comrades on crude stretchers. A truly exhausting effort for all concerned. The need to carry their wounded and the long night march, combined with a lack of time to prepare food, was slowly sapping and exhausting everyone. Some of the centurions had suggested that they halt for the night and make a camp, but he'd said no to that. They had to push on. They had to keep moving.

Fergus grunted as he reached over to readjust the sling in which his left arm was resting. The arm was aching and in addition to that he was suffering from a raging headache. Glancing around to look behind him, he could see that the darkness to the east was already a very dark blue. Sunrise was not far away.

What was he going to do when he reached the Euphrates? The plan once they reached the river was to head south from there to Babylon and hopefully find and link up with the emperor's troops. Grimly he lowered his head. He was in command. His men were counting on him to lead them to safety. That was his job and his duty but what if the rebellion had spread to the kingdom of Osrhoene? What if Zeugma was suddenly on the front line. What if the people of Zeugma had risen too. Did he as a father and husband not have a duty to protect his family? Were his soldiers more important than his own family? Carefully he reached up to touch the stained, dirty bandage that was wrapped around his forehead. Galena and his daughters house was on the banks of the Euphrates. All that he would have to do was take a horse and follow the river home. He could be home in a few days if he rode fast.

"Where is the commander? Where is Fergus?" a voice suddenly called out from the darkness behind him.

"I am here," Fergus replied in a loud voice as he turned to peer into the night.

In the darkness a horse snorted and a few moments later a rider appeared from the gloom. It was Dio. Finally recognising Fergus and his staff, the centurion slowed his beast and started to keep pace with Fergus.

"Well, what is it?" Fergus growled impatiently.

"Sir are you going to make us march until we drop dead," Dio snapped, and the strong disapproval in his voice was clear. "I have men back there in the rear-guard who are not going to last much longer. When you led us out of Seleucia you told us that you would lead all of us out of this mess. All of us. That's going to mean fuck all if we don't halt soon. Our line of march is going to be littered with corpses. Men that did not need to die. Please Sir. Order a halt. If only for an hour or two so that we can sort ourselves out."

Fergus took a deep breath as he kept on walking.

"We will halt at dawn, centurion," Fergus said sharply. "You can sort out the stragglers then."

"Thank you, Sir," Dio said in a tense, toneless voice and a moment later he was gone, vanishing into the night.

***

Fergus was woken by laughter. He'd been sitting with his back slumped up against a tree. Opening his eyes, he hastily raised his head in alarm. He'd only meant to close his eyes for a few brief moments. It was morning. In the crop-covered fields that stretched away along the banks of the Royal river he could make out narrow irrigation ditches and a few scattered palm trees. The smell of fresh manure lay heavy on the land and annoying flies were buzzing around his head. Amongst the crops, parties of legionaries had flung themselves to the ground. Their body armour and helmets gleamed in the sunlight. Some of the soldiers seemed asleep whilst others were busying themselves with repairing equipment, preparing cooking fires and their breakfast. Out in the fields two horses were grazing on a patch of grass and up on the earthen dyke that ran along the canal, a couple of sentries were leaning on their spears. All seemed peaceful. Quickly Fergus turned in the direction where Dio and a few of his fellow centurions were sitting together in a circle around a small camp fire. The officers were laughing.

"What are you laughing about?" Fergus called out.

Dio paused as he turned to glance at Fergus and the centurions fell silent.

"I was telling the boys here Sir the story about the time that I was taken prisoner by King Decebalus of the Dacians," Dio replied with a little amused smile.

"I didn't know that you had been captured," Fergus growled as he slowly got to his feet and ambled over to the group.

"Yes Sir, it happened when I had just joined the army, straight out of basic training," Dio said with a chuckle. "The army sent me to some god forsaken outpost along the Dacian frontier. Soon after I arrived the Dacians surrounded us and my commander chose to surrender rather than fight it out. I was held as a POW for nearly a year, a guest of the king, as my captors like to call it."

"So, what's so funny?" Fergus muttered.

"We were joking about the Batavian regiments Sir," Dio replied quickly. "It's nothing."

"No go on," Fergus said sharply. "My father served his entire career with the 2nd Batavian Auxiliary Cohort. He spent fourteen years on the Danube. About the same time that you were there. So, if you have something to say, then just say it."

Quickly Dio exchanged glances with his fellow officers and for a moment none of them spoke.

"Go on," Fergus snapped. "I would like to hear your story."

"Well it was like this Sir," Dio said taking a deep breath as he looked up at Fergus. "After I and my comrades were taken prisoner, the Dacians, marched us back to their homeland. We must have walked two or three hundred miles. It was fucking awful. The worst time in my career. In some of the border villages through which we passed, the locals were friendly and would come out of their houses and place buckets of water at the side of the track. They were meant for us, so that we could drink. But our guards would kick the buckets over. They treated us like shit."

Dio paused and lowered his eyes to the ground as the memories came back to him.

"I was telling the boys here Sir," he continued, "that I remember one day marching beside a Batavian soldier. The Batavians have these distinctive helmets. You know the ones with a feather sticking out. Well this Batavian prisoner, he was being picked on by one of the guards. A proper sadistic Dacian arsehole. Not a moment went by when this guard didn't try to humiliate and bully him. But on this day the Batavian seemed to have had enough for when his guard came up to him, he floored him with the most perfect punch I have ever seen. Knocked him out with one blow." Dio paused. Then he sighed and looked up at Fergus.

"As we marched on I tried to get this Batavian to swap helmets with me," Dio said, as his voice turned melancholic. "His friends urged him to swap positions in the column with them and hide his appearance. Anything to make the guard confused. We were all worried what the guard would do in revenge. But my Batavian friend told me, no way would he give up his cap with his regimental insignia. He just flatly refused to hide. He was that proud of his unit." Dio sighed and turned his eyes to the ground. "So, a few hours later we are still marching down this road and the sadist returns. And he is looking for revenge. He's fucking pissed. And as soon as he spots my Batavian friend, he comes up to him and stabs him in the throat; murders him right in front of us. We were not even allowed to bury his body. I shall always remember that Batavian. He had courage. He had guts."

Dio fell silent and Fergus stood motionless looking down at the ground. An awkward silence descended on the group of officers.

"Get the men ready to move right away," Fergus snapped at last. "We have wasted enough time. We need to keep moving. See that it is done."

And with that he abruptly turned around and started out towards the dyke and the Royal river. Dio's story had not been what he'd been expecting. It had caught him off-guard, but he had no time for stories. He was in command and it was a lonely job. The responsibility of leading his men out of danger and the lack of news concerning Galena and his daughter's safety, were getting to him, irritating him, weighing him down. But that was his burden to bear; to be born alone and in private.

***

The Euphrates river gleamed in the sunlight and beyond, the wide-open and empty desert extended to the horizon. Carefully Fergus surveyed the river and the thin strip of greenery that extended along its banks. It was nearing noon and out on the blue waters, there was no sign of any people or ships. Three full days and nights had passed since their night-time retreat from Seleucia.

"I never thought I would be glad to see this river again," Britannicus said wearily, as he too gazed at the placid and wide waters.

Fergus remained silent. Along the banks where the Euphrates and the Royal river merged his men were resting, grouped together in their units. And as he turned to look at them, he felt a tiny spark of elation and hope. They had made it this far. They had managed to escape from Seleucia. But now he faced a choice. The original plan called for him to head south along the banks of the Euphrates to Babylon; the last known location where emperor Trajan and his forces had been based. If the rebellion was as widespread and serious as he feared, then the emperor would need him in the coming fight. But if he turned north he would be able to retreat towards Zeugma, Galena and his daughters. In the chaos of the uprising who could blame him if he retreated northwards. Fergus sighed. He had a decision to make.

Just then a shout rose from one of the Roman pickets placed along the river bank. Turning to stare in the direction of the noise, Fergus suddenly caught sight of horsemen galloping towards his men's positions across the open ground. In the fields the legionaries rose to their feet in alarm, but as he stared at the newcomers Fergus could see that they were few, barely more than twenty riders. And there was something oddly familiar about their armour and uniforms.

"I think they are ours Sir," Britannicus exclaimed in a puzzled but excited voice, as he raised his hand to shield his eyes from the sun.

Fergus muttered something to himself as he watched the horsemen thundering towards him. Britannicus was right. They looked like Roman cavalrymen. Without saying a word, he started out towards the newcomers, striding across the open stony and barren ground. A crowd of legionaries were milling around the horsemen as Fergus hastened up to them. The riders were sitting on their horses looking lost. They were covered in dust and they looked utterly exhausted. But they were Romans. What looked like the remnants of a legionary cavalry turma, squadron.

"Who are you? Where have you come from" Fergus called out, as he pushed his way towards the small band of horsemen.

In reply one of the cavalrymen turned to Fergus.

"Are you in charge," the man cried.

"I am the commanding officer," Fergus shouted back as he came towards the man. "We're the 1st Cohort of the Fourth Legion, formerly the garrison of the city of Seleucia. Who are you?"

"Sixth squadron of legionary cavalry of the Third Legion Sir," the cavalrymen gasped, with sudden relief in his voice. "Thank fuck we found you. You are the first friendly faces we have seen. We're all that's left from our patrol. Bastard Parthians ambushed us to the north near Doura-Europus. That was five days ago. We have been heading south along the river ever since. Do you know what is going on Sir? We have been trying to evade Parthian cavalry for days and my men have not eaten in two."

"We will give you some food," Fergus replied. "What news do you have?"

On his horse the cavalry decurion slowly shook his head.

"All we know is that Doura-Europus has risen in revolt. The locals massacred the garrison. There was no warning. We were lucky to escape. The city belongs to the rebels Sir. I don't know what has become of the rest of our units. They seem scattered to hell. It's all one big cluster fuck."

Slowly Fergus nodded as he took in the news.

"Any news from further north?" he called out in a tense voice. "Any news from the kingdom of Osrhoene or Zeugma? Have they joined this rebellion? Has the uprising spread to those regions?"

"I wouldn't know Sir," the cavalryman said with a shrug. "All I know is that Doura-Europus is no longer under Roman control. We were hoping that you would be able to tell us more."

Deflated, Fergus allowed his shoulders to sag.

Chapter Six – The Hollow Square

Fergus crouched, his head bowed to the ground, his eyes and mouth firmly closed as he tried to protect his face with his arms from the raging sandstorm. In the flurry of dense whirling sand and small pebbles it was impossible to make out a single object, even though he knew his men were close by. Calmly he forced himself to breathe through his nose, supressing the thought that he was about to choke. This was not the first sandstorm he'd been caught up in, but nevertheless panic hovered close by. There was nothing he could do but be patient and sit it out. Each man would be in a world of his own – struggling with the same thoughts and fears. Nothing could move in such a storm. But the storm would pass. It would end.

Three days had passed since the encounter with the Roman cavalrymen from Doura. Fergus groaned as a small flying pebble painfully struck his head and silently he cursed about having given that girl his helmet. It had taken a whole day and a half for his engineers to make the rafts which had ferried his men across the wide, placid Euphrates to the western bank. But they'd done it and their crossing had not been contested by rebel forces. He'd turned south along the Euphrates. Avoiding the marshy, reed and crocodile-infested river bank and the narrow strip of green, irrigated fields sandwiched in between the river and the desert; he'd kept his men out in the open, barren and stony desert, where they could easily see danger approaching.

At last the fury of the buffeting, whirling and whining sandstorm seemed to slacken. Cautiously opening his eyes, Fergus raised his head and looked up to see the blue sky once more. It was noon. The sling in which his left arm was resting was filled with sand and small stones and for a moment, he struggled to clear it out. Around him his men were slowly rising to their feet, strange shapes covered in dust and sand. Hastily Fergus got to his feet and turned to survey his troops. The column was strung out on the gravelly desert, a hundred yards from the edge of the green strip of land that ran along the river. As he looked around, men's voices started to call out as the legionaries checked up on each other. Close by, Fergus's military staff, his cornicen and standard bearer slowly got to their feet. Their faces were completely covered in fine dust and as the standard bearer caught Fergus staring at him, he grinned. Then he spat something from his mouth.

"Would be nice to have a swim in the Euphrates Sir," the standard bearer said, as he turned to shake the sand and dust from the vexillation standard. "Get rid of this sand and dust. The shit's gotten absolutely everywhere."

"We keep heading south," Fergus said. "There is no time for swimming. Cornicen, give the order that the march is to continue."

"Yes Sir," the trumpeter said hastily, as he reached up to wipe his mouth and lips. Then hastily cleaning his trumpet, he raised the instrument to his lips.

As the trumpet rang out across the desert, Fergus started walking.

"Let's go. Let's move, we head south," Fergus cried out as he made his way along the columns of dust-covered soldiers. Along the edge of the irrigated belt where the pleasant green land abruptly gave away to the grey yellow of the barren desert, the legionaries were milling around, forming up and hoisting their marching packs over their shoulders. A few of their luckier comrades mounted on horses came riding past. The beasts too were cloaked in dust, giving them an alien appearance.

Pausing beside a column of wounded, being carried along on crude, improvised stretchers by their comrades Fergus spoke a few encouraging words to the men. The need to carry eighty-five wounded and sick men with them was clearly slowing down the column, but they had made it this far and there was not a man now who advocated abandoning their comrades to their fate. The determination that they were all going to make it, had united them.

The small fortified Parthian watchtower and fort stood on its own, looking forlorn and abandoned. Its gates had been half-torn from their hinges and the mudbrick walls showed signs of having been attacked. After entering and examining the place the scouts had returned, reporting that everything of value had been looted long ago. Idly Fergus turned his attention to the south as he strode through the desert. A quarter of a mile away from the fortified watchtower, along the green, fertile banks of the Euphrates, the small village was nothing more than a collection of mudbrick huts. It looked poor. Out in the patchwork of irrigated fields that surrounded the small settlement, a few farmers, their families and farm animals were at work amongst their crops. Batting away the desert flies that buzzed around his head, Fergus turned to gaze on the locals, as the Roman column marched on by. The Parthians had stopped what they were doing and were staring at the Romans in silence. They seemed unafraid and made no attempt to run or hide. In an enclosure a herd of goats was bleating noisily and out of sight a dog was barking. This was a strange war Fergus thought, as he walked on, gazing at the villagers. It was hard to know who was friendly and who was the enemy. One moment the locals were doing deals with you, the next they were at your throat. The column had been moving for the best part of an hour since the sandstorm and this was the first settlement they'd come across.

"Sir," a voice called out and looking up, Fergus saw Britannicus striding towards him. The tribune's face was covered in fine dust apart from a trickle of sweat that had made its way down his cheek.

"What is it?" Fergus growled, as he left the party of wounded and strode over to his deputy. Britannicus seemed to be in a bullish, confident mood.

"Some of the men are wondering how long it is going to take us to reach Babylon Sir" the young tribune said quickly. "I told them that we will be there soon. But what if Trajan and his troops have already moved on Sir? There is no way of knowing where the emperor could be? Is it not prudent that we make plans in case Trajan has already left Babylon?"

"If you mean that we should be moving north along the Euphrates instead of south," Fergus replied sharply, "then the answer is no. If Doura has risen in rebellion the route north will be blocked. We head south and find the emperor. Trajan will need us.

We have a duty to recover Seleucia. That's the plan. That is what we are going to do."

"Of-course Sir," Britannicus said smoothly. "I just thought I should mention it."

Fergus was silent for a moment as he gazed at his protégé. Ever since he'd successfully managed to hold the palace, back in Seleucia, there had been a new cockiness about Britannicus. An overconfidence and aggression that was annoying and worrying him. Fergus was just about to raise the issue and reprimand Britannicus, when a cry of alarm rang out from the small band of Roman cavalrymen guarding the desert flank of the column. Turning in the direction of the horsemen Fergus saw them turn and start to race towards him.

"Shit, trouble," Fergus hissed.

The cavalrymen did not need to explain themselves. Out in the desert, on the horizon, a cloud of dust was approaching, and it was not another sandstorm.

"Who are they?" Britannicus snapped, as he peered out into the desert and the fast approaching cloud of dust.

"We will find out soon enough," Fergus said. "But anything moving that fast will be on horseback."

With sudden urgency he turned to his cornicen.

"Give the order for the men to halt and take up positions to receive enemy cavalry. We will form a hollow square, three ranks deep. Britannicus, I want our slingers arrayed in a line facing the desert. They are to stand in front of the legionaries and be ready to use their slings. Get the wounded into cover inside the square. Now go. Hurry. Go."

As the trumpet rang out and Britannicus hastened away yelling his orders, Fergus gazed at the approaching cloud of dust.

"Could be Parthian cavalry Sir," the standard bearer said as he too gazed at the approaching cloud of dust.

"Maybe," Fergus said sternly. "Wait and see."

As the officers screamed at their men, the legionaries rushed to take up their positions in the hollow square formation that was rapidly taking shape. The front ranks of the formation were down on one knee, their shields lined up next to each other, forming a protective wall. The butts of the men's pila were wedged into the ground and their gleaming iron spear-heads were pointing outwards, bristling like a hedgehog. Their colleagues in the second and third ranks were standing upright, shoulder to shoulder, tightly packed together. Their armour and shields gleamed and reflected the fierce sunlight. Calmly Fergus surveyed the preparations. The high quality of his legionaries training and drill was showing itself in the smooth and efficient way in which each man knew exactly what to do. As the last of the stretcher bearers came running into the hollow square formation and placed their charges on the ground, Fergus called out to his staff and hastened towards the side of the square that faced the desert. His staff followed at a run, just as the eighty slingers came racing up to take their positions.

Jogging to the front of his men some instinct made Fergus turn and gaze at the villagers. The locals too had noticed the cloud of dust approaching out of the desert and were running back to their huts. Whoever was coming towards them, the locals seem to know who they were. They looked spooked.

"Have your men ready to use their slings," Fergus shouted at the auxiliary centurion in command of the slingers. "If they press their attack your men are to fall back behind the legionary lines. Got that."

"Yes Sir," the centurion shouted.

Fergus came to a halt and turned to gaze out into the desert. On the horizon he could make out figures on horseback. There were at least two-hundred of them and they were galloping straight towards him. Peering at the approaching riders, Fergus suddenly grunted in surprise. Amongst the horsemen were camel riders. As they drew nearer he saw that the riders had nomadic and Arab style keffiyeh scarfs wrapped around their faces and heads. Hastily Fergus retreated to behind the slingers. The newcomers were not Roman or from any auxiliary alae that he recognised.

"Slingers let them know we are here," Fergus shouted. "Bring them down."

Close by, the auxiliary officer opened his mouth and roared an order in his native Hispanic language and in response the slingers raised their slings and confidently began to whirl them high above their heads. Out in the open, flat desert the horsemen made a perfect target. Faster and faster the slings spun around as the little men from the Balearic isles steadied themselves and took careful aim at the approaching horsemen. Another shout from the auxiliary officer and, with a quick flick of their wrists the slingers released, and their small stones and lead bullets went shooting away with incredible force and accuracy. Out in the desert horses, men and camels went down in a furious, screaming tangle. With grim satisfaction, Fergus watched as the remaining horsemen swerved away and beat a hasty retreat. But after a hundred paces or so they seemed to regroup and turn once more to face the Roman column. In front of the ranks of legionaries, the slingers had reloaded and wore once more whirling their deadly slings above their heads. Out in the desert however the riders had come to a halt and seemed content to watch the Roman column from a safe distance.

"Stand down. Save your ammunition," Fergus yelled at the slingers. The riders were clearly too few to pose a serious threat to the Roman column.

"That will teach them Sir," the standard bearer said in a satisfied voice. "The lesson is. Don't fucking approach a Roman column like that."

Fergus was peering at the horsemen. They were milling about, gesturing and shouting but they were too far away for him to understand what they were saying.

"They are not Parthians," he snapped at last. "They look like desert nomads. Arabs or Bedouin from one of the desert tribes. I have met these men before. They are fiercely independent. They are raiders preying on the trade caravans. They owe no loyalty to anyone but to their tribe."

"But why are they here Sir?" the standard bearer replied. "Why attack us? There are far too few of them to take us all on. It would be madness Sir."

Slowly Fergus shook his head as he gazed at the riders out in the desert. "I don't know, but if there is anything that I learned about these desert men, it is that they are not mad. They will have come here with a purpose."

"Maybe that explains that ruined Parthian fort back over there, Sir," the standard bearer said quickly. "Maybe that was put there to keep the villagers safe from these Bedouin raiders. Fuck lot of good it's going to do them now."

"Maybe," Fergus muttered.

"What are your orders Sir?" the cornicen called out.

For a moment Fergus hesitated. The Arabs did not look like they were about to retreat. What were they waiting for? What did they want? Quickly Fergus turned to look at his men. The legionaries were massed in their impregnable position, gazing impassively at the enemy.

"Go find Dio and Britannicus and bring them here. I need to speak to them both," he snapped.

As the trumpeter sped off in search of his two most senior officers, Fergus turned to gaze at the desert raiders. The Bedouin seemed content to stay where they were. Amongst their ranks he caught sight of a black banner flapping in the breeze. Staring at the men from the desert, he was reminded of his time as commander of the 7th Auxiliary Alae of Numidians in charge of policing the desert road from Sura to Palmyra. That had been his first independent command and the first time he had encountered these men from the desert.

"Sir," Dio called out as he and Britannicus, accompanied by the cornicen hastened towards him.

"We need to keep moving. Babylon cannot be much further," Fergus said quickly, as he turned to address his officers. "We will continue our march in a hollow square. Have the men of the third row take care of carrying our wounded. We will keep them in the centre of the square for protection. Dio, I want you to take that cavalry squadron on up ahead and use them as scouts."

"The decurion from the Third is a capable man Sir," Dio said quickly. "He can handle a scouting mission."

"No," Fergus said patiently shaking his head. "We are nearing Babylon. If Trajan is still in the city there will be Roman outposts and patrols. If we run into the emperor's patrols or outposts I need you to be there. I don't want any misunderstandings. It's fucking easy to get killed by one's own side out here. No fuck ups. I don't want to lose any more men, not after coming this far."

"Sir," Dio said in an obedient voice.

"Britannicus," Fergus said turning to his young protégé. "Take a single company and bring up the rear-guard. See to it that you bring all the stragglers with you who will drop out from the column. I don't want anyone left behind, not with that fucking band of thieves and robbers watching us out there. Stay with the stragglers and guard them. If they attack, take up a defensive position. Stay in position. Understood?"

"Yes Sir," Britannicus said in a quick confident voice. "What do you think they want Sir" he added, gesturing at the Arabs. "They are just sitting there as if waiting for something."

"I know what they want," Fergus growled as he lowered his gaze. "It's the same thing that these nomads always want. Slaves and loot. They must think that we look vulnerable and ripe for an easy picking. They are going to go after our stragglers. Our high-quality weapons, shields, armour, equipment. It will all be useful to these Bedouin."

"Fucking hell," Britannicus snorted with sudden disgust, as Fergus's words sank in. "Slaves and loot. We're the fucking Roman army. No one is taking me as a slave."

***

The silence of the desert was disturbed by the rattle and clink of equipment and the crunch of hundreds of army boots on the gravelly desert floor. As the Roman column headed south along the banks of the Euphrates, high in the blue sky the fierce afternoon sun glared down on them. Swarms of desert flies buzzed around the men's heads. Keeping abreast of the legionaries who were moving along in a hollow square formation, Fergus grimly turned to glance at the Arabs. Out in the desert the nomads were following and shadowing them from a safe distance. There had to be around one hundred and fifty of them. Some were mounted on camels and others on horses and all were wearing their traditional long flowing robes with keffiyeh wrapped around their heads and faces. Their encounter with his slingers had not put them off. Contemptuously Fergus looked away. The decision to march in a protective hollow square had slowed his progress but it would provide near immediate all-round defence if the nomads attacked or they were ambushed. Up ahead Dio and the twenty or so cavalrymen from the Third Legion had nearly vanished from sight on the horizon.

"Sir looks like Britannicus and his men are falling further behind," a centurion called out.

Turning to look towards the rear Fergus grunted, as he saw that Britannicus and his men were indeed lagging. The need to cajole and keep the stragglers and those men who couldn't keep up with the column moving, had already created a gap, a third of a mile wide from the main column.

"Shall I order the column to a halt Sir," the centurion called out. "Give them time to catch up with us."

Fergus came to a stop as he gazed back at the rear-guard. If he ordered the column to a halt, then effectively he would be conceding that they would be moving at the pace of the stragglers. That could put them in danger if the Arabs were just the advance party of a larger force. Irritably he bit his lip. The Arabs were smart. By threatening his stragglers, they were slowing his progress. Yet he had to keep moving. There was safety in mobility. In other circumstances the stragglers would have been placed on the supply wagons and a strong force of cavalry would have protected the rear-guard, but he had neither wagon's or cavalry.

"We keep moving," Fergus called out to the centurion. "But if the gap grows any larger we will call a halt and let them catch up."

Fergus was just about to move on, when out in the desert the Arabs turned around and started to gallop away towards the Roman rear-guard. Perplexed Fergus watched them go. The Bedouin were crying out to each other. Suddenly they divided into two parties. The camel-born infantry trotted straight towards Britannicus and his men, whilst the horsemen raced away in a lazy curving move that brought them around the rear of the party of Romans. As he watched the manoeuvres, Fergus felt a sudden and growing sense of alarm.

As the camel riders came on they began to extend into a wide line. They seemed intent on attacking the Romans. Amongst the rear-guard Britannicus had seen the threat and his men and some of the stragglers were rushing to form a defensive formation. Closing in on the Romans, the camel riders came to a halt, dismounted and stormed towards the Romans on foot, shouting and brandishing their weapons.

"Call the column to a halt," Fergus yelled at his cornice, as he saw the danger. "Get a company down there to re-enforce Britannicus. Go," he shouted at the centurion. Tensely Fergus watched as the first of the Romans started to hurry towards their comrade's aid. To the rear Britannicus had formed his men in a small defensive box, bristling with gleaming spear points. It was text book. Fergus grunted in approval. If Britannicus sat tight he would be able to see off the desert raiders until his comrades came to his aid.

Close by the trumpet rang out, ordering the Roman column to a halt. All by now had seen the fast-moving Arab strike against the rear-guard. In the desert the Arabs on foot were closing with the legionaries but just as they seemed to get drawn into hand to hand combat, the Bedouin suddenly began to retreat. Stay in your position Britannicus. "Stay in your fucking position," Fergus hissed to himself, as he stared at the confrontation. Then he groaned in dismay. Instead of remaining in their tight defensive box Britannicus and his men raised a cry and went charging off in a wild pursuit of the enemy. In an instant the tight defensive formation was shattered and lost. "No, no," Fergus cried out. But there was nothing he could do. The distance between the main column and the Roman rear-guard was only a third of a mile, but the company hastening to their comrades' aid was not going to get there in time.

Fergus's eyes widened in horror, as on cue the Arab horsemen came charging in from the rear where they'd been biding their time waiting to attack. Too late Britannicus and his men seemed to spot the new threat. Caught spread out in a disorganised state across the desert floor there was no time to form a defence. Within a few moments, the Arab horsemen were in amongst the legionaries, their horses' hooves kicking up small clouds of dust, as they cut down the men with swords, bows and spears. The cavalry attack was so sudden and furious that it caught many by surprise and the consequences were devastating. Screams and yells erupted across the desert and men went crashing and tumbling to the ground. Triumphantly the Arab infantrymen turned and joined in the battle.

Fergus started to run and, as he did he sensed the whole column doing the same. Up ahead all was shrieking confusion as the legionaries did their best to defend themselves. But they were outnumbered and disorganised. As the Romans closed the gap, the Arab horsemen suddenly fled, galloping away into the desert with loud blood curdling cries. The camel-mounted infantry still locked in vicious hand-to-hand combat with the legionaries, also broke away and began racing back to their mounts. Fergus cursed. He was too late. Across the desert floor the bodies of dozens of legionaries lay scattered about. Only a small band of men had managed to come together and seemed to have fought back-to-back and had survived. On the ground the wounded were screaming in agony.

As he reached the scene of carnage and saw the blood and the corpses strewn across the gravelly desert floor, Fergus shook with rage. This debacle had been avoidable. But there was no way he could seek vengeance on the Arabs or pursue them. He had no cavalry. Rushing up, the legionaries fanned out, trying to do what they could for their wounded comrades, but the scale of the disaster was clear to all. Slowing to a walk, Fergus made his way through the devastation towards the small band of weary men still clustered together in their tight defensive position. They had survived because they had stuck together. The twenty or so legionaries covered in dust and some smeared with blood, had held their own. Around their battered position a dozen Arabs had been killed and several more badly wounded. Amongst the band of men, Fergus suddenly recognised Britannicus. His protégé face was splattered with blood and he was clutching a blood-stained gladius.

Britannicus's eyes widened as he saw Fergus striding towards him. His shoulders sagged in relief and he was just about to speak, when Fergus slapped him hard across his face. The force of the blow sent the young tribune staggering backwards where he tripped over a corpse and landed on his back in the dust. A moment later the sharp point of Fergus's gladius was furiously hovering over Britannicus's throat.

"You disobeyed me. I told you to hold your position," Fergus roared, his voice shaking with fury.

***

The massive and spectacular mud-brick walls of the ancient city of Babylon rose up from the earth. The two and a half-thousand-year old city occupied both banks of the Euphrates with the river running through the heart of the metropolis. Its rectangular walls seemed in good condition. Fergus, surrounded by his staff and principal officers, stood in the desert gazing at the famous settlement where Alexander the Great had died. At his side the standard bearer was proudly holding up the square vexillation standard of the Fourth Scythica. Behind the officers the Roman column had come to a halt and the legionaries and slingers were resting and sitting around in the desert. A day had passed since the debacle with the desert raiders. The Arabs had not returned but the fight had cost him fifty-one dead and wounded. Fergus's face looked stern and hard and something seemed to have changed in him. Gone were his handsome youthful features and instead he seemed to have grown older and more mature over the past few days. Standing around him his officers, clad in their plumed helmets and body armour, their hands resting on their belts, remained silent, as all gazed at the city a mile away.

"There Sir," a centurion called out suddenly as he pointed at a small party of horsemen riding towards them. The party of riders was kicking up a cloud of dust as they hastened towards the Roman column. Patiently Fergus watched as the horsemen drew closer. At last he recognised Dio.

"Well," Fergus demanded as the centurion and his men came galloping up to him.

Dio hastily wiped the dust from his face.

"Emperor Trajan's camp is a mile south of the city on the right bank of the Euphrates," the centurion called out, as his face lit up in a grin. "The city of Babylon is still under Roman control. Trajan is here Sir."

Chapter Seven – An Audience with an Emperor

The playing-card shaped Roman army marching camp stood on the banks of the Euphrates within a mile of the walls of the shimmering city of Babylon. It was late afternoon and, in the bright blue sky, not a cloud was to be seen. On the side facing the river the local levees protected the camp, whilst landwards the only defences were a shallow V-shaped ditch and a low, rudimentary earthen rampart. Beyond the fixed defences Fergus could make out long rows of dusty army tents pitched in the fertile fields. A few guards were standing up on the embankment and a moment later, from within the camp, a trumpet rang out. Up ahead, at the camp entrance, more and more soldiers were rushing up and gathering, as news of the new-comers arrival spread. Fergus, marching at the head of his silent column, his left arm still stuck in its dirty, torn and stained sling, led his men straight towards the entrance. He looked stern and unsmiling. Just behind him came his staff, holding up the proud square vexillation standard of the Fourth Scythica Legion. Behind them, as if on parade, came the legionaries carrying their spears, marching packs and shields - in smart and neat ranks of eight men abreast and led by their officers. The main column was followed by a convoy of wagons he'd requisitioned in Babylon. The carts were of all sorts and upon them he'd placed the wounded, sick and those who couldn't keep up. Dio and the twenty of so cavalrymen of the Third Legion brought up the rear walking their horses calmly towards the Roman camp.

Approaching the entrance into the camp, Fergus was aware of the hundreds of curious and eager faces peering and craning their heads to get a glimpse of him and his men. Fergus kept his eyes fixed on the horizon. Now that they'd had confirmation that Emperor Trajan was present, he was determined to make his men's entrance into the camp as grand and perfect as possible. It would be a shame to let an opportunity slip by to make an impression on the old emperor. Marching into the camp, Fergus led his men straight down the main avenue towards the principia, the centre, where a collection of grander and larger tents indicated an HQ. Along the sides of the track the legionaries clustered, gazing at the newcomers in silence. The rhythmic tramp of the legionaries' boots dominated the silence as the proud vexillation of the Fourth came on in their smart unit formations.

Close to the HQ tents, a party of senior legionary officers had gathered and were standing waiting for him to reach them. The sunlight gleamed and reflected from their magnificent body armour and plumed helmets. As he marched up to them Fergus suddenly raised his voice.

"Column will come to a halt," he roared and abruptly he stopped in front of the group of officers, straightened up and rapped out a smart salute. Behind him the legionaries and slingers came to an immediate halt. Silently and stiffly the men remained standing in formation, gazing straight ahead, as if waiting to be inspected on the parade ground.

"Sir," Fergus cried in a loud voice as he addressed himself to one of the legionary legates. "Vexillation of the Fourth Scythica Legion reporting for duty Sir."

***

The army tent was large and spacious, much larger, grander and luxurious than Fergus was used to. Around the edges stood an array of expensive and finely crafted furniture, a chest, a table, a camp bed and a rack on which hung a splendid coat of armour. Several burly and tough looking praetorian guards were standing outside the entrance, the sunlight reflecting from their armour and helmets. One of them was holding up an imperial banner. The bronze Imagine depicted the face of emperor Trajan. Two more hard faced praetorian guards were standing stiffly to attention at the entrance that led into the secluded and curtained off main section of the tent. Fergus licked his lips, as he sat gazing at a jug of water that stood on the table opposite him. His face and red hair was still covered in a fine layer of dust and his beard was an untrimmed riot. Behind the heavy curtains he could hear voices, but they were muffled, and he could not hear what was being said. Nor did he have any idea of what was going on. They had told him to sit here and wait. That had been some time ago. There had been no time to get a wash or have his arm checked out by the legionary doctors. The debrief had lasted for more than an hour. The officers on Trajan's staff had wanted to know everything. The situation in Seleucia. The strength of the rebels. Names of their leaders. Their supply situation, levels of support. The state of the defences. The questions had gone on and on until Fergus had the feeling he was just repeating himself. It was only at the end of the debrief that he'd been able to mention to the senior officers that he would be sending Britannicus home in disgrace.

Suddenly the heavy curtains parted, and two senior officers appeared, heading purposefully for the exit. Hastily Fergus rose to his feet and quickly saluted and, as he did he recognised one of the officers. It was Lusius Quietus, his former commanding officer who had sacked him from his command a year and half ago. As Quietus glanced at him in passing and recognised Fergus, the small, darkish-skinned Berber cavalry general looked equally surprised. For a moment he paused in the middle of the tent gazing at Fergus. Then a little amused smile appeared on his lips, as if he was recalling some memory, and without having uttered a word he turned and disappeared out into the daylight.

"He will see you now," a voice said sharply. The voice had come from behind him.

Fergus turned around to see a tribune standing beside the heavy curtains. Hastily he crossed the floor of the tent and followed the officer through the gap in the curtains. Beyond, he found himself in a dim, stuffy and airless space. Several comfortable looking couches lined the sides of the tent and the middle of the room was dominated by a large wooden table, upon which lay a large-scale map, several papyrus scrolls, writing materials and a solitary sheathed gladius. A group of senior officers were standing to one side, but all were silent. Amongst them Fergus recognised the aquilifer, the legionary eagle standard bearer. The soldier was clutching the aquila, the sacred gold and silver eagle standard of the Sixth Legion. The eagle's beady eyes gleamed in the dim light and with its outstretched wings the eagle seemed ready for take-off. Its razor-sharp talons were outstretched, gripping the base of the standard.

"So, this is the man who has brought me a thousand valuable soldiers," a voice called out breaking the silence. Coolly Fergus turned to look in the direction of an old man sitting on his own on one of the couches. Trajan, conqueror of Dacia, Armenia and Parthia, emperor of Rome, father of the Roman people and lord and undisputed master over a quarter of the world's population, looked old, tired and unwell. But his physical ailments did not seem to have affected his mind. The sixty-three-year old emperor was studying Fergus keenly from his couch. He was clad in a purple cloak and fine, personally tailored body armour. His fingers were adorned with glittering rings and he was bareheaded, his hair trimmed short.

Instinctively and hastily Fergus turned, straightened up and saluted smartly. There was no mistaking who this man was. Trajan might be old and unwell but, as he stared at the emperor, Fergus quickly became aware of Trajan's formidable and fearless eyes examining him. It was easy to see why this old soldier and grizzled warrior remained boundlessly popular within the army and the populace. There was a greatness about him that was hard to describe but it was there.

"Sir," Fergus said quickly, unable to think of any other way in which to address the emperor.

"Stand at ease son," Trajan growled in a weary voice. "And come a bit closer so that I can get a good look at you."

Obediently Fergus took a few steps forwards and Trajan grunted. For a moment the tent remained silent.

"I remember you now. It's your red hair. That's unusual. You served under Quietus last year," Trajan said at last, as he looked up at Fergus. "Commander of the 7th Auxiliary Alae of Numidians. You were at Elegeia when king Parthamasiris of Armenia surrendered to me. You are one of Hadrian's men."

"Correct Sir," Fergus said stiffly. "At Elegeia I provided the escort for Parthamasiris Sir."

For a moment Trajan gazed at Fergus in astonishment. He had clearly not been expecting that. Then a little bemused smile appeared on the old warrior's lips and he looked away. Fergus remained silent. It had been Trajan himself who had ordered him to execute the Armenian king and make it look as if Parthamasiris had died whilst trying to escape. The "death trying to escape version" had become the official story.

"And now in this time of great crisis and betrayal you have brought me nearly a thousand highly valuable men," Trajan said with a sigh. "I can see why Hadrian trusted you. You are his man. Did you know that I have promoted him to overall commander of our Syrian and Armenian armies? You must be pleased. He's now effectively my deputy in this war." Trajan paused, as a brief distasteful look crossed his face. "I thought it wise in case something was to happen to me."

"I was not aware of this Sir," Fergus replied. "Maybe Sir, you have met my father," Fergus said quickly and boldly. "His name is Marcus. He is a senator back in Rome

Sir. He served with the 2nd Batavian Auxiliary Cohort. And my wife Sir. She is friends with your wife and niece."

"Marcus," Trajan said slowly, savouring the name. For a moment the emperor remained silent as he pondered on the name. "Ah yes Marcus," Trajan said at last. "The senator who opened that veteran's charity. Quietus was talking about him. Yes, I believe that I have met him a few times back in Rome. A good man I believe. He has raised a fine son."

"Thank you, Sir."

"I placed you in command of the garrison in Seleucia," Trajan said rounding on Fergus in a tired sounding voice. "Why did the people of Seleucia rise-up against me? I was lenient with them. I treated them fairly. Did you fuck it up?"

Fergus lowered his eyes and took a deep breath. The question had come up in the debrief, but he'd not been expecting to be asked again. Trajan was looking up at him and there was a sudden streak of cunning in the old warrior's, wise and fearless eyes. As if he was about to judge him on the answer he provided. Across the room Fergus was suddenly conscious of the group of officers closely observing him. For a moment he paused. He had to be careful in what he said if he wanted to avoid having the uprising blamed on him.

"I did not fuck it up Sir," Fergus replied. "I treated the civilian population with respect and according to the rules set down by your staff. I guess it is the nature of men everywhere to crave freedom. There was just not enough time to teach them to be loyal to Rome, but I tried Sir. Everyone under my command tried and when it became apparent that we were going to fail, I decided to lead my men to safety and bring them here to you. I guessed that you would be needing us Sir."

Trajan did not reply. Then slowly the emperor rose to his feet and patting Fergus on the shoulder, he walked across to the table and gazed down at the map.

"Relax," Trajan said sharply. "No one is accusing you of a dereliction of duty. I have been a soldier for forty years and I can tell when a man is telling the truth. You did the right thing in evacuating your men and bringing them here. Seleucia is not the only city to have risen in revolt. I have received reports that Doura too has risen, as have Edessa in Osrhoene. Hatra too and Nisibis and apparently most of Armenia. They have all chosen to defy me, to betray me. Quietus heads north, as I speak, to gather our forces to crush the rebellions in Osrhoene and northern Mesopotamia. The Consul Maximus is trying to delay Sanatruces's advance and in Armenia the governor Severus will no doubt have his hands full. So, Seleucia is just another fucking headache amongst many and it doesn't look like it's going to get better any time soon. Prince Sanatruces marches on Ctesiphon with an army intent on liberating the Parthian capital. I must face him in battle, but I can't, not yet anyway, not with just two understrength legions and a few praetorian cohorts."

"Ctesiphon and Babylon remain loyal Sir," Fergus said quickly. "And most of the countryside we passed through is quiet and peaceful."

"Yes, yes," Trajan said in an irritable voice. "Ctesiphon and Babylon remain loyal because my presence here scares them shitless. That's the only reason. But if Prince Sanatruces manages to liberate Ctesiphon then every fucking Parthian peasant and his dog is going to feel entitled to rebel against us."

With a sudden and surprisingly swift move for such an old man, Trajan slammed his fist down on the table.

"It must not happen," the old, worn out looking warrior cried. "It will not happen. I will defeat Sanatruces in battle and crush these Parthian peasants and their presumptions if it is the last thing I do. This uprising will not succeed. These Parthians will learn to fear me. We shall bring them back under the shadow of our eagles. Once the rest of the troops arrive you and I, Fergus, are going to march out to confront this Parthian prince and we're going to kill him."

***

Carefully the doctor raised Fergus's left arm and peered at the scab that covered the knife wound. Stoically and bare-chested Fergus sat on the chair, as he waited for the army doctor to finish his examination. The two of them were in Fergus's sparsely decorated tent. A day had passed since his audience with Trajan and he and his men had been assigned quarters in the camp. It had been a welcome improvement to finally be able to sleep on a camp bed under shelter from the elements, have time to prepare a proper dinner, repair his equipment, have a wash and tend to his beard and scars.

Muttering something to himself, the doctor lowered Fergus's arm.

"Has it healed?" Fergus asked in an anxious voice.

"Looks all right," the doctor said. "You were lucky that it did not get infected. The sling can come off, but you should use your arm sparingly. You should make a full recovery, gods willing."

"Thank you," Fergus growled in relief, as he reached for his tunic.

As he started to dress himself and the doctor packed away his medical equipment, Fergus turned to the surgeon with a quizzical look.

"I saw you in the emperor's tent yesterday," Fergus exclaimed. "I thought I recognised you. You were there when I had my audience with Trajan. Are you the emperor's doctor? Are you tending to him?"

The doctor sighed. "I am an army doctor," the man replied, as he turned to leave Fergus's tent. "I belong to the Sixth Legion. The emperor has his own personal doctors that take care of him."

"I have heard rumours that Trajan's health is deteriorating. Is that true?" Fergus asked quickly.

At the exit leading out of the army tent the doctor paused.

"The emperor is in denial," the doctor snapped at last. "All I know is that he is refusing to believe what his doctors are telling him. But yes, his health is deteriorating."

And with that, the army surgeon stepped out into the daylight. For a moment Fergus gazed thoughtfully at the exit to his tent. Adalwolf had been right when at Antioch he'd told him about Trajan's declining health. Stiffly Fergus turned, slipped into his tunic and reached for his body armour and belt. As he dressed himself, his hand brushed against the Celtic amulet hanging around his neck. The finely woven iron work felt refreshingly cold as it touched his skin. Pausing Fergus looked down at the amulet. According to Trajan the kingdom of Osrhoene had risen in rebellion and Zeugma was right on the front line. But he could not dwell on his family's fate. He had to trust that they would be all right. It would be impossible to continue otherwise.

"Sir," a serious sounding voice said suddenly. Looking around, Fergus saw Dio standing in the entrance to his tent. The centurion had removed his helmet and had tucked it under his arm. He looked grave.

"May I have a word Sir?" Dio asked.

"Go on," Fergus replied, as he turned to fasten his belt around his waist.

A moment later the flap to his tent was pulled aside and a group of officers from his vexillation entered. Calmly Fergus stopped what he was doing and straightened up. What was going on? Dio and the centurions silently formed a semi-circle around him. Looking at them, Fergus saw that nearly every centurion from his command was present, their faces grave and serious looking.

"It is regarding Britannicus Sir," Dio said. "We are here to plead leniency on his behalf. All of us here feel the same way Sir."

"Britannicus disobeyed orders," Fergus snapped. "I am sending him home in disgrace."

"He is young. He was rash. He made a mistake Sir, but he is nevertheless a good man, a good officer," Dio replied quietly. "He saved all of us by holding the palace in Seleucia. He is devastated by your decision to send him home in disgrace. His career will be over. He will be a broken man. We ask you to reconsider Sir. Give Britannicus a second chance Sir."

Fergus turned to look away in silence. Then he sighed. The intervention by his officers irritated him, but deep down he knew that as overall commander he was ultimately responsible for everything that went on under his command. He too shared responsibility for the debacle out in the desert.

"I will consider your request," Fergus said brusquely as he turned to look at Dio.

Chapter Eight - There is always a Cost

On the pontoon bridge that had been thrown across the Tigris, thousands upon thousands of legionaries, praetorian guards, auxiliary infantry, Batavians, Numidian cavalry, wagons, camels, archers, slingers and artillery from across the empire, were on the move. The Roman column was endless. The rhythmic tramp of thousands of hobnailed boots, the cries of the officers, the snorting of horses, the baying of mules and the trundle of hundreds of wagon wheels filled the evening with noise. Out on the water, under the big cloudless skies, a solitary fisherman had cast his nets into the river and was gazing in silence at Trajan's army as it crossed the Tigris. With the setting sun to his back, Fergus led his men up onto the bridge and as he did, he peered at the eastern bank of the wide, peaceful river. Amongst the arid fields and clumps of palm trees, Roman engineers and work parties of legionaries were busy constructing the marching camp. The evening light reflected from their armour and pick-axes. Fergus licked his cracked lips, as he turned his attention to the Tigris. His deeply tanned face, hair and body armour were covered in a fine layer of dust and sand and streaked with sweat. The sling and the bandage around his forehead had gone and he could use his left arm again, although it remained a little stiff. Maybe, later tonight when he'd completed all his duties, he would get the chance to have a quick dip and swim. He'd been on the move since dawn and even though the intensity of the day's heat was receding, he could feel the sweat and sand clinging to him.

As he made his way across the pontoon bridge and approached the eastern bank, he caught sight of a group of senior officers standing on the bank observing the troops as they crossed. The officers were easily identifiable by their fine cloaks, armour and helmets. Moving towards them at the head of his eight hundred strong vexillation, Fergus turned his head to the officers and snapped out a quick salute, which was returned. Fergus marched on, following the unit ahead of him. Two weeks had gone by since he'd led his men into the emperor's camp at Babylon. The time for rest and recovery had been short, for within days other Roman contingents had arrived and the camp had quickly swelled to over twenty thousand men. And a few days later Trajan had decided that the time had come to march east to confront Prince Sanatruces. The news had been greeted with relief and eagerness by the men. A major and decisive battle was coming. Every man knew it. But with it came the hope that the battle would crush the uprising once and for all.

The unit ahead of him was moving towards the marching camp that was still being constructed and, as he followed them, Fergus turned to snatch a quick glance over his shoulder. Striding on behind him with his staff officers was Britannicus. The young tribune looked glum and depressed. Since they had arrived in the emperor's camp he'd kept himself to himself, avoiding any social contact or occasion with his fellow officers. It was as if he was deeply ashamed of himself. And rightly so Fergus thought, as he turned away. By rights he should have sent Britannicus home in disgrace. The tribune had disobeyed orders and his mistake had gotten men needlessly killed. There was no excuse for that. But in the end, Fergus thought with sudden weariness, he too shared blame for the debacle. And so, he had decided to give Britannicus a second chance. The reprieve however had not done anything to alleviate the strained relationship that now existed between him and his former protégé.

***

It was getting late when Fergus at last managed to get away from supervising his men's camp building duties. Slinging a towel over his shoulder and slipping a sponge into his tunic pocket, he headed for the banks of the Tigris. A quick swim and wash in the river was just what he needed. Around him, the huge army camp was a hive of activity. Long rows of white army tents stretched away in neat ordered lines and men, mules and horses were moving along the paths in between the tents. Striding towards the river bank he suddenly paused. In the fading light he caught sight of the distinctive uniforms and helmets of a Batavian cavalry alae. The Batavians occupied a section of a long row of white army tents and most were huddled around their small cooking fires, busy preparing their evening meal. They were speaking in low voices and in their native language and, as he listened Fergus recognised a few words. Gazing at them with sudden interest, Fergus turned and strode up to a group of Batavians who were tending to their horses.

"Are any of you from the 2nd Batavian Cohort?" Fergus called out.

The cavalrymen turned and gazed at Fergus in silence as he approached. Repeating his question haltingly in the few Batavian words he'd learned from his father, Fergus paused.

"We're from the Ninth Sir," one of the troopers replied at last in Latin, as he reached up to stroke the nose of one of the horses.

"My father served with the 2nd for 23 years," Fergus replied with a friendly nod. "His name is Marcus. He commanded the Cohort during the Brigantian uprising in Britannia." Fergus paused and took a deep breath as he recalled Marcus's words. "He gave a speech to his men once."

"So, trust in the man beside you and do your duty for in the coming days I want our enemy to cry out in alarm as they see us approach. I want to hear them shout: Ah shit. Here come those damned Batavians again."

For a moment the Batavian troopers remained silent, as they glanced at each other. None of them looked a shade over twenty-five.

"It was before our time, but we know the speech Sir," one of the Batavians replied politely in heavily accented Latin.

Fergus nodded again and grinned, trying to engage the young troopers in conversation, but they seemed reluctant to do so. An awkward silence followed. The real motive for approaching them, he knew, was because he was hoping that against the odds they would have news about his father and his family back on Vectis. The Batavian community was small but tightly knit and its members were spread across the empire. Maybe they had heard rumours, snippets, anything? But as the realisation dawned that they had no news, Fergus looked down at the ground.

"Very good," Fergus said looking up quickly with a friendly smile. "Very good. Carry on."

Turning awkwardly away from the group, Fergus started out once more in the direction of the river. But he had not gotten far when he heard running feet coming towards him. In the gloom he saw the runner from his staff and as he recognised the man, Fergus groaned. Some instinct warned him he was not going to get a chance to have a swim after all. The runner seemed to be looking for him. He was in a hurry.

"I am over here," Fergus called out from the gloom.

Hastening towards him, the legionary quickly rapped out a salute.

"A message from the legate," the soldier said hastily. "He says you are to report to his HQ right away Sir."

***

"What's going on Sir?" Fergus asked, as he strode along at the legate's side. The two of them were hastening towards the central section of the camp, where the emperor and his entourage had set up their tents.

"I don't know," the commanding officer of the Sixth Legion replied. "Trajan has called a meeting of all his senior officers. It's unexpected. Something must have happened."

Fergus remained silent as they approached the encampment. His seven hundred and fifty strong vexillation had been attached to the Sixth, to whose legate he now reported. In the evening sky the first of many twinkling stars had appeared. Dozens of praetorian guards were on duty around the cluster of imperial tents. Making their way towards a large pitched tent, Fergus glanced around. There was a tension amongst the Roman officers converging on the HQ. He could see it in their faces and the urgency by which they approached. Something indeed must have happened.

Oil lamps had been fixed to the sides of the tent and in their flickering, reddish glow Fergus could see that well over fifty senior legionary and auxiliary officers were present inside the spacious tent. They were talking to each other in low, urgent and hushed voices.

Taking a spot at the back of the gathering, Fergus and his commanding officer patiently and silently waited for the emperor to appear.

As at last Trajan entered the tent, accompanied by a squad of stern and hard-faced praetorians, the officers silently and respectfully stepped aside to allow him to move towards a chair and a small table that had been readied for him. Eagerly Fergus peered at the emperor. There was no doubt that his physical health was deteriorating but Trajan's spirit seemed undimmed. If anything, he looked more determined than ever. Without saying a word or acknowledging anyone, Trajan made his way to the chair and tiredly lowered himself into it. For a moment the old warrior gazed down at the table, lost in thought. He looked sombre.

"Gentlemen," Trajan called out at last without looking up. "I have received news in the past hour. Bad news. The consul Maximus and his troops have been routed by the Parthians. Maximus is dead, killed in battle. Prince Sanatruces advances on Ctesiphon with his army. He is a mere forty miles away from us as of tonight."

A murmur arose amongst the gathered officers.

"Tomorrow we will break camp and advance to meet Sanatruces on the plains east of Ctesiphon, where we shall bring an end to his career," Trajan called out and as he spoke, he lifted his head and gazed up at his officers. Despite the bad news Fergus found his lips forming into a grin. The old warrior's confidence and resolve rang true and were infectious. Trajan was a leader. A formidable leader - for when he spoke men believed him. There was no doubt about it. His presence filled the tent with confidence.

"We shall halt the Parthian advance and avenge Maximus," Trajan called out. "We shall crush this uprising and restore order. Mesopotamia and its people belong to Rome. We are not going to give up all the hard-won territory that we have conquered these past two years. No fucking way. No, fucking way," Trajan cried out in a louder voice.

For the briefest moment the large tent remained silent. Then a stir rippled through the assembly and as one, the officers raised their voices and cried out in fierce agreement. Some began to stamp their boots on the ground and suddenly the chant swept through the tent.

"Parthicus. Parthicus. Parthicus!"

Fergus joined in crying out the honorary title that the Senate back in Rome had voted to bestow on Trajan earlier in the year for his unprecedented conquests of Armenia, Osrhoene, Adiabene and Mesopotamia.

As the officers started to file out of the tent, a young tribune came up to Fergus and the legate of the Sixth and motioned for them to stay behind.

"Sir," the tribune said quickly, addressing himself to the legate and handing him a small letter bearing Trajan's personal seal. "Here are your new orders. See that they are carried out immediately."

***

Standing in his command post out in the desert, Fergus peered across the flat, arid, and brown ground towards the gates leading into the square Parthian fort. The high mudbrick walls of the enemy stronghold were strengthened by four towers, one to each corner, and on the western side the fort was protected by the wide, placid waters of the Tigris. The water sparkled in the clear dawn sunlight. On the battlements, he could make out armed men gazing back at him. Fluttering from the top of one of the towers was a defiant Parthian banner. There could be no more than a few hundred defenders Fergus thought, as he studied the defences. Clustered around Fergus, his officers - clad in their sturdy body armour and wearing their plumed helmets, remained silent. All his officers were gazing at the solitary figure hastening towards them across the two hundred yards of no man's land that separated the Roman siege lines from the Parthian fortification. Fergus remained motionless, his hands resting on his hips as the figure approached.

A day and a night had passed since he had been ordered to break away from Trajan's army, march south and take this small but strategically important Parthian fort. For, from its position on the eastern bank of the Tigris, twenty miles south of Ctesiphon; the square stronghold threatened Roman supply lines and controlled the river traffic between Charax in the deep southern delta and Ctesiphon to the north. The battle group's new orders had been greeted with dismay by his officers, for all feared that it would mean that they would miss the decisive battle against prince Sanatruces. But orders were orders. The Parthian fort had to be taken. The old redoubt had been abandoned until only a few days ago, when a force of rebels from Seleucia had managed to sail downstream, reoccupy it and start to disrupt the river traffic.

"They say no," the vexillation standard bearer said suddenly breaking the silence as he peered at the figure hurrying towards them. In his hand the signifier was holding up the square vexillation banner of the Fourth Scythica and his helmet was covered in a wolf's head.

Fergus remained silent as the Parthian translator closed the gap. As the translator caught sight of Fergus he quickly shook his head.

"Sir," the translator gasped, as he made it to the command post. "They refuse to surrender. They told me they shall fight to the death. They told me to tell you to stuff your demand up your arse."

Disappointed, Fergus shifted his attention from the translator and back to the fort. He had his answer. It had been a worth a try to get the enemy to surrender. If time had been on his side, he could have minimised his casualties and settled down to starve the enemy out, or undermine his walls with siege tunnels, but those options were closed. His orders were to take the fort and take it quickly and then to re-join Trajan's army with all possible speed. The emperor it seemed, needed all available troops to be present for the coming battle against Sanatruces.

"Have the scorpions start to shoot at those battlements," Fergus growled, as he turned to his officers. "Target the men above the gateway to keep them guessing as to where our main assault will come."

Quickly Fergus turned to Britannicus. The young tribune was watching him tensely and anxiously.

"I want you to take the battering ram and strike the eastern wall," Fergus said in a clear voice. "Make sure that you protect the ram, for it is the only one we have. Use your archers to provide cover and have your men form a testudo. Batter down that wall. Once you have made a breach - storm the fort. I shall lead the main force into the stronghold. No prisoners. They had their chance to surrender. I want this stronghold captured before nightfall today. Is that clear?"

"Yes Sir," Britannicus said in a quick, eager voice as his face lit up with sudden relief and determination. "Thank you, Sir. You can count on me. Today I shall win back your respect. The fort shall be ours before nightfall."

As Britannicus hastened away, Fergus watched him go. He still wasn't completely sure that giving the tribune a second chance was the right thing to do. But it had been the easiest thing to do. The strained relationship between them had not however improved. Britannicus, terrified of the shame of being sent home in disgrace, had responded to his reprieve, by becoming more and more desperate to prove himself. He had become terrified of being denied his chance to redeem himself. Pride in oneself meant everything to him. Disgrace and humiliation were worse than death. Fergus sighed. Every soldier he'd ever met had had that same fierce self-respect, a pride that meant more than almost everything else. But Britannicus was taking it to a new level. If he had ordered Britannicus to singlehandedly attack the fort it was likely the tribune would have done so.

The sound of the battery of scorpions going into action, made Fergus turn to look to his right. The carroballistae, giant cross bows mounted on wagons, had started to hurl their massive bolts at the defenders above the gates. The twang and crack of the Roman light artillery reverberated across the open desert. From under the simple canvas sheet held up by wooden poles that passed for his command post, Fergus silently observed his troops as they began to move up into their assault positions. His battlegroup built around the seven hundred and fifty or so legionaries of his own vexillation had been reinforced by a company of Syrian archers, three squadrons of Numidian light cavalry, a battery of cart-mounted artillery and a detachment of combat engineers who were manning the battering ram. Close by and being held in reserve, the ninety or so Numidian cavalrymen upon their small shaggy horses, were gazing at the Parthian fort. Quickly Fergus's eyes swept the desert to his rear. But there was no sign of trouble from that direction. There had been no time or resources to build proper siege fortifications, but a scattering of anti-cavalry caltrops and sharpened wooden stakes provided some protection to their rear, if Parthian cavalry did show up and try to relieve their besieged comrades.

A shriek of pure terror rang out from the men above the gates, as one of the scorpion bolts decapitated a man with brutal force sending his body and head flying backwards into the stronghold.

"Direct hit Sir," one of the officers nearby growled, in a satisfied voice.

Fergus didn't reply. His attention was firmly fixed on the movement of Britannicus's troops and the solitary battering ram, that was slowly rolling towards the eastern wall. The wheeled battering ram, a heavy wagon with a long wooden beam suspending on ropes beneath a protective shed-like structure, was attracting a lot of Parthian attention, but their missiles were bouncing harmlessly off its iron and hide clad roof. On either side of the ram, two companies of legionaries, a hundred and sixty men, were slowly advancing on the wall, tightly packed in their enclosed testudo formations, their shields raised above their heads, front and flanks. As he gazed at the war machine's progress, Fergus was suddenly reminded of the fortresses in Dacia which he had helped to reduce. Compared to those formidable stone monsters, perched on their lofty impregnable cliff tops, this was going to be a relatively straightforward task but as with every military operation, there would always be a cost. A cost counted in men's lives.

"Once that ram reaches the enemy wall," Dio said quietly, as he came up to Fergus, "it will be only a matter of time before that wall collapses. Should we not move the main assault force into position so that we can exploit the breach as soon as possible Sir?"

"No keep them facing the gates," Fergus replied sharply. "I want the enemy to keep guessing until the last moment from which direction the main blow will come. I will give the order when the time is right."

"Very well Sir," Dio said quickly, as he lowered his eyes.

That was his job as commander Fergus thought, as he peered intently at the progress of his troops. To move amongst his men, to encourage them, to judge situations and make the right decisions at the right time and in the right place. If he could successfully do that, then victory would surely follow.

Along the eastern wall of the Parthian fort the defenders seemed to be throwing everything they had into stopping the slow but inexorable progress of the battering ram. Arrows and stones went hurtling and zipping through the air, pounding the roof of the ram and the accompanying legionaries. From the ramparts, the Parthians were screaming and shouting; working themselves up into a fever pitch. In reply the eighty Syrian archers, with their distinctive pointy helmets and loose chain mail armour, were down on one knee out in the desert; their beautiful composite bows pointing upwards as they sent volley after volley of arrows at the defenders.

Tensely Fergus watched the battle unfolding and, as he did his fingers started to fidget with the pommel of Corbulo's old gladius. Choosing the right moment to commit his main assault force was going to be crucial. But it was even more important that his men saw that he was willing to take the same risks as they had to. As the battering ram and the testudo finally reached the Parthian wall, Dio, standing beside Fergus, hissed in delight and clenched his fist. For a moment nothing happened. Then Fergus saw the massive, suspended wooden beam with the copper head of a ram at its point, swing out of its protective shed before slamming back into the wall with a dull thud. Once more the combat engineers working inside the shed, swung the massive beam backwards before letting it slam back into the wall, hitting it at the exact same spot. Up on the wall the Parthian defenders had responded by lowering a large leather bag filled with hay. They were trying to swing the bag into position, so that it would soften the blows from the battering ram, but the effort failed as the man holding the rope was struck by two arrows in quick succession and dropped the rope, causing the bag to fall to the ground.

"Not long now Sir," Dio said excitedly.

Fergus said nothing as the ram's head crashed once more into the wall. Dio was right. That wall was not going to remain standing for long. Already he could see cracks appearing along it. On the ramparts, the Parthian defenders too had sensed the impending collapse and had given up on their efforts to defend the wall. They were retreating from the point of danger.

"Have the men form up on me," Fergus snapped, turning quickly to Dio. "Flying wedge. No prisoners. We go in through the breach."

As Dio hastened away and started to relay his orders to the five hundred heavily armed legionaries crouching behind the command post, Fergus's attention remained fixed on the wall. A legionary from the squad assigned to him for close personal protection, hastily handed him his large infantry shield and helmet. Quickly Fergus slid the ordinary legionary's helmet with the wide cheek guards and flat-rimmed neck guard over his head and raised the large shield. The shield's grip and helmet brought back a hundred memories, but he refused to think about them. With a suddenness that took everyone by surprise, a section of the wall seemed to sway and then with a tumbling, chaotic crash the mudbrick wall collapsed, sending a cloud of reddish dust billowing into the air. For a moment all was silent. Then a triumphant cry rose from the Roman ranks.

Pulling his sword from his sheath, Fergus raised it above his head.

"Follow me," he roared.

Without waiting to see if the men were following, he started out at a run, heading straight towards the breach in the walls. The shield felt heavy, and as he reached the base of the wall his left arm was already aching from the effort of holding it. An arrow zipped past, striking the ground. Shocked, Fergus looked up to see the Parthian archers shooting at him from up on the wall. Another arrow shot past narrowly missing him. But this was no time for second thoughts. In the tumbled mass of mud bricks and broken debris, the men from Britannicus's two infantry companies were already clambering over the broken masonry and pouring into the fort. Clouds of dust, kicked up by the collapse, obscured his view but briefly Fergus caught a glimpse of Britannicus's fine red-plumed helmet vanishing into the enemy stronghold. Fergus swore as his boot caught a sharp piece of broken masonry. Hastily he clambered up over the mound of broken bricks, half choking on the dust. Behind him, the five hundred legionaries came charging after him in an extended V shaped formation with Fergus at the very apex. As Fergus slithered down into the fort in an undignified manner, a Parthian shrieking in a high-pitched, outraged voice, launched himself at Fergus swinging a captured Roman spear. Fergus just had time to block the blow with his shield, stumbling backwards as he did. As the Parthian came at him again he was impaled by a legionary's spear. Behind Fergus, more and more legionaries came slithering and streaming into the fort.

"Kill them all. Kill them all," a Roman voice screamed.

Wildly Fergus looked around him. All was chaos and confusion. Clouds of reddish dust obscured part of his view but inside, the fort seemed to consist of a single storey building surrounded by an open parade ground. Corpses and the wounded were strewn across the sandy, bone-dry ground. Ignoring the shrieking, confused and merciless hand-to-hand combat that was raging all around him, he set out towards the building at the heart of the small fort. He'd gone no more than a few yards, when he was set upon by three Parthians. The men came charging towards him, wielding swords and knives, their faces contorted in rage and hatred. Taking a blow on his shield, Fergus jabbed at one of the men and was rewarded by a shriek of pain. Then the men assigned to his close protection were suddenly all around him, stabbing and driving the Parthians backwards.

But the defenders were not so easily beaten and within seconds, the small group of Romans with Fergus at their centre, was surrounded by a vicious, snarling mob. Instinctively the nine Romans bunched together, forming a small tight circle as they desperately fended off the Parthian attacks and blows with their shields and stabbed at their opponents. Fergus suddenly found himself unable to move or raise his hand. His shield was torn from his grip. All he could do was stand up. The tight press of bodies around him was squeezing him, making it hard even to breath. Grimly Fergus struggled to stay on his feet as the mass of screaming, yelling men around him tried to kill each other. If he slipped now he would be trampled to death within seconds. This way and then that way, the mass of bodies swayed and moved, buffeted by the vicious, swirling fighting with Fergus unable to do anything about it.

Then abruptly the Parthian assault collapsed. More legionaries appeared, savagely cutting their way through the enemy ranks with their short stabbing swords. There was no one better at this sort of close quarters fighting than the Roman legionary. As the pressure around him eased, Fergus was able to raise his sword. Nearby, a Roman collapsed as he was struck by a thrown spear, and from the ramparts a body came tumbling down into the debris with a sickening crunch. Grimly, Fergus stooped and picked up a discarded legionary shield and began to move towards the building, where upon the roof a Parthian banner was still defiantly flying.

"Tear that fucking flag down," Fergus roared, gesturing at the Parthian banner with his sword.

But there was no time for the men to carry out his order, for within a few seconds the Parthians seemed to have regrouped. A group of them, formed into a V shape wedge, came charging straight towards Fergus. Their momentum tore a gap in the Roman line, sending the legionaries scattering and stumbling backwards. As the lead man came at him, Fergus however caught him square on his shield and stabbed him in the head stopping the man's wild charge dead in its tracks. Around him all was chaos, as men hacked and stabbed at each other in a wild, screaming melee. Suddenly Fergus's face was splattered by someone else's blood. Hastily he raised his sword arm to wipe the blood from his eyes. Nearby, two men were wrestling on the ground, locked in a fight to the death and a few yards away, a wounded legionary was choking to death, his hands pressed in vain to a nasty neck wound.

"Kill them all boys. Kill them all," a Roman voice screamed.

Determinedly Fergus started out again towards the entrance into the building. Dimly he was conscious of his bodyguards hastily regrouping around him. The Parthians seemed to have marked him out as the Roman commander for his bodyguards were struggling to fend off the increasingly desperate Parthian attacks and lunges. The enemy were out to get him. But how could this be so. How had they managed to mark him out as the Roman commander? He was clad in an ordinary legionary helmet and was holding a legionary shield. With a rush Fergus suddenly realised that he was still wearing his tribune's cloak. He had forgotten to take it off.

"Tear down that banner," Fergus roared again.

Around him the Parthian resistance was beginning to grow disorganised. As more and more legionaries appeared and came pouring into the fort, the Romans started to drive the enemy back up against the western wall. There was no way out for the Parthians. They were trapped. But as the enemy resistance started to splinter into small bands of isolated and desperate men, there was no question of surrender. Nor did the Parthians seem to wish for it. They looked like they were going to stay true to their word and fight to the end. Grimly Fergus made it to the entrance to the building. A squad of legionaries were already there and were trying to batter their way inside, but the stubborn door refused to budge. With a venomous kick Fergus launched his foot against the door but he too was repelled.

With an annoyed look Fergus turned away. His chest was heaving from exertion. Around him, across the open parade ground, the scene that met his eyes was one of absolute carnage. The bodies of the fallen lay scattered around, lying on their own or in groups on top of each other. Discarded weapons, shields, decapitated heads, severed arms, boots, feet and helmets were strewn about. A few wounded were shrieking and crying out in pain and a solitary figure was trying to drag himself through the sand, leaving a bloody trail behind him like snail. But the bloody fight was nearly over. The fort was about to fall. Trying to calm his breathing, Fergus paused to stare at a column of legionaries who had made it up onto the western wall and had begun to clear it of its last defenders. Closer by, a knot of determined defenders had retreated to a corner of the fort and were fighting furiously and valiantly as they kept the legionaries at bay.

"There is no need to close with them. They are finished," Fergus roared at a centurion, as he angrily gestured at the knot of Parthian defenders boxed in against the walls. "Bring up the Syrian archers and have them finish off those men."

Abruptly turning away Fergus once more lunged at the door into the building, but it still refused to budge. He was about to try again when he saw Dio running towards him. The centurion's fine armour was splattered in blood and dust and he had lost his helmet. Something in Dio's expression made Fergus hesitate.

"What?" he roared at his subordinate.

"Sir," Dio's face was ashen. "It's Britannicus Sir. He's dead. His men say he got separated from the company. He tried to kill the Parthian leader by himself. He's over there, Sir."

"What?" Fergus growled in confusion, as a little colour shot into his cheeks. "Dead?"

"I am afraid so Sir," Dio gasped.

"Shit," Fergus hissed, as he quickly looked away. Then he swore again in a softer voice as the realisation sank in. There was always a cost.

"Shit."

Chapter Nine – Battle

Fergus to his dearest Galena,

Tomorrow is the big day. Tomorrow we at last face Prince Sanatruces in battle. It is night as I write this letter to you my love. I am with Trajan's army some distance east of Ctesiphon. I can see the camp fires of the enemy less than two miles away. They say that the Parthians outnumber us two to one. It is not very nice out here in these arid wastelands and I do miss the green woodlands and meadows of Britannia and Vectis. The past few weeks have been tough, but I am well. We have heard that the kingdom of Osrhoene has joined the uprising. If this is so, I pray that you and the girls have sought refuge and are safe and well - for you know that you and our girls mean everything to me.

I do not know if you have received my previous letters. The postal system has become unreliable in these unstable and dangerous times. If I manage to survive the battle tomorrow I shall write again. If not, you should know that I am happy to die for Rome and I willingly give my life for all of you. I will not send this letter but keep it on me. The thought that you all are well is sustaining me and I hope that what little good I have been able to do in this life will not be forgotten in the other.

I shall pray for you and the girls tonight. Give them each a kiss from me. Fergus to his Galena

Fergus stopped writing and for a moment he looked lost in thought, as he sombrely gazed down at the neat letters scratched into the small, soft wood tablet. Then quickly he closed the letter and slipped it into his tunic. Across the big and clear night sky, thousands upon thousands of stars were visible, twinkling and glowing peacefully in the darkness. It was a most magnificent sight, but Fergus seemed not to notice. Reaching for the oil lamp he rose from his chair and holding up the lamp, he started out into the darkness. Around him, stretching away for several miles the camp fires of Trajan's army seemed to mirror the stars.

It was time to do his rounds Fergus thought. With a major battle likely within the next few hours it was important that his men saw him amongst them. Alone, he made his way through the camp, pausing here and there to speak a few words to his legionaries. The men were sitting huddled around their camp fires, resting, sleeping, eating and preparing for the coming battle. They seemed pleased to see Fergus and as they recognised him, some of them called out his name, offering to share their food and wine with him. Declining all invitations, Fergus kept on moving. It was in times like these, he had discovered, that having a good memory served him well for it allowed him to remember men's individual achievements and actions. And seeing and hearing their commander remember, praise and call out what they had done, had a huge morale boost on the men.

When at last he had finished his rounds, spoken to his centurions and checked the sentry posts, the night was already well advanced. Wearily Fergus sat down on the looted Parthian chair that had been placed near his tent. For a moment he closed his eyes, but he could not sleep even though he knew he must. Opening his eyes, he turned to gaze in the direction of his gear and personal belongings. There was not much, just a worn army blanket, a metal army cup, all Galena's letters, a ration of grain, dried beans and the bag containing Britannicus's ashes. After the capture of the Parthian fort on the banks of the Tigris, he'd ordered the fort and its walls to be demolished. The stronghold was too strategic and important for it to be allowed to be used again as a rebel base, and there were no Roman troops available to hold the place. As for the enemy dead and his own casualties, he'd ordered them to be burned. The slain had been gathered together in great heaps and after a few simple funerary rites had been said, petroleum had been poured over the bodies and they had been set alight. The flames and smoke would have been visible for miles, but he hadn't cared who would see it. Wearily Fergus stared at the bag containing Britannicus's ashes. Then he bit his lip. It had been the easiest option to give Britannicus a second chance, but had it been the right decision? After the battle he'd ordered Britannicus's body to be honoured and burned separate to the others. Dio had performed the religious funerary rites, and afterwards Fergus had collected the ashes and placed them in a bag. He had vowed that if he survived the war and was able to make it back to Britannia, he would hand the tribune's ashes back to his family in Londinium, so that they would be able to bury their son in his native soil.

***

The sight of twenty thousand Roman legionaries and auxiliaries drawn up ready for battle was truly awesome. It was morning and Fergus, clad in his body armour, greaves, cloak, and wearing a tribune's plumed helmet, sat upon his horse directly behind the front line, accompanied by his staff and bodyguards. Stoically Fergus turned to look around at the massed Roman army formations. Across the flat, arid plain on either side of his position, stretching for two miles, was a continuous line of Roman soldiers, standing shoulder to shoulder. The sunlight reflected from the legionary's and auxiliary's armour, and the men's shields were resting against their legs. In their hands the soldiers were clutching their spears. The Romans were arrayed three ranks deep, their unit standards proudly on display. Their centurions, identifiable by their plumed helmets, stood with their men in the front row, whilst their optio's stood at the back of the third row, ready to force any man back into position with their wooden staff's. Amongst the cohort formations small gaps had been left for the skirmishers. The lightly clad slingers and javelin men were drawn up in a ragged thin line, directly in front of the heavy infantry. It was their job to harass the enemy before the main clash of the heavy infantrymen. And despite the huge numbers of men, the battlefield remained eerily silent.

Carefully Fergus allowed himself to exhale. He had fought in countless skirmishes, sieges and small battles during his twelve years of army service, but never in anything like this; never on this scale. This was going to be a new experience. The only thing to which he could possibly compare it to, were his father's experience at Mons Graupius in Caledonia and old Quintus's war stories. The stories he'd eagerly listened to as a boy growing up on Vectis - about Corbulo, his grandfather, and how Corbulo had fought in the great battle that had brought the destructive reign of the barbarian queen to an end.

As Fergus studied the mass of silent, disciplined troops, he felt his mount stir uneasily and nervously beneath him. The horse could sense what was coming. The seven hundred or so battle fit men of the vexillation of the 4th Legion had been placed right in the centre of the Roman battle-line, flanked by the cohorts of the 6th Legion. His men occupied a seven hundred feet long section of the main battle line, each man taking up three feet of space. From within their limited space, packed closely together it would be impossible for an ordinary legionary to see more than a dozen yards left or right. They were confined to their little world with just their comrades, officers and weapons for company. Slowly Fergus turned his gaze towards the left and then to the right, but it was impossible to see the distant Roman and auxiliary cavalry formations who would be guarding the army's flanks. A pall of dust had gathered to the south, but there was no way of knowing what was happening along that section. Had the Parthians attacked? Had a unit routed? Grimly Fergus looked away. It was pointless speculating. His job was simple. To focus on the seven hundred feet of front line ahead of him and make sure that his men held their own. This was no independent command. He had to be ready to quickly and efficiently execute the orders of his superiors when they came and that was that. Carefully Fergus licked his lips. His mouth was parch-dry despite the generous water ration he'd consumed that morning. It was just nerves, a natural fear that came to every living being, Quintus had once told him, when trying to describe standing in the line facing the barbarian queen. And if you could handle that fear without running, without forgetting your job, without disgracing yourself - then you were a proper soldier. Slowly Fergus exhaled again. All seemed ready. His men were in position and had been so for nearly an hour. But the order to advance on the enemy lines had not yet come.

Grimly Fergus turned his gaze across no-man's land towards the massed ranks of Parthian warriors who were drawn up facing the Roman lines, a half a mile away. The Parthians were too far away to make out their clothing, armour or weapons, but there was no doubt that they significantly outnumbered the Romans. Their ranks looked at least ten or twelve men deep.

Sat around him on horseback, were his cornicen and standard bearer, holding up the square vexillation banner of the Fourth Scythica, together with the eight legionary bodyguards who were on foot. The cornicen's trumpet hung suspended across his chest and the standard bearer's helmet was covered by a wolf's head. The legionaries' shields were resting on the ground, leaning against the men's legs and, in their hands, the men were clutching their pila, throwing spears. All were staring across the open, arid plain towards the enemy lines.

"Looks like we are facing Prince Sanatruces's own guardsmen Sir," the standard bearer called out, gesturing at the massed Parthian infantry ranks facing them. "The skirmishers say they spotted men holding up Parthian royal banners. Looks like it's going to be a tough fight. They say Sanatruces's personal guard are the best of the best Sir."

For a moment Fergus didn't reply, as he studied the enemy army.

"I have met Sanatruces once before," Fergus said at last, and as he did his staff and the men around him, turned to look at him in surprise. Fergus hesitated as he remembered the rescue of Adalwolf a year ago. "It was on a Parthian vessel anchored off Derbent on the Hyrcanian Ocean. I helped rescue a friend from aboard Sanatruces's own ship. He was trying to ransom him for gold."

"What happened Sir?" the cornicen asked eagerly.

"I threw a knife at Sanatruces and jumped overboard," Fergus replied. "Shame that I missed or else we wouldn't be here right now, would we."

"Shit Sir," the standard bearer exclaimed, as his lips slowly cracked into a grin. "That's a fucking brilliant story. You never told us Sir."

"Sir," the decanus in charge of his eight bodyguards called out suddenly in an urgent tone. "Imperial banners approaching Sir."

Hastily Fergus turned to look in the direction in which the decanus was pointing, and there coming towards him along the rear of the Roman battle line, was a group of horsemen. "Oh, fuck its Trajan," Fergus exclaimed in surprise, as he caught sight of the imperial banners being carried by the horsemen. Hastily Fergus urged his horse around so that he was facing the group of riders. Leading them, Trajan was clad in a splendid coat of armour and purple imperial robes, but he was bareheaded. As he rode on past, surrounded by his senior officers and mounted praetorian guards, Fergus and his staff quickly rapped out a salute. On his horse the old warrior emperor turned and idly glanced at Fergus, and as he seemed to recognise him, a little crooked smile appeared on Trajan's aged face. Raising his right hand slightly, the emperor clenched his hand into a fist making sure that Fergus had noticed. Then he was gone, riding on further down the line.

***

Across the battlefield multiple Parthian horns and trumpets suddenly rang out, shattering the eerie silence that had existed until then. Fergus tensed. This was it. The battle was about to begin. Across the half a mile of flat open ground that separated the two armies, the Parthian infantrymen had started to advance towards the Roman lines. As they came on, banging their weapons against their shields, their shrieks, yells and shouts grew in volume. Tensely Fergus watched them approach. Amongst the ranks of Roman legionaries, not a man made a sound as they grimly awaited contact. Out in front, the lightly clad skirmishers were already in action. Whirling their slings high above their heads and throwing their javelins at the great advancing masses of Parthian infantry. But their efforts went barely unnoticed and, as the Parthian infantry began to close, the skirmishers hastily fled, filtering through the narrow gaps in the main Roman battle line.

From the Roman lines a trumpet suddenly rang out and, as it did the signal was quickly picked up by more trumpets. As Fergus recognised the signal, he calmly turned to his cornicen.

"Signal the men to start their advance," he snapped.

A moment later the cornicen's trumpet rang out. The sound was swiftly followed by a few shouted orders. In front of Fergus, the long lines of Roman legionaries had picked up their large shields, decorated with thunder and lightning bolts and had started to advance at a slow, but steady walk, straight towards the oncoming Parthian masses. Tensely Fergus observed his men. They were maintaining their close formation, each man's shield nearly overlapping with that of their comrades beside them. The legionaries had raised their pila above their shoulders, their long iron spear heads pointing at the Parthians. There was no need to tell the men what to do. The legionaries were professionals. Each man had been trained for this, prepared for this moment but nevertheless, as he watched his men, Fergus was deeply impressed by their discipline. It required utmost self-control and self-discipline to calmly and silently keep walking straight towards the great masses of shouting, screaming Parthian infantry, who were bearing down on them. Urging his horse on behind the ranks, Fergus could do nothing but watch.

Closer and closer the two armies moved until, when they were less than a hundred yards apart, the Parthian ranks raised a mighty roar and charged. Fergus felt the hair on his neck stand up, but the spark of panic passed as quickly as it had come, and his training took over. Ahead of him, the silent legionaries were still advancing at their slow but steady walk, directly into the oncoming flood of running, screaming men. Then as the enemy had closed to less than twenty yards, the legionaries as one, flung their spears straight at the great mass of Parthian infantry, tore their short swords from their scabbards and charged, and as they did a great defiant and furious roar rose from the Roman ranks. The volley of spears at such close range had a devastating effect on the Parthian charge. Men went down in great numbers and those that fell were swiftly trampled underfoot, by their comrades coming on behind them. Here and there the Parthian charge seemed to lose some of its impetus. As the two battle lines made contact, a furious, screaming melee developed. Huddled behind their large shields and tightly packed together, the Roman legionaries formed a solid wall of wood and iron, from behind which they stabbed and lunged at their opponents with their short gladius swords. Shrieks and screams filled the air, but as he looked on from his horse, Fergus could see that his men had stopped the Parthian charge dead in its tracks.

"Hold them boys. For fuck's sake hold," a deep Roman voice screamed above the din.

All along the battle line, screaming, yelling men were shoving and pushing at each other with their shields as they sought to find an opening into which they could thrust their swords and spears at their enemy. Then abruptly the two sides recoiled from each other, swiftly creating a space of ten or fifteen yards wide between the two armies. Grimly, furiously, gasping and panting for breath, the men in the front lines stared at their opponents as they sought to build up the courage and the momentum for another charge.

"Wedge formation," Fergus roared, as he hastily urged his horse on down the line behind his men. "Wedge formation. Get stuck into them. Break them apart. Break them apart."

Along the Roman battle line as far as he could see the Parthian and Roman infantry were locked in furious hand to hand combat, that rippled forwards and backwards as men made contact and recoiled from the ferocious, savage stabbing contest. Fergus had just turned his horse and was racing back down the line, when a Parthian spear shot passed him and struck his cornicen full on in the chest, knocking him clean out of his saddle and onto the ground. There was no time to see if the soldier was still alive. In the front line some of the legionaries seemed to have heard his orders, for led by their officers and with a loud savage cry, they charged the Parthian line. Here and there the legionaries had begun to form small V shaped wedges, some composed of only three or five men, as they tried to hack their way into the solid Parthian line. The hand to hand combat was frantic. Shrieking, screaming, desperate men fighting for their lives, filled the morning with noise, but Fergus was not listening. Yelling encouragement at his men, he rode along at the back of the battle line oblivious to the fine target he made for enemy missiles.

In the front line the legionaries had started to make inroads in the Parthian line. With grim, savage determination the Romans, led by their officers, were hacking their way deeper into the Parthian ranks. Using their large shields to protect each other's flanks, the legionaries short stabbing swords flashed and lunged at the enemy with deadly efficiency. Block, stab, move forwards. Block, stab, move forwards. Block, stab, move forwards. The Roman equipment, discipline and superior training was beginning to tell.

"Sir, for fuck's sake get yourself a shield," the standard bearer screamed, as he rode up to where Fergus was shouting encouragement at a group of legionaries struggling to make headway. Fergus ignored the man and instead, urged his horse on down the line. This was no time for such matters. A critical moment in the battle was approaching. He could sense it. Beyond the Roman lines the Parthians were putting up a stout resistance, but their men lacked the Romans quality body armour and organisation. Some instinct told him that they were not going to be able to endure this ferocious contest for much longer.

"Sir, please Sir," the standard bearer yelled, as another spear narrowly missed him. For the briefest moment Fergus turned to stare at his standard bearer. Then reaching across, he snatched the square vexillation standard from the man's surprised hand and, digging his heels into his horse's flank, he cried out and started off back down the line.

"No, no, no Sir," the standard bearer shrieked, as he realised what Fergus was about to do.

Charging down the battle line behind his men, Fergus held up the proud banner for all to see and as he did he roared, before sending the standard flying over his men's heads and deep into the Parthian ranks. From behind him, he heard a strangled, desperate cry of sheer horror. To lose one's battle standard was the ultimate shame, a shame that belonged to every man in the unit and which would never be erased. A shame that would endure for all eternity.

"Bring me back my standard," Fergus roared as he reigned in his horse. "Bring me back my standard. You are men of the Fourth Scythica. You are not going to lose your battle standard. Not today. Not today!"

It was impossible to tell what effect his dramatic action had on the men, or even if they had noticed, but some had. Immediately in front of him, the Roman assault took on a new frantic aggression and purpose. With furious, fearless violence the legionaries renewed their attempts to break through the Parthian line. Hacking, shoving and stabbing at their opponents, the Romans forced their way deeper and deeper into the Parthian masses. The screams of the wounded rent the morning air and, along the contact line the bodies were beginning to pile up. With a savage expression, Fergus stared at the fighting. He had no fresh reserves to commit to the battle, nothing by which he could force a result except his men's pride in themselves and their unit. Would it be enough, or had he just committed his men to an eternity of shame and contempt?

Dimly he was aware of his standard bearer screaming at him, but the man's words would not register. Nothing else mattered but to win this contest, this frantic, savage, bloody and murderous fight to the death. And he was going to win. They were going to break the enemy.

Suddenly his horse was struck by a spear and, with a startled cry Fergus was flung from his saddle and tumbled to the ground. He landed with a painful thump and for a moment he was unable to move. Staggering to his feet, the sound of the battle just yards away came back to him, as a loud frantic rush of noise. For a moment Fergus struggled with a blurred vision and his breathing was causing him pain. As he turned to look around, a loud triumphant cry rose all along the Roman line. Turning to stare at the fighting, Fergus gasped as he saw that the Parthian resistance was beginning to crumble. A trickle of men had started to flee and within seconds, the panic and confusion spread, and more and more Parthians turned and began to run. The collapse was sudden and had come without warning and as the Parthians fled, the Roman legionaries set off in pursuit. The battle had turned.

Pulling Corbulo's old gladius from his scabbard, Fergus raised it in the air and grimly started to follow his men as they charged after the routed enemy. Gazing to his left and then to his right, Fergus saw that the whole central section of the Parthian battle line had collapsed into chaos. The Parthian infantry were in full retreat, streaming away across the plain in huge panic stricken and disorganised masses. This then was the moment, after all organisation had been lost, when the battle turned from a contest into a bloody massacre. As he stumbled along after his victorious men, Fergus paused as one of his bodyguards came hurrying towards him. The man was clutching the vexillation banner of the Fourth Scythica. Handing it back to Fergus, the soldier glared at him silently with wild, furious and accusing eyes.

"We were never going to lose it," Fergus growled, as he turned away and started out after his men.

Ahead of him across the plain the Parthians were running for their lives. The bodies of the slain and wounded lay scattered across the arid ground, but the legionaries were not in the mood to show mercy. As he staggered on after his men, clutching the soiled vexillation standard, Fergus suddenly became aware that the ground was shaking. To his right clouds of dust were being kicked up into the air, and suddenly he caught sight of figures on horseback racing across the plain. The Numidian and Batavian horsemen had struck the Parthian centre from the rear and were mowing down the fleeing men with contemptible ease. The rout was turning into a massacre. Close by, a Parthian infantryman was down on his knees and trying to surrender. The man was holding up his arms in a pitiful attempt whilst crying out in his foreign language. But it did not save him from a legionary who viciously stabbed him in the neck and the man crumpled to the ground. Fergus kept moving. Ahead of him across the corpse-strewn plain, the legionaries advance was beginning to slow and come to a halt, as the men paused from exhaustion and turned their attention to finishing off the enemy wounded. The task of completing the enemy rout now belonged to the cavalry who were superbly well equipped for this role. Fergus had just caught up with the front ranks, when an excited cry rose a hundred yards away. Turning to gaze in that direction he caught sight of a group of legionaries milling about in excitement.

"What the fuck is going on over there?" Fergus roared, as he started to walk towards the group of men.

As he approached he caught sight of Dio standing amongst a group of legionaries. The centurion's body armour was splattered with blood and he was clutching his gladius in one hand. Spotting Fergus, Dio turned and hastened towards him, his eyes and face filled with raw excitement and triumph.

"We think we got him Sir," Dio yelled in savage delight. "Come and have a look. We think its him."

"Who? Who are you talking about?" Fergus shouted.

"Prince Sanatruces Sir," Dio yelled. "He's dead. Come and have a look. It must be him Sir. We got the bastard. It was us Sir. The Fourth Scythica who got him. It was us. We just fucking killed Sanatruces."

Chapter Ten – Return to Seleucia

Autumn 116 AD

Fergus finished washing himself with his sponge, stuck it into his belt and raised the small shaving knife to his chin. The cool, refreshing waters of the Tigris tugged at his body, but the current was not strong. It was morning and he stood in the river, not far from the muddy bank, stripped to his waist. Closing one eye, he raised his chin and carefully applied the knife and began to shave himself. A couple of hundred yards away, the massive city walls of Seleucia came right up to the water's edge and across the wide, placid river, just visible on the opposite eastern bank, he could make out Ctesiphon, the Parthian capital. Hidden behind the tall green river reeds along the embankment, a battery of Roman onagers, catapults were hurling their projectiles at the besieged city. The desultory crack and whir of the war machines had started at dawn, but the bombardment of Seleucia seemed to be having a minimal impact on the rebel defences.

Ten yards away, two prostitutes were washing themselves in the river and trying hard to catch his eye. They were making a good show of letting him see their breasts, and as they chatted they kept on glancing in his direction. Ignoring the girls, Fergus continued to shave himself. He was in good physical shape, he had money and his seniority meant he could have had any of the hundreds of desperate local women who had flocked to the Roman army encampments that surrounded Seleucia. But he'd abstained. He had stayed faithful to Galena. It had been hard, sometimes very hard, but somehow, he'd managed it. It was not something many of his fellow officers could claim. It was not something his grandfather Corbulo or his father Marcus or even his mother Kyna, had been able to do. But he had. So too had Galena. He was certain of that. She too would remain faithful. It was what he loved about her. Glancing at the prostitutes, Fergus sighed. Watching the girls washing themselves in the river had suddenly reminded him how good it would be to see his wife again. It had been nearly a year since he'd last seen her and his five daughters. He had tried not to think about them too much for that would not do him any good, but now in this unguarded moment he could not help himself.

"Sir," a voice suddenly called from the bank. "You are needed over at the legate's HQ. They said that you should come right away."

Fergus paused shaving and slowly turned to look at the soldier standing on the shore. There was always something or someone interrupting him. It was the inevitable consequence of his rank.

"All right," he growled. "Give me a moment to finish this."

***

The legate's tent had been pitched in the centre of encampment B, one of several Roman camps that hemmed Seleucia in on three sides. As Fergus approached, the two legionaries on guard duty stiffly snapped out a salute. The military situation remained finely balanced Fergus knew. Several weeks had passed since the great battle that had killed prince Sanatruces and routed his army. There had however been little time to celebrate the victory. Ctesiphon and Babylon had refused to join the rebellion, no doubt overawed by Trajan's presence but Seleucia, stubborn Seleucia on the Tigris, had refused to surrender and was prepared to fight it out with the legions. Trajan had left the task of forcing a surrender to two of his legionary legates and had moved northwards to try and quell the rebellious cities in northern Mesopotamia, taking half of his army with him.

Entering the tent, Fergus was struck by its lavish furnishing. All of it looted. Along the edges of the tent stood a fine couch and a table, covered in an abundance of food and drink. Expensive looking carpets had been placed on the ground and, in a corner stood a stone bust of the emperor. For a moment Fergus said nothing as he allowed his eyes to adjust to the gloomy light. The two legionary legates who were in command of the Roman troops besieging Seleucia, were engaged in a deep earnest conversation. Nearby, a mock-up of the besieged city stood on a table in the middle of the tent.

"Sir, you wished to see me," Fergus said.

"Ah Fergus," one of the legates replied, beckoning him over. "Yes, come and have a look at this," the legate said, gesturing at the mock-up of Seleucia. "We have just received some good news from the north. Quietus has sacked Edessa. The city is back under our control."

Fergus nodded and obediently he approached the table and looked down at the model made of stone, wood and sand. The mock up clearly showed the city's walls, gates, the Roman camps, siege lines and the course of the Tigris.

"We need your opinion on how best to take Seleucia," the other legate growled. "You were its former garrison commander. You know the layout of the city better than any of us. Well, what can you tell us about the city's weaknesses?"

For a moment Fergus remained silent as he stared at the model.

"Listen Fergus," the first legate interrupted sharply. "I will explain the situation. Our losses have been heavy. We are stretched. We have only nine thousand men to besiege Seleucia, garrison Ctesiphon, Babylon and half a dozen other settlements, plus guard against any hostile Parthian moves from the east. Our supply lines to the north and west are threatened by the rebels in Doura-Europus and Hatra. Trajan has ordered that men are not to be sacrificed unnecessarily. We just don't have the man power anymore. Nor can we replace our losses. So," the legate paused. "We need to come up with a plan to recapture Seleucia that involves minimal casualties, and we must do it quickly. Trajan wants Seleucia taken as quick as possible. The city's continued resistance could be an inspiration to others."

"So that rules out a direct assault," the second legate growled. "And we do not have the time to sit here for weeks or months and starve the city into submission. That leaves only one viable option, subterfuge."

"It seems that you have already decided on what course of action to take Sir," Fergus said with a forced smile, as he looked up at the legates.

"I believe," the first legate said in a stern voice. "That you were responsible for capturing Seleucia the first time by using subterfuge. We need some ideas on how we can repeat that feat. Well?"

Fergus remained silent as he turned his attention back to the model of the city. Then at last he cleared his throat, reached forwards and with his fingers, tapped the section where the docks protruded into the Tigris.

"The city walls are massive and well laid out," Fergus said with a sigh. "The gates into Seleucia too, are well protected. There are huge crossbeams that need half a dozen men to lift into place. But once in place they will keep those gates standing. They have been designed to withstand a battering. They are made of solid wood – reinforced by iron cladding, impervious to fire and two feet thick. But set within the gates there are smaller doorways. When we were in control of the city we closed the gates at night but kept the smaller doorways open. They are easily defendable and locked in an emergency and it meant we did not need to constantly open the gates. A city like Seleucia has a lot of traffic going in and out."

"So, what are you suggesting?" one of the legates growled.

"I know the city and its streets fairly well, as do my men," Fergus replied, looking up at the Roman officers. "A party of volunteers and a raft, say eight or ten men, dressed in civilian clothing could be launched from here, just upstream from Seleucia. The operation would be conducted at night and with a massive diversion; say an artillery barrage to catch the defender's attention. The party would enter the city through the docks, make their way to the northern gates here, kill the guards and open the doorway letting in your troops."

Abruptly the tent fell silent, as the legates stared at the model of Seleucia.

"How would you open the doorways in the gates? Presumably the rebels will have locked and barred them."

"I have the keys," Fergus replied quickly. "I have the keys to the city. When we were forced to evacuate from the palace during the uprising, I took the spare set of keys with me. Each gate had a spare set in case the originals were lost. They were kept in the former governor's mansion. Obviously, the keys can only be used to open the door from the inside, but I thought maybe one day they would come in handy."

The two legates stared at Fergus in stunned silence. Then slowly one of them shook his head in disbelief.

"Shit Fergus," the officer hissed. "And you only thought about telling us this now. You are full of surprises."

Fergus shrugged. "I am telling you now," he replied sharply. "And I would like to lead the mission into the city. Seleucia was my responsibility. It was my job to hold the place and I know it's streets. I would like to have the opportunity to be able recover the city for Rome Sir."

"Agreed," one of the legates snapped. "Handpick your men. We want this done as soon as possible."

Fergus turned to look down at the model of the city.

"May I ask Sir," he said. "What will become of Seleucia once we have recovered the city?"

"The city will be sacked and burned," one of the legates replied grimly. "Anyone who surrenders will be sold into slavery, the rest killed. Anyone who dares rebel against Rome will suffer the consequences."

Fergus nodded and lowered his eyes.

***

The raft bobbed up and down on the gentle current. In the cloudless night sky, the stars twinkled and glowed. Fergus lay stretched out on the raft, his legs protruding into the cold water. He was clad in civilian clothing and his face and forehead was camouflaged with mud, that had been smeared into his skin. Ahead in the darkness, he could make out the rebel camp fires along the docks. Slowly and silently the raft drifted towards the river harbour. The night was quiet. On either side of the raft a man was in the water, clutching hold of the craft, swimming and guiding the vessel towards a spot along Seleucia's river front. The remaining six men, all hand-picked volunteers, all clad in civilian garb, lay beside Fergus, stretched out on the raft. They too were gazing intently and silently at the approaching harbour. The docks ahead looked crowded and congested by all kinds of river vessels, large transport barges, fishing boats, pleasure craft, all driven into the harbour by the Roman naval blockade on the Tigris, north and south of Seleucia. As the raft drew closer to the mass of ships, Fergus suddenly heard voices in the darkness. They were Parthian. Turning his head, he gazed at the Greek translator who had volunteered to come with them. The translator, sensing Fergus looking at him, shrugged.

Suddenly to the south the night sky was lit up by three flaming projectiles that went arching gracefully through the air, over the tall walls and into the city. They landed with a crash and instantly the night was rent by uproar. Along the southern wall it was as if a thousand voices were shouting and screaming. Moments later another barrage of Roman missiles went arching through the sky towards Seleucia. Grimly Fergus stared at the spectacle. The diversion had begun. Along the harbour front the Parthians were crying out to each other in the darkness. In the light from their camp fires that partially illuminated the water front, Fergus caught sight of shadows flitting through the gloom. Slowly but steadily the raft drew closer and closer to the docks. When they were but a few yards from a large moored river barge, Fergus silently slithered off the raft and into the river. The water was cold. Holding onto the raft with one hand he and the other men silently pulled the craft into contact with the larger vessel. Quickly Fergus turned his head to listen.

Nearby Parthian voices were calling out to each other, but from the tone of their voices the rebels didn't seem too concerned by the bombardment to the south. A moment later a laugh punctured the darkness. Carefully Fergus raised his head and peered at the stone embankment. A dozen yards away, along the waterfront, a camp fire was blazing, and in its light, he caught the outline of a sentry peering out into the river. The man was armed with a spear and a flaming torch. Calmly Fergus's gaze swept along the embankment. There were more camp fires stretching all the way along the docks. Clearly the rebels had realised the danger of an attack from the river. Closing his eyes, he tried to picture the layout of the docks and the streets leading to the northern gate as they had been, when he'd been the city's garrison commander. Once they were on land they would have to move fast. There was no room for cock-ups or missed turns. One slip up and they would be done for. He hadn't needed to volunteer for this mission Fergus knew. It would have been much easier to do nothing, to keep his head down but the legates would have just sent other men to do the job and that was not right. Seleucia had been his responsibility. It had been his duty to hold the city. And it was his job to erase the shame and humiliation of being forced to withdraw his men, sneaking away under the cover of night as if they were thieves.

Opening his eyes, Fergus turned to his men who were crouching silently on the raft behind him. In the darkness he could not make out their faces. Boldly he reached up and began to hoist himself up over the side of the river barge. After a few frantic exhausting moves, he managed to haul his body up and over the side of the hull. For a moment Fergus lay on his back staring up at the stars, as he tried to regain his breath. Along the southern edge of Seleucia, the burning Roman artillery missiles continued to arch through the sky like blazing meteors. Having regained his breath Fergus carefully raised his head to peer at the sentry, but the man had not noticed anything. Silently Fergus began to crawl along the empty boat towards the embankment. There was no way they were going to be able to sneak into the city without the sentry spotting them. He had to be taken out.

Reaching the embankment, Fergus pressed himself up against the cold, damp stone work and glanced upwards. The sentry was no more than a few yards away. The man was softly humming a tune to himself, completely oblivious to danger he was in. Lazily he began to pace up and down. In the darkness Fergus felt around until his hands found the small ladder that led upwards onto the waterfront. Swiftly he pulled a pugio army knife from the folds of his civilian clothing and as quietly as possible he started to climb. The sentry had his back turned, when Fergus swiftly rose up behind him. With a few quick steps he reached the man, clamped his hand around the sentry's mouth and swiftly cut his throat. The man's spear clattered to the ground and his torch tumbled into the river where it sizzled and died. The action had taken no more than a few seconds. The dying man was spilling a huge quantity of blood down his throat and across his chest, as Fergus hastily lowered him to the ground. Crouching beside the corpse, Fergus turned to look around him, but in the dim firelight he could see no one. No had noticed the attack. So far, so good then.

A few moments later, Fergus sensed movement out on the river. Grasping hold of the corpse, he quickly rolled it over and holding onto the arms he lowered the body into the river, where it vanished into the darkness. Quickly Fergus picked up the sentry's spear and discarded it too into the Tigris. As he crouched in the shadows, his men appeared, hastily and silently clambering one by one up onto the embankment. When they'd all made it up onto the land, Fergus raised his fist in the air and gestured for them to follow him. Pulling his hood over his head, he boldly started out towards the main street leading away from the docks.

The darkness to the south was still being punctured by the spectacular Roman artillery barrage. Clutching his knife in his hand, Fergus silently and purposefully led his men in single file through the harbour area. Around him, the docks were clogged with a chaotic mass of crates, barrels, sacks of grain, cranes, large numbers of amphorae and piles of wood. The place stank of fish. The siege and rebellion had meant that all commerce and trade had come to a stop. Somewhere in the darkness amongst the merchandise, a man was snoring loudly. Up ahead blocking the entrance into the narrow street that led away from the docks, Fergus caught sight of another camp fire. Three armed figures were standing guard around the fire, warming their hands and chatting to each other. Calmly Fergus strode straight towards the men. As the rebels noticed him they turned to face Fergus, and one of them called out to him. Fergus quickened his pace, strode straight up to the nearest figure and before the man could do anything, he stabbed him in the head. A horrified scream of alarm rent the night, but it died as quickly as it arose, as the men with Fergus pounced on the other two guards and quickly silenced them. The fight was over within seconds. Dragging the corpses into the shadows, Fergus turned to peer down the narrow street. It looked deserted. In the buildings that lined the road there were no lights showing. Most of the city's inhabitants seemed to be asleep.

"Follow me," Fergus hissed turning to his men. "We don't stop until we reach the northern gate. Keep your eyes open. Kill anyone who gets in our way."

Calmly but quickly, followed in single file by his companions, he began to move on down the darkened, deserted street, keeping to one side of the road. High above him in the night sky, the stars twinkled and glowed. To the south, the Roman missiles seemed to have set a building on fire, for flames were flickering and leaping up into the darkness. Fergus hastened onwards. The street was just wide enough to allow two donkeys with paniers to pass each other and the paving stones were stained with old squashed animal droppings. As he moved on deeper into the city, Fergus strained to listen, but apart from the Roman barrage all seemed quiet and peaceful. He was approaching a cross roads, when suddenly he caught sight of a large group of torches coming towards him down the street. The crunch of boots and men's voices accompanied the torches.

Hastily Fergus shot into an alley filled with rubbish and pressed himself up against the wall, as his men scattered into the shadows. A few moments later a large troop of well-armed men came marching past. Silently Fergus stared at them as the men headed off down the street towards the docks. How long before the missing sentries would be discovered? How long before the alarm was raised? Poking his head out of the alley, he turned to look up the street, but it seemed clear. Silently Fergus slipped back into the street and shot across the cross roads. The soft patter of feet followed him. Crouching in the shadows, he paused to allow his companions to catch up. Then he was off again, slipping quickly through the darkened street. Pausing again at another crossroads, he turned to get his bearings. If he remembered correctly the northern gate was not far away now.

"It's that way Sir," the translator whispered, as he hastily crouched beside Fergus and pointed down one of the streets. "I remember Sir. I am sure of it."

Fergus grunted as he turned to stare in the direction in which the Greek translator was pointing. The darkness was disorientating but something in the translator's voice sounded truthful.

"All right let's go," Fergus hissed.

Hastening across the intersection, he darted into the street to which the translator had pointed. In one of the homes a man and a woman were having a loud, furious argument and in another a baby was crying. As he pushed on down the narrow road, a dog suddenly started to bark. Ignoring the noise, Fergus paused as he reached the end of the street. Crouching in the shadows he suddenly hissed in frustration. Ahead in the dim light, across an open space he could see the outline of the city walls and the massive gatehouse that housed the northern gates. But the rebels seemed to have constructed another makeshift wall across the entrance to the gates, blocking them off completely. As he peered at the defences Fergus hissed again. The only way to access the outer doorway for which he had the keys, was by going through the main gatehouse; the only entrance being a narrow, no doubt locked, and guarded doorway set in the walls.

"What's the problem Sir?" a Roman voice whispered from behind him.

"They have blocked the gates with a second wall," Fergus whispered. "It means that the only way to get to the outer doorway is through the main gatehouse and fuck knows how many guards could be inside or up on those walls."

Grimly Fergus bit his lip as he tried to decide what to do. He was rapidly running out of time, for the missing sentries would surely soon be missed. And then the hunt would be on. He had to do something, and he had to do it quickly. Behind him he could hear his men's soft laboured breathing as they crouched along the wall.

"We could go over the wall Sir," the Greek translator whispered as he quickly pointed at the makeshift wall that the rebels had constructed. "Look at how it had been constructed. It's a poor, hasty job Sir. There should be enough ridges and edges for a man to clamber over."

Fergus frowned as he leaned forwards and peered at the wall in the dim light. It was impossible to see for sure, but the translator's idea could work. If he could get across the wall, the outer doorway set into the gates would be only a few yards away.

"Why the hell did you volunteer for this mission?" Fergus whispered as he tore his eyes away from the gatehouse and turned to peer at the Greek crouching behind him. "You did not need to do so. You know that."

"To earn your respect Sir," the translator whispered. "I have to share all the same dangers and hardships like you soldiers do, but no one has ever given me credit for anything."

Fergus leaned his head back against the wall and raised his eyebrows in surprise and for a moment he wanted to laugh.

"Well if this works," he hissed at last. "Then you shall have my respect." Then quickly he turned and hissed at the men crouching along the wall. "I, Timo and Antonius will go for that wall. We climb over it. If you see us get across you all follow. Beyond are the gates. You know what to do."

Turning his head, Fergus peered at the wall. Then he shifted his gaze up towards the top of the massive city walls. In the darkness he could see a few flaming torches moving about on the battlements. Slowly he tightened his grip on his knife. It was now or never.

"Go," he hissed as he leapt to his feet and raced across the open space that separated the homes from the city walls. As he reached the newly built wall, he launched himself at the masonry. The translator had been right. The rebels had done a poor job and the wall was uneven and lined with edges, handholds and ledges. With furious energy, Fergus reached up, grasped hold of an edge and heaved himself upwards. A few moments later he heard his two companions start to do the same. The task was simpler than he had expected and after a few moments of laborious activity, he had reached the top. Directly ahead, in the confined space beyond the makeshift wall, he caught sight of the massive wooden gates. They were shut and the huge cross bars had been raised into position just as he had expected. There was still no response from the guards up on the walls. With a grunt, Fergus slid his legs over the top of the wall and slithered to the ground, landing painfully on his arse.

Pulling his knife from his belt, he rose to his feet and turned towards the doorway to his right, that was set into the walls and that led into the gatehouse. It was closed. If there were guards inside he could not hear them. Two torches had been affixed to the stone walls in iron holders either side of the gates and, in their flickering, hissing light, he caught sight of the small outer doorway set into the massive wooden gates. Silently Fergus moved up to the gates and tried the doorway. It was locked just as he had expected. As his two companions made it over the wall and slid to the ground, Fergus turned and gestured for them to take up position beside the door leading into the gatehouse. Fumbling within his civilian tunic, he produced the solid iron keys and inserted one of them into the lock. With a metallic snap, something turned and with a push the outer door swung open. Softly Fergus swore in triumph. Beyond the doorway the night remained silent and peaceful. There was no hint in the darkness that three thousand Roman soldiers were about to storm the gate.

A soft noise alerted Fergus that the rest of his men were coming over the wall. He'd just managed to turn around, when he heard a loud voice call out from within the gatehouse. Without warning the door leading into the gatehouse swung open and a figure poked his head out of the doorway. Without thinking Fergus launched himself at the man. With a crash Fergus slammed into the guard and his momentum sent both careening into the guard room. A startled cry rang out. It was followed by another. Savagely Fergus punched his opponent in the face. Then he stabbed him and was rewarded with a shriek. Staggering to his feet, Fergus was just in time to see the surprised faces of three guards staring at him in horror. Then Fergus's companions were onto them. The legionary's short swords flashed wickedly in the light, cutting down two of the men before they even had a chance to respond. The third man managed to yell a loud warning and make it onto the first step of the stone staircase that led upwards onto the battlements, before Fergus caught him in the back with his knife. Savagely Fergus silenced him, allowing his body to collapse onto the stone floor of the guard room. The man he'd punched in the face was groaning and trying to drag himself across the floor. Quickly Fergus stepped towards him and cut his throat. A moment later the translator and the rest of his men came storming into the guardhouse, clutching their swords. Wild eyed they paused to stare at the bloody chaos and the four corpses strewn across the room.

"You five - get up onto the battlements and silence the sentries up there," Fergus hissed in an urgent voice, gesturing at the narrow stone stairs that led up onto the top of the walls. "The rest of you hold the guard house."

Just as he finished speaking a loud cry of alarm rose from above their heads. "Hurry, hurry," Fergus cried as he stuffed his knife into his belt, turned and shot out of the doorway through which he'd just come. In the confined space beyond, the door set into the gates was open. Hastily Fergus reached up and yanked the two torches from their iron holders. Holding the flaming torches in both hands, he kicked the door so that it opened wider. Then he slipped on through it and into the dark night beyond. For a moment he could see nothing. On top of the walls an alarm bell suddenly started to ring out, its urgent dong, dong, dong shattering the tranquillity.

Raising the two torches high above his head, Fergus turned to face the darkness. Then quickly he crossed the torches and repeated the sign three times. It was the signal to confirm that the gates were open.

On top of the walls an outraged bellow was suddenly followed by a shriek and, in the darkness close by, a body came tumbling down from the battlements, hitting the ground with a thud. From the darkness beyond the walls Fergus suddenly heard a Roman voice. It was followed moments later by the sound of running feet and the clink of metal against metal.

***

The wide colonnaded avenue that ran the length of Seleucia was filled with frantic people, wailing women, crying children, harsh male voices and the sound of cracking whips. Under the elegant Greek style covered walkways, the stoas, that lined the avenue on both sides, every shop and business of the once flourishing mercantile district was closed, looted or abandoned. It was afternoon and in the clear blue sky the sun shone supreme. Fergus, clad in his body armour and army uniform, accompanied by Dio, the Greek translator and a few legionaries, strode along the avenue casually gazing at the long lines of prisoners and slaves. There had to be thousands of them. The lines stretched away into the distance. In the street the citizens of Seleucia were kneeling on the paving stones, arranged in long parallel lines, their hands clasped behind the back of their heads, their faces turned to the ground, as the slave merchants and their lackeys, armed with whips and iron chains secured and inspected their catches. In the direction of the ex-governor's palace and former Roman garrison HQ, part of the city was already on fire. Thick, black columns of smoke were belching up into the sky.

Fergus looked tired but satisfied. Seleucia had fallen. The siege was over. The great city was once more under Roman control. The disgrace he'd felt at having been forced to abandon Seleucia had been wiped clean. Dark circles had formed under Fergus's eyes and his cheeks were covered in a fresh layer of stubble. The operation the previous night to secure the northern gate and let in the main army had been a success. Once the legionaries had gained a foothold, the street fighting that everyone had been expecting had fizzled out surprisingly rapidly and most of the city had surrendered without a fight. It seemed that many of the citizens of Seleucia did not after all, have the stomach for a protracted battle. A few die-hard holdouts still refused to surrender, but their position was hopeless. Seleucia was to be torched and if they refused to surrender, they would die in the flames. Grimly Fergus turned to gaze at the long columns of people kneeling in the street. It seemed that half the population of the city had fled before the siege had begun but those that had remained behind were now about to learn what it meant to rebel against Rome.

"What a fucking mess. Look at them. Fools," Dio hissed, as he strode along gazing at the long lines of kneeling, miserable and broken people who were being enslaved. "Did they not think? Did they not realise that this is what would happen? And look at their city. It will be nothing but rubble and ash by the end of the week. What a mess."

Fergus did not reply as he continued along the avenue, keeping under the covered walkway. The rules of war dictated that the victor might do with the vanquished what he pleased.

However, as he approached the cross roads where the main avenue was intersected by another wide street, a sudden commotion caught his eye. Out in the street a slaver, clutching a coiled whip, had raised his voice and was trying to take something from a girl, one of the slaves. The girl looked around ten years old and she was putting up a spirited fight. In her hands she was protectively holding onto a magnificent plumed Roman officer's helmet. The slaver was trying to take it from her, but the girl was having none of it and their fierce quarrel was getting noisier and noisier. As he caught sight of the helmet, Fergus's eyes widened. That was his helmet. The helmet he had given to the beggar girl whilst he had taken refuge in her mother's house during the start of the uprising.

"Heh you," Fergus bellowed, as he left the shade of the walkway and strode out into the street straight towards the struggling girl and the slaver. "Leave her alone. Back off."

Seeing Fergus and Dio approaching, the slaver let go of the helmet and hastily stumbled away.

"Get out of here," Fergus roared at the slaver.

Then he turned to look down at the girl. She was staring back up at him in alarm and defiance. Her bare feet were dirty and shoeless, her clothes were torn and soiled and she had an angry purple bruise across her left cheek. Fergus grunted, and at his side Dio swore softly under his breath as both recognised her. It was the same girl. The little beggar who had warned them about the uprising and who had saved their lives. There was no mistake. For a moment Fergus remained silent as he stared at her.

Crouching beside her he gestured at the helmet.

"That's mine," Fergus said in Latin. "May I have it back?"

On the ground the girl was staring at him with her large eyes. It was clear that she had not understood a word of what Fergus had just said. Fergus sighed and turned to glance up at the translator. The Greek was about to speak, when the girl reached out and hastily placed the helmet into Fergus's hands. Surprised, Fergus looked down at his tribune's helmet. He had not been expecting to see it again. Turning to the girl he nodded his gratitude. Then fishing into his tunic pocket, he produced a silver coin and held it up in the air. As she caught sight of the gleaming coin, the girl suddenly smiled.

"What is her name? Ask her?" Fergus said sharply glancing up at the translator.

Obediently the Greek translated the question. The reply came quickly.

"Hera," the translator replied. "She says she is called Hera. Wife of Zeus, King of the Gods," the Greek added with a note of pride in his voice. "And she says Sir that you are her friend."

"Ask her what has become of her mother and family," Fergus said as he handed the girl the silver coin which she boldly snatched from his hand.

"She says her mother is dead and her father has not come home. She doesn't know where he is. She has no one else Sir. She begs for food every day," the Greek said as he translated the girl's muttered words.

Fergus nodded and then straightened up and turned to look down the street.

"They should have got out of the city before the siege," he growled. "I warned her mother. I told her to get out." Then he sighed and turned to look down at the girl. "Tell her that I am taking her as my slave," Fergus said. "Tell her that she will no longer need to beg in the streets. She is coming with me back to Zeugma. Galena can always use another household slave."

"Sir," Dio exclaimed in surprise. "You want to take her with you? On campaign, during this uprising?"

"She saved our lives," Fergus replied, as he turned to look at Dio. "And she's an orphan just like you are. So, yes, I am taking her as my slave. She will have a much better life with my family than with these slave traders. You know what those men will do with a girl like her." Fergus paused and then he reached out and slapped Dio on the shoulder. "Cheer up. Maybe something good has come out of this mess after all," Fergus said with a grin.

Chapter Eleven – This is Not a Retreat

The wide, placid waters of the Euphrates cut through the desert, a refreshing and reassuring sight in the bleak, featureless landscape. Fergus, accompanied by his staff and a small mounted escort, rode on down the flank of the long plodding column of legionaries and auxiliaries. Their horse's hooves kicked up little clouds of dust. It was afternoon. Fergus clad in his body armour, plumed helmet and tribune's cloak had fastened a Bedouin keffiyeh scarf around his face, but the desert sand and dust had still managed to get into his eyes, ears and nostrils. Ignoring his discomfort and the swarms of little flies, he glanced at his men as he rode on past. The three and a half thousand men of his battle group were heading north along the Euphrates. After the fall of Seleucia, he had watched the city burn. Rome's revenge had been brutal and thousands upon thousands of citizens had been sold into slavery and thousands more had died. It had been a tragic end to an old and famous city, for Seleucia would probably never recover from this. A few days later, he had been given command of a battle group formed around his own vexillation and ordered to march north and retake Doura-Europus, which was still in rebel hands. Fergus sighed. Officially this was not a retreat, for he had orders to retake Doura, but it felt like a retreat. The possibility that he would see the grand walls of Ctesiphon again was remote. Slowly Fergus bit his lip as he trotted on down the side of the column. He was going back to Doura. The place from which the advance into central Mesopotamia had started less than a year ago. It would be the second time that he would be attacking the city and the thought was depressing.

Grimly he studied his men. They looked worn out and covered in dust. Morale was holding up so far but there was no doubt that the long relentless campaign was having an impact. What his men needed was some proper time to rest and recover, repair their equipment, heal their wounds and receive replacements for the heavy losses they had suffered. But there was little chance of that. The uprising and hostility to Rome showed no signs of abating. With the six hundred or so battle-fit legionaries from the 1st Cohort of the Fourth Legion as its core, the battle group had been re-enforced by the remnants of vexillations from the Third Cyrenaica and the First Italica, several units of slingers, combat engineers, Syrian archers and the Ninth Batavian Auxiliary Cavalry Alae. All units were understrength, some severely so. The losses in men had become a growing problem but there was no chance of them being replaced, not in the short term at least. For that, the war would have to end. For some army officers it had become an unspoken scandal that no provisions or preparations had been made for a system of replacements, capable of sustaining the field army. No new legions had been raised for the war. That, Fergus had heard it whispered, was Trajan's failure. The growing manpower problem, Fergus had heard it acknowledged amongst the senior Roman commanders, was beginning to dictate strategic choices.

"Sir, look," the centurion accompanying Fergus suddenly called out, as he pointed out into the desert.

Turning to look in the direction in which the officer was pointing, Fergus grunted. Just visible and far out into the desert, tiny figures on horseback were galloping along parallel to the Roman column. The horsemen were moving in the same direction as he was and kicking up a cloud of dust as they sped along. Fergus said nothing as he studied the distant figures. Prince Sanatruces may have fallen in battle and his army routed, but there was no doubt that in the past few months the Parthians had recovered their warlike spirit and determination. The humiliation of seeing their capital city captured, occupied and a Roman consul made governor of Mesopotamia had undoubtedly focussed Parthian minds and resources.

"They must be either Bedouin out of the desert or Parthian cavalry Sir," the centurion said as he peered at the riders. "Not enough of them to attack us. They are shadowing us. Somehow, I don't think the rebels in Doura are going to be surprised to see us. Shall I order the Batavians to drive them off?"

"No, leave them alone," Fergus replied, as he lowered his keffiyeh. "Let them report on our progress. We were never going to surprise the rebels."

Fergus turned to look away. The enemy scouts were the least of his problems. Doura was still at least two days march to the north and it would be four or five days before he would be ready to assault the city. His real problem was a lack of supplies. The countryside between the Tigris and the Euphrates had been stripped bare of wood, food and animal fodder during the previous nine months of active campaigning. It meant no resources from which to construct assault ladders and his horses were dangerously low on fodder and hay. Turning in his saddle, Fergus looked back towards the rear of the column where the massed ranks of Batavian cavalry and a unit of slingers formed the rear-guard. Amongst the column of supply wagons being pulled along by oxen and water buffalo, was a solitary battering ram. The vehicle, with its massive bronze-headed ram protruding from its protective shed, was surrounded by a unit of combat engineers. Crossing the Euphrates at Fallujah they had nearly lost the war machine, when one of its axels had broken and the ram had threatened to roll into the river. The delay in fixing the battering ram had cost a whole day. But without the war machine the assault on Doura would be impossible.

**

The light had started to fade and in the Roman marching camp along the edge of the Euphrates most of the men were still busy erecting their tents and preparing their evening meals. Out on the desert perimeter, guarded by a few Batavian cavalry squadrons, work parties were out spreading anti-cavalry caltrops across the desert floor, whilst others were digging a V-shaped trench and constructing an earthen embankment. As he hurried through the camp towards the river Fergus however, paid the work no attention. Up ahead on the banks of the river the work details had stopped what they were doing and were lining the embankment. The men were staring at the river and some were calling out to the sailors manning the small fleet of boats that had suddenly appeared out on the wide waters. The ships had come from the north but were carrying Roman banners. Pushing his way through the crowd of curious soldiers, Fergus made it to the front. Pausing on the steep embankment, he gazed down at the river barges that were pulling into land beside his camp. The ships were laden with cargo, amphorae and other supplies.

"Who are you?" Fergus cried out in a loud voice, as he searched around trying to spot whoever was in charge.

"We're bringing supplies down river," one of the sailors shouted in good Latin from a boat nearest to the shore. "They are destined for the garrison at Ctesiphon and Seleucia. We're mighty glad to see you boys. May we anchor here for the night? There are hostile forces just to the north."

"How did you get past Doura?" Fergus shouted back.

"Doura is in rebel hands," the sailor cried, as a grin appeared on his face. "Presume that you lot are heading north to recapture the city. We snuck past them last night. We had no lights, just kept our distance and let the current do the work. The rebels never even noticed us passing. Fucking amateurs."

Carefully Fergus turned his gaze to the mass of supplies piled up on the boats. Then he licked his lips.

"What news from the north?" Fergus shouted.

Along the water's edge, several of the supply vessels had thrown their anchors into the river and a few sailors were busying themselves with securing their vessels and lowering their sails.

"Not much," the captain shouted back across the peaceful waters. "Hatra continues to hold out against us and most of Osrhoene and Armenia are completely lawless, but Quietus has managed to torch Edessa, and the last I heard, he has also managed to recover Nisibis. We would be in a whole load of deep shit if it wasn't for Quietus. If you want my opinion Sir, Trajan should have made Quietus his deputy and not that useless prick Hadrian, who sits in Antioch doing nothing. Anyway, are you all right with us spending the night here. My men are exhausted. We have had a long journey. We could do with your protection."

For a moment Fergus remained silent, as his gaze swept over the small fleet of supply boats.

"Fine, anchor here for the night," he shouted back. "But my men are low on supplies. We will take from you what you were going to deliver to the garrison at Seleucia. And we're going to need those supplies right away so start unloading them."

Onboard the captain stared at Fergus in stunned surprise. "Sir, I have orders to deliver them to Seleucia. The men there need those supplies. I can't just surrender them to you."

"Seleucia is a burnt-out ruin. There is no Roman garrison anymore. We were it," Fergus shouted back, his voice rising angrily. "Have you not heard. We took the city weeks ago and burnt it. It is no more. So, fuck your orders and start unloading those supplies. My men need them."

***

87

The tent was lit by two oil lamps and in their soft glowing light Fergus watched Hera eat as he sat quietly on the ground repairing a hole in his tribune's cloak. It was late and through the gap in the tent the night sky was filled with stars. Close by, stretched out in his hammock, Dio, still in his body armour, was fast asleep, snoring gently, his head resting on his arm. Outside the tent, the Roman camp was quiet, the peace punctured by the occasional shout and the noise of voices conversing. Quietly Fergus observed Hera. The slave girl was hungrily devouring her soup. She had ignored the spoon he'd given her and instead was pouring the liquid straight into her mouth. Once she was done she hastily reached for the loaf of hard, black bread and tore away a piece before stuffing it into her mouth, chewing furiously. Fergus smiled and looked down at the ground. He'd placed her on one of the supply wagons at the rear and had assigned a wounded soldier to watch her. There was no way the girl would be able to do the twenty-mile plus daily marches. At first Hera had seemed confused and frightened by her unfamiliar surroundings but she had not run away even though she'd had ample chance to do so. She had trusted him Fergus thought with satisfaction and for that he was glad for it meant he would not need to discipline her. She was a slave after all even though she probably didn't realise it yet.

"Hera," Fergus said suddenly looking up at her and using her name to catch her attention. "When this war is over you will become part of my family's household. You will go where we go. You will live with us, but you cannot leave. Maybe when you are older you will regain your freedom." Fergus paused and lowered his eyes. "I have a wife. Her name is Galena and five daughters. A few of my girls are your age. Galena is strong willed and very beautiful. She will be strict with you, but she has a good heart. You must do what she tells you to do." Fergus paused again and looked up at Hera. "I haven't seen my family in nearly a year and I miss them, but I know that you will be happy in my household. Our home is far-a-way in Britannia. It is a beautiful green land filled with great wild forests like you have never seen before."

Across from him Hera had abruptly stopped chewing and was staring at him. Fergus sighed and looked away. The girl had not understood a word he'd said.

Chapter Twelve – House to House

Once more the massive bronze head of the battering ram came swinging out of its protective shed and crashed into the gates, sending a dull thudding and cracking noise reverberating across the open desert. From his vantage point some two hundred yards behind the ram, Fergus watched the war machine doing its work. It was morning and along the western wall of Doura-Europus, a few defenders were pelting the battering ram and the Roman testudo with missiles. But the defenders were few and their efforts strangely half-hearted and ineffective. Massed across the open flat desert, around Fergus, were nearly two thousand heavily-armed legionaries. The silent men were standing, grouped together behind their company and cohort standards, their large shields resting against their legs. In their hands they were clutching their spears. The sunlight gleamed and reflected from their body armour and helmets. Every single man was staring at the gates leading into the besieged city, waiting patiently for the order to storm the place. The ram was doing an effective job and it was clear to all, that the wooden gates would not last long.

Stretching away on either side of the main assault force, arrayed in positions that sealed the city off from the landward side, parties of Syrian archers and slingers were bombarding the walls with a barrage of arrows and lead bullets. And further back, protecting the Roman camp, Fergus could see the Batavian cavalry squadrons who were being kept in reserve. All was ready. The decisive moment was coming. Fergus turned to peer at the defenders on top of the walls. He had been expecting more resistance from the rebels. If this was all they could manage then Doura would fall quickly and that was just as well, he thought grimly. It was imperative that he took the city today. For his cavalry scouts had warned him that a large force of Parthian cavalry was lurking just a day's ride south along the Euphrates. If he wasn't careful his men would be caught between the city walls and Parthian horse archers.

Fergus turned his attention to the group of officers standing close to him. He had originally decided to place himself at the head of the assault and personally lead his men into the city. A commander should lead from the front after all, like any centurion. But in a rare act of rebellion, his senior officers including Dio, had flatly refused to allow it, arguing that he was too valuable and that the risks were too high. No amount of arguing had been able to change their minds. So instead, as a compromise, he would be going in with the second wave. Grimly Fergus lowored his hand until it rested on the pommel of Corbulo's old gladius. Then he sighed. He did not relish what was coming. The rebels should have surrendered. Doura was going to fall. The city was going to fall today and when it did, he would be forced to make an example out of its citizens, an example that they would never forget.

With a loud shattering crack, the bronze head of the Roman battering ram broke through the gates, sending them swinging inwards. The noise was greeted by a great triumphant roar by the Romans. Moments later a trumpet rang out and the legionaries surged forwards. Up on the walls the defenders were crying out in alarm, but their few pitiful missiles could do nothing to halt the attack. Tensely Fergus watched, as the first companies led by their centurion's stormed through the gates. Then quickly he turned to the legionaries around him.

"Let's go, go, go," Fergus roared, as clutching his shield he began to calmly walk towards the shattered gates.

As he reached the entrance into the desert city, Fergus could see that the gates had nearly been torn from their hinges. Wood splinters and the remains of the broken cross beam together with a few corpses, lay scattered about in the street. The bodies were oozing blood onto the paving stones. On either side of him legionaries were rushing into the city and further away, he could hear screams and confused shouting. Without reaching for his gladius, Fergus calmly strode into Doura-Europus and as he did, a spear knocked down one of the men ahead of him. Up ahead, blocking the narrow street was a makeshift barricade made of an overturned wagon, stones, barrels and debris. The legionaries trying to force their way through were being held back by determined resistance and their advance had stalled. Hastily Fergus turned his gaze to the right and then the left. The two other narrow streets leading away from the gates were also blocked by similarly defended barricades. A large group of legionaries were trying to force their way through but were being held back. As another man went down, felled by an arrow, Fergus bit his lip. Then a Roman voice cried out in warning. Suddenly rebels had appeared on the roof tops of the buildings that surrounded the gates. With frantic, desperate energy they began to pelt the Romans down below in the street with stones, darts, roof tiles, arrows and spears. Fergus growled in dismay as he and the men with him quickly veered into the relative shelter of the gatehouse. So, this was why the defenders had not put up much resistance on the walls and in front of the gates. It looked like they were going to make the Romans fight from house to house.

"Get up on those roofs," Fergus roared. "Drive them from those roofs. Bypass those barricades. We go house to house. Get up on the roof."

Pulling his gladius from its sheath, Fergus poked his head around the edge of the wall and snatched a quick look at the rebels on the roof tops. Then calling out to his bodyguards, he broke cover and sprinted across the street, launching himself at the doorway into one of the nearby buildings. His shoulder struck the wooden door but instead of crashing through into the room beyond as he'd expected, the door refused to budge and instead Fergus went bouncing painfully and embarrassingly backwards onto the paving stones. Around him the city was filled with shrieks, shouts and the noise of desperate fighting men. As he lay on the ground, a roof tile came hurtling through the air and smashed into a hundred fragments, narrowly missing him. Startled, Fergus scrambled to his feet just as one of his bodyguards kicked open another door and vanished into the darkness beyond. Storming after his men into the dark, cool building, Fergus caught sight of one of his men disappearing up a flight of stone steps. Racing on after him Fergus shot up the stairs and a few moments later emerged into bright daylight and out onto the flat roof of the single storey building. Close by, one of the rebels standing on the roof turned and came at Fergus, lunging at him with a knife. With a yelp Fergus stumbled backwards as the tip of the man's knife raked across his body armour. Then with a swift, savage and powerful blow, Fergus punched his sword into his attacker's neck, killing him instantly. Nearby, the bodyguard was locked in a vicious fight to the death with another man. The two of them were grappling with each other, frantically rolling across the roof as they tried to stab each other. But there was no time to go to the legionary's aid. With a furious, high-pitched scream, a woman came at Fergus slashing the air with a long scythe. Fergus's eyes widened in horror and once again he staggered backwards as the woman's blade swept in towards him. Behind his assailant stood a boy who looked no older than six or seven. The woman seemed intent on protecting him. The boy's face was pale with terror. Blocking the scythe with his shield, Fergus quickly forced the shrieking, furious woman backwards and then finished her off by stabbing her in the abdomen and kicking her off the roof and into the street below, where she hit the pacing stones with a thud. On the rooftop close by, the legionary had finally gotten the upper-hand and was slowly throttling his opponent to death with his hands. Gasping for breath, Fergus whirled round but the only person left on the roof was the young boy. He was standing rooted to the floor, his eyes filled with horror, his lip trembling as he stared at Fergus, but he had not moved an inch, nor did he make a sound. Ignoring him Fergus leapt to his bodyguard's aid, but his help was not needed. Grimly the legionary staggered to his feet, just as more Romans came surging up onto the roof, their hobnailed boots clattering on the stone stairs.

"House to house," Fergus roared. Across from him on the adjacent roof several rebels were pelting the Romans in the street with missiles. Without hesitating Fergus took a running leap and launched himself across the narrow gap that separated the building from the next roof. He landed on his feet, but his momentum sent him crashing and tumbling into one of the rebels. Losing his shield on impact, Fergus went down in a tangle of arms and legs. The man he'd crashed into was shrieking and trying to stab him. As they grappled with each other, Fergus tried to stab his opponent, but the man had a firm grip on his arm. With a ferocious cry Fergus slammed his forehead and helmet into the man's face and was rewarded by a high-pitched shriek of pain and the man's grip on his arm weakened. Tearing himself free, Fergus staggered to his feet and kicked his opponent in the groin with his hobnailed boots. The blow forced the rebel down onto his knees, but before the man could do anything or make another sound, a legionary had stabbed him in the back. Close by, someone screamed. A moment later something thudded onto the ground. Staggering backwards Fergus was suddenly aware of a searing pain in his leg. Looking down he saw something had gashed his upper leg and blood was welling up, but it was not a serious wound.

In the corner of the roof an old man was the only survivor. Slowly and warily the man backed away, his eyes darting from one face to another as several legionaries closed in on him. He looked very old. In his trembling hand the man was clutching a knife. Fergus grimaced as he felt his leg stiffening up. Then before any of the legionaries could attack, the old man swiftly raised his knife and cut his own throat. As the blood gushed out, he toppled silently over the side of the building.

"Sir are you all right," the decanus in charge of the bodyguards cried out, as he saw the blood seeping from Fergus's leg.

"I am fine," Fergus snapped irritably. On the flat roof from where they'd just come from, more legionaries had appeared and were leaping across the gaps between the roofs. In their midst, ignored by all, like a stone statue, the small boy stood silent and unmoving, completely frozen in fear and horror. Down below and around the barricades the sound of fierce fighting could be heard and, across the street from him, Fergus caught sight of more legionaries. The Romans were moving, leaping and fighting their way across the roofs of the terraced houses, trying to make their way towards the centre of Doura. As Fergus stooped to retrieve his shield, one of the legionaries was hit by a spear and went tumbling down into the street.

"Keep moving," Fergus yelled at his men and, ignoring the pain in his leg, he launched himself across the gap and onto the next building. The roof of this house was deserted but as Fergus landed, the floor abruptly gave way under his weight and with a startled cry he disappeared through the roof and into the dark room below. Fergus landed on a table with a painful cracking crash and the impact shattered the wooden table, sending splinters of wood flying in all directions. For a moment he lay on the ground too stunned to move. In the darkness close by, a woman suddenly screamed and something in her shrill voice made the hair on Fergus's neck stand up. Staggering to his feet, Fergus just had enough time to see the woman coming at him clutching a stone. With all her might she swung at Fergus, intending to bash his head in with the stone, but he ducked, and the woman missed. Before she could recover, a legionary came dropping down from the roof above and landed right on top of her. The force of his impact broke the woman's neck.

In the gloomy light, Fergus hastily turned to look around. The building however seemed to consist of just one room and the woman had been the only occupant. With a crash another legionary jumped down into the house and then another. Grimacing, Fergus hastened towards the door, opened it and cautiously poked his head out. In the narrow street beyond he could see a barricade blocking the road. A group of men, women and boys were standing behind the barricade, lobbing a barrage of stones and missiles at the legionaries who were trying to force their way through. Quickly Fergus withdrew his head and pressed his back up against the mud brick wall as he tried to steady his breathing. In the room his companions were watching him, as more of his men came jumping down through the hole in the ceiling. Hastily Fergus picked up his shield from the ground.

"Barricade is to the right, twenty, thirty paces away," he gasped, as he straightened up. "We have to clear the street. Right, follow me."

And with that, Fergus took a deep breath and shot out of the doorway and down the narrow street towards the group of defenders. Most of the rebels had their backs to him and did not see the Romans charging towards them. But a few did and as their warning cries rang out, the defenders panicked and tried to scatter. Catching a man in his shoulder with his sword Fergus bowled him over and onto the ground, stamping on his face as he charged on towards the barricade. He had covered half the distance to the obstruction, when ahead of him men came pouring out of doorways. There were dozens and dozens of them. At the same time a stone slammed into Fergus's helmet, making him gasp in pain and shock.

"There are too many of them Sir," a Roman voice cried out, from behind Fergus.

"Back," Fergus yelled as the rebels stormed towards him down the narrow street. "Back. Back into the house. We will defend the doorway."

Hastily the eight Romans beat a retreat down the street, as more missiles rained down on them from above. Piling back into the house Fergus slammed the door shut after the last of his men had made it inside. Outside in the street he could hear confused shouting, and a moment later someone tried to force their way inside. Straining and grunting the legionaries pushed back and the door remained closed. Fergus stumbled backwards into the room and turned to look around but there was nothing useful which he could use. Unlike the other building there was no stairs leading up onto the roof. He and his men were trapped. Frustrated, Fergus swore out loud. What was he doing, trying to personally lead his men into battle. That was not his job. He was in command of the whole assault force. He should have been directing the battle, not getting himself cornered like this.

Outside in the street, confused shouting had broken out, but no one tried to force their way into the building. Around Fergus in the gloomy light the legionaries were staring at each other in silence. Their sweat drenched, stoic faces were trying to figure out what was going on outside. Suddenly the voices in the street seemed to recede and Fergus heard running feet followed by a scream. Pushing one of the legionary's out of the way, Fergus boldly opened the door a crack. There was no response and quickly he opened it wider and cautiously peered around the corner of the doorway. The rebels had gone but a few of them remained behind the barricade. The street, that had been filled with armed men just a few moments ago, was now practically deserted bar a sleuth of corpses, discarded weapons, stones and broken roof tiles. A noise from one of the roofs made Fergus look up. He was just in time to see a figure leaping across from one roof to the next. Across the narrow street a door was open, and through the doorway Fergus saw a ladder protruding up into a hole in the ceiling. A trail of blood had stained the dusty floor.

"Follow me," he hissed. Then he shot out of the doorway and across the street and into the building opposite them. As he entered the dwelling, a groan made him raise his sword. In the back room, slumped on the floor with his back leaning against the wall was a wounded man. The rebel had his hands pressed to a wound across his abdomen and he looked in a bad way. As behind him his bodyguards piled into the building, Fergus ignored the dying man and turned his attention to the ladder, that led up onto the roof. Quickly he peered up at the hole. Then grasping hold of the ladder with both hands he started upwards. Poking his head out, he saw that the roof was deserted. Hastily he clambered up out of the hole, crouched and surveyed the scene. One by one his men came climbing up and scuttled across the roof. Fergus bit his lip as the pain in his leg manifested itself again.

Across the strange and weird landscape of flat roofs and under a clear blue sky, small parties of legionaries and rebels were moving, fighting and hurling projectiles at each other. The cries and shouts were everywhere. It was impossible to know where the Roman and rebel positions were or indeed, who occupied a building or street. This was unlike any battle he'd ever fought in. There were no battle lines, no strategic moves, nothing but confusion, Fergus thought as he turned this way and then that way. The assault on Doura had become a chaotic and confused fight, involving small squads of men fighting to the death in a labyrinth of narrow streets and alleyways. A game of cat and mouse. One in which the rebels had the advantage for they knew their city better than the Romans did and they'd had time to prepare. This was their plan. He could see that now. Fergus grunted as he came to a decision. He had to get back to his main force. He needed to try and direct the battle, that was his job. What was needed was a plan to methodically seal off and clear a section of the city at a time. Every house and street had to be cleared and its defenders rooted out, their barricades torn down. There was no doubt that Doura would fall, now that his men were in the city, but he could not afford to take high casualties. He had to try and minimise his casualties and end this crazy urban battle as quickly as possible. Catching sight of the city gate and walls Fergus swiftly rose to his feet and jumped across the gap onto the next roof.

***

Smoke was rising into the clear blue skies from the mounds where the dead were being burned - out in the desert. Holding his hand to his mouth and nose, Fergus stared sombrely at the fires. Gathered around him, his bodyguards were doing the same. The stench of the corpses and the sheer number of the dead had quickly become a hygiene threat, and fearing the spread of disease, he'd ordered that the corpses be burned as quickly as possible. However, throughout the city they were still finding and bringing in the dead and many of the wounded were still succumbing to their injuries. It was late in the afternoon. From his vantage point up high up on the wall, Fergus had a good view of the city and the Euphrates that ran along its eastern walls. A week had passed since the assault and successful capture of Doura-Europus. His plan to seal off and methodically clear each district had worked and despite ferocious, at times fanatical resistance, the rebels had been methodically isolated from each other, cornered and cut to pieces. Thousands had died. Men, women, children, the elderly, the young, the sick. Some had perished in the flames when the legionaries, out for bloody revenge after the hard fight for Doura, had set fire to a district of the city. Others had killed themselves and their families, preferring that to a life of enslavement. Most had died in the fighting. Fergus knew that the bitter resistance that the Romans had encountered had surprised everyone and had enraged and shocked his men.

Sombrely he turned to look at the eight wooden crosses that stood out in the desert, lining the approach road coming from the north-west. He had a decision to make. A decision that he alone had to make. A decision that could not be put off for much longer. He'd crucified the remaining rebel leaders, as a warning to anyone thinking about joining the rebels. It was his right, but much to the slavers annoyance he'd stalled on the terms of enslavement for the city's surviving populace. Doura had refused to surrender, and because of that decision, the populace had forfeited their right to be called free men and women. To decide the fate of the populace was a right that belonged to the victors. Selling the survivors to the slavers who had accompanied his task force, was not something Fergus was however thrilled about. But his men were eager for the transaction to take place, for the profits from the sale would be shared out amongst every soldier. Fergus sighed. Slowly he turned around and gazed back out across the city. He would not be able to postpone the decision forever. If he went ahead and agreed the transaction, no one would think it unusual and yet there was no honour in such an action even though he had the right. But, if he decided to be magnanimous and refuse to agree to the transaction his men would be severely pissed off.

Along the top of the wall, Fergus suddenly noticed a legionary hastening towards him. As he came up to Fergus the soldier saluted.

"Sir, you are needed at HQ," a legionary said quickly. "Centurion Dio is asking for you. He says it's important Sir."

Without saying a word, Fergus turned and started off down the ramparts followed quickly by his close protection detail. As he strode along the battlements, Fergus cast a final glance at the crosses standing out in the desert. A few scavenger birds were circling overhead. The matter must be important he thought, for Dio did not make it a habit of calling for him unless it was indeed urgent.

The mansion of the former Parthian governor of Doura had been badly damaged during the fighting and it was missing most of its roof, which had gone up in flames. Black scorch marks adorned the walls and the once fine floor mosaic, was covered in soot, debris and old bloodstains. Some of the Roman wounded had been placed out in the gardens in neat, ordered rows. The men were lying on mattresses and looted couches, whilst an overworked doctor and some of his slaves and students busied themselves amongst them. Further away along the mansion's perimeter wall, groups of legionaries and auxiliaries were busy preparing their meals over small cooking fires. The smell of freshly baked bread wafted across the gardens. The guards at the entrance to the Roman HQ saluted, as Fergus strode into the building.

As Fergus came into the main chamber of the house, he caught sight of Dio and a few of his centurions. The officers were standing about taking to each other in quiet, solemn voices that ceased abruptly as Fergus entered. All eyes turned to stare at him. In a corner, the standard bearer of the Fourth Scythica hastily rose to his feet from where he had been reclining in a chair.

"Well what is it?" Fergus growled, as he turned to Dio.

In response Dio cleared his throat. The centurion looked troubled and refused to meet Fergus's inquiring gaze and Fergus felt a sudden unease. Not much ever bothered Dio but something was certainly bothering the old veteran officer now.

"Sir," Dio said quietly. "An imperial messenger has just arrived in the last hour. He says he has come direct from the emperor's camp. Trajan was encamped close to Ctesiphon when the messenger left them. That was several days ago. The man has brought us new orders. He brought us this," Dio added, holding up a tightly rolled papyrus scroll. "Apparently," Dio said in a deliberately breezy voice, "Trajan sent us three messengers, all three taking different routes to find us and all three carrying the same instructions. Just in case one or two of them got caught. I expect the other two messengers will probably be arriving soon. There is nothing like a bit of proper Roman planning and organisation is there."

Fergus was staring down at the sealed scroll.

"I take it that the fact that the wax seal has been broken means that you have read the letter," Fergus growled.

"I have Sir," Dio replied in a grave voice. "And I believe the letter is genuine. Trajan's hardened soul shines through in the writing. It's a proper master piece of literary genius. Shame it could not have gotten here a bit earlier."

"Well," Fergus replied raising his eyebrows. "What does it say?"

"It says Sir," Dio said taking a deep breath. "that Trajan, in all his great wisdom, has decided to officially depose the king of kings of the Parthian throne. That maggot Osroes has been sacked and the Parthians have got a new king. A boy named Parthamaspates is to become the new ruler of Mesopotamia. He is to act as a puppet and client king of Rome and because of that, there will no longer be any need for Roman garrisons in Mesopotamia. Trajan has decided to pull out Sir. He is abandoning Ctesiphon and all our other conquests. He is retreating northwards."

"What about Doura-Europus?" Fergus snapped.

"The city and its people shall be handed over to Prince Parthamaspates," Dio replied and the anger in his voice suddenly became palpable. "Doura will come under his jurisdiction as part of the agreement with Trajan. We have been ordered to evacuate the city and head north Sir."

Dio paused, and then without warning, he flung the letter onto the ground with sudden rage.

"One hundred and seventy-three of our men died to take this fucking city," the centurion roared. "And it now seems they died in vain. If these orders had reached us a week ago those men would still be alive. It's a fucking disgrace. Trajan has given up. He has abandoned us. Everything we have fought for and bled for this past year, has been for nothing."

Fergus was staring at the scroll lying on the floor. Then slowly he looked up and turned to his officers. All seemed to share Dio's disappointment and anger, but Trajan's new orders had spared him from making the difficult choice over the fate of the town's population.

"North? Where does Trajan want us to go?" Fergus asked at last in a calm voice.

"We have been ordered back to Zeugma," Dio hissed, trying to control his anger. "They are sending us back to our old legionary base. We are going home, Sir," Dio added in an icy voice.

Chapter Thirteen – A Letter from Hadrian

January 117 AD

Along the road leading to the legionary fortress at Zeugma the bodies of crucified rebels lined the highway, one bloody mutilated corpse after the other. Perched on top of the crosses, the silent scavenger birds had paused in their feasting and were watching the weary Roman column making its way through the bleak, arid countryside. From the state of the corpses they must have been there for some time, Fergus thought sombrely, as sat on top of his horse, he led his men towards their camp. It was around noon, but it was a cold, overcast and miserable day. To the east where the peaceful Euphrates meandered its way through the countryside, several ominous columns of black smoke were just visible on the horizon. For a moment Fergus peered at the smoke. The Euphrates marked the border between the Roman province of Commagene and the client kingdom of Osrhoene to the east and it was clear that the uprisings against Roman rule had spared neither.

Looking tired and unshaven, Fergus sombrely turned his attention back to the legionary fortress. The vexillation's long journey from Doura to Zeugma was over. They were nearly home. Coming on down the road behind him, eight abreast, were the remnants from the First Cohort and the legionary cavalry from the Fourth Scythica Legion. The deeply tanned legionaries had their marching packs and spears slung over their shoulders and their shields were in their protective dust covers. The tramp of their hobnailed boots on the stones; the metallic rattle and clink of their equipment and weapons; the thud of horses' hooves; the bellow of a water-buffalo and the trundle of wagon wheels were so familiar to him that Fergus no longer noticed them. The mood amongst the men was grim. No one seemed willing to break into any of the usual bawdy marching songs they'd sung on their way south, at the start of the conquest of Mesopotamia. As he approached the fortress gates, Fergus sighed. The homecoming was no triumph. It felt like a defeat, a bitter disappointment. He'd led over a thousand men out of these gates a year ago and now, barely half were returning. Casualties had been heavy, and they had precious little to show for it.

Along the ramparts of the legionary base, Fergus suddenly caught sight of figures manning the battlements. The soldiers up on the walls were staring at the approaching column. Just then, from inside the fortress, a trumpet rang out and moments later the gates began to swing open. The garrison were welcoming them home. Grimly, Fergus turned to the standard bearer and his new cornicen who were riding their horses behind him. The standard bearer, a wolf's head drawn over his helmet, was proudly holding up the square vexillation banner of the Fourth Scythica.

"Announce the return of the vexillation," Fergus growled, addressing himself to the trumpeter.

"Yes Sir," the cornicen replied.

As Fergus stiffly and silently led his men through the gates and into the fortress, he was conscious of hundreds of pairs of eyes watching him. The eager, curious legionaries manning the walls and lining the main street, were gawking at their comrades as they marched on past. From their youthful, inexperienced faces and their posture, the soldiers of the fortress looked like a cohort of brand new recruits still undergoing basic training. Here and there though, amongst the eager crowd welcoming him home, Fergus caught sight of a familiar face and a couple of weapons instructors saluted smartly, as he slowly rode on past. Leading his men out onto the large open parade and exercise ground opposite the long rows of barracks blocks, Fergus finally brought his legionaries to a halt in the centre of the square.

"The vexillation will form up for inspection. Give the order," Fergus snapped, as he turned once again to his cornicen.

As the trumpet rang out and the legionaries silently began to form up in rows, Fergus urged his horse forwards and then turned the beast around so that he could inspect his men. Behind the vexillation, the crowd of curious new recruits had spilled out into the parade ground and were gazing at their comrades. From the corner of his eye Fergus suddenly noticed a small group of senior legionary officers hastening towards him. Amongst them he recognised Gellius, the legionary legate, resplendent in his gleaming cuirassed armour and red cloak. Dismounting stiffly from his horse, Fergus saluted as Gellius and his staff came up to him.

"Good to have you back Fergus," Gellius called out as he reached out to lay a hand on Fergus's shoulder.

"Thank you, Sir," Fergus replied stiffly. "Permission to address the men Sir?"

For a moment Gellius said nothing as he peered at Fergus. Then his gaze shifted to the legionaries and cavalrymen drawn up ready for inspection. At last, turning back to Fergus, Gellius nodded.

Handing the reins of his horse to one of the young tribunes, Fergus calmly and without hesitation strode out into the parade ground, a lone figure out in front of the massed legionary ranks. The homecoming may have felt like a defeat, a disappointment but Dio was right. It could not end this way. He would not allow it to end this way. He had to try and salvage something from this military debacle. Calmly Fergus turned to face his men and as he did, the large exercise ground abruptly grew quiet. The legionary officers and standard bearers were standing out in front of their companies and amongst them he caught sight of Dio.

"Soldiers," Fergus's voice boomed out across the parade ground. "I am proud to have led you into battle this past year. We have been through a lot. You have all proved yourselves worthy. Let no man ever dispute that. Wherever you met the enemy you proved victorious. That is a credit to yourselves and your officers. In this grand conflict, that has already lasted nearly three long years, we have played only a small part, but for us this war was never about maps and territory. We fought for each other. We fought for the honour of the legion. We fought for the glory of Rome and our gods."

Fergus paused as his stern gaze swept across the massed ranks of legionaries. The men were staring straight back at him.

"Often alone, outnumbered and besieged we watched and waited as the enemy tried to annihilate us, only to be thrown back," Fergus continued in a loud voice. "Yes, we lost good friends and comrades, all of us did. But we came back after long months, from the jaws of death and out of the mouth of hell, while all of Rome wondered, when shall the reputation and courage of the men of the Fourth Scythica fail. With your actions, courage and resolve you have set an example of what it means to be a legionary of the Fourth. An example that I am sure is being talked about in the halls of the gods and the abodes of our forefathers. An example that will act as inspiration for future generations. When in the long years to come, men come to talk about us they shall look back on what we have done and say, "do not despair, do not yield to doubt, remember the men who captured Seleucia and Doura, who killed prince Sanatruces and who brought back their vexillation banner in good order. They marched straight forward, and they died if need be – unconquered. They brought honour to the Fourth Scythica. That is what you have achieved. That is all that could ever be asked of you. That is your victory!"

As Fergus fell silent his eyes swept over the troops standing stiffly to attention on the sandy exercise ground. Not a sound could be heard. Then slowly at first, but swiftly gaining in strength, the legionaries began to stamp their boots on the ground and a cry rose that was taken up by hundreds upon hundreds of voices.

"It is yours," the legionaries cried out, "it is yours. This is your victory Fergus. This is your victory."

Swiftly the chanting changed, and the men began to call out Fergus's name as they stamped their feet on the ground.

***

As Fergus finally finished his verbal report and debrief, the stuffy and packed room inside the camp's principia, HQ, remained silent. Out in the corridor and crowding around the doorway into the office were more officers and men, all eager and keen to hear what he had to say. Reaching out to his cup of wine, Fergus took a sip. The vexillation had been away for nearly a year and Fergus sensed that many of the officers and men wanted to know what had become of friends and comrades who'd not returned. Around him in the cramped legate's office, a host of sombre looking senior officers remained silent as they pondered what had been said. Some of the tribunes were gazing down at the floor whilst others were fidgeting with their cups. At last, Gellius the legate, motioned for the slaves to refill the officer's cups.

"You brought back the vexillation standard," Gellius said, turning to Fergus and breaking the oppressive silence. "That's all that truly matters. This war was ill conceived from the start, but no one can find fault with the performance of the Fourth. You did well Fergus. I am going to give you and all your officers and men a three-day pass starting at midnight tonight."

"Thank you, Sir," Fergus replied stiffly.

"The latest news that I have is that Trajan is besieging Hatra," Gellius growled as he turned towards a large map that hung from one of the walls. "I would have given you and your men a longer period of leave, but the situation is serious. I need every man that I have got. Most of the rebellious cities in Northern Mesopotamia have been recaptured, but Armenia is still in a state of open revolt and I doubt that spineless boy Prince Parthamaspates is going to last long in Ctesiphon, when King Osroes returns to claim his throne. If Osroes does overthrow our Parthian puppet, then Trajan is going to have to make peace with Parthia or plan a new invasion. My money is on a peace treaty, especially if the emperor listens to Hadrian. Osrhoene too, is still an unsettled kingdom," Gellius growled, as he tapped the map with his fingers. "Eight of our cohorts are spread out across the territory trying to maintain law and order. It's a mug's job. The locals clearly don't want us there. Trade and commerce have all but ground to a halt. There is no tax money coming in and my men are exhausted. There was some sporadic fighting when the uprisings started, but since Quietus sacked Edessa things have calmed down. Still I expect that we shall have to abandon Osrhoene soon."

"Why is that Sir?" Fergus asked with a frown.

"Our manpower is being stretched to the limit," Gellius replied sourly. "The troops are needed everywhere at the same time. Have you not heard? Uprisings have not only taken place in Mesopotamia and Armenia but across all our eastern provinces. It feels like they have been coordinated. Probably by the Parthians and their allies. There is rebellion in Egypt, Cyrenaica, Cyprus and Judea. Many of the uprisings are being led by the Jews. On Cyprus they massacred the non-Jewish population. Tens of thousands have died; whole towns destroyed. Quietus has been despatched to Judea to put down the revolt there. It's a fucking mess and it's not helped by the fact that Trajan's health is rapidly declining. Some think he will not survive the summer and if the War Party refuse to accept Hadrian as the next emperor, we could be looking at civil war - gods forbid."

Tactfully Fergus lowered his gaze to the floor and resisted the temptation to speak his mind. Had he not warned Hadrian about the potential for serious unrest and rebellion financed by Parthian gold? Had he not implored his patron to take his warnings seriously? And what had Hadrian done about it. Absolutely nothing. For instability in the east seemed to suit Hadrian. It meant he could argue for a defensive military strategy, a key aspect of the Peace Party's grand strategy.

"So, what happened to Britannicus?" Gellius asked softening his tone as he turned to face Fergus.

In reply Fergus stooped and rummaged around in his personal kit before placing the bag containing Britannicus's ashes on the table for all to see.

"He died leading the assault on a Parthian fort," Fergus said, as he looked down at the bag. "He died leading from the front. I had his body cremated and have promised to return his mortal remains to his family in Londinium. He was a brave man and a good soldier."

Sombrely Gellius and the officers in the room stared at the bag. Not a man made a sound. Then at last the legate sighed and looked away.

"One more thing before you go on leave Fergus," Gellius said, snapping his fingers at a slave and sending him off to fetch something. "Ten days ago, an imperial messenger arrived here carrying a letter for you. He had come all the way from Antioch. You had better read it. It looks important. The letter carries Hadrian's personal stamp."

***

"What are you going to do with your leave?" Fergus asked, as he and Dio strode alone across the open exercise ground of the Roman fortress.

"I am going to take my dog for a walk along the Euphrates," Dio replied with a serious looking face. "The bitch will have missed me. After that I don't know. Some of the officers are planning a visit to Zeugma but I am not so sure I will join them. It would be good to spend some time alone. Maybe I will go fishing."

Fergus nodded and for a few moments the two of them remained silent as they strode across the exercise yard. As they reached the street leading to the fortress gates Fergus came to a halt.

"Well I'm afraid our paths diverge from here," Fergus said, forcing a grin onto his face. "I am going home to see my family. I will catch up with you in three days."

Dio too had come to a halt and for a moment the old veteran gazed down at the sand in silence as if lost in thought. Then he looked up.

"That was a good speech," Dio muttered. "A damn fine speech. The men liked that. Thank you and for what it's worth it has been a privilege and an honour to serve under you, Sir. You led us into battle and you brought us home again. The men will remember that. I will remember that."

Then swiftly and without warning Dio straightened up and saluted and, as Fergus returned the salute, for a moment the two officers stood stiffly to attention facing each other in the street. At last Dio nodded, turned and quickly strode away without saying a further word.

***

As Fergus caught sight of the lonely villa on the banks of the Euphrates he sighed with relief. The stone building looked undamaged. It was getting late and around him darkness was closing in rapidly. Resisting the growing anticipation and excitement he brought his horse to a halt and gazed at the villa, savouring the moment. Beyond the house the wide peaceful waters of the Euphrates were just visible, and the gardens looked in good shape. Idly his fingers reached up to touch the iron amulet around his neck that Galena had given him all those years ago, when as a young decanus he'd left for the German frontier. The amulet had powerful magic that would protect him. A good luck-charm and so it had proved up till now. On his belt hung Corbulo's old gladius and the bag containing Britannicus's ashes. Sharing the horse with him was Hera, the Parthian slave girl from Seleucia. The little girl had not said a word since they had left the legionary fortress and even though they could not talk to each other he sensed that she knew where they were going. The girl was nervous and kept picking at her fingernails.

Urging his horse onwards Fergus started out towards the villa. As he approached a sudden excited shriek rent the evening air and two young girls came charging out of the doorway towards him. Catching sight of Briana and Efa, Fergus grinned and hastily dismounted, leaving Hera sitting alone on the horse. His daughters were crying out in excitement and joy as they rushed up to him flinging their arms around his waist. Lifting them both up, Fergus laughed with joy. Then another startled cry erupted from within the villa and moments later Galena, carrying young Athena and together with Gitta and Aina, came rushing out of the doorway towards him. As she reached him Fergus caught sight of tears in Galena's eyes. Hastily and silently his wife buried her face into his chest, clinging to him tightly, her whole body shaking. Fergus chuckled, as for a moment all he could do was remain standing upright as Galena and his girls pressed around him, their joy and relief nearly overwhelming him. His daughters were speaking so fast and through each other, that it was impossible to answer any of their questions. Instead Fergus affectionately lowered his face until it was resting on Galena's head. The stress of not knowing for a year what had become of him, seemed to have taken a toll on Galena. His wife was sobbing silently, her body trembling as she refused to look up at him.

Gently Fergus broke free from the embraces and turned to look at Hera. Briana and Efa too had noticed the slave girl sitting on the horse and were gazing up at Hera with curious, uncertain expressions.

"This is Hera," Fergus said. "She is a Parthian slave and will be joining our household. She does not speak any Latin or Greek. You are all to treat her with respect. She saved my life in Seleucia."

Close by, Briana and Efa exchanged startled glances with each other.

"She is welcome in our house and we will teach her our language," Galena said in a hoarse voice, as she turned to look at the slave girl. "Come inside Fergus," Galena added, as she wiped the tears from her eyes and turned to look up at him with a sudden smile that broke through like a ray of sunlight on a rainy day. "There is much that we need to talk about. There has been news from Kyna on Vectis. A letter has come. But gods am I happy to have you back with us. You have no idea how hard it is to sit here waiting and wondering whether or not you will be coming home."

**

The night was already far advanced when Fergus slipped out of bed. Try as he may he could not sleep. Under the sheets Galena muttered something but she did not wake up. In the villa all was quiet. Everyone seemed asleep. Leaving his wife in bed Fergus, stark naked, silently moved from the bedroom and out onto the garden terrace. The night air was cool and along the banks of the Euphrates in the distance a few man-made lights were glowing in the dark. Looking up at the night sky, he grunted at the amazing array of brilliant stars. It was a truly wonderous sight. Lowering his gaze, he sighed and peered out across the dark and wide river. Galena had been right to say that there had been news from Kyna, his mother, on Vectis.

The letter however had been nearly eighteen months old when it had finally been delivered. In it Kyna had confirmed what Aledus had already told him when he'd met him in Antioch a year ago. That she and Marcus had been forced to leave Rome and return unexpectedly to Vectis and that the future was uncertain. That Nigrinus, leader of the War Party and one of the most powerful men in Rome, seemed hell bent on killing Marcus and destroying the family. The news was a disaster, a reversal of fortune that he could still barely comprehend. Kyna too, had written about Elsa's betrayal and the outrageous news that Armin, Elsa's little brother, had also disappeared together with the bulk of the gold coins which he, Fergus had brought back from Dacia. Marcus had kept the gold at the farm on Vectis for safekeeping and its loss was a severe blow. It meant for starters that Marcus's position on the senatorial lists was now under threat, because to qualify for a seat on the senate a man had to prove he had wealth of over a million denarii. Wealth the family no longer possessed. Kyna had ended her letter by saying that Marcus was going to try and find Armin and recover the gold fortune. But that had been nearly eighteen months ago. Anything could have happened since then. Nigrinus could have succeeded and murdered his whole family by now. Moodily Fergus rubbed his eyes. Marcus, his father had to solve this feud with Nigrinus by himself. He'd gotten himself into this mess and he needed to get himself out of it too. Slowly he shook his head in dismay. Marcus had sent Aledus to find him and ask for his help, but there was precious little he could do from the other side of the world. All he had been able to do was send a message to his father telling him to have hope and at the same time plead with Hadrian to use his influence to protect Marcus and his family on Vectis. Had it been enough? Had it worked? He didn't know. He didn't even know whether Hadrian was aware of his plight or had decided to help him.

At the thought of Hadrian, he suddenly remembered the letter that Gellius had given him. In the emotion and excitement of seeing his family again he had completely forgotten about it. Quietly he stole back into the villa, found his tunic and cloak and retrieved the sealed papyrus scroll. Appearing back on the terrace, clutching a small oil lamp, Fergus sat down on a chair, placed the lamp on a table and turned to study the wax seal. The imprint was Hadrian's all right. He easily recognised that stamp. Maybe here at last was Hadrian's answer to his pleas to help his family. Gently breaking the seal, Fergus slowly unrolled the letter and in the flickering light of the lamp he started to read.

Adalwolf to Fergus,

Greetings old friend. I trust that this letter finds you well and in good health for I have good news for you. Hadrian has instructed me to write to you to tell you that in his capacity as the emperor's official deputy he has promoted you to legate of the Twentieth Legion based at Deva Victrix in Britannia. Your promotion has been confirmed by Trajan. Hadrian wishes you to take up your new post as legate with immediate effect. You are to present this letter to the Governor of Britannia upon your arrival in Londinium. He may have further instructions for you. Letters have already been despatched to Deva to alert the legion to the change in commanders. So dearest friend, as you see Hadrian has come through for you in the end. He will of course expect your loyalty and that of your troops when he becomes the next

*emperor, but I have assured him that in this respect he has nothing to fear from you.
I remain your faithful friend, Adalwolf.*

With a trembling hand Fergus lowered the letter onto the table and as he did a fierce blush of pride shot across his cheeks. Legate of the Twentieth Legion. He had been promoted to legate of the Twentieth. That had been his dream and ambition from the moment he had joined the legion as an eighteen-year old youth straight out of basic training. And now he had made it. The dream had become a reality. He had risen to the very top. He had gone from being an ordinary legionary to commander of the Twentieth. It was some achievement. Slowly Fergus exhaled and tried to steady his breathing. Then abruptly he turned to look up at the stars. What would Corbulo, his grandfather, make of this? There was no way of knowing for sure, but it was a good bet that tonight, Corbulo would be proud, very, very proud of him indeed. Fergus raised his hand to his mouth. And that was what it had always been about. To make something of himself. To make his grandfather proud. And now he had.

"What are you doing out here all by yourself?" Galena said suddenly from the doorway into their bedroom. As she emerged into the light from the lamp she frowned as she saw him sitting at the table, stark naked.

"What is it?" Galena added in alarm, as she suddenly caught sight of the scroll.

Fergus was gazing up at his wife. Then he grinned.

"We are going back to Britannia," he said as he rose to his feet and came towards Galena. "Hadrian has promoted me to legate of the Twentieth Legion. We are going back to Deva Victrix, all of us."

Chapter Fourteen - Resolve

Summer 115 AD

The fresh sea breeze was buffeting the Hermes's red sail and the choppy waves were slapping into her prow, making the ship pitch and roll and sending fine white spray flying over the deck. The groaning and creaking of the timbers was accompanied by the screeching of the sea gulls as they rose and dived down on the ship. High up at the top of the mast, the proud pennant depicting the face of Hermes - messenger of the gods, was streaming in the wind. Standing alone by the bow of the small grain vessel, Marcus held onto the rigging and gazed out across the sea at the coastline of the Isle of Vectis, a mile away. He looked old, gaunt and his cheeks were unshaven. Yet despite his age there was a toughness and a flinty hardness in his eyes. A simple brown cloak was fixed around his neck by a broach. Hanging from his belt was an army pugio and on his fingers several rings gleamed in the noon sun. Without taking his eyes off the coastline, Marcus slowly reached out with his right hand to rub the three remaining fingers on his left and try to stop the uncontrollable shaking in his left arm. The strange and worrying trembling of his arm had started in Rome soon after he'd become aware of Elsa's betrayal. He should have gone to a doctor but there had been no time.

"It feels good to be coming home doesn't it," a female voice said coming up behind him.

Turning around Marcus saw Kyna. His wife was standing watching the coastline with a peaceful, contented look. For a moment Marcus peered at her. Leaving Ahern, her son behind in Rome had left Kyna unsettled and distraught for weeks but lately her old and quiet resolve seemed to have returned and for that, he was glad. Despite the summer weather Kyna had wrapped herself in a thick, white woollen cloak with a hood that was draped over her head. Slowly Marcus nodded as he turned his attention back to the coastline. Kyna was right. The view of the green island, his family's home, was a most welcome sight after all these weeks at sea. He had not realised just how much he had missed the place.

Ignoring his wife, Marcus gazed at the coastline. To the west, towering cliffs rose up out of the sea. At his side Kyna stirred and quietly and contentedly slipped her arm under his, and for a while the two of them stood gazing out at the wide, long sandy beach where he had so often taken his dogs for walks and where Fergus learned to swim. Alexandros, the captain was steering the little ship straight towards the marshy estuary that clove deep into the island's north eastern coast. Once they were in the estuary he would be able to see the villa. They were nearly home and as he thought about that, Marcus suddenly lowered his eyes. His relationship with Dylis, his half-sister had not always been cordial. Often there had been friction between them. The girl was strong-minded, stubborn and unpredictable, traits he could only think she must have adopted from Corbulo. Gently Marcus rubbed his fingers as he tried to stop his left arm from shaking. He had agreed to legally split the ownership of the villa and the farmlands with her, but in all practical terms it was Dylis who ran the farm. It was she who had done all the hard work. It was she who had raised three children on the farm and had agreed to take in and look after Elsa, Armin, Ahern and

Cunomoltus whilst he had been away serving in the army and in Rome. She had made it all work. It was she who had masterminded the expansion, the improvements and who had turned the place into a profitable business. He was the head of his family, but he was no farmer, nor was he suited for such enterprise. He was a soldier. That had been his profession. He could not claim to have built the family business. That was Dylis's achievement. So, what would his half-sister make of his unexpected arrival? Marcus took a deep breath as he gazed at the coastline. Dylis had a right to be angry with him for through his actions he had put all she had ever cared for and built up - at risk. The deadly feud with Nigrinus had put everything at risk. That was his failure. His shame. His alone. He had placed their home, the lives of his whole family and that of the children in mortal danger. There had been barely any time to warn Dylis that he was coming apart from the messenger he'd sent to her as soon as Elsa had told him about stealing his gold. There had been no chance to tell her what had happened in Rome or about the disastrous feud with Nigrinus. The flight from Rome had been too chaotic, too sudden and too unexpected.

***

As the anchor crashed down into the water, Marcus climbed up the ladder and onto the deckhouse roof where Alexandros, the one eyed Greek captain was standing beside the tiller, bellowing orders to his wife and Jodoc.

"The waters are too shallow to go any further," Alexandros growled as Marcus straightened up and turned to look around at the marshes that lined the banks of the small estuary. "I will lower the small boat and you will have to row ashore. You had better hurry. I want to leave on the next high tide."

Marcus nodded and for a moment he remained silent. "Thank you, old friend," he said at last, in a quiet voice. "Without you and the Hermes I doubt we would have made it very far. Once again you have saved us. I will not forget. You and your family shall always have a friend and a home on this island."

"I know, I know," Alexandros grunted before bellowing another instruction to his wife who was standing at the bow. "But we cannot stay. I want to make it to Londinium as soon as possible. I have work to do and the winds are favourable right now."

"You are still planning to go ahead? To return to Hyperborea?" Marcus asked, as a little impressed smile appeared on his lips.

"Yes," Alexandros replied. "In Londinium I am going to look for a crew and I need supplies. Now that the Hermes has been repaired and is seaworthy, I am going to sail her back across the western ocean. The plan is to leave in spring of next year. I am going to find that western passage to the land of the Chin and India. That is my dream, Marcus. I am going to open that new trade route and, with my newly acquired wealth I am going to build a trading company the likes Rome has never seen. And when I die Calista, my daughter and Jodoc shall continue the business and turn it into a dynasty." With a determined look the one eyed Greek captain turned to Marcus. "I have toiled for others all my life. Now I have a chance to work for myself and that feels good my friend. That feels damn good. You wait and see. I am going to find that passage to the west. It exists. I know it does."

In reply Marcus reached out and laid his hand on Alexandros's shoulder and nodded.

"You are a brave man and I hope you make it," Marcus replied. "But do me one favour. Come back to Vectis one last time before you leave on your voyage. To say goodbye. Will you do that Alexandros?"

The big Greek Captain hesitated for a moment. Then quickly he nodded.

"I will Marcus," Alexandros said. "I will visit you before I leave and if you and your family want to come with me, we will have a place for you."

***

In the small wood that dominated the higher ground above the marshy estuary, the forest floor was covered in beautiful, colourful flowers and the warm, optimistic scent of summer was everywhere. Bees and butterflies buzzed and fluttered amongst the vegetation and, in the ancient trees, birds were calling out to each whilst small animals were rustling unseen in the undergrowth. Marcus, weighed down by the personal belongings they'd managed to take with them on their flight from Rome, led the way up the narrow forest path followed by Kyna, her slave girl and Indus, the burly Batavian bodyguard who was bringing up the rear. Above his head, through the gaps in the forest canopy, a fierce blue sky was hosting the sun and bathing the forest in glorious sunlight. Stoically Marcus peered ahead, hoping to get a glimpse of the villa, but the trees shielded the house from his eyes. It had been Corbulo, his father who had first settled his family here on Vectis, when the farm and its land had still belonged to Agricola, former governor of Britannia. Agricola had given Corbulo the task of looking after and managing the villa, for Agricola himself had spent very little time there, preferring his estates in the south of Gaul. Corbulo had died soon after and when Agricola too died some years later, the great man had given the house and its farmlands to Marcus in his will. Marcus had become the new and sole owner of the property. Marcus frowned. Agricola had never really explained his decision, but it must have been out of respect for Corbulo, a final recognition of his father's loyalty to him. And when he died, Marcus thought, the house and its estates would pass on to Fergus as sole owner. Both he and Dylis had agreed on that.

As he finally caught sight of the house through the trees, Marcus paused. In the sunlight the finely constructed stone villa with its smart red roof tiles and its wooden outhouses looked in good condition. All looked peaceful and well ordered. A thin column of smoke was rising from the kitchens. In their stables and pens Marcus could see horses, pigs and chickens and, out of sight, he could hear cows mooing. The rectangular house had been built on a gently rising slope and together with the stables, slaves' quarters and agricultural storage buildings, it formed a courtyard that was enclosed on three sides. A rutted and unpaved track led away northwards and a simple wooden fence marked the boundary of the property. Nearby Marcus could see the remains of the old defensive palisade he'd once built to protect his home. But apart from that there was no sign left of the bad times that had once befallen the estate. Beyond the house to the west, a line of slaves were at work in fields filled with acres of golden wheat. The slaves were singing as they worked and nearer to him, standing beside the well, drawing water with a bucket, was a slave woman. Two of the slave woman's young children were standing beside her, playing with a small leather ball. Turning his attention away from the house Marcus grunted in surprise. To the northwest of the house a chalk ridge of high ground rose sharply from the estuary and along its south-facing slopes were rows upon rows of neatly ordered vines. The vineyard was new. It had not been there the last time he'd been here. Dylis must have planted it in the past year. Did she really think she could produce wine in Britannia? Slowly Marcus shook his head. His half-sister was indeed full of surprises.

Abruptly Marcus's attention was wrenched away from the vineyard by loud barking. Bounding towards him across the field were two of his hunting dogs. A fond expression appeared on Marcus's face as the dogs charged up to him and excitedly began whirling around his legs, sniffing, snapping and barking. A few moments later a cry rose from within the courtyard and a figure emerged from the house, paused and gazed in Marcus's direction. Then swiftly the figure turned and in an excited voice shouted something into the house, before starting out towards Marcus. At the entrance into the villa a couple of figures rushed out of the doorway and came to a halt in the courtyard. All were staring at the newcomers. Then an excited shout rang out and the figures started to run towards him.

"It's Marcus. It's Marcus and Kyna," Cunomoltus cried out.

As his half-brother reached Marcus, Cunomoltus was grinning with delight from ear to ear. Quickly and forcefully he embraced Marcus and then Kyna and then with a swift and sharp verbal command, he silenced the dogs. Cunomoltus was followed moments later by Dylis's twins, their long blond hair decorated with summer flowers, their faces beaming with joy.

"Gods Marcus, this is a welcome surprise," Cunomoltus, gasped as he took a step backwards to look at him and Kyna. "We were not expecting to see you so soon. Is everything all right? Where is Ahern?"

"Good to see you too brother," Marcus said with a grin. Then he raised his eyebrows in mock surprise and opened his arms wide, giving each of Dylis's twins an affectionate hug. The girls were no longer children. They had grown up. They had both turned eighteen last year. They had become young women Marcus thought, but he still found it hard to accept how quick they'd grown up.

"You look beautiful, both of you," Marcus said with a smile as he gazed fondly at his nieces. "Time to get you married soon, I reckon."

In response the girls quickly and nervously glanced at each other and blushed.

"All well here?" Marcus asked turning back to Cunomoltus.

Cunomoltus quickly lowered his eyes. "The farm is prospering Marcus," he replied in a guarded voice, "but I'm afraid not all is well. Armin has vanished and so has the bulk of the gold which we buried on the farm. It's a disaster. We can't find Armin anywhere. Dylis thinks that he stole the gold. Only we knew where it was buried. He must have discovered where."

Marcus's face darkened but he said nothing. The news then was as he had expected. Across the field, Marcus caught sight of Jowan hastening towards him. Dylis's husband, his hair tied back in a ponytail, was clutching a hayfork and was wearing a wide-brimmed sunhat and a dirty leather apron. At the same time coming towards them from the house, at a walk, was Dylis. His sister's clothes, arms and face were covered and stained with splashes of paint and in her hand, she was clutching a brush. As Jowan came up to Marcus he dipped his head in a respectful and courteous manner, flung his hayfork onto the ground and quickly embraced Marcus and Kyna. The last to reach them was Dylis and, as she smiled and silently hugged Marcus and Kyna, the excited dogs bustled silently and excitedly around Marcus's legs. Stepping back, Dylis turned to Marcus and gave him a puzzled look.

"Well it's good to see you both. This is a surprise. We were not expecting you so soon," Dylis said as her eyes moved from Marcus to Kyna and back. "Has this something to do with Armin's disappearance or did you finally get bored of Rome?"

For a moment Marcus said nothing, as sombrely he turned to look at the house. Finally, he turned to his little sister.

"Gather the whole family together. I need to speak to all of you. The situation is very serious," Marcus said in a grave voice.

***

It was late in the evening and in the long dining hall of the villa the fire crackled in its hearth. On the walls oil lamps lit up the room in a dim flickering light. Marcus stood beside the window, looking out at the night and the moon that presided over the dark wheat fields, a cup of Posca in his right hand. Slowly he reached out to try and steady the shaking in his left arm but to no avail. Along the large wooden dining table that dominated the hall, Jowan, Cunomoltus and the twins were sitting gazing down at the polished oak in shocked silence. The rich, generous dishes of food and jugs of wine, posca, water and milk had barely been touched. In a corner Petrus, the Christian boy whom Corbulo had once rescued from Londinium, was leaning against the wall stroking his beard thoughtfully. The others, Dylis, together with her fifteen-year-old son and Kyna, were sitting beside the hearth staring silently into the flames. Only Indus, the big bald Batavian bodyguard seemed unaffected by the news Marcus had just shared.

"So now you know what has happened to us in Rome," Marcus said at last as he turned to face his family. "Now that you know about Elsa and Armin's betrayal the question arises - what are we going to do?"

"What a fucking bitch," Jowan suddenly swore with uncharacteristic anger. "We treated her and her brother like one of us. They were one of us. Why did I not see that coming?"

"None of us saw Elsa's betrayal coming," Kyna replied in a weary voice. "But she and Armin had been planning this for some time. The damage has been done. None of us are at fault. We must move on."

"If the situation is as bad as you describe," Cunomoltus said, quickly turning to look at his half-brother. "And this senator. This Nigrinus will be coming for us, then I see no other alternative. We must leave Vectis. We should go north or east. Corbulo still has family living around Camulodunum and Galena has family in Deva. We should seek shelter with them."

"Don't be stupid," Dylis hissed as she angrily rounded on Cunomoltus. "Did you not hear what Marcus just said? There will be a bounty on Marcus's head. He's a fugitive from the law. He murdered two prominent senators in his own home. There is clear proof. No one will protect him now. No one will harbour us. No one will want to touch us. Once news of that reaches the province we will not be safe anywhere."

"Well we can't stay here," Cunomoltus retorted. "If this Nigrinus is as powerful and influential as Marcus says, we won't be able to fight him. All we can do is flee. That is the sensible option. Think about the children."

At the mention of her children Dylis's face darkened and she looked away.

"Ahern refused to come with us," Kyna said suddenly. "My son chose to stay behind in Rome. If Nigrinus finds Ahern, what do you think they will do to him? I don't know why he chose to stay but I have faith in him." Slowly Kyna turned to look around the room. "We must have faith. All of us. We must believe in each other. Whatever we decide it must be unanimous. United we stand, disunited we fall."

"I know some Christian brothers who would be willing to shelter us," Petrus said quietly, but no one seemed to be listening to him.

"Fine words are all well and good," Dylis hissed bitterly as she turned on Kyna. "But if it wasn't for your husband's foolishness and recklessness, we would not be in this position."

Defiantly and angrily Dylis turned to glare at Marcus. "Well its true isn't it? You got us into this trouble. This whole mess is your fault. You have put us all at risk. What do you propose to do about it?"

All eyes suddenly turned to Marcus standing beside the window. For a moment he said nothing, his face grave and serious.

"What is done cannot be undone," Marcus said at last, as he turned to look at his family. "There is no point arguing about what has happened. The damage is done like Kyna's says. I have become a fugitive from the law. Elsa and her brother Armin have stolen our gold and we have been run out of Rome, and it is highly likely that Nigrinus or his minions will come here looking for me. I know that man. He will not rest until he has what he wants." Marcus paused, as he took a sip from his cup. Then he lifted his chin with sudden resolve. "We must look towards the future and we will see this crisis through to the end," he said in a grave but confident voice. "This is not the first crisis we have faced. We have endured before and will do so again. We will survive. But I am not going to leave this house, this farm. This is our home. This is where we belong. There is nowhere else to go. I will be damned if I am going to run again from a weasel like Nigrinus, even if he and his cohorts come here with the full backing of imperial authority and the law. If we are to die, then let it be here in this house where my father first made his home. We are staying put, all of us. We will defend our property like we have done before. I am done with running. That is my decision."

For a long moment the dining hall remained silent. Then slowly Cunomoltus shook his head.

"This is madness," he muttered. "What hope do we have against the full force of the law and the power of the War Party?" Anxiously Cunomoltus looked up at Marcus. "Brother, this is not like earlier, when Priscinus tried to steal our farm from us. These people Marcus, these people who have become our enemies; they are vastly more powerful and dangerous than Priscinus ever was. How can we fight them? It's madness. It's suicide."

"What about my children?" Dylis snapped. "Whatever happens the children must survive. You cannot expect them to fight, Marcus."

Marcus turned to gaze at the twins and Dylis's teenage son, all three of whom were anxiously watching him. For a moment Marcus remained silent, his face hard and grim.

"They are no longer children. They are old enough to face our enemies," Marcus said at last. "The girls are old enough to be married and the boy can wield a sword. I have trained him myself. He is ready. The time has come for them to grow up and see what the world is really like. How else are they going to survive out there? No, they shall stay here with us. I am not sending them away. We must stick together."

A tense and oppressive silence descended on the hall as Marcus slowly turned to look at each member of his family in turn. Then slowly Jowan got to feet, crossed the room and stooped to kiss Marcus's hand.

"I am with you Marcus," Jowan said with a little respectful nod. "You are the head of this house. You and Corbulo have always been wise. You have always made the right decisions. I shall do what you decide."

One by one the others silently rose and did the same, kissing Marcus's hand and, as they returned to their places the silence in the dining hall seemed to lighten.

"Great so now what?" Cunomoltus growled unhappily. "What do we do now?"

"We need to find Armin and retrieve our gold," Marcus replied quickly, "that's our first task. We will start tomorrow, and I am going to need you all to tell me everything you know about that boy."

***

Alone in their bedroom Kyna came up behind Marcus and gently reached out to grasp his shaking left arm. For a moment the two of them stood together, not speaking.

"It's getting worse," Marcus said, as he felt his wife press her face into his back. "The shaking. It's getting worse. I can't control it."

"It doesn't matter. You are still the same man whom I knew all those years ago," Kyna replied in a quiet voice, as she reached up on her toes to fondly kiss his neck. "You still have the same spirit, the same courage, husband. It is what I love about you. You are a rock that stands in the ocean and endures."

Marcus grunted as he felt Kyna press herself into his back.

"I will be by your side come what may," Kyna whispered. "You and I, Marcus shall share the same fate. I shall not be parted from you. Cunomoltus may have his doubts but I do not. I shall stand at your side and defend this house, for you are right, without this place we have nothing; we are nothing. We will stand and fight. I want you to know that I will be there for you. I will be there for all of us."

Slowly Marcus turned around and fondly looked down at his wife.

"Listen, do you remember all those years ago," he said softly, "when here on Vectis I made a contract with the immortals. The agreement I made with the gods. If they were to keep Fergus alive and out of harm's way, I would do what the gods commanded?" Slowly Marcus shook his head. "They may demand my life Kyna and if they do I shall willingly give it to them, but you have made no such promise. You must survive Kyna. You must survive for Fergus and his family. They are the future. They will need you. The family will need you. When the time comes I do not want you to share my fate. I want you to live."

Chapter Fifteen – Petrus Delivers

The forest was quiet and peaceful as Marcus and Petrus strode on down the narrow, overgrown and twisting path back towards the villa. It was late in the afternoon and the fine summer weather bathed the wood in light and warmth. In between them, resting on their shoulders, hanging suspended from a wooden pole, was the carcass of a small deer. Blood from the arrow wound where Petrus had brought down the animal had stained its light fur and its large sightless eyes were staring at the ground. A week had passed since Marcus and Kyna had returned to Vectis. Leading the way, Petrus turned his head to give Marcus a little triumphant grin. The hunt had been a success and tonight the family would dine on fresh wild meat.

"So, your Christian god does not mind you killing animals. I thought the basis for your religion was love, love of all things." Marcus said as he noticed the small wooden cross hanging from around Petrus's neck.

"A man still has to eat," Petrus replied with a shrug, as he led the way through the forest. "But I do not eat pigs. They are filthy animals. They are not like this noble beast of the forest. Tonight Marcus, at dinner, a word of thanks from you for my highly developed hunting skills would be a nice touch. I am the best hunter on Vectis, but no one ever thanks me for what I bring to the table."

"I wonder why," Marcus said sourly, as he followed Petrus through the wood. "Maybe it's because you are never on the estate to help with the farm work. Maybe it's because people think you are lazy. Tell me, how much time do you spend hunting. From what I hear you also like to get drunk in the taverns on the mainland?"

"There is nothing wrong with liking a drink," Petrus said defensively. "But I do my share of the work. The family benefits from what I bring back and it was I who helped Esther disappear or have you already forgotten our little trip to Rome."

Marcus grunted as he remembered the fraught journey to Rome with Petrus and Esther, the Christian slave who together with Dylis, had murdered her master Priscinus and who needed to disappear before Priscinus's vengeful family could catch her. It had been on that visit to the eternal city that Marcus had made friends with Paulinus and had become re-acquainted with Lady Claudia.

"What about Armin?" Marcus said, abruptly changing the subject. "Did you ever take him hunting?"

"Armin," Petrus exclaimed with a frown. "He was a strange boy. Bit of a baby. Didn't say much. Can't say I ever took him hunting. He spent a lot of time in the stables. He loved the horses and he seemed to pine after his sister's company. Sometimes I would find him out in the forest crying his eyes out. It was strange."

"So, you never spoke to him?" Marcus asked in a disappointed voice.

"Not really," Petrus shrugged. Quickly he raised a finger in the air as he seemed to suddenly remember something. "No, that's not correct," Petrus said hastily. "There was this one time, about eighteen months ago. I was heading to Reginorum on the mainland. A horse show was taking place in town, which I really wanted to see and so, on the spur of the moment, I invited Armin along for I knew he liked horses."

So, the two of us come walking into town and of course the first people we have to run into are a couple of priests from the temple of Neptune and Minerva." Petrus sighed as he continued down the forest path, clutching the wooden pole that protruded over his shoulder and upon which hung the carcass of the young deer. "You know the history between me and those priests. Scumbags all of them. Give them a copper coin and they will say that Minerva will grant you wisdom. Give them a silver coin and they will say Minerva is your best friend. It's pathetic, a fraud. Anyway, so, one thing leads to another and words are exchanged between me and them. Harsh words. But we don't come to blows. The priests don't see me as a threat because I am the only Christian in these parts. I think they see me more as a freak. So eventually they leave me alone and Armin and I go on to watch the horse show."

Up in front of Marcus, Petrus suddenly seemed to grow agitated.

"But I am not afraid of those priests," Petrus snapped. "I really am not. So, after the show I decide to take Armin to the tavern where I know those priests like to drink. Just to show them that I am not afraid of them. All goes well."

Suddenly Petrus paused and behind him Marcus frowned, as the two of them came to an abrupt halt in the forest.

"I know he is only eighteen," Petrus exclaimed, "but I give Armin one cup of wine and it gets him pissed. He starts talking. After one cup of wine! Extraordinary. Have you ever heard of that before? Anyway, we start talking, the first and only proper conversation that I have had with that boy and he tells me that he misses his father and sister. Then he tells me that he has extended family amongst the Batavian community living around Ulpia Noviomagus Batavorum. He knows where they live. He knows their names. Armin tells me to my face that he has never met his extended family but that he would like to see them one day."

On the forest path Petrus turned to look back at Marcus. "Did you know that Armin and Elsa had kin across the sea in the Rhine delta?"

***

Out near the golden wheat fields the slaves had paused in their work of clearing a thorny and overgrown hedge and were sitting together under the shade of an oak, resting, drinking and eating their midday meal. Their wide brimmed sunhats and simple white tunics gave them some relieve from the scorching heat. Around the slaves an array of pick-axes, hayfork's, knives, spades and other agricultural tools lay discarded in the grass. A little further away at the edge of the wheat fields, the family too had gathered together and were sitting quietly in a circle in the grass, eating their lunch of bread, goats cheese, honey, slices of cold mutton washed down with water, wine, milk and mead. They were all there, Dylis, Jowan, Kyna, Cunomoltus, Petrus, the twins and Dylis's teenage son, together with the three hunting dogs. It was just after noon and in the clear blue skies the sun shone supreme. Jowan and Cunomoltus were wearing sunhats like those worn by the slaves, but the women had opted for fine, expensive-looking linen umbrella's too shade themselves from the fierce glare of the sun. Petrus lay stretched out in the grass, his eyes closed as if he was asleep whilst Cunomoltus busied himself with feeding the dogs small pieces of offal. No one, apart from Kyna and Dylis, seemed to be paying any attention to Marcus as he spoke.

"Yesterday Petrus told me something very interesting," Marcus said as he sat cross-legged in the grass speaking to his family in a calm, clear voice. "It seems that Elsa and Armin still have family living near Ulpia Noviomagus Batavorum. I didn't know about this. Elsa and Armin's father was called Lucius. That was his Roman name, but he was a Batavian officer. I knew him well. We served together in the Second Batavian Auxiliary Cohort, in the north and in Caledonia too. So, it is quite possible that Armin still has family amongst the Batavians on the Rhine frontier. It's possible that this is where Armin has gone. It's possible he fled across the sea and has sought refuge amongst his extended kin. I think Armin must have had help preparing his plan. That gold is heavy for a start and it would be highly dangerous for a boy of his age to travel alone with such a fortune. So, it's possible Elsa instructed her extended family to help her brother. It makes sense. The boy as I recall, was not the smartest spark and Petrus says Armin told him that he was keen to see his extended family."

"You killed him, didn't you?" Petrus called out with a lazy yawn as he lay stretched out in the grass sunning himself. "You and Cunomoltus murdered Lucius didn't you."

Marcus's face darkened as he turned to glare at Petrus. For a moment Marcus remained silent, as next to him the twins lowered their eyes and nervously picked at their fingernails. Slowly Marcus reached out for a cup of water and downed it. There were a dozen retorts and justifications he could offer to Petrus, but he sensed that Petrus, being his usual rebellious and antagonistic self, was just trying to annoy him.

"Where is Ulpia Noviomagus Batavorum?" Kyna asked helpfully breaking the awkward silence.

"It's across the German sea in the province of Lower Germania," Marcus growled, giving Petrus an annoyed look. "The coast is maybe three days sail from here with a favourable wind. After that it's a two day ride on horseback. Batavorum is the capital city of the Batavians. It's their Oppidum. Their city where they come together to trade and do business together. It's also the main place where the army recruits for the Batavian cohorts. The town lies on the banks of the Rhine."

"I am just saying," Petrus interrupted as he lay in the grass with his eyes closed. "Because it was I and your father Corbulo who killed Lucius's brother in Viriconium, when we were on the run from the anti-Christian pogroms in Londinium. Bestia I believe he was called. A deserter from your regiment. A right turd of a man. I was only twelve, but I remember that day like it was yesterday. Corbulo had a bitter ongoing feud with Bestia, something to do with what happened during his attempt to find and rescue you in Caledonia."

Petrus paused, opened his eyes and sat up leaning on his elbows, his wooden cross dangling from his neck as he turned to gaze at Marcus.

"So, I think I can see why Elsa and Armin don't particularly like us. We killed both their father and her uncle. That is enough spilt blood for anyone to develop a life-long hatred. Did it never occur to you Marcus that Elsa or Armin might seek revenge one day?"

"Shut up," Marcus growled.

"Yeah, shut up Petrus," Cunomoltus snapped as he threw a piece of offal at Petrus.

"So, what do you plan to do Marcus?" Dylis interrupted.

"I think Armin has fled across the sea to be with his extended family," Marcus snapped. "So, the plan is simple. Indus and I will go to Batavorum, find him and retrieve our gold. I still have some contacts amongst the Batavian community who will be able to help. We need that gold. We shall leave tomorrow. The rest of you shall remain here."

"How long will you be gone for?" Kyna said her face suddenly looking anxious. "And what happens if Nigrinus or his men come here looking for us? What should we do then?"

"We may be gone for a month, I don't know - as long as it takes." Marcus replied grimly, as he turned to look at the anxious faces peering back at him. "As for Nigrinus, we will have to take the risk and trust that he has still not got his act together. Nigrinus is an important and powerful man. He is one of the few who has access to the imperial postal system. If my capture was his top concern, his men would already have found us by now. It takes only nine days for a message to leave Rome and reach Londinium. But I suspect he has other more important and weightier issues to deal with right now. He is an important man, but he is also busy and short on time. He is, after all, trying to become the next emperor. That is far more important to him than going after me."

"So, you are basing our wellbeing and survival on the idea that our great enemy is too busy to come after us right now" Petrus said in a sarcastic voice. "That is an even flimsier excuse than that which Marvina gave me when she refused to marry me. Do you honestly believe that Nigrinus will do nothing? Don't you think he will just send one of his men to Britannia with orders to find us."

"We need to retrieve that gold," Marcus hissed angrily. "I know the risks, I understand the dangers, but we have no choice. This must be done. Without that gold we stand no chance at all. If Nigrinus sends men to find us, you will tell them that you have not seen or heard from me."

For a moment Petrus gazed at Marcus in silence.

"So, you do have a plan on getting us out of this mess?" Petrus said at last, as a little conspiratorial smile appeared on his lips.

"Of-course I have a fucking plan," Marcus bellowed. "But I need that gold for it to work."

Angrily and hastily Marcus forced himself to look down at the grass. He had allowed Petrus to make him lose his temper. For a moment the picnic remained silent.

"Marcus," Jowan said at last in a calm voice. "Should I start to construct defences around the house like those we built against Priscinus?"

"No, that will not be necessary," Marcus said in a calmer voice, as he slowly shook his head. "If all goes well the gold that Fergus brought back from Dacia will be our walls. Nothing and nobody is impregnable to money. That is our best chance and I still have a friend or two in Rome. I want you all to carry on as before. Indus and I will return with Armin and the gold."

"Don't forget Fergus," Kyna said in a hopeful voice, as she turned to look at the faces around her. "We sent Aledus, Fergus's army friend to find him in Antioch and tell him about our situation. Fergus will help us. I know he will. I have faith in him. I have prayed to the gods. Fergus will come to our rescue."

"If you say so," Petrus said, in a weary dispirited voice, as he lay back down in the grass and closed his eyes.

"Marcus," Dylis said suddenly. His sister got to her feet. "Before you leave you should visit Efa's grave and pay your respects. Let's go there now."

Marcus frowned but said nothing as he got to his feet and started to follow Dylis across the grass. Catching up with his sister, Marcus glanced at her. The two of them were alone as they made their way towards a solitary carved and decorated headstone that stood on a small rise shaded by an oak tree.

"Kyna is worried about you," Dylis said in a business-like voice as the two of them strode towards the headstone. "She is nervous Marcus. She knows what happened to Corbulo. She knows how he died. She thinks that you are planning to go the same way as our father. You should speak to her."

Marcus sighed and looked away.

"All will turn out well in the end," Marcus replied.

Chapter Sixteen – The Watch on the Lower Rhine

Onboard the merchant ship, the two old veteran warriors, both well into their fifties, their brown riding cloaks flapping around them in the breeze, stood gazing out at the wide, funnel shaped estuary where the Rhine ran into the German sea. Marcus's old, crinkled, weather beaten face was as hard as granite. At Marcus's side, Indus his stoic Batavian bodyguard, was also staring at the coastline. Hanging from their belts were sheathed short swords and army pugio knives and, slung over his broad shoulders, Indus was carrying a sturdy looking leather satchel, a hunting bow and a quiver filled with arrows. It was afternoon and in the overcast skies a fresh south western wind was blowing the small cargo vessel straight across the choppy sea, towards the Roman naval base of Batavorum Lugdunum. Further out on the grey sea, three warships from the Classis Germanica were heading northwards on patrol, their square sails bulging in the wind. Along the banks of the Rhine estuary, sandbanks and salt marshes lined the shoreline and to the north, amongst the sand dunes, emperor Caligula's half completed and abandoned stone lighthouse stood alone - a forlorn construction amongst the natural splendour of the dunes. Marcus squinted as he gazed at the shore. Despite having served with the 2nd Batavian Auxiliary Cohort for twenty-three years he had never been to the ancestral homeland of the Batavians.

"Batavorum Lugdunum," Indus said pronouncing the name carefully and respectfully. The big bodyguard was speaking in his native Batavian language, his tone sombre and an uncharacteristically melancholic look had appeared in his eyes. "This is the place Sir from where I first shipped out as a new eighteen-year old recruit with the Ninth. I have never been back since. They say that that before the invasion of Britannia the emperor Caligula drew up his troops and artillery here on the beach and then declared war on Neptune. Afterwards he had his troops gather sea shells as war booty and built that lighthouse over there, as a monument to his victory."

Marcus raised his eyebrows as he gazed at the sand dunes and wide sandy beaches that formed the coast of the province of Germania Inferior. It was the first time that he'd heard Indus speak at such length, since he had first interviewed the old homeless soldier, in Rome more than two years ago.

"Do you still have family living in these parts?" Marcus asked.

"No Sir," Indus quickly shook his head. "No. No family. I served the Ninth and now I serve you Sir. I serve a senator of Rome," Indus added with a hint of pride in his voice.

"Yeah, well I am not so sure I am a senator anymore," Marcus replied sourly. "Best to keep our identity hidden when we go ashore. If people inquire, we are just two old veterans, returning home from service abroad."

Indus nodded in agreement.

Quickly Marcus glanced up at the overcast skies. "It's too late to set out for Ulpia Noviomagus Batavorum today," he said. "We will find somewhere to sleep tonight. Then tomorrow I will purchase a couple of horses and we will set off inland. By my calculation it should take us two days to reach Ulpia. I have an old friend living in the town who may be able to help us."

"When we find Armin Sir, do you want me to kill him?" Indus said lowering his voice. For a moment Marcus did not reply. "No," Marcus said at last. "No that won't be necessary. I have other plans for him."

***

Night had come and, out in the dunes, the small camp fire glowed in the darkness; the flames spitting and crackling as it devoured the dry wood. Marcus and Indus sat around the small fire, silently eating their evening meal, their cloaks drawn around their bodies, their faces turned red in the light from the fire. A hundred yards away or so across the dark, wild, undulating, heather-covered sand dunes the dull boom of the waves could be heard breaking onto the beach. Closer by, but hidden in the darkness, seagulls were crying out as they sat atop the ruins of Caligula's lighthouse. A half a mile away in the sand dunes, a few pinpricks of light in the darkness indicated the position of the Roman fortified port of Batavorum Lugdunum. Finishing his meal, Marcus replaced his pugio in his belt, took a swig of water from a flask and glanced at his companion.

"That shaking in your left arm Sir," Indus said gesturing at Marcus's arm, with his knife. "Does it hurt? Can the doctors do nothing about it?"

Marcus turned to look down at his arm. The uncontrollable shaking had started again.

"It doesn't hurt but it's fucking annoying," Marcus replied.

"Some would say that the shaking has started because you have been touched by the gods," Indus said, staring soberly at Marcus from across the fire. "Maybe it is a sign Sir. A sign of things to come. Maybe the gods have given you a new purpose."

"Yeah or else I am just getting old."

Indus looked down at the sand as he finished his meal.

"The gods like to send us signs Sir," Indus said with a serious expression. "They like to play games with men. They like to test us. They never tire of testing us. May I tell you a story Sir?"

A little bemused smile appeared on Marcus's lips as he turned to gaze at Indus. "You have become quite talkative since we landed on these shores haven't you," Marcus exclaimed. "For two years in Rome and on Vectis you barely spoke a word. What has changed Indus?"

"I honestly did not expect to see these shores again Sir," Indus replied in a quiet, rather glum voice. "Returning here has reminded me of many things that I had forgotten about. I have no family and yet I have stories that I now feel it is my duty to pass on. Knowledge that must be passed on. It is the duty of every Batavian to keep these stories alive for they are the story of our people. I will not live forever and before I die I need to pass on my knowledge so that it benefits the next generation. Will you listen Sir?"

"Of-course I will listen," Marcus replied. "Although I am hardly the next generation."

"Thank you, Sir," Indus said in a humble and grateful voice.

For a long moment the only sound around the fire was the crackle of the flames and the dull booming of the waves crashing onto the beach.

"I remember Sir," Indus began in a solemn voice, "when I was still a young lad growing up beside the river, that my father and mother had a tradition of storytelling. Each winter, during the long, cold nights, when the lakes and streams froze, and you could see the steam coming off the farm animals, they would gather the family together by the fire and tell us about our heroes and the origins of our tribe. They would sing the stories to us - stories that they in turn had learned from their ancestors all the way back to the first men and women. For our tribe does not write down its history like you Romans do. We only remember it in song, Sir."

For a moment Indus paused, seemingly lost in thought. "I still remember their voices Sir. My parents had rich, powerful voices. They are as clear to me as daylight. They told me that when I became a father it would be my duty to pass on this knowledge to my children. Except I never had any children Sir, at least none that I know about."

"Go on," Marcus said, as Indus seemed to falter.

"They told me about the origins of our tribe; of us Batavians," Indus said, as he threw another stick onto the fire, sending a cloud of sparks shooting upwards into the darkness. "They told me that many generations ago our ancestors lived far to the east in the vast, wild forests beyond the Rhine. We were part of the great Chatti confederation in those days, before the arrival of Rome. But as Rome pushed northwards and finally reached the Rhine, my ancestors quarrelled with the other tribes. The quarrel was about how to deal with Rome. Most of the Chatti chiefs and elders favoured hostility to Rome, for the legions were encroaching on their homelands. But my ancestors, the chiefs of the Batavians, they had a different view. They argued in favour of an alliance with Rome, for they could see the benefits of such an arrangement. The quarrel became insolvable; the differences too stark." Indus paused; his eyes staring into the flames; his face serious. Then abruptly he looked up at Marcus. "So, my ancestors decided to leave. Our whole people, all ten thousand of us, left our homes with our horses, our sick and elderly, our belongings, our cattle and began moving westwards. We followed the great river downstream and, as we went in search of a new homeland, my ancestors were led by a man, a great warrior whose left arm was shaking just like yours Sir."

***

The horses' hooves thudded on the gravel, scattering the seashells, as the two horsemen came riding down the road in single file, heading eastwards towards the rising sun. It was morning and warm, but ahead of them in the dull overcast skies, dark storm clouds threatened. Out on the Rhine a convoy of Roman supply barges, filled with wood and great quantities of amphorae, their sails bulging in the fresh breeze, were heading downstream towards the cavalry fort of Praetorium Agrippina. Idly, Marcus turned to gaze at the barges. He and Indus seemed to be the only people out on the road this morning. The Via Militaris, the newly constructed Roman military road, five yards wide, slightly elevated and flanked on either side by drainage ditches, had been built on the higher ground directly above the southern bank of the Rhine and seemed to be following the course of the river. To the south and north beyond the narrow corridor of sandy higher ground, the uninhabited, treeless, peat bogs, fens, marshes and wetlands of the delta, stretched as far as the eye could see. Numerous water channels criss-crossed the green, low-lying, impassable land and herons and egrets stalked the wetlands unchallenged. Marcus grunted. On their journey inland from the sea, he had seen few people and even fewer native settlements. It made sense for the vast wetlands and peat bogs would not be able to support a large population. Turning his attention back to the Rhine, Marcus peered out across the wide, peaceful waters to where the great river split in two, forming a narrow, low lying grass covered island, before the water channels re-joined. The island was not much more than a large, soggy sandbank but facing it on the southern bank, close to the water, was a solitary Roman watchtower.

"The river spirits are always restless and unpredictable Sir," Indus suddenly called out, as he nudged his horse alongside Marcus and the two of them slowed their pace. For a moment the big bodyguard peered fondly at the river. "I grew up along the Rhine. We prayed to the spirits of the great river every night. The water spirits are constantly on the move, constantly trying to find a new path to the sea and they are unstoppable. They never rest Sir. They are the true masters of this land. The water spirits demand much. To prevent flooding and ruining crops, they must constantly be appeased with gifts. Tonight," Indus nodded solemnly, "when we stop to make camp, I shall make an offering to the spirits that live in the river so that, tonight at least, we shall not get our boots wet."

Marcus remained silent as the two of them trotted towards the Roman watch tower.

"When I was a young boy Sir," Indus continued, with a frown as he gazed about him, "I remember that this land was covered in forests. Beech, hazel, elm, lime and oak trees. They were beautiful forests, but I see they have all gone now. The Romans must have cut down the trees to build their ships and forts." Indus sighed as a pained expression appeared on his face. "The water spirits will not be happy," he muttered to himself with a little bewildered shake of his head.

Marcus was only half listening to what Indus was saying. He was peering at the Roman watchtower that stood on the high ground at the water's edge. Constructed solely on the southern levees of the Rhine, they had come across a manned watchtower every mile and a half since they had left Batavorum Lugdunum. The standard wooden army construction reminded him of the time in Caledonia when he and Corbulo had been on the run from Emogene and her band of vengeful Caledonians. On the narrow balustraded platform that ran along the top floor of the watchtower an auxiliary, clad in chain mail armour and clutching a spear was standing guard. The soldier was watching the traffic on the river but, as Marcus and Indus rode on past the silent watchman turned to stare at them.

It was afternoon when up ahead on the road Marcus caught sight of a party of workmen and horse-drawn carts blocking the way. The wagons were filled with building materials, sand, stones, gravel and great heaps of seashells, used to cover the road surface. Slowing his horse to a walk, Marcus and Indus cautiously approached and, as they drew closer Marcus saw the reason for the blockage. Along a low-lying section of land, the Rhine had broken through its banks, washing away the substructure and gravel surface of the Roman road. The workmen were trying to repair the highway. Some of the men were knee deep in the water as they tried to plug the breach in the embankment. Carefully Marcus urged his horse into the muddy water and slowly rode on, splashing through the inundated land until he reached the road again on the other side. Up ahead, a half mile away, a Roman fort stood right on the very edge of the river, its dirty, muddy-brown wooden walls and watchtowers re-enforced by revetments and sandbags. Wooden jetties and a simple harbour protruded out into the river, alongside which lay a moored cargo barge.

Out in the river a solitary Roman warship on patrol was slowly making its way downstream. As they rode towards the fort, Marcus glanced curiously across the river at the northern bank and, as he noticed the small tributary river that flowed into the Rhine, he grunted. It was as he had begun to suspect. Access to the river and an unobstructed and commanding view seemed to have been more important to the military engineers than the fear of flooding. The main Roman forts along the river, he had noticed with an experienced military eye, were situated much closer together than the forts he remembered seeing on the Danube frontier. They were smaller too. Seemingly catering for a single cohort of auxiliaries, around five hundred men. But what seemed remarkable, was that the forts along this scarcely inhabited section of the frontier had all been placed opposite or alongside tributary rivers or navigable peat brooks. No doubt to prevent ship-borne raiders and smugglers from crossing into Roman territory. It confirmed what he had suspected. The Roman forts, watchtowers and naval vessels were watching and guarding every possible avenue that offered a chance to attack and infiltrate the lands to the south.

It was getting late, when Marcus at last reined in his horse and slowed the beast to a walk. In the fading light, along the road to the east the threatened thunder storm had not materialised and there had been no rain. Cautiously Marcus turned to stare at the Roman watchtower that had been constructed on a slight rise along the banks of the Rhine. On the viewing platform an auxiliary was gazing back at him. Quickly Marcus turned to examine the flat, grassy countryside.

"We will make camp here for tonight in the shadow of that tower," he said, as he urged his horse on towards the river bank. At his side Indus was gazing up at the solitary watchtower.

Riding up to the square wooden construction, Marcus dismounted and raised the palm of his right hand, calling out to the watchman standing on the narrow walkway.

"Friend, we are going to camp out here for the night. We are two army veterans passing through on our way to Ulpia Noviomagus Batavorum. Is that all right with you?"

"Sure," the auxiliary called out in reply.

Gesturing for Indus to dismount, Marcus led his horse down the grassy slope to a narrow stream and for a moment he allowed the beast to drink and nibble at the grass. Then tying the horse to the stump of a dead tree, he strode back up to the high ground where Indus had already found a spot to make camp. Close by, in the watchtower, Marcus was conscious of the sentry watching him. As Indus set out to gather some firewood Marcus turned to gaze out over the Rhine. In the dying light the river looked magnificent. A wide, gleaming, spectacular ribbon of water dividing the land on its way to the sea.

***

Marcus and Indus sat around the camp fire, each content to be alone in their silence. In the summer night sky there was no sign of the stars or the moon, but it remained dry and warm. As a shower of glowing sparks shot up into the dark sky, Indus reached out and tossed another piece of wood onto the fire. Marcus sat cross-legged staring thoughtfully into the flames. Now and then he would reach out to take a sip of wine from his simple wooden cup. Tomorrow they would reach Ulpia and the search for Armin could begin in earnest. But Petrus had been right. He was taking a risk in leaving Vectis. If Nigrinus acted quicker and more decisive than he had expected, the family would be in trouble. He had to find Armin and the gold quickly, but that was easier said than done. He was going to need help. Across from him, Indus suddenly rose to his feet and turned to face the Rhine, the banks of which were only a few yards away. Muttering something to himself Indus quickly flung an object into the water which disappeared with a distant plop.

"The spirits of the great river will not trouble us tonight," Indus announced in a solemn but confident voice, as he sat back down beside the fire.

Marcus nodded without saying anything. He was just about to raise his cup to his lips when a voice, close by, cut through the darkness. The voice had come from the direction of the watchtower.

"You there by the fire. Have you got any beer? We have run out of beer. We have got some birds eggs - if you would like to trade?"

Swiftly Marcus and Indus rose to their feet, as an auxiliary soldier appeared out of the gloom. The man's chainmail armour and helmet gleamed in the firelight. The soldier nodded a cautious greeting at Marcus and then extended and opened his hand revealing three fine bird's eggs.

"No beer," Marcus replied quickly. "But we can share some of our wine with you and your men."

"Boys," the auxiliary shouted as he turned in the direction of the watchtower. "He says he has no beer, but he has some wine?"

"Wine will do," a voice shouted back from the darkness.

The auxiliary turned back to face Marcus and nodded. In reply Marcus gestured at Indus who stooped and produced a flask of wine from his satchel.

"You said you were veterans," the auxiliary said in a curious voice as the trade was swiftly completed.

"That's right," Marcus replied as he looked down at the bird's eggs. "Second and Ninth Batavian Auxiliary Cohorts. We're on our way to Ulpia to see an old friend. Where are you boys from?"

The auxiliary nodded as he silently took in what Marcus had just said. "We're from the south," the soldier replied at last. "When you have been based on the lower Rhine frontier as long as I have, you can easily tell newcomers from locals. Their boots are still dry." The soldier laughed. "We've been out here manning these watchtowers for five years now. Sometimes I think the real enemy are not the barbarians across the river but the river itself. We spend more time battling the water than any barbarians. Lucky for you its summer. Every fucking winter and spring we get flooded out. It's impossible to keep the water out. It gets everywhere. We must endure wet feet, damp supplies and now and then the floods cut the road in two leaving us marooned out here. That's when you want to have a good supply of beer. And when it freezes you are constantly falling on your arse. All very annoying. Between you and me we can't wait to be transferred. Egypt sounds nice."

"You should try praying to the spirits of the river," Indus growled disapprovingly.

The auxiliary half turned to Indus, frowned and hesitated. Then he turned back to Marcus clutching the wine flask under his arm.

"Why don't you and your pal come inside," the man said in a friendly manner, gesturing in the direction of the watchtower. "It can get pretty boring out here and I know all the lad's jokes. Would be good to have some new company. You Batavians have a good reputation. We can drink the wine together."

"All right," Marcus replied. "That is kind of you."

***

It was afternoon on the following day when Marcus caught his first glimpse of the walled town of Ulpia Noviomagus Batavorum. The large city of five thousand people, capital and main settlement of the Batavians, had been built on the southern banks of the Rhine. As he and Indus rode towards it, Marcus could see that the city walls were in good condition. Out on the water the river traffic was heavy. Ships and barges of all sizes and designs were converging and leaving from the city's harbour, guarded by two artillery armed warships from the Classis Germanica. Further to the southeast on higher ground, stood the imposing stone legionary fortress that had been constructed by the Tenth Gemina Legion. A sprawling vicus of civilian buildings, shops, temples, whorehouses, bathhouses, taverns, workshops and homes had grown up around the fortress and, just visible, was a huge amphitheatre.

"Your friend Sir," Indus asked as the two of them approached the city gates. "How are we going to find him? It's a large place."

"Not we," Marcus snapped, as he sharply reined in his horse and brought the beast to a halt by the side of the road, "you are going to find him." For a moment he peered at the town. Then slowly he reached out and raised the hood of his cloak over his head. "We must be careful from now on," Marcus growled, as he glanced at Indus. "It will not do for Armin or his extended family to recognise me or hear that I am in town. Armin won't recognise you. That's why it is you who is going into town to find my friend. Don't worry. He is an old army buddy from my days in the Second. Find the nearest tavern and make some inquiries. Pay for the information if you must. If people ask, tell them that you are an old army comrade of his. I shall wait for you here; there in that copse of trees."

For a moment Indus looked doubtful. Then quickly he turned and nodded. "Leave it to me Sir," he said as he urged his horse on towards the gates.

It was several hours later, with the sun low on the western horizon, when Marcus stirred as he caught sight of Indus, accompanied by another man, coming out of the town. As the two figures drew closer, a little smile cracked onto Marcus's lips as he recognised the one-armed man walking beside Indus. Calmly Marcus broke cover and started towards the two men and as he did, the stranger raised his one arm in greeting and cried out.

"Thunder and lashing rain, so Wodan cometh," Hedwig shouted, as a huge smile appeared on his face as he recognised Marcus. "So, trust in the man beside you and do your duty, for in the coming days I want our enemy to cry out in alarm as they see our approach. I want to hear them shout: Ah shit. Here come those damned Batavians again."

Coming up to Marcus, Hedwig swiftly embraced his old commander. "I remember Sir. I remember that speech like you had given it just yesterday," Hedwig said beaming with delight. "So, what brings you here?"

Chapter Seventeen – The Plan

Relaxing in the steaming hot bath, Marcus reached out for his cup of wine. Hedwig had broken open his finest barrel for him and it did indeed taste good. Condensation was running down the stone walls of the private bathhouse and, set into the tiled floor, a second-rate mosaic artist had tried to create several hunting scenes. Close by, on a chair in a corner, a stark naked young female slave was playing a few soft notes on a gigantic harp. Hedwig's private bathhouse was just large enough to comfortably accommodate the three old, battle-scarred warriors. Sitting across from Marcus in the piping-hot, greenish water, Hedwig had been thoughtfully rubbing the stump of his amputated arm, as he'd listened to what Marcus had to say, whilst Indus had retreated into his usual silence, his naked upper body showing a mass of angry scars, tattoos, whip marks and old wounds.

"A good wine," Marcus said at last, breaking the silence as he raised his cup in a salute. "A fine bathhouse. An obedient wife. You seem to have it all Hedwig. But why come back here to the land of the Batavians? I thought you had made your home in Aquae Sulis."

In the baths Hedwig shrugged. For a moment he stared pensively at the water. Then he looked up.

"I am a Batavian," he replied in a serious voice. "I was born in this country. I came home Marcus because this is where I want to die. The spirits of my ancestors are here and one day I shall go to join them."

"But not yet old friend," Marcus growled. "Not yet. I need your help."

"Like you said," Hedwig replied, turning to inspect his stump with a serious look. "It sounds like you are in a lot of trouble Marcus. So, of course I will help you. The whole Batavian community may be no larger than the population of Londinium, but half of them are spread out across the delta and the other half are living in the vicus or here in Noviomagus. It will make the search more difficult, but I shall make some inquiries as to the whereabouts of Lucius's extended family. I have a nephew who can help. If Armin is hiding out here I will find him. In the meantime, you and Indus shall remain here in my house as my guests."

"I am grateful," Marcus said.

In the baths, Hedwig stirred and reached for a small sponge.

"You did well in coming to me, Marcus," Hedwig said. "You may be a legend amongst the Batavian cohorts, but Lucius's extended family are not just going to give up their boy and they certainly won't want to be parted from that gold. You must be careful. It would be best if you stayed indoors until I have found the family and where Armin is hiding. It would do your cause no good if you had tried to do this on your own. Noviomagus may seem huge to those locals who have never been further than twenty miles from the Rhine, but as you and I know, this is not a large place. It's a close-knit community. Strangers are noticed. People talk. If you had started poking around on your own, making inquiries and such like, news of this would surely have reached Armin and his family. After that you could forget about ever finding Lucius's son. The boy would simply vanish into the forests beyond the Rhine to the east where it would be impossible to track him."

"No. That would not do," Marcus nodded. "My family's fortunes rest on finding that boy and I need to do so quickly. I can't afford to be away from Vectis for long."

"I understand," Hedwig replied in a serious sounding voice. "But to avoid raising suspicions and alert Lucius's extended family, we must do this properly and it is going to take some time."

"How do you plan on finding Armin? You mentioned that you had a nephew?" Marcus pressed. "How can he help?"

Hedwig paused. Then carefully he began to apply the sponge to his body. "The treaty of alliance between Rome and us Batavians," he said as he washed himself, "stipulates that we shall be free from paying taxation in return for providing the Roman army with an annual quota of soldiers. It is an alliance that has endured for over one hundred and fifty years."

"I know this. How does this help?" Marcus said.

"This summer there is a new intake of recruits," Hedwig replied solemnly. "You were never part of this, because you joined and trained with the Second Cohort in Britannia. So, since the start of summer the army has been conducting the usual extensive field training and exercises. Parties of horsemen fording and swimming across rivers in formation. Weapons drill. Camp building. Route marches. Endurance training. Mock battles. It's all very inconvenient for us civilians for the army clogs up everything, the roads, the river, the taverns, the shops. The Roman officers like to put the new recruits through their paces and they also like to show off to the local populace. Showing that the old alliance works has propaganda value. But it means that right now the whole delta is full of troops on exercises."

"Sounds like fun," Marcus growled.

"The eldest son remains to inherit and look after the family farm," Hedwig continued in his serious voice. "The younger sons join the Roman army. That is how it has been for us Batavians since the treaty was first made. My nephew," Hedwig paused. "His name is Wolfgang. My nephew failed the physical entry requirements of the army. He has a crooked foot. He really wanted to join and see the world. Instead he now runs his own business. He is a good lad. For him these army exercises are a boon. He spends his days following the troops around the countryside with a pushcart, selling them food, drink and snacks. It's a good business and he has an uncanny ability to know exactly where the soldiers are when on exercises. He can find them in all weather, day or night. It's amazing. The auxiliaries stationed along the Rhine and the legionaries of the Ninth here at Noviomagus; they love him. He's become famous amongst the soldiers. So, I shall ask him for help in finding Armin. If anyone can, it will be Wolfgang."

***

Marcus looked tense and fed up, as he sat hunched over the board game. Across the table, Indus was thoughtfully staring at the pieces on the chequered board, as he contemplated his next move, seemingly oblivious to Marcus's mood. A week had passed since they'd arrived in Ulpia Noviomagus Batavorum. A week in which nothing had seemingly happened. A week in which they had been forced to remain inside the confines of Hedwig's house, whilst time slowly and relentlessly ticked away. The waiting had become deeply frustrating. Every day that he was away from Vectis was becoming harder and harder to bear. Marcus stirred restlessly. If Nigrinus and the War Party acted quickly and decisively, then his family were in grave danger and he would not be there to protect them. Stirring again, Marcus clenched his mutilated left hand into a fist, making Indus look up. But he needed that gold Marcus thought. The gold that Armin and Elsa had stolen from him. Using the gold was his only realistic hope of stopping Nigrinus from taking revenge.

"Your move Sir," Indus said as he looked up again at Marcus.

Irritably Marcus turned to gaze down at the board game. He had lost count of how many times he and Indus had played the game whilst they waited for news.

Just then there was a commotion at the entrance into the house and, as Marcus and Indus turned to look in the direction of the hallway, Hedwig appeared with a triumphant look on his face. Accompanying Hedwig was a smaller, younger man with black curly hair. As the newcomer caught sight of Marcus, he blushed. The younger man was limping and as Marcus looked down he saw that the man had a deformed foot.

"We found Lucius's extended family," Hedwig said triumphantly, as he flung his cloak onto a couch and reached for a jug of water. "Wolfgang here tracked them down to a couple of farmhouses close to the great temple of Magusanus."

"You found Armin?" Marcus blurted out as he rose to his feet.

"We found Lucius's family Sir," Wolfgang replied, as he gazed at Marcus and Indus in awe. "It's them Sir. But we don't know Armin or what he looks like. Only you can verify if he is amongst them. But its progress Sir."

"How far away from here is the temple of Magusanus?" Marcus snapped.

Wolfgang hastily glanced at his uncle, his cheeks blushing furiously. Then he took a cautious step towards Marcus. The young man looked in his mid-twenties.

"Sir, may I say that it is an honour to meet you," Wolfgang said quickly in a humbled voice. "I have heard all the war stories about you and my uncle. You are a living legend Sir. Everyone around here has heard about your speech and how you saved the Second from annihilation. In this town there are a hundred men who would gladly buy you drinks all night long and an equal number of women who would gladly tear their clothes off for you Sir. I am just a humble snack merchant, but for you Sir all my food will be free of charge. I hope you will try some of what I have to offer. I sell good stuff. A recommendation from you would allow me to expand the business. Maybe we can discuss it later. Anyway, it is a privilege to have you staying here with us Sir."

As Wolfgang finished talking an awkward silence descended on the room. Marcus stood staring at Hedwig's nephew, his face incredulous.

"All right, all right, Wolfgang," Hedwig said at last in a weary but patient voice. "I am sure that Marcus appreciates your words but enough of the sales pitch. Marcus is not here to taste your snacks. Tell him about what we found?"

"Of-course," Wolfgang blurted out, as he blushed again. "Sorry Sir. You asked about the great temple of Magusanus. The temple is north of here, beyond the river, on the island of the Batavians. It's not far. Maybe ten or fifteen miles away. Lucius's extended family occupy a small settlement of two farms. There are sixteen people, adults and children. Their home is about a mile away from the great temple."

"Can you take me there?" Marcus said sharply.

"Of course," Wolfgang replied, glancing hastily at his uncle. "But it would not be wise for you to show your face."

"I need to know wherever Armin is with them," Marcus said. "If he not hiding out with them then I have just wasted everyone's time. I need to know as soon as possible. I don't have much time."

"We can go tonight Sir," Wolfgang replied. "Lay up under the cover of darkness and observe the farms during the day. That could work. But there is something else that I discovered. One of the members of Lucius's extended family has been boasting that he and his family have struck it rich. Apparently, he got drunk in a tavern here in town and was heard saying that his family have recently acquired a vast inheritance in gold. I don't know whether it's true or just beer talk, but people are talking. No one knows how they managed to get such an inheritance for no one around here has such wealth. You may not know this Sir, but our community, us Batavians are sharply divided between those who left to join the Roman army and see the world and those that remained behind on the ancestral farms. When the leavers finally return home, they are different men to their brothers who remained behind. The leavers have seen the world Sir. They have become Romans in outlook and in citizenship too. They like different foods, the likes of which we have never seen before in these parts. They like to eat from a plate and drink from a beaker like the Romans do. They say our local food is boring and they prepare their food differently. They prefer Roman pottery to our own native produce. They wear different clothing made of foreign textiles. Some of the leavers return home honouring foreign gods and others bring foreign women back with them. I can tell you Sir; it is leading to tension with those who remain true to the old ways. It's like we have become two different tribes. Now as a businessman I must tread a very careful path between this divide."

"Wolfgang," Hedwig interrupted sharply. "Enough. Stick to the point. Marcus is not interested in your business."

"No, it's all right, let the boy speak," Marcus replied, raising his hand. "If what he says is true then that can only mean that Armin is here and so is the gold. This could be good news. Thank you. I appreciate your help."

"So, what do you want to do now Marcus?" Hedwig said.

"If Armin is hiding out in this settlement with his extended family," Marcus said thoughtfully, "then I must find a way of getting to him. I also need to recover all that gold."

"There are sixteen people living on those two farms," Wolfgang said quickly. "You can't just go and knock on the front door."

"I can't help you take Armin, Marcus," Hedwig said quickly. "Neither me or Wolfgang can be seen to be getting involved. We live here. There would be consequences for us if we were seen to be having a role in his abduction."

"I know. I know," Marcus replied with a little nod. "I am not asking you to take part in the seizure of Armin. I just need to find a way to get to him."

A long pensive silence descended on the living room.

"I have an idea," Wolfgang said at last, as he turned to Marcus. "The summer festival to honour Magusanus is coming up soon. The people are going to honour the great god at his new temple. That means placing offerings, witnessing the rituals and afterwards a feast, eating, drinking and partying. It should go on all night. The festival has been growing in importance ever since Trajan came here eleven years ago and poured money into the temple's renovation project. The spot on which the new building now stands has long been a holy place for us. My bet is that Armin's extended family will visit the festival at some point. They will not want to upset Magusanus by not paying their respects to him on his feast day and the temple is only a mile or so from their home."

"So, when they leave for the temple," Marcus interrupted, with a sudden gleam in his eye. "When they are at the festival paying their respects to Magusanus. That's when we strike, swoop on the farm and take Armin. Yes, that could work."

"It's risky," Hedwig muttered. "What happens if not all of them go? What happens if they take Armin with them to the festival?"

"It's possible," Marcus nodded. "But I suspect they won't want to show him off in public just in case people start asking questions. The alternative is that we strike at night but that will be harder and even riskier, but I can't think of anything better."

"Are you going to kill him?" Wolfgang asked gazing at Marcus.

"No, I need Armin for something else," Marcus replied.

Once more a pensive silence descended on the room.

"I say we do it Sir," Indus said at last, in a calm, quiet voice. "The two of us can handle it. We will have the element of surprise and in my experience that counts for a lot."

Marcus nodded in agreement. "All right," he said making up his mind. "We will take Armin when his family are distracted. When is the festival due to take place?" he added, turning towards Wolfgang.

"In ten days' time Sir," Wolfgang replied.

"Great," Marcus hissed as his face darkened in frustration.

Chapter Eighteen – Festival Day

The four silent figures lay stretched out on their stomach's, observing the two farm houses from the long, dry grass that covered the earthen embankment. The sun had just risen, and from their hidden position along the dyke, Marcus had an excellent view of the small settlement. The two byre houses - crude barbarian dwellings made of wood, thatch and mud had been carefully positioned on higher ground away from the numerous watercourses that crisscrossed the land. There steeply sloping and thickly thatched roofs reached nearly all the way down to the ground. Out of sight, a cock was crowing, but there was no sign of any people. The column of smoke rising from the smoke hole in one of the houses, was the only sign that anyone was at home. Across the flat, green fields that surrounded the two isolated farms, a herd of cows and horses were grazing. The smell of manure hung in the still air and there seemed to be no fence marking the border of the owner's land. Carefully Marcus turned to peer up at the sky. It looked like it was going to be another fine, hot and cloudless day. Slowly he turned his attention to the peat brook that meandered away southwards towards the Rhine. The stream was just narrow enough for a man to jump across and not get his feet wet. Close by Indus was calmly and patiently staring at the farmhouses. At his side the bodyguard had laid his bow and arrows out in the grass. Next to him, Wolfgang in contrast to Indus, was staring at the farms like a starving wolf that had spotted its prey; his cheek twitching with tension and excitement. Hedwig however had his eyes closed and seemed to be asleep. Grimly, Marcus turned to look back towards the copse of tall trees where they had left the four horses, two of them packed and prepared for a long journey. The moment of truth was nearly upon him. Soon he would know whether Armin was indeed hiding out here on these isolated farms. Soon he would know what had become of the gold that Elsa and Armin had stolen. Or maybe not. Maybe Armin and the gold were not here, and he'd made a serious miscalculation and wasted precious time. The thought of failure made him want to be sick.

"I have been here before," Wolfgang whispered, as he turned to Marcus. "The army likes to use this brook as an assault course. They make the new recruits charge across it in full armour, shields and gear. The soldier who gets his feet wet must do it again until he manages to get across with dry boots. They are a hungry lot after that training. That's when I strike with my pushcart. On a good day I can sell them everything that I have got. Before you and Indus go you should taste some of my snacks. They are the best in the delta."

"Wolfgang. Shut the fuck up," Hedwig hissed in an annoyed voice as he lay stretched out in the grass with his eyes still closed. "No one is interested in your fucking snacks. Stop trying to refine your sales pitch. It's getting boring."

Ignoring Hedwig, Marcus glanced at Wolfgang. Then slowly he turned his attention back to the farmhouses.

"This feud between me and Armin's family," he said speaking in a quiet, sombre voice, "it has been going on for over thirty years now. It started with Bestia, my decurion and commanding officer in the Second Batavian Cohort. You did not know him Hedwig because it was just before you joined us. We fought together at the battle of Mons Graupius in Caledonia, but the man was a piece of shit. A violent bully who liked to use his whip on us troopers as if we were his cattle. We all hated and feared him. Anyway, the trouble started when Bestia deserted and tried to murder my father Corbulo. That's a long story for another time. A few years later my father managed to catch up again with Bestia and kill him in Viroconium. That should have been the end of the feud but unfortunately it wasn't, for Bestia had a brother and his name was Lucius and he too served with us in the Second."

"I remember," Hedwig said quietly as he lay in the grass with his eyes closed. "I remember Lucius. Who can forget him? He so badly wanted to be a Roman; he changed his name."

"Lucius was a good man, unlike his brother," Marcus said glancing quickly at Wolfgang before turning to peer again at the farmhouses. "He was my friend. We fought together in Hibernia and during the great northern uprising in Britannia he was my second in command, after Cotta our prefect had got himself killed. Lucius never understood why his brother had deserted and what had become of him. He was always making inquiries about Bestia's fate. So," Marcus continued in a weary voice, "eventually he discovered that it was my father who had killed his brother. So, Lucius took his revenge out on me and betrayed me to the enemy during the fighting in the north. No doubt he did not expect me to survive but I did."

"And afterwards you went looking for Lucius and killed him," Wolfgang murmured. "But Lucius had two children, Elsa and Armin, and before you killed him, Lucius made you swear to look after his children which you did by adopting them."

"That's right," Marcus said with a surprised look.

"Hedwig told me the whole story," Wolfgang said with a little indifferent shrug. "And now it was Elsa and Armin's turn to betray you and seek vengeance for the murder of their father and uncle. I get it. It's not the kind of story that you would want to tell your children right before they go to sleep."

"Bloodshed seeks only to shed more blood," Marcus growled. "I thought I had brought an end to the feud, this cycle of vengeance, by adopting Elsa and Armin, but it seems I was wrong. I underestimated Elsa for it is she who is leading this. She is the brains behind the plan to ruin my family."

"Sir, look," Indus said softly.

Across the green open fields, figures had appeared outside the thatched farm houses. Tensing, Marcus peered at them trying to spot Armin, but he was too far away to make out individual faces. The figures seemed to be preparing horses and a wagon. As he gazed at them, a man led a barking dog out of the house and proceeded to chain the beast to a wall where it continued to bark.

"I count four adult women, Sir," Indus said quietly, as he peered intently at the figures. "Five adult men, one of whom could be Armin's age. Six children. If what Wolfgang said was correct, then we are missing one person. Maybe he is still inside."

"Could be Armin," Wolfgang muttered trying to hide his excitement.

"They are moving out," Hedwig hissed. "Looks like they will be paying the festival a visit. Seems Wolfgang was right."

"Let's hope so," Marcus replied.

For a long moment none of the watchers lying hidden in the long grass said a word, as all gazed at the activity amongst the farmhouses. The cock on its perch was still crowing and, as the figures mounted their horses, climbed onto the wagon and began to move out down the rutted track the dog kept up its ferocious barking.

"They have left the children behind," Indus said quickly. "All six of them. Look they are going back into the house. Strange."

Marcus said nothing as his eyes moved from the farm houses to the departing figures and back again. Suddenly his body tensed, and his face darkened.

A figure had come out of the farmhouse and seemed to be admonishing the barking dog and it was not one of the children.

"That's Armin," Marcus hissed.

"Are you sure? I can't make out his features from here Sir," Indus replied quickly.

"No, it's him," Marcus snapped. "I know - it's him. He's here."

"So, we found him," Wolfgang said excitedly.

Quickly Marcus turned to look at Hedwig. "You and Wolfgang should go back to the horses. Wait for us there. Indus and I will finish the job."

Without waiting for an answer, Marcus swiftly rose to his feet and started to run towards the two farmhouses. Leaping across the ditch he landed in the grass with a painful grunt. Ahead of him the dog was barking as it tried to break free from its restraining lead, but there was no sign of the figure who had just appeared from out of the house. As Indus came effortlessly leaping across the ditch, Marcus staggered to his feet and started to hurry across the field towards the farms. At his side Indus was clutching his bow.

As he reached the first house, Marcus slowed his pace, gasping for breath. Cautiously he paused to peer around the corner of the building at the second thatched byre house from which he'd seen the figure emerge. But apart from the barking dog, there was no one about in the courtyard. The animal had seen them by now and was wildly trying to break loose from its restraints. Just then, the thick animal skin that covered the entrance into the long house opposite Marcus was thrown aside and the young man came out into the courtyard again and once more started to admonish the barking dog in an irritable voice. Catching sight of the boy, Marcus's face hardened.

"Armin. Armin," Marcus bellowed furiously as he left his position and strode across the courtyard towards the young man. "Come here you little piece of shit."

At the door where the dog was chained to the wall, the young man nearly jumped into the air as his name was called out. Startled, he whirled round to stare at Marcus and, as he recognised him, Armin's face grew pale with horror. For a moment he looked physically sick and unable to move as Marcus bore down on him. Then in panic he turned and rushed back into the house with Marcus close behind. Inside the large, gloomy interior, a fire was burning beneath the smoke hole in the roof and sitting around it were six startled and scruffy-looking children. Trapped and with nowhere else to flee to, Armin turned in panic to face Marcus, frantically waving a small knife as he screamed abuse at him. Without hesitating Marcus swiftly drove Armin back up against the wooden wall, kicking him hard in the groin and forcing him to drop the blade. Armin screamed in pain as he slithered to the ground. Grasping hold of Armin's long hair, Marcus yanked his head backwards and then slammed the young man's face into a solid wooden wall post, breaking his nose with a sickening crack. As Armin crumpled to the earthen floor, a sudden movement around the fire nearly caught Marcus by surprise. Whirling round he was just in time to see one of the children, a blond boy of around ten, bravely charging towards him, his child's fingers clenched into small fists. But before the boy could reach him he ran straight into Indus, who squatted him aside, flinging the boy against the wall as if he was a sack of hay. With a startled cry the boy however recovered and before Marcus or Indus could do anything he had shot out of the doorway and vanished.

"Where is my gold? The gold that you stole from me," Marcus bellowed as he stooped and dragged Armin back up onto his feet.

Blood was pouring from Armin's broken nose and his eyes were rolling about in agony and he could barely stand.

"If you don't tell me where you have hidden my gold I will personally cut every one of these children's throats and leave them to die in their own blood. Do you hear me Armin? They are all going to die because of you," Marcus roared. "Because of what you did."

Armin tried to speak, but the noise that came out of his mouth was inaudible. Around the fire the remaining children had started to cry and shrink backwards in terror as Indus loomed over them.

"I will cut their throats, all of them," Marcus bellowed as he glared at Armin "Where is the gold? What have you done with it?"

"It's…" Armin howled. "It's in the ground. We buried it over there under that stack of fire wood. I swear. I swear. Fuck my nose. Please. Don't harm the children."

"Show me," Marcus snapped, and without ceremony he pushed Armin towards the large stack of firewood that stood against the wall.

As Armin collapsed to the ground and began to pick at the wooden sticks, Indus quickly shoved him aside and began removing the firewood, rapidly tossing them aside.

"It's in the ground, just there," Armin whimpered at last as he pointed at the cleared earthen floor.

"Dig it up Indus," Marcus snapped as he forced Armin down onto the ground and began to tie the young man's hands behind his back with a stout rope. Around the fire the remaining children were staring at him in silent terror. "The boy who ran away," Marcus hissed as he finished binding Armin's hands. "Where will he go?"

"It's festival day. He will go to warn my family," Armin groaned in a miserable voice. "They are only a mile away at the temple."

Quickly and silently Marcus glanced at Indus. They didn't have much time. Hastily Marcus reached into his pocket, produced a blindfold cloth and began to firmly bind it around Armin's head and eyes.

At his side Indus suddenly grunted and reached down into the hole in the earth he'd made. Pulling out two large sacks, he dumped them at Marcus's feet and as he did the sacks made a clinking metallic noise.

"Looks like they are filled with gold coins Sir," Indus said, as he peered into the sacks. Then quickly he rummaged through the bags with his hands and pulled out a coin examining it with his teeth and then his eyes. "Yup, its gold all right. A lot of gold Dacian coins bearing the head of king Decebalus."

"Is this all of it?" Marcus growled as he slapped Armin across his head. "Is this all the gold that you stole from me?"

"Most of it," Armin groaned miserably. "We spent some but the majority of it is there."

"You are not lying to me, now are you?" Marcus hissed.

"I am telling the truth," Armin squealed as he felt the sharp blade of Marcus's pugio press into his neck.

Silently Marcus gestured for Indus to firmly close and take the sacks. Then swiftly he hauled Armin back up onto his feet.

"Let's go," Marcus growled. "We have a long journey back home to Vectis."

As the three of them emerged into the daylight, Marcus quickly turned to look in the direction of the temple of Magusanus, but on the rutted track leading away from the small settlement there was no sign of anyone. Pushing Armin ahead of him, Marcus started out across the field towards the spot where they'd left their horses, whilst at his side Indus came on carrying the two heavy sacks of gold.

"You are a spineless idiot do you know that," Marcus hissed as he guided Armin across the field. "Did you really think that I would slaughter those children? I may be many things, but I am no monster."

"You killed my father," Armin muttered.

"Shut up," Marcus snapped as he slapped the young man across his head. "Where is your sister? Where are Elsa and Cassius hiding?"

"Fuck you," Armin hissed defiantly as he stumbled on across the field.

"Do you want me to make him talk Sir?" Indus said.

"No, he will talk," Marcus said in a confident voice. "He is going to do a lot of things. But let's just get out of here first."

***

Hedwig and Wolfgang were standing in the small copse of trees beside the four tethered horses. Forcing Armin onto his knees Marcus took the two sacks of gold from his bodyguard and leaving Indus to guard the young man he strode over to where the two Batavians were waiting for him.

"You got him. You retrieved the gold," Hedwig said, as a grin appeared on his lips.

"We did," Marcus said in a grateful voice. "Thanks to you and your nephew." Marcus paused. "I want to thank you, old friend, for all you have done. I want to compensate you and Wolfgang for your time. I have gold."

But Hedwig shook his head. "No Marcus," he said quickly. "We do not want your gold. What we did, we did for you and the honour of the Second. That is more precious than gold. We shall always be veterans of the Second."

Marcus nodded with a little smile. Then his face grew sombre.

"So, I guess this is goodbye then," Marcus said, and as he spoke he had a sudden sense that this would be the last time he would be seeing Hedwig. Across from him Hedwig too seemed to sense it.

"Thunder and lashing rain so Wodan commeth," Hedwig muttered as he took a step towards Marcus and the two old warriors embraced, their foreheads touching each other.

***

The flat, green fields seemed to stretch to the horizon, interrupted here and there by ditches, streams and tiny settlements of two or three farms. Following the peat brook southwards towards the Rhine, Marcus, with the bound and blindfolded Armin sitting in front of him on the horse, set the pace with Indus following, the reinforced sacks of gold firmly secured to his saddle. They had only gone a couple of miles before Indus suddenly cried out in alarm. Twisting round Marcus swore as across the fields, galloping towards them he caught sight of five figures on horseback. Marcus's face darkened. Armin's family had found them. As if sensing that rescue was near at hand Armin suddenly opened his mouth and started to scream for help at the top of his voice.

"Ride, ride," Marcus yelled at Indus as he urged his horse onwards. "We will lose them at the river."

As the two horsemen started to pick up the pace, charging across the open fields, sending clumps of mud flying into the air, Armin continued to scream and holler until Marcus silenced him by striking him hard across his head.

"Shut up. They will not take you alive," Marcus hissed. "I will make sure of that if they force us to fight."

Quickly twisting round in his saddle Marcus saw that the five riders were gaining on him. It was only to be expected, his horse and that of Indus were heavily laden. They were not going to be able to outrun their pursuers. Was he going to have to fight after all? He and Indus would have a tough time against five armed men and if they were trained fighters they would stand little chance. Where was the damned river? Leaping across a ditch the two horsemen fled across the fields. Ahead, the land rose up to a steep natural embankment. Veering towards it Marcus sensed his horse starting to tire. The beast was snorting and panting from the effort of carrying two men. Its pace was slowing. It was nearly spent. Behind them their pursuers were closing in and their triumphant cries and yells were clearly audible. Surging up the slope of the embankment Marcus gasped as beyond he suddenly caught sight of the wide waters of the Rhine glittering in the sunlight. Close by, Indus came charging up the slope and before Marcus could act the bodyguard had slid down from his horse and had pulled his bow from his back. Calmly Indus knelt on the ground, notched an arrow, took careful aim and released. With a scream one of the horsemen racing towards them went crashing and tumbling to the ground. Hastily Indus notched another arrow and brought a second horseman down into the grass. Abruptly the three remaining horsemen brought their horses to a halt. Milling around uncertainly, they gazed at Marcus and Indus in helpless fury. Grimly Indus notched a third arrow to his bow as he knelt on the top of the embankment pointing his weapon at the riders.

"Go Sir," Indus cried out. "I will cover you and join you on the southern bank. "Go now before they find their courage."

Without hesitating, Marcus cried out to his horse and, storming down the side of the embankment the beast went splashing head first into the Rhine and began to swim. Grimly Marcus held on as the cold water came surging up to his waist and the horse snorted and gasped. The current was strong and soon the beast was struggling. Twisting round Marcus was just in time to see Indus and his horse splashing into the river. Frantically Indus's beast began to swim out into the open channel with Indus urging it onwards. Marcus hissed. The Batavian horses could swim and carry a soldier in full armour across a river but not two men. They were not going to get across. On the northern embankment four of their pursuers had suddenly appeared, one of them limping along on foot and were shouting to each other as they gazed at the two desperate horses swimming across the Rhine. But the men made no attempt to follow them into the water.

As he sensed his horse starting to panic Marcus swore and grasping hold of Armin's long blond hair with his right hand he boldly flung himself and Armin from the horse and into the river. Armin's head went under and as he resurfaced, spluttering and coughing, he cried out in panic for his hands were tied behind his back and he was still blindfolded.

"Cut me free. Cut me free," the young man yelled in a panic-stricken voice as he struggled to keep his head above the water.

Gripping the young man's hair, Marcus forced Armin to keep his head above the water. Close by, the horse was starting to pull away towards the southern bank.

"Where are Elsa and Cassius hiding?" Marcus bellowed, as he furiously kicked his legs to keep them both afloat. "Tell me where your sister is, and I will cut you free."

Armin's head went under again and, as he resurfaced spluttering and gasping for breath he cried out in panic.

"Elsa's still in Rome. She's in Rome. She never left the city."

Angrily Marcus turned to look back at the stationary horsemen up on the embankment. The fifth man had now joined them on foot and was silently gazing at him from the shore. His pursuers were making no effort to continue the pursuit and as the current continued to push them downstream the distance between them was growing. Gasping for breath and struggling to keep himself and Armin afloat, Marcus turned and finding his strength he started to swim towards the southern bank dragging Armin along with him. Out in the river his horse, relieved of its heavy burden, was starting to swim in a more regular fashion, its head bobbing up and down in the water. Snatching a glance in Indus's direction, Marcus saw that the Batavian was directing his horse towards Marcus's mount with the intention of grasping hold of the reins and preventing the beast from bolting or swimming the wrong way. As he noticed Marcus looking at him, a cheeky, triumphant grin appeared on Indus's face. They were going to get away.

"You promised to cut me free," Armin cried out in between a spluttering and coughing fit. "You promised."

"I lied," Marcus hissed, as he grimly held onto the young man and dragged him through the water.

Chapter Nineteen – News from Rome

As the two horsemen trotted down the rutted country track towards the villa, a sudden commotion broke out ahead of them and Dylis's twins came rushing out of the forest where they'd been picking mushrooms.

"They're back. They're back," the girls cried excitedly.

Raising an arm in greeting, Marcus examined his farm as he and Indus rode towards the gates leading into the villa's courtyard. Sitting directly in front of Marcus was Armin, a blindfold bound around his eyes and his hands tied behind his back. He looked miserable and exhausted. Marcus's riding cloak was splattered with dried mud and his face covered in a fine layer of dust and sweat. He looked worried. But the villa and its outhouses seemed in good shape. All looked just like it had been when he'd left the place over a month ago. There was no obvious sign that Nigrinus or his men had paid a visit. Relieved, Marcus allowed himself to take a deep breath. The thought that something terrible had happened had grown worse the closer to home he'd gotten.

It was afternoon and in the golden wheat fields a party of slaves had stopped working and were staring in the direction of the two horsemen. The fine-looking stone-built house with its smart red roof tiles gleamed in the fierce summer sun and in the glorious blue skies not a cloud could be seen. Glancing sideways Marcus grunted as he saw another party of slaves at work amongst the newly planted vines along the south facing ridge. As he and Indus reached the gates into the courtyard, Kyna and Jowan came hurrying towards him, their arms raised in greeting. Dismounting, Marcus pulled Armin from the horse and forced the silent young man down onto his knees. Then Kyna was upon him, flinging her arms around her husband. She was swiftly followed by Dylis's daughters. The young women's faces looked happy and they were laughing excitedly. Jowan, clutching a pickaxe, silently inclined his head in a respectful greeting as he quickly reached out to shake hands with Marcus.

"Is everything all right?" Marcus asked as the women milled around him.

"Everything is fine Marcus," Kyna replied with a broad smile. "Dylis is away in Londinium on business. She has taken her son with her. Cunomoltus and Petrus are out with the dogs, hunting. They should be home before nightfall. We did not know when you would be back."

"Good. Good," Marcus muttered in a relieved voice. "No unexpected visitors. No trouble?"

"No trouble," Kyna beamed joyously. "But whilst you were gone a messenger arrived with two letters. They are addressed to you Marcus. I think they have come from Rome. We have been waiting for your return before opening them."

"Letters," Marcus frowned. "From Rome!"

"That's what the messenger said," Kyna replied with a little shrug. "Both letters were delivered by the same man, but they bear different seals. They look important Marcus. The messenger belonged to the imperial postal service."

Looking puzzled, Marcus turned for a moment to gaze at where Jowan and Indus had untied the two sacks of Dacian gold and were carefully examining the coins. Then turning to the blindfolded Armin, whose hands were tied behind his back, Marcus forced the boy up onto his feet.

"I recovered the gold," Marcus growled. "Or most of it anyway and look who I found hiding out across the sea."

Opposite him, Kyna's face drained of all emotion and her features hardened. For a moment she said nothing as she stared at the miserable blindfolded figure in front of her. Then without warning she raised her hand and slapped Armin hard across his face, eliciting a startled yelp of pain.

***

In the night sky the stars, tiny pinpricks of light in the vast darkness, lit up the heavens, forming a fine tapestry of light. Outside on the villa's terrace the family had gathered together around the large oak dining table. The slaves had carried the table out onto the terrace so that tonight the family could eat outside beneath the stars in the still, balmy summer air. Seated around the table, in the glow and the crackle of a large camp fire, Cunomoltus, Kyna, Jowan, Petrus, Indus and Dylis's two daughters were silently and sombrely picking at the evening meal, as they listened to Marcus recounting his and Indus's journey. The cooks had prepared a feast and the table was crammed with fine cutlery and plates of apples, dried beans, bread, meats, cheese, honey and olives, together with jugs of milk, water, mead and wine. At the very end of the table two empty chairs and plates stood untouched and respectfully left alone.

"So, what are we going to do now?" Cunomoltus said as Marcus fell silent. "Before you left you mentioned that you had a plan?"

Marcus took a sip of wine from his cup and then slowly reached out with his right hand to steady the shaking in his left arm.

"The gold that Fergus brought back from Dacia will allow us to defend ourselves," he growled. "It is the only defence capable of stopping Nigrinus and his associates. These are powerful men. The gold is our only hope. We cannot fight Nigrinus like we did with Priscinus."

"But maybe we shall have to," Petrus said with sudden foreboding.

"Fergus will come to our aid," Kyna said calmly, her eyes gleaming with the certainty of someone who was utterly sure of herself.

Ignoring his wife, Marcus gently rubbed his left arm.

"Armin has told me where Elsa and her husband Cassius are hiding," he said. "Armin says they are still in Rome. He knows where she is." Marcus paused as his face grew thoughtful. "I still have unfinished business with Elsa," he said. "So, I am going to be sending a message to Elsa. I am going to tell her that I am holding her little brother and that if she wants him to stay alive, she should present herself to us here on Vectis. She should come here to Vectis."

Around the dining table the family quickly exchanged startled glances.

"Do you think she will really come?" Petrus exclaimed. "After what she did to us? Do you really think she will risk coming here, even for her little brother?"

"I don't know," Marcus replied with a shrug. "We shall see. But if she doesn't, Armin will die, and his death will be on her conscience. That is the choice I am forcing her to make."

"Elsa is close to her brother," Kyna interrupted in a sharp and unforgiving sounding voice. "When Marcus first adopted her, she agreed to come with him on condition that she and her brother would never be separated. She will come. She will come here to Vectis for Armin. I know she will."

"Then she is a brave girl, despite what she did to us," Petrus said, raising his eyebrows and looking around the table.

Silence descended around the table and, for a long moment, the only noise was the crackle and spitting of the camp fire.

"And if she does come here," Jowan said at last in a quiet voice, "what are you going to do to her Marcus?"

Around the dining table all eyes turned to gaze at Marcus. For a moment Marcus did not reply, his eyes smouldering in the eerie glow of the fire.

"This feud with Bestia, with Lucius, and now with Elsa," he said as grimly he looked up at the faces around the table. "It has been going on for over thirty years now. It has blighted our lives. I am going to bring it to an end. If Elsa decides to come here to us on Vectis, I am going to end it once and for all."

***

It was late when Marcus wearily sat down at his desk in his small study and gazed down at the two tightly rolled scrolls of parchment that lay on the table before him. He was alone. Next to him on the table, a small portable oil lamp shaped like a human foot was burning and hissing quietly in the darkness. Picking up the first scroll he examined it. The letter bore the mark of the fiscus, the imperial treasury. Surprised Marcus raised his eyebrows. It must have come from Paulinus. Breaking the seal, he unrolled the parchment and started to read.

Paulinus to Marcus, greetings old friend. It is my sombre duty to warn you that Nigrinus has had the senate declare you a fugitive and a murderer. You have been accused of being a traitor, a murderer and an enemy of the senate and the people of Rome. Nigrinus has had you stripped of your right to sit in the senate and has had your name removed from the senatorial lists. You and your family have been banned from standing for any government positions or for bidding for government contracts.

Your house here in Rome has been confiscated by the state, your veteran's charity shut down and every mention of you as a senator and magistrate is being erased from all government documents and records as I write this letter. The senate has even decreed that none may be permitted to ever mention your name again in the halls of the senate. Such animosity and rage, Marcus. I honestly have not seen such bitterness since the days when the senate plotted the overthrow of Domitian. Every government official is now legally obliged to have you arrested but news will be slow in reaching the most distant provinces and I suspect that not all officials will be so keen to carry out these orders.

Still you should be under no illusion as to the precariousness of your position. Nigrinus knows where you are. He knows about your family on Vectis. If he catches you Marcus, he will kill you and your family. Even in this matter goes to court, expect any trial to be merely a show, a charade. Your Roman citizenship will provide scant protection. Nigrinus will never let you go. He is after your head. He told me that himself. Apparently one of the senators found dead in your home was his cousin. As you know Nigrinus is a busy, important man, the leader of our War Party faction. I do not think therefore that he has the time to leave Rome and personally travel to Britannia to find you. Instead he has announced and made it public knowledge that he is offering a private reward for your capture. It is a sizable amount of money, likely to stir the interest of the professional bounty hunters or such like scum. Your enemies are thus multiplied and may not be obvious to you at first. Do not underestimate Nigrinus. He is a powerful, influential and resourceful man. Be on your guard, Marcus.

The good news is that you still have some supporters here in Rome. Take heart my old friend. I like to believe that friendship is stronger than politics. Lady Claudia and I have managed to discreetly spread the word amongst the senate that the charges against you are politically motivated. Hadrian's faction, the Peace Party seem more receptive to such arguments than our own colleagues. But do not expect them to intervene. They too are outraged at the death of the two senators. We have also let it be known that your son Fergus is a close ally of Hadrian. I do not know what impact this will have but any government official looking to have you arrested may think twice about it when they realise the politics involved and the powerful connections that your family have.

These are uncertain times here in Rome Marcus. I sense the mood is changing. It is with a heavy heart that I confess to believing that it is now more likely than ever that Hadrian shall become the next emperor. The signs are increasingly pointing to that outcome. Your son Fergus seems to have gambled on the right man, unlike us. It is ironic, for if Hadrian does become the next emperor, it is I who will be relying on your family's mercy and friendship for my survival. There is little chance that Hadrian and the Peace Party will spare or forgive me, the War Party's chief accountant. I miss our little chats old friend. Rome is not the same without you. May Fortuna look kindly on us both. Your friend, Paulinus to his Marcus.

Thoughtfully Marcus lowered the scroll. Then quickly he read the letter again. When he was done he reached out for the second scroll and examined the seal.

Lady Claudia to her Marcus. My dearest Marcus, will you let Kyna know that her son Ahern is safe and well under my protection. I am sure she worries about him every day and I wish to allay some of that burden. Ahern wishes you to know that his decision not to come with you was not done out of spite or bitterness. Despite the dangers he feels he is not yet ready to leave Rome and the exciting projects he wants to be part of. He feels that if he left the city now he would never again get a chance to be part of all that is new, innovative and exciting in his chosen scientific field. I hope you understand and I want you and Kyna to know that I shall always protect him. I am your friend and always will be.

Here in Rome Marcus, I fear that the signs are that Hadrian shall become the next emperor and I am not alone in that judgement. Hadrian's star is rising. It fills me with dread for the future. Internal discipline and loyalty amongst our faction, the War Party, is starting to fracture. Nigrinus has begun to see enemies everywhere. His suspicions are such that no one, not even his closest allies, are safe from his growing wrath and paranoia. Morale is falling. Some of our supporters are preparing for the worst, others I suspect are planning to switch sides like rats abandoning a sinking ship. I however am too old for such nonsense and cowardice. I have made up my mind that whatever happens I shall remain true to the War Party and despite what he has done to you, also to Nigrinus. He is after all the leader of our faction. Once one has chosen a side one must stick to one's decision until the end. I do not fear death Marcus. I urge you not to despair. These days men of true courage and nobility of heart are rare in Rome, but such men cannot ever be broken. They may die but they can never yield. They are the favoured amongst the gods. I shall pray to Diane, the huntress to protect you and your family. Farewell Marcus. Your loving Claudia.

In his small gloomy study Marcus sighed and looked down at the neat handwriting. Then reaching out he fondly traced his finger over the words.

Chapter Twenty – Dylis

Under the late summer sun and a glorious blue sky, the golden wheat fields were full of activity. Wiping the sweat from his forehead Marcus straightened up and grimaced as he stretched his aching back. He was clad in loose-fitting farmer's clothes. A wide brimmed sunhat gave him some protection from the burning heat and, in his right hand he was clutching a long-bladed scythe. Spread out in a line across the fields, the slaves and the whole household were hard at work harvesting the wheat with their scythes and small handheld knives. The slaves were singing as they worked, and, on the edge of the field, Jowan was shouting instructions to the men bringing up the ox drawn wagons. The animals were bellowing loudly. Gazing at the work, Marcus sighed. He was no farmer. He had never been cut out to labour on the land. He was a soldier but now that the harvest time had come he saw why every hand was needed. It was a mammoth task. The work was hard, but it looked like they were going to have a fine harvest this year and the knowledge that they would have a plentiful supply of food, seemed to have raised everyone's spirits.

A sudden cry from near the gates to his property made Marcus turn. Two riders were approaching down the rutted track, their heads covered in wide-brimmed sunhats, their hands raised in greeting. Peering at the newcomers, Marcus recognised Dylis and her son. As the pair rode towards the villa, Dylis's twin daughters started to hurry across the fields towards their mother. Leaving his position in the line, Marcus also strode over towards his half-sister, raising his scythe in greeting as he did.

"You are back then," Dylis called out with a little smile, as she caught sight of Marcus. "Was your journey to the Rhine a success?"

"I recovered most of the gold and Armin is locked up inside the house," Marcus called out. "How was Londinium? What were you doing there anyway? You have been gone for a long time."

"I had business to take care of that could not be rushed. There were some business associates I needed to visit. It was interesting," Dylis replied evasively, as she dismounted and quickly and warmly embraced her twin girls. Then gesturing to her teenage son to lead the horses to the stables, she turned back to Marcus. "There is something that I need to discuss with you. But it can wait. You said that you brought Armin back?"

"Yes," Marcus said. "The miserable little shit is inside the house."

"I want to see him," Dylis said sharply, her face hardening. "I want to see him right away."

Sitting with his back against the wall in the small windowless room, his hands tied behind him, Armin looked utterly miserable, a broken shell of a young man. The smattering of a beard had appeared on his pale face and he looked like he had been crying. As Dylis, followed by Marcus, stepped into the room, the boy hastily struggled to his feet and backed away, his eyes widening in fright. Slowly Marcus folded his arms across his chest, as for a long moment Dylis glared at Armin in contemptuous silence.

"Why have you kept him tied up?" Dylis said at last as she turned to Marcus. "This is the most secure room in the house. He is not going anywhere."

"It's in case he tries to harm himself," Marcus growled. "I need him alive. I have sent a message to Elsa demanding that if she wants to keep her little brother alive - she should come here to Vectis and present herself to us."

"He knows where Elsa and Cassius are hiding?" Dylis said raising her eyebrows.

"They are still in Rome," Marcus replied.

For a moment Dylis said nothing as she stared at Armin. Then she took a step forwards and quick as a striking snake she caught hold of the young man's chin with her hand forcing, Armin to look at her.

"We took you and your sister in," Dylis said in a voice that crackled with fury. "We adopted you both. We treated you like you were family. We loved you like you were our own children and this is how you repay us. You conspire to ruin my family and my farm. You plot to put us in mortal danger. You steal our gold. You threaten my children. You are not worth the dirt on my boots."

And with that Dylis spat into Armin's face and sent him staggering backwards against the wall.

"You should kill him Marcus," Dylis said harshly, as she turned and strode out of the room. "You should kill him and his bitch of a sister. Only that way will this feud end once and for all."

***

Out on the villa's terrace, the camp fire was slowly burning itself out. In the balmy night all was peaceful. The slaves had long since cleared the evening meal away and most of the family had retired to bed, leaving Marcus and Dylis as the last ones sitting around the table, each with a cup of wine in their hands.

"You mentioned that you wanted to speak to me about something?" Marcus said at last, as he turned to look at his sister.

"Yes," Dylis muttered with a faraway look. "Whilst you were gone looking for Armin I spoke to our neighbours. In fact, I spoke to all the villas on Vectis. They have agreed to warn us if strangers are spotted on the island. Ninian, our business agent in Reginorum has agreed to do the same. It may give us some extra time if Nigrinus's men come looking for us."

"That's good," Marcus said with a nod.

"But that's not what I wanted to talk to you about," Dylis continued, as she gazed out into the darkness that covered the fields.

"Whilst I was in Londinium, I discovered something," she said, slowly turning towards Marcus. "It concerns Corbulo, our father. Did you know that he was writing an account of our family history?"

"No, I didn't," Marcus replied frowning. "He never mentioned anything like that. Why, what did you find?"

"Well I went back to bank that used to be run by Falco. Remember him? I wanted to see what interest rates they offer. It's not important," Dylis said with a quick dismissive wave of her hand. "But to my surprise I discovered that they had kept all Corbulo's old business files. So, whilst rummaging through them I found this account, an incomplete account of our family's history. Corbulo seems to have started writing down everything he knew about his ancestors, but the account is incomplete. It's just a few paragraphs. It had got stuck in amongst a mass of business receipts and orders. That's why Falco never found it."

"Really?" Marcus said turning to look at Dylis with sudden interest. "What did the old man say about our ancestors?"

Fondly Dylis gazed out into the darkness. Then she raised her cup of wine to her lips and took a sip.

"He was always full of surprises, Corbulo," she said with a sigh. "I have brought the account back with me if you would like to read it," she said. "Nothing really unusual in it except that Corbulo says that one of our Roman ancestors was present at the meeting where Hannibal and Carthage surrendered to Rome and Scipio Africanus after the battle of Zama. Apparently, he was there when Carthage sued for peace and the terms were agreed. Corbulo even claims that Hannibal knew him and spoke highly of him."

"What?" Marcus frowned. "Carthage's surrender? Hannibal. That must have been well over three hundred years ago. Corbulo never mentioned anything to me about an ancestor being present at the peace conference."

"Well it's all there in writing, our father's writing," Dylis replied. "I think it's true. So, it seems we have an illustrious forefather in our family."

"Extraordinary. Did Corbulo give a name?"

"No, no name," Dylis replied with a little chuckle. "But from the way he wrote about it. I would say that our father was mighty proud of our ancestor."

Chapter Twenty-One - The Dogs of War

"Marcus, Marcus, where are you? Wake up," the urgent voice cried out. A moment later the door to Marcus's bedroom was flung open and Cunomoltus came marching into the room. In his hand he was holding a small oil lamp. In its dim hissing light, Marcus saw that Cunomoltus was clad in a well-worn and dust-covered riding cloak. He looked flushed and agitated.

"What," Marcus snapped in an annoyed voice, as if he had just been woken. Next to him in bed Kyna groaned and, keeping her eyes closed, she rolled over and away from the intrusion pulling the covers with her.

"What is it?" Marcus said reaching up to rub his eyes. "Do you know what time it is? It's still dark outside."

"Trouble," Cunomoltus hissed.

Instantly Marcus was awake. In the dim light from the lamp he gazed at his brother. Then hastily he swung his legs out of bed and reached for his tunic and belt.

"What," Marcus snapped, as he fumbled with his clothes. "What has happened? Weren't you supposed to be selling your dogs to the army at Isca Augusta. You were not supposed to be back for a few days."

"To hell with the dogs. I have ridden two days without stop. I rode through the night to get here," Cunomoltus exclaimed, as he took a step backwards. Leaning against the wall Marcus suddenly noticed how exhausted his brother looked. "We're in trouble Marcus," Cunomoltus stammered in a shaky voice. "A shed load of shit is on its way as I speak. You had better wake the others. It's serious."

"Talk to me brother," Marcus said in a calm voice, as he hurried to put on his clothes.

"Well you are right," Cunomoltus stammered. "I went to meet my army contact at Isca as per usual to sell him my dogs. Normally it's a formality. He inspects the dogs and then quotes me a price. We settle on the amount and the transaction is completed. Only this time my contact is not interested in my dogs. Instead he is reluctant to even meet me. No, not reluctant, he was afraid Marcus. He was afraid. Said that the deal and any future deals were off."

"Why?" What has made him change his mind?"

Cunomoltus took a deep breath. "So, I finally managed to speak to him," Cunomoltus said. "Turns out he knows something about us. He tells me in all confidence that a centurion from the Second Augusta by the name of Flaccus and fifty legionaries left Isca on foot the day before and guess where they are heading and what they have gone to do?"

"Shit," Marcus muttered as he looked away.

"That's right," Cunomoltus snapped, nodding vigorously. "Centurion Flaccus and his fifty men have been ordered to march to our farm here on Vectis and arrest you. Gods know what they are planning to do with you, but I don't think they are there to escort you to a tribunal. They are on their way as I speak. I have been told that they have orders to take you dead or alive and kill anyone who stands in their way."

"Fifty legionaries," Marcus said quickly, running his hand over his head. "Who gave these orders?"

"My contact didn't know," Cunomoltus replied. "But it must be one of the senior legionary officers. Probably a friend of Nigrinus and the War Party. My man told me that our name and our business has suddenly become toxic. He says no one will want to work with us anymore. He told me to my face that he never wanted to see me or do business with me again. The arsehole. After all the high-quality dogs that I sold him over the years."

On his feet, Marcus swore again. Then fastening his belt around his waist, he turned to Kyna. She was sitting bolt upright in bed, very much awake, with the covers drawn around her neck, staring up at Marcus and Cunomoltus in silent horror.

"Wake the others," Marcus growled, as he reached for his sheathed gladius and pugio army knife. "Gather them together in the dining hall. I want to speak to everyone and get the slaves to prepare three horses. We will set out straight after breakfast. You did well, brother. Get some rest whilst you can."

"Set out?" Cunomoltus blurted out in confusion. "Where? Who? Why?"

But Marcus was already striding out of the room and the questions went unanswered.

***

The straight Roman road cut through the forest, vanishing over a small rise in the distance. It was around noon and in the high summer's sky a few clouds were visible. In the verges running alongside the drainage ditches that lined the highway, colourful flowers poked their heads above the long grass and insects buzzed and darted around on the cool, peaceful and scented forest breeze. Marcus stood in the long grass, his gladius and pugio stuffed into his belt, his hands resting on his hips, as he peered at the lone rider trotting towards him. The horseman's beast was kicking up small clouds of dust as it clattered along on the gravel-covered road. The man seemed to be in no hurry. At the edge of the tree line, holding onto the three horses, Cunomoltus and Indus too were gazing at the approaching rider. Across his back Indus had strapped his bow and quiver. Cunomoltus was clutching a massive and ancient looking battle-axe in addition to a gladius and a knife that hung from his belt.

As the rider came towards him Marcus silently stepped out onto the road and raised his hand in a greeting.

"What news Ninian?" Marcus called out.

Up on his horse Ninian raised his hand returning the greeting. The family's commercial agent and grain broker sighed, his face sombre as he glanced in the direction of Indus and Cunomoltus. Then he turned to look down at Marcus.

"I sent my boys out, north and west," the agent exclaimed. "Like we discussed. My eldest has just reported back. He says he spotted a party of legionaries marching down this road. They are heading towards Reginorum as we suspected. They are coming in from the west. He says he counted fifty men plus an officer. All on foot with a single ox drawn wagon in support. Gods know what they need that for. My eldest says it's empty. All the men are armed to the teeth, wearing their armour and carrying shields. He says that if they keep going they should be here within two or three hours. Are you sure you want to do this Marcus? It is not too late to consider the alternatives."

"You want me to run," Marcus said with a little sarcastic smile. "Thank you, old friend, but we shall wait here for the soldiers. I am done with running."

Up on his horse Ninian nodded wearily. "I thought you would say that," the agent muttered. "So, what's the plan Marcus?"

"The plan," Marcus replied calmly, "Is not to get killed or arrested."

Ninian nodded again but he looked doubtful. At last, with another sombre sigh the broker nudged his horse on past Marcus and started out down the road towards Noviomagus Reginorum, Chichester.

"I hope to see you again soon Marcus," the man called out, as he raised his hand in farewell. "You are a good client."

"You have proved a faithful friend to me and my family, Ninian," Marcus called out as he turned to watch Ninian move off down the road. "I shall not forget it. You will see me again."

Then hastily Marcus left the road and strode over to where Indus and Cunomoltus were waiting with the horses at the edge of the forest.

"Are you sure about this Marcus?" Cunomoltus hissed and, as he spoke Marcus could see how nervous his brother was. His hand was trembling and sweat was trickling down his forehead. Gently laying his hand on Cunomoltus's shoulder, Marcus nodded.

"We have no choice," Marcus muttered. "When they come, try not to show any fear. They will not be expecting us. It may give us a small advantage. Let me do the talking. If it all goes tits-up, flee. Ride back to the farm and get the others to safety like we discussed. Under no circumstances are you to come back for me. Have you got that, brother?"

Cunomoltus nodded.

"Do not ask me to do the same Sir. I will not flee," Indus growled in a menacing tone. "I have sworn an oath to the gods that I will protect you. My place is at your side. I shall die before I break my word Sir."

"I know, I know," Marcus murmured, as he reached out to grip the big and old Batavian on his shoulder.

***

It was several hours later when the party of legionaries appeared, coming over the rise. Their body armour, helmets and shields gleamed and glinted, reflecting the sunlight. In their hands they were clutching their large shields, emblazoned with lightning bolts and the men's throwing spears were slung across their shoulders; the sharp iron spearheads pointing up to the sky. As they came on down the road towards him Marcus quickly gestured at Indus and Cunomoltus to prepare themselves. Then calmly he strode out into the centre of the road and halted. Placing his hands on his hips Marcus gazed at the heavily armed professional soldiers marching towards him. The party was led by a centurion, his fine and unmistakeable plumed helmet made of horsehair, making him look taller than he was. In his hand the officer was clutching his vine staff. Bringing up the rear, a solitary ox-drawn wagon rumbled along tended by two slaves. As the soldiers drew closer, Marcus forced himself to stand his ground in the middle of the road. Near the edge of the forest Cunomoltus had mounted his horse and was clutching the reins tightly, his huge battle-axe resting on the horse's back.

"Centurion Flaccus," Marcus suddenly bellowed, raising his hand when the party were no more than a dozen yards away.

On the road the centurion and his men kept on coming towards Marcus, the steady and relentless tramp of the soldiers hobnailed boots growing louder and louder.

"Centurion Flaccus," Marcus bellowed again, as he boldly moved forwards to physically block the officer's way.

And as he did the centurion at last came to a halt, his face twitching in a mixture of annoyance and surprise.

"How the hell do you know my name?" the officer cried out as he peered at Marcus. "Stand aside citizen before I kick you off this road."

"Are you or are you not centurion Flaccus?" Marcus snapped.

"I am Flaccus," the centurion retorted with a confused frown. "Now get off the fucking road."

Behind the centurion the party of legionaries had come to a halt and all were staring at Marcus in surprise.

"No Sir," Marcus said firmly shaking his head. "I will not stand aside. My name is Marcus. I am the owner of the villa on Vectis to where you are heading. I am the man that you are looking for."

For a moment Flaccus looked too stunned and surprised to say anything. Then he blinked and slowly raised his hand to rub his chin. He was a short man of around forty, with bulging arm muscles and a green tattoo of a snake on his neck.

"You are Marcus?" the officer exclaimed at last pointing at Marcus with his vine staff. "You are really Marcus? The man with the villa on Vectis?"

"I am the man you have been sent to arrest," Marcus growled. "Retired soldier and former prefect of the Second Batavian Auxiliary Cohort. Veteran of the battle of Mons Graupius and ex-senator of Rome. I am your man, centurion."

"Fucking hell," Flaccus bellowed as a little amused grin appeared on his lips. "That's a good one. If what you are saying is true, then you have got balls. I will grant you that. But how do I know you are speaking the truth? How do I know that you are the man I am looking for and not some imposter? Anyone could know what you have just told me. I am here on important state business."

Menacingly Flaccus raised his vine staff in the air. "If you are fucking wasting my time citizen I will beat the shit out of you. This is no joking matter."

In response Marcus raised the three remaining fingers on his left hand in the air.

"Did your superiors not tell you that the man you were looking for has only three fingers on his left hand. Well here they are," Marcus retorted.

"Shit," Flaccus swore softly and a little colour shot into his cheeks as he caught sight of Marcus's mutilated left hand.

"I heard that you and your men were coming to pay me and my farm a visit," Marcus said sternly, his eyes fixed on the centurion. "So, I thought I would head you off. Save you getting your boots wet crossing over to Vectis."

"That's kind of you," Flaccus retorted in a sarcastic voice and, flashing Marcus a quick fake smile.

"Listen," Marcus continued. "I have no argument with you or your superiors. I don't know what lies they have told you about me or what they have promised you. I am here because I think you and I can make a deal."

"A deal," Flaccus blurted out as he raised his eyebrows in surprise. "My orders are to find you and bring you back to Isca dead or alive. That's the deal. You have got a hell of a nerve standing there telling me what I should be doing. What is stopping me from ordering my men to seize you right now?"

Quickly Flaccus turned to look at the forest on either side of the road. "Or are you going to convince me that you have a hundred armed-men hiding amongst the trees just waiting to fall on us. I don't think so."

"You are not listening," Marcus snapped, as his face darkened. "Sure, your soldiers can overpower me. You have the numbers. You have your orders. But you, you are not going to be one that takes me. See those two men of mine over there at the edge of the forest." Marcus paused, without taking his eyes from Flaccus. "The one pointing his bow at you right now. I have seen him kill a man with a single shot from twice that distance. So, if you are feeling confident go ahead and order your men to seize me, but I can assure you that you won't be around to witness all the fun afterwards."

Carefully and coolly Flaccus turned to gaze in Indus's and Cunomoltus's direction. Standing near the trees away from the road, Indus had notched an arrow to his bow and was crouching and carefully aiming the weapon directly at the centurion.

"Fuck you," the officer hissed.

"You and I are going to make a deal," Marcus growled. "It's either that or both of us are going to die right here on this road. The choice is yours. Tell me what your superiors promised you as a reward for my capture?"

Slowly Flaccus turned to gaze at Marcus, his face calm and devoid of emotion and for a long moment the officer said nothing.

"Ten gold coins," Flaccus snapped.

"I will give you twenty gold coins to turn your men around and fuck off back to where you came from."

"I want fifty gold coins," Flaccus retorted quietly, as he took a step towards Marcus. "And I am going to need another twenty gold for my superior, plus another fifty to keep my men from talking. You got that kind of gold, arsehole?"

"Done," Marcus snapped. "I have the gold. And when you return to Isca you will tell your superiors that you could not find me or my family. You will tell them that we have vanished. And I want you to remember something. I have eyes and ears in Isca. They will be watching you. If I learn that you have reneged on our deal, I will cut your balls off. Is that clear enough for you dick-head?"

Across from him, Flaccus gave Marcus a contemptuous look. Then idly his eyes settled on Cunomoltus and Indus.

"If you have the gold," Flaccus muttered. "Then you must be keeping it nearby. Maybe I will just take it from you and get paid twice."

"It's buried in the ground," Marcus replied. "Only I know where and I am not going to tell anyone. You see I have been tortured before in Caledonia by druids. Trust me, they know how to inflict pain on a man. But here's the rub," Marcus snapped, as he took a step towards Flaccus, his eyes flashing dangerously. "I don't think I really care anymore whether I live or die. Maybe I am just tired of life. When a man reaches my ago and has seen what I have seen, sometimes he just really doesn't give a shit anymore. Have you ever had that feeling centurion?"

Flaccus turned to stare at Marcus in silence. Then slowly he shook his head.

"You are fucking crazy old man," the centurion hissed. "Just get the gold and we will be on our way."

**

"He's back," Cunomoltus yelled as Marcus came out of the doorway to his villa and started to hurry across the courtyard. "Indus is back."

As Marcus approached the gates of his home in the noon sunshine he frowned as he caught sight of the solitary horseman trotting towards the farm. Several days had passed since he'd successfully managed to bribe Flaccus and his men on the road to Noviomagus Reginorum. But soon after they had started out on their return journey home, Indus had vanished without explanation. There had been no point in trying to look for him and Marcus had resigned himself to the belief that Indus would return when he wanted to.

"Where the hell have you been?" Marcus roared, as accompanied by Cunomoltus, he opened the gates and strode out onto the rutted track towards the horseman. "Care to explain why you left us without saying a single word?"

Indus said nothing as he slowed his pace. Then reaching the position where Marcus and Cunomoltus were standing waiting for him, the big Batavian warrior calmly dismounted and grasping the reins of his horse, he led the beast up to Marcus. The Batavian looked his usual stoic, quiet and unexcitable self.

"Well," Marcus growled in an annoyed voice as he stared at Indus.

"Sorry Sir," Indus muttered. "I couldn't tell you what I had to do, for I know you would not approve but it had to be done."

"What?" Marcus snapped as his eyes narrowed with suspicion. "What did you do Indus?"

"Well it's like this Sir," Indus replied in a calm, quiet voice. "After I left you, I went looking for those legionaries and that centurion. Finally caught up with them close to Aquae Sulis. That centurion, Sir. The man called Flaccus. When he went to visit a whorehouse in town one night. I cut his throat and dumped his body in a lake. The man was an arsehole."

"You did what?" Marcus exclaimed.

"I killed him Sir," Indus replied in a calm voice. "Don't worry. There were no witnesses and they won't find his body. Like I said, I didn't like the look of him and he was threatening you. He was always going to remain a threat. So, now the next man thinking about taking you on will think twice before coming here. I killed Flaccus as a deterrent, Sir. No one knows it was us, but everyone knows it was us, if you understand what I am saying Sir."

"Jupiter's balls," Marcus groaned as he lowered his head, closed his eyes and rubbed his hand across his face.

"Yeah and I brought back sixty-five gold coins that he took from you Sir. Couldn't get the rest from those legionaries," Indus replied, as fishing inside his tunic he produced a leather bag and stuffed it into Cunomoltus's startled hand.

Chapter Twenty-Two – Visitors

November 115 AD

Out of the grey, dull, overcast skies the rain came pelting down. It was a cold morning and inside their pens the farm's cows were mooing as they waited impatiently to be milked. Marcus was in one of the workshops helping Jowan fix a new wheel to one of the farm's wagons when Petrus appeared at the barn door. His hood and cloak were drenched.

"Marcus," Petrus called out in an urgent voice. "The slave on watch reports that there is a man at the gates. He says he's been sent by one of our neighbours. He wants to speak to you. Says its urgent."

For a moment Marcus gazed at Petrus. Then, exchanging a quick glance with Jowan, he got to his feet and reached for his cloak that was draped over the side of the wagon. Without saying a word, Marcus strode out into the rain, pulling his hood over his head as he did. He was swiftly followed by Petrus. On his belt Marcus was carrying a sheathed gladius and his army pugio. As the two of them squelched through the puddles towards the fence that marked the boundary of his property, Marcus peered at the solitary horseman waiting patiently by the closed wooden gates. Close by, languishing atop the newly erected watchtower, a slave was clutching an old army surplus trumpet and trying to keep himself dry.

"Fine weather in which to be out riding, friend," Marcus called out, as he raised his hand in greeting when he recognised his neighbour's youngest son.

Atop his horse, the young man nodded. "Marcus," the boy called out lowering his hood, his face squinting in the rain. "My father sent me to warn you. Strangers have been spotted coming ashore to the north. They are heading your way."

"Strangers," Marcus growled guardedly, his face darkening.

"That's right," the boy nodded. "Nine of them including two women. They have horses, but they didn't seem to be in a hurry. They will be here within the hour."

And with that the boy nodded a quick farewell, turned his horse around and went trotting away through the rain.

For a long moment Marcus watched the boy ride away. Then thoughtfully he raised his hand to rub his chin.

"Bounty hunters?" Petrus exclaimed in a tense voice.

"I don't think so," Marcus growled. Calmly he turned away from the gates and started back towards the villa. "Alert the others," he snapped as Petrus hastily caught up with him. "I am not going to take any chances. Have the whole family and the slaves gather together in the house. Everyone is to be armed, including the slaves and tell Indus to fetch his bow and take up a position in the watchtower. I will meet these visitors at the gates and tell Kyna to join me. Hurry."

"Who do you think they are?" Petrus said in an anxious voice.

But Marcus was not listening. His old, weathered face had become hard as flint as he stomped away through the rain.

***

As one by one the nine riders appeared on the muddy, rutted and puddle-strewn track, the slave up on the watchtower quickly raised his trumpet to his lips. The short warning blast from the trumpet rang out across the villa and the sodden fields beyond. Beside the closed gates, Marcus, with the hood of his cloak drawn over his head, stood peering at the visitors. It had finally stopped raining, but the skies were still dull and heavily overcast. At his side Kyna had wrapped a fur cloak and hood around her body and was watching the newcomers with a strange, calm resolve. Up on the platform in the watchtower, Indus slowly notched an arrow to his bow and casually turned to point the weapon at the horsemen. The riders however seemed unconcerned that they had been spotted. Walking their horses down the muddy track, they slowly came on towards the gates. They were led by a small, slim figure wrapped in a long mud-splattered riding cloak and with a hood drawn over their head. And as they drew nearer, Marcus's hand slowly tightened into a fist.

Reaching the closed gates, the riders came to a slow halt and for a moment no one spoke or moved. Then calmly, Elsa reached up and lowered her hood from around her head and shook free her long blond hair. From atop her horse, her hard, fearless eyes slowly fixed on Marcus. Across her chest, strapped into a small ingenious leather harness, a small baby was sleeping peacefully. Behind Elsa her companions had spread out into a single line. The seven men and one women were all armed and amongst them, Marcus suddenly thought he recognised some of the men who had chased him and Indus across the Rhine. Across the space that separated them the tense, silent, standoff lengthened.

"So, you came," Marcus called out, as he turned his attention back to Elsa. "That was a brave thing to do. I see you have brought your extended family with you. But where is Cassius? Where is your husband? I don't see him with you."

"Cassius chose not to see you," Elsa replied in a cold voice from atop her horse. "Where is my brother? What have you done to Armin?"

"He is here," Marcus growled as he glared at Elsa. "He lives."

Marcus paused. At his side Kyna was studying Elsa intently, her face a mask of quiet female resolve.

"If your husband, my former secretary, does not dare face me then he is a coward," Marcus bellowed. "You married a coward, Elsa."

"I have not come here to argue with you," Elsa shot back. "I have come here to take Armin back home to where he belongs."

"Who says that he is going back with you," Marcus shouted, his eyes boiling over with sudden anger. "Who says that any of you are leaving this place? From the moment you and your companions set foot on this island you belonged to me. You betrayed me and my family. You tried to ruin me. There is a price to pay for such treachery and you will pay it."

On their horses Elsa's companions stirred and Elsa glanced quickly in the direction of the watchtower from where Indus was aiming his bow at her.

"What do you want Marcus?" Elsa hissed.

Behind him, Marcus was suddenly conscious of movement. Glancing over his shoulder he saw Dylis, Jowan, Cunomoltus and the others streaming out of the house and walking across the courtyard towards him. All were armed. As she came up to the wooden gates, Dylis caught Marcus's eye, her expression utterly merciless.

"What do I want?" Marcus growled, turning to look at Elsa, his eyes blazing. "What do I want?" Marcus bellowed. "I read your letter. I know now what you think of me. But I kept my word. Long ago I made a promise to Lucius, your father. I said that I would look after his children and that is what I did. That is what I still intend to do. We took you in Elsa. You and your brother, we treated you like family. We did not deserve your betrayal. It was a cowardly thing to do. It is not what your father wanted for you. So, you ask me what I want? Well I don't want revenge. I summoned you here to make peace. This feud between our families has gone on long enough. It is going to end. It ends today, right now, right here and you are going to end it Elsa. That is the price you are going to pay."

"You should kill the bitch and her brother," Dylis called out in a harsh voice as she lifted a spear up into the air.

"No," Marcus replied sharply. "No. This feud ends right now. Fergus, my son shall not get caught up in this cycle of violence and vengeance." Quickly Marcus turned to Petrus. "Go and fetch Armin and bring him here," he snapped. Then turning back to Elsa Marcus glared at her.

"I am going to give Armin back to you, unharmed and without retribution or conditions," Marcus called out. "I am going to forgive you and your brother for what you did. You will all be free to ride out of here. You have my word."

"You are forgiving her?" Dylis spluttered in surprise as she rounded on Marcus. "After everything she and her brother did to us? No, this is not right."

"The sword will not end this feud. It will only prolong it. Only real forgiveness has the power to end this feud," Marcus shouted, as ignoring his sister he looked across at Elsa. The young woman had lowered her gaze and was silently staring at the muddy ground.

No one spoke. No one moved. As the tense, silent standoff deepened, Marcus turned to look back at the house. He was just in time to see Petrus emerge from the doorway escorting Armin out into the courtyard. Armin looked miserable and dejected as he came towards the gates, but as he looked up and caught sight of Elsa sitting on top of her horse, his expression abruptly changed to one of outright joy. Leaving his position beside the gate, Marcus strode over to Armin and roughly grabbed him by his neck before turning to look at Elsa.

"So, are you and I going to bury this feud once and for all?" Marcus bellowed. "We have a chance to stop this now. A real chance."

On her horse, Elsa was gazing at Armin. Then slowly and carefully she dismounted and as she did, her companions did the same. Handing the reins of her horse to one of the men, Elsa turned and came towards the gates, her face calm, fearless and composed.

"Have they treated you well little brother?" she called out looking across at Armin.

"Marcus broke my nose," Armin replied in a trembling voice. "But apart from that and being slapped and spat at, they have pretty much left me alone."

Elsa nodded and for the briefest moments a little fond smile appeared on her lips as she gazed at her younger brother. It vanished as she turned to Marcus.

"Very well," Elsa snapped as she raised her hand to gently rub her sleeping baby's head. "Does the memorial stone to Corbulo still stand near the stepping stones across the river? If so I would like to go there and say a prayer to my father Lucius. It is his forgiveness and permission that I must seek."

"The stone still stands," Marcus growled. "You know the way."

***

On the higher ground away from the stepping stones that provided a bridge across the swampy river and which led towards the wide sandy beach beyond, everyone had silently and sombrely gathered around the old moss-covered stone memorial to Corbulo. In the sodden grass Elsa was kneeling before the stone, her face turned to the ground, her eyes closed, whilst both her hands were outstretched with the palms facing upwards. She was speaking quietly, using Batavian words. Then, when at last she was done, she stiffly rose to her feet and turned to face Marcus.

"It is done," she said coldly. "My father's and uncle's restless spirits are at peace. They give me permission to end this feud. The quarrel between us is over."

"I am glad," Marcus said with a little nod. "And you will remember that I kept my promise to your father. Now take your brother and get off my land."

Chapter Twenty-Three – Westward Bound

Spring 116 AD

With an eager, broad and unshakable grin that seemed permanent, Cunomoltus dipped the oars into the water, pulled backwards and propelled the small boat across the inlet. It was morning and a fresh breeze was blowing in from the west. On Vectis's swampy shoreline and amongst the forests on higher ground, the winter snows had finally melted, revealing a new and fragile layer of greenery. As the small boat ploughed across the gentle waves, a formation of nine geese came gliding over the inlet, flying in formation. After the long winter, spring was at last in the air. Opposite Cunomoltus, sitting at the end of the boat, Marcus was staring across the waters at the Hermes. He looked old, his grey tattered beard was playing in the breeze and his left arm was shaking uncontrollably. In his right hand he was holding a small wicker cage containing a solitary cackling chicken. Out on the water, the little ship looked in fine condition, fully restored with fresh, solid-looking timbers as it lay at anchor with its main sail furled. At the ship's bow, close to the waterline, a large and freshly painted eye was visible on the hull.

As they approached the vessel Marcus saw figures moving about up on the deck. As he raised his hand in greeting a figure on-board the Hermes paused and then quickly returned his greeting.

"Have you lost your way captain?" Marcus bellowed in a happy voice. "Permission to come aboard Sir."

"I believe we have not," Alexandros yelled back, with a wide grin. The one-eyed captain, sporting his black eye patch, stooped and then threw a coil of rope out to Marcus. "Tie her up and come aboard. We have been expecting you Marcus."

As Cunomoltus busied himself tying up the small rowing boat, Marcus, clutching the small cage, clambered awkwardly up the netting that was draped over the Hermes's hull. Stumbling onto the deck, he was swiftly surrounded by familiar faces. Quickly Cora and then Calista came up to him and gave him a quick joyous hug. They were followed by Calista's eleven-year-old daughter. The girl had been born in Hyperborea and looked just like her mother. Then it was Jodoc's turn. The druid's son was unable to hide a grin, as he quickly embraced Marcus and then did the same to Cunomoltus as he clambered onto the deck. Shyly Jodoc retreated a little, placing his hands on his daughter's shoulders as the two of them gazed silently at Marcus and Cunomoltus. The last to embrace Marcus was Alexandros. The big, one-eyed Greek captain was chuckling to himself with delight as he examined Marcus from top to bottom.

"So, are you still going ahead with your plan," Marcus exclaimed as he gazed at Alexandros with a broad grin. "You still planning on heading west, back out across the ocean to Hyperborea?"

"That's right," Alexandros chuckled. "Like I promised. We came back to say goodbye to you and Cunomoltus. We are bound for the west, to Hyperborea and beyond. We are going to make our fortune out there in the west, Marcus."

"Just the five of you?" Marcus frowned, as he turned to look around the deck.

"Well at the moment yes," Alexandros replied, quickly lowering his gaze. "We do all know how to sail though," he added in a defensive voice. "The little sailor girl over there," he said, gesturing at Calista's daughter, "she has known no other home apart from the Hermes and neither has her mother. After we dropped you off, we sailed to Londinium where we berthed for the winter. I was hoping to find some more crew in the city, but we found no one willing to make the passage. Everyone thought I was completely mad. Jodoc thinks he may be able to convince a couple of acquaintances in Hibernia to come with us. We are going there after we leave here. I was however hoping to find some desperate hardy souls when we came to see you. Do you perhaps know anyone who would be willing to make the journey across the ocean?"

A little grin appeared on the corner of Marcus's lips. "If you are asking me whether I would like to go with you, the answer is no I'm afraid. My home is here on Vectis."

"It's not too late to change your mind," Alexandros replied. "What with all that trouble in Rome and with this Nigrinus after you. Maybe you should think about it Marcus. Leave all your troubles behind. You know what lies out there. You could begin again, a clean slate for you and your family."

"Ah, you are a persuasive man Alexandros," Marcus said with a gentle smile. "But my home is here on Vectis. I am not leaving. I am waiting for my son Fergus to return home."

"Fair enough," Alexandros replied with a grin, as he slapped Marcus across his back. "I understand."

"So, when are you are setting out?" Marcus asked turning to look around the deck.

"Not tonight," Alexandros boomed with a mighty laugh. "No, tonight my friend you and Cunomoltus will be our guests. The Hermes is in fine shape and well stocked with provisions. Your gold made that happen. We're vastly better prepared than the first time. No, tonight Marcus we are going to drink to the old, sturdy lady who never let us down. Tonight, we are going to drink to us."

"Sounds like you already began, old man?" Cunomoltus called out in a cheeky voice as he gazed across at the big Greek captain.

"Shit," Alexandros said, slowly shaking his head as he turned to look at Cunomoltus. "Remind me again why I never had you thrown overboard? How many weeks did we have to endure your misery after you were forced to leave that Hyperborean girl behind. Even the ship's cat was sick of you."

"You are a funny man Alexandros," Cunomoltus retorted, the broad grin plastered across his face. "It's just that I can smell the wine from here."

"It's good to see you Alexandros," Marcus interrupted in a serious voice as he stepped forwards and caught hold of the captain's arm. "I am glad you came back to say goodbye. Of-course we shall drink with you. Your journey must start well." Quickly Marcus indicated the small cage at his feet. "I have brought this chicken with me and will slaughter it as an offering to Neptune and the water spirits. I shall ask them for your safe passage across the ocean. Allow me to do this old friend."

Slowly Alexandros looked down at the solitary chicken inside its cage.

"It looks terrified," the Greek captain growled. Then a broad grin appeared on his lips and he kicked the cage, sending it sliding over the deck in his wife's direction. "Fancy some chicken tonight Cora," Alexandros boomed with laughter. "Your recipes are the best in the world."

***

In the night sky a few stars were visible. Aboard the Hermes near the deck house at the stern, the seven of them were gathered together, sitting cross-legged in a circle on the wooden deck. Oil lamps hung from the rigging, creating an eerie, flickering light and the motion of the sea was gently rocking the ship. Curled up in Cunomoltus's lap the black ship's cat was dozing contentedly. Across from Marcus, Calista's daughter had difficulty in keeping her eyes open. The mood was relaxed, and all the adults had cups of wine in their hands. Alexandros was recounting what had happened to them during the winter in Londinium, his powerful voice drifting away across the dark waters of the sheltered inlet. When at last he fell silent, Marcus looked down at the deck and then reached out to fondly touch the planking with his left hand. Raising his cup of wine to his lips he downed the contents and quickly placed his cup down on the deck. Then without warning he took a deep breath and began to sing in a deep voice and as he did, the others quickly and smoothly joined in, singing the mournful and beautiful Hyperborean songs they had learned from their time in the new world. And as their voices rose together into the darkness, the seven of them linked hands and arms and Marcus turned to gaze at the faces around him. In the flickering reddish light all were smiling and grinning at each other, as the memories of their epic sea voyage returned and with it the fierce comradeship that had sustained them.

"Will you keep this safe, Marcus," Cora asked as the singing finally died away. From under her cloak she suddenly produced a small leather-bound wooden box that was sealed with strips of cloth. "It's the entire written account of our journey to Hyperborea from twelve years ago including my hand drawn pictures. Everything is in it. I want you to have it."

"In case we do not return," Alexandros said quietly, as he fixed his eyes on Marcus.

Marcus nodded as he took possession of the box. For a moment he ran his fingers over the wood. Then he glanced quickly at his brother.

"I hope you succeed," Marcus said quietly, turning to look around the circle. "I hope you find what you are looking for like I did on our first voyage. Hermes is the messenger of the Gods. Let her take you onwards and into eternity. She is a good ship and she is crewed by fine people; among the finest I have known."

Chapter Twenty-Four – Summoned

A week had passed since Marcus had said goodbye to Alexandros and the Hermes. His last image of the small ship had been seeing the Hermes's red sail disappear behind the towering cliffs as it headed away westwards along the coast. Now, trotting down the straight Roman road, the three horsemen brought their horses to an ambling halt, as across the open fields they caught sight of Noviomagus Reginorum. The gates into this small prosperous market town were open and traffic, pedestrians, horsemen and ox-drawn wagons, were coming in and out of the settlement. Out in the fields that surrounded the town, farmers were planting the next harvest. Along the settlement's earthen embankment and wooden palisades, a party of workmen were replacing the old defences with a brand-new stonewall. Marcus grunted as he carefully surveyed the scene. At the rate that the workmen were going, it would be many years before Reginorum had its new defences.

"Maybe I should go on ahead and see what Ninian wants," Cunomoltus said, as he peered at the town from atop his horse. "I know Ninian is a longstanding friend - our reliable business partner, as Dylis likes to call him, but this summons seems rather odd. Normally he would ride out to our farm if he had something important to tell us. You know how much he likes to see Dylis and he does work for us after all. So, why summon us now to Reginorum without bothering to tell us why it is so urgent and important? Something smells fishy, Marcus."

"Could it be a trap Sir?" Indus asked eyeing the town. "Maybe Ninian is a good man but someone else is forcing him to summon you to his office in town. Maybe someone is trying to lure you away from the farm Sir?"

Marcus said nothing, as he gazed across the fields at the town. Then slowly he shook his head.

"You are both being paranoid," Marcus growled, as he began to move forwards, urging his horse down the road towards the town gates. "Clear your heads," he called out. "If someone wants to ambush me they would have done it when we landed on the mainland or in the forest - that we just passed through. No. If Ninian says it's important then it will be important. I want to hear what he has to say."

Clattering past the armed city guards and into the town, Marcus turned to look around. On the corner of a street nearby stood the tavern, where twelve years ago, he'd spent the night before setting out on the final leg of his long journey home from the Dacian frontier. That too had been the day when Cunomoltus had first appeared and had followed him to Vectis, claiming to be his long-lost half-brother. It had been on that same day too, that he'd learned of Ahern's existence and Kyna's infidelity. But he himself was hardly blameless and innocent in that respect.

Further along the main street that ran the length of the town, the splendid and rich looking Temple of Neptune and Minerva, whose priests had given Petrus such a hard time, was gleaming in the afternoon sunshine. Beyond the temple, a queue of people had formed and were patiently waiting for their turn to enter the newly-completed stone bathhouse. No one seemed to be paying him any attention, as Marcus slowly walked his horse past the terraced shops and houses and down the narrow and congested street, with Cunomoltus and Indus following closely behind. Dismounting in front of the grand temple, Marcus paused for a moment to gaze at the marble dedication slab that had been proudly erected in front of the temple doors. Then on foot and leading his horse, he headed towards Ninian's small office, that was squashed in between the temple and a row of buildings. As he approached the broker's office, Ninian appeared in the doorway and quickly raised his hand in greeting.

"Marcus, good to see you," Ninian called out. "I know its irregular, but I am glad you came. I'm afraid that the matter is urgent and important."

"What is so urgent and important that you could not tell me earlier?" Marcus asked, as he clasped hold of Ninian's arm in a formal greeting.

"I was concerned you would not come if I told you," Ninian replied evasively and, as he did, he glanced hastily towards the doorway into his office. "You had better come inside. There are two men waiting here to see you. They have been here since yesterday morning."

"Who? What men?" Marcus snapped, as he shot the doorway a quick suspicious look.

"Important men, Marcus," Ninian replied sharply, as he raised his eyebrows. "They are speculatores - law enforcers on the governor's staff, old friends of mine. They have come from Londinium," Ninian added. "The governor has sent them. They wish to speak to you, that's all."

Slowly Marcus turned to peer again at the dark doorway leading into Ninian's office. Then without any further hesitation, he abruptly strode towards the entrance and ducked into the building, swiftly followed by Ninian and Indus, leaving Cunomoltus outside to tend to the horses.

Inside the gloomy broker's office, two men were sitting around a table upon which stood a jug and a couple of cups. As Marcus came striding into the room, the men swiftly rose to their feet. They were clad in good quality clothing and both looked to be in their forties, with stylishly trimmed beards.

Marcus paused in the middle of the office and silently gazed at the strangers, as Ninian quickly slipped past him and smoothly positioned himself in between the two parties.

"I am Marcus. I believe you two gentlemen wanted to speak to me?"

For a moment the two men did not reply. Then the taller of the two, a man with a broken nose, raised his chin and peered at Marcus.

"My name is Felix," the man said, speaking confidently in good clear Latin. "Forgive me for arranging our meeting here and not at your farm. Ninian and I go back a long way and I thought it would be better and more discreet if we did it here. My colleague and I are speculatores, law enforcers on the staff of the newly appointed governor of Britannia, Marcus Appius Bradua."

"Bradua!" Marcus interrupted. "I didn't know there had been a change of governor?"

"Marcus Appius Bradua took up his position at the start of this year," Felix replied in a patient voice. "He arrived in Londinium a month ago. He has instructed my colleague and I to inform you that the senate in Rome has declared you a fugitive and an enemy of Rome. You stand accused of conspiracy and treason against the state and the murder, in your own home in Rome, of two leading senators. Furthermore, I am instructed to inform you that your name has been erased from the senatorial lists, that your property in Rome has been seized and that your family are forbidden from applying for any government contracts until the outcome of your trial. You are also forbidden from standing for election to any government positions. I hope you understand the seriousness of these charges."

"Of-course I understand the seriousness of the situation," Marcus snapped. "And I know Bradua from my time in the Senate."

Quickly, Felix exchanged glances with his colleague.

"The governor has instructed me to inform you that you are to stand trial," Felix said in a stern voice, as he turned to Marcus. "The court date has been set for the sixth day of June, the trial is to be held at the governor's palace in Londinium. You are a Roman citizen and therefore have the same rights as all citizens. You will be allowed to defend yourself in court, but I warn you, that if the charges of treason and murder are proven, you will likely receive the death penalty."

"I am no traitor," Marcus replied calmly. "I have served Rome faithfully. I was a soldier for twenty-three years with the Second Batavian Auxiliary Cohort. I lost these fingers fighting on the Danube. The charges against me are politically motivated. They will not stick."

"Well we shall let the court and the law decide that," Felix said quickly. "My job is just to inform you of the charges against you and summon you to court. Out of respect for your former position and status as a senator of Rome and your long-standing acquaintance with him," Felix continued, "the governor feels that you are no flight risk. He doesn't think you will run, so he has agreed to grant you the privilege to remain at liberty until the day of your trial. However, you shall pay a bail sum of ten thousand denarii. We have instructions to take receipt of the bail money. We expect the money to be delivered to us here within the next three days."

"Who will be the judge? Will it be a trial by jury?" Ninian said quickly.

"The governor Marcus Appius Bradua has jurisdiction and will preside over the case as the judge," Felix replied. "He has a duty to uphold Roman law in the province. The prosecution team will be appointed by members of the senate in Rome and the trial outcome will be decided by an appointed jury of twelve leading citizens of Londinium."

"Why the delay in the court date?" Marcus growled. "I am ready to defend myself now. Why such a long wait?"

For a moment Felix hesitated.

"The prosecution needs more time to collect evidence against you," Felix replied at last. "Their investigators are already in Rome searching for witnesses. The governor is determined that this be done properly, so it will take some time before they are ready."

"No doubt it will be Nigrinus who puts together the prosecution," Marcus snapped.

"You have been informed of the governor's instructions and you are ordered to comply with them," Felix said sharply. "You have three days in which to raise the bail money and bring it here. As for the legal proceedings, the governor has a solemn duty to uphold the law and ensure that you get a fair trial. He wishes you to know that that is exactly what he intends to do."

"I am sure he does," Marcus replied. "But that little shit Nigrinus doesn't."

***

"Marcus Appius Bradua is a member of the War Party," Marcus said, as he sat at the table in the dining hall of his villa. "I met him a few times in Rome. He is a decent man, a former Consul of Rome but he is a friend of Nigrinus. He may not be within the War Party's inner circle, but he is loyal to Nigrinus. No doubt the governor is acting on Nigrinus's instructions. If Bradua must choose between me and Nigrinus, he will always choose Nigrinus. He will not take my side. He will faithfully carry out his orders. That's the kind of man he is; a loyal dog who doesn't like to take risks."

"So, we are fucked then," Cunomoltus exclaimed angrily, sending a grape flying across the table and onto the floor.

Around the dining table in the hall, Kyna, Dylis, Petrus and the others were sombrely and silently gazing down at the oak table. It was evening and outside, darkness cloaked the land.

"Maybe, maybe not," Marcus replied, as he glanced at his brother. "One thing is for sure. Nigrinus is going to pack that jury with his supporters. Men who will do his bidding. That's the real reason why the court date has been delayed. He needs time to bribe the jury members."

"What about the charges?" Dylis said, looking up.

"The charge of treason against the state is preposterous," Marcus snapped, his face darkening. "There is no evidence for that, but the second charge is more problematic. I did kill those two senators in my house."

"Only after they came to us demanding that you kill yourself," Kyna cried out, her face flushed with sudden emotion. "It's not fair. You were set-up Marcus. You have done nothing wrong. Those men died because they gave you no choice. You have always worked in the interests of Rome, all your life. Everyone knows that."

"What about offering to pay compensation to the families of the two dead senators," Petrus exclaimed. "Would that work?"

Marcus sighed. "Maybe if the circumstances were different, but Nigrinus wants my head. He is not going to accept any money."

A sombre and oppressive silence descended on the room and, for a long moment no one seemed to want to speak.

"So, what do we do Marcus?" Cunomoltus asked at last in a weary voice as he sent another grape rolling across the table.

"We could run," Petrus interrupted. "All of us. We could disappear."

"And go where?" Dylis retorted sharply. "Leave our home and everything we have worked for behind. I don't think so."

"I am not running from that little shit Nigrinus," Marcus replied in a calm voice, as he looked up at Petrus. "No, I shall go to Londinium and fight this case. We have time and I may still have some friends and allies in the city."

"And we have gold," Cunomoltus blurted out, in a hopeful voice.

"You are going to need a good defence lawyer," Dylis said, as she turned to look at her brother. "I have business associates in Londinium who may be able to help. I will leave for the city tomorrow."

Sitting at the table, Marcus nodded in agreement. Then slowly he turned to look at each member of his family in turn, his gaze grave but confident and indominable.

"I do not want any of you to despair," he said. "You are all to hold your heads up high. We will not be bullied by the powerful. We shall not be cowed by might. We are Corbulo's people and we fear nothing. I am going to win this trial. We are not going to be beaten by that man. We are going to win."

Chapter Twenty-Five – Friends and Enemies in the Capital

The Roman bridge across the Thames looked spectacular in the sunshine, as it stretched away across the wide river. There was nothing like it in the whole of Britannia, Marcus thought. A proud statement of Rome's technical and engineering prowess and a subtle propaganda reminder, if anyone needed it, that things were now definitely better under Roman rule. Sturdy wooden piles, rammed into the riverbed, held up the four-hundred-yard long, wooden construction. Across the bridge, in both directions, a vast multitude of pedestrians, soldiers, horsemen and convoys of wagons was crossing. The noise created by the traffic was astonishing and reminded Marcus of the Forum in Rome. As he rode his horse down Watling Street and towards the bridge, accompanied by Dylis and Indus, Marcus could see that on either side of the approach road to the bridge and the scattering of suburban houses, the Thames had broken through its banks and flood defences. The devastation that the river had caused was terrible. The floodwaters had spread out over a wide area, submerging homes, buildings, mudflats, marshes, tidal channels and creeks and making the Thames in places look nearly a mile wide. As he gazed at the natural disaster along the southern bank, a man emerged from one of the semi-flooded homes, wading through the water and clutching a pile of belongings. Further along a woman was on her knees crying, as she gazed at her ruined home.

"We used to live just over there," Dylis said, breaking the sombre and reflective silence that had existed between them since dawn. She pointed at one of the houses. "When our father was still in the stone-haulage business. Corbulo and my mother Efa had made their home just over there. But that was thirty years ago now."

Marcus glanced in the direction that Dylis was pointing, but said nothing and neither did Indus. Their faces remained masks of stoicism.

The squad of soldiers from the governor's personal guard, who were guarding the southern end of the bridge, barely noticed Marcus, as he and his two companions joined the congested traffic crossing northwards into the city of Londinium. Out on the sparkling and gleaming waters of the river and to the right of the bridge, ocean-going ships were approaching the harbour, whilst dozens of other vessels lay tied up against the massive wooden quays. Their cargos were being lifted out of the holds by an army of wooden cranes. Idly Marcus gazed at the harbour front. It had been from here that he and the Hermes had set out on their epic voyage across the western ocean to Hyperborea. The city, Marcus thought, struggling with a sudden melancholy, contained many memories and wherever he looked he was reminded of them.

Up on the higher ground, on the northern bank of the Thames, stood Londinium, capital and largest city of Britannia with sixty thousand inhabitants. There was no city wall but, rising majestically above the mass of terraced buildings and grid-like pattern of city streets, the massive Basilica and Forum dominated the city's skyline. Walking his horse across the bridge, Marcus gazed silently at the awesome stone construction, several storey's high. It was the very heart of the city, where the merchants, banking and legal guilds had their offices and stalls and where the city council met. It had been some time since he had been back to Londinium and the signs of rapid change and booming growth were everywhere.

Slowly Marcus turned his attention to the governor's palace, whose grounds came right up to the waterfront to the left of the bridge. Beyond the outdoor pool and river-front terrace, a proud imperial banner was flying from the top of the fine-looking building. For a moment Marcus gazed at the palace. It was from this building that Rome ruled Britannia. It was from here that orders would be dispatched to the three legionary legates and the commanders of the fifty or so auxiliary cohorts, stationed in the province. It was rumoured too, that it was beneath the palace, in the warren of tunnels and tiny prison cells, that the enemies of Rome - rebels, traitors and Christians were tortured in the most gruesome manner, before finally being put to death. There seemed to be some truth to the rumours Marcus thought. For thirty years ago, Corbulo, his father had managed to rescue Efa, his wife, from those very same dungeons, during the time of the Christian pogroms. Marcus turned to look away. There were still two weeks to go before his court date, but Dylis had insisted that they leave for Londinium well before then, to prepare his defence. His sister had hired a defence lawyer. One of the best in town she had claimed, and now they were on their way to stay at his house.

***

It was evening and Marcus, Dylis and Senovarus, his defence lawyer, were reclining on their individual couches around the dinner table, picking at the considerable array of food dishes. The richly decorated dining hall was lit by flickering oil lamps and, near the door leading to the kitchens, a crackling brazier was heating up the room.

"May I speak candidly, Marcus," Senovarus said at last, as he reached out to take a sip of wine from his cup. The lawyer was a thin and wiry man with a head that seemed out of proportion to the rest of his body.

"Of course," Marcus replied. "That's why we came to see you, isn't it? That's what I am paying you for."

Senovarus shot Dylis a quick bemused glance, before carefully clearing his throat and placing his cup back on the table.

"I have known your sister, Dylis for a long time," Senovarus began smoothly. "She has briefed me on all the details surrounding your case. It is an unfortunate business and it has complications now that the new governor has become personally involved. The situation is especially delicate because it involves imperial politics. We must tread carefully."

"Can we win the case or not?" Marcus shot back, as he fixed his eyes on the lawyer.

The lawyer grinned and for a moment he said nothing.

"I will be open and honest with you Marcus," Senovarus said at last. "I am a supporter of Hadrian and the Peace Party. I have been so for a long time. Most of the populace in Londinium are supporters of Hadrian. In my mind there is no doubt that Hadrian will become the next emperor. I have it on good authority that Trajan's health is beginning to deteriorate. It will not be long now before we have a new emperor. It is just a matter of time."

"Or maybe we shall have civil war," Marcus replied.

"I doubt it," Senovarus said, with a quick dismissive gesture. "Hadrian's influence and control over the legions grows ever stronger and Trajan will officially nominate him as the next emperor before he dies. Plotina, Trajan's wife will ensure that. The army will not follow Nigrinus. They may follow Quietus, but Hadrian will take precautions to ensure that Quietus will not get the chance to do so."

"You seem very confident of yourself," Marcus said.

"It is my job to appear confident and sure of myself," Senovarus said, with a little amused grin. "How else can I convince the jury that you are innocent?"

"Tell my brother about our defence strategy," Dylis interrupted.

"Right," Senovarus replied. For a moment he hesitated. "The new governor has a reputation for being incorruptible. I doubt he can be bribed. It is my belief however that our new governor Marcus Appius Bradua, also knows that it is likely that Hadrian will become the next emperor," the lawyer exclaimed. "As a prominent member of the War Party and an opponent of Hadrian, I believe the governor is primarily concerned with saving his own skin and rescuing his career. He may have doubts about the wisdom of prosecuting someone like yourself, Marcus."

"Why is that?" Marcus shot back in a sceptical voice.

"Well you are not just a nobody, Marcus," Senovarus said gingerly. "You are a former senator of Rome, a war veteran and a hero in some quarters. You have money; you have land; you are a leading Roman citizen. Prosecuting a man like that makes Rome look bad. It's like turning on one of your own. It's bad publicity, especially in the provinces. But Bradua will most likely be concerned because of your son, Fergus, and his close association with Hadrian," the lawyer replied. "Dylis told me how close your son is to Hadrian. That will work to our advantage. Bradua will know that your family have connections to Hadrian. It will make him more cautious. He will fear Hadrian's reaction; offend the next emperor and it is likely that his career will be over. Do you understand what I am saying?"

"I do," Marcus growled, as he reached out to the bowl of olives. "But I know Bradua. I worked with him in the senate in Rome. He is a loyal dog. He is even more scared of Nigrinus than of Hadrian. He will do exactly what Nigrinus tells him to do."

"Maybe, maybe not," Senovarus replied. "I am however convinced that Bradua harbours doubts about prosecuting you. What we need to do is encourage his doubts to the point where he abandons the case. We need to get Bradua to change his mind. The governor is in a difficult position. Prosecute you - a former senator, and he will no doubt offend Hadrian and ruin his career but do nothing and he will offend Nigrinus and be accused of failing to uphold the law. I think Bradua is looking for a way out. He is searching for a compromise that will allow him to emerge without damaging his career."

"And you think that will work?" Marcus snapped.

The lawyer nodded.

"Marcus," Dylis said sharply, as she leaned forwards and gazed across the table at her brother. "What we are saying is, that in order to conduct an effective defence, we need you to become a firm supporter of Hadrian and the Peace Party and we need you to declare your allegiance to Hadrian in public."

Marcus raised his eyebrows, and for a long moment he said nothing as he stared back at his sister.

"I have already prepared a full programme of speaking engagements and public appearances here in Londinium," Dylis went on, unperturbed by Marcus's silence. "The people of Londinium need to know where you stand, Marcus. They need to hear your support for Hadrian. They need to realise that this trial is politically motivated. In that way there can be no doubt in the governor's mind, as to the risk that he is taking by prosecuting you. We must get the people on our side. It is crucial. The crowds love an underdog, Marcus. They love a fight between the small man and the powerful. Most of the people of Londinium support Hadrian. We need them to be on your side during the trial. That matters because the jury is to be chosen from amongst them."

"Your sister has already been spreading the word amongst the business and mercantile community that your son Fergus is a close ally of Hadrian," Senovarus added. "She is right. You must now publicly declare your allegiance to Hadrian and the Peace Party. I can then argue in court that this trial is not about murder or treason, but about politics, and that you are being persecuted for your politics. That is the only way in which I can save you from being convicted."

Dylis and Senovarus peered at Marcus expectantly, but on his couch, Marcus said nothing, his eyes staring down at the floor. Then slowly he raised his head to look at his two dining companions and, as he did there was something indomitable in Marcus's gaze.

"I swore an oath of allegiance and loyalty to the War Party," he said sternly. "A solemn oath. Nigrinus may have become my mortal enemy and I may no longer be an active member of the War Party, but I still swore an oath. Such a thing cannot be undone. What you ask from me is dishonourable. No, I will not now break my word. I will not change sides and support Hadrian just to save my skin. A soldier's oath once given, cannot be taken back."

***

The narrow city street was filled with noise and activity as Dylis led Marcus and Indus through the morning crowds and onwards in the direction of the Forum. Two days had passed since their arrival in Londinium. Leading the way down the street, Dylis looked tense and unhappy, as she cut a determined path through the crowds. Despite Marcus's refusal to renounce his oath of allegiance, she had insisted that they proceed with her plan anyway. The compromise that they had settled upon was for Dylis to do all the talking, whilst Marcus remained silent, standing at her side.

Grimly Marcus gazed at his sister as they strode on down the busy street. It was a messy and unsatisfactory compromise, a dysfunctionality at the heart of his defence, that would not and could not work. The speaking engagements and public appearances that Dylis had planned, were not going to sway the populace as soon as they discovered that his heart and loyalty were not with Hadrian. They were going to make a mockery of him, but Dylis had insisted and there was no doubting her determination.

Around them, the busy street was teeming with shoppers and merchants and, from their simple, terraced two-room dwellings, the advertising cries of the shopkeepers mingled with barking dogs, bellowing oxen, shrieking children and the rundle of wagon wheels on the paving stones. At Marcus's side, Indus, armed with his short sword and a knife, was gazing at the people in his usual silent and stoical manner; his alert eyes darting from one face to the next.

The odour of unwashed bodies hung heavily over the crowds but, as they headed eastwards, the stench of raw sewage grew stronger. Soon they reached the small wooden bridge over the Walbrook and the source of the stench became clearer. The locals were using the small stream, that cut Londinium in half, as a sewer and rubbish dump. Wrinkling his nose in disgust, Marcus crossed the bridge as he followed Dylis eastwards along Watling Street. To his right, down an alley, he caught sight of the stone temple to Mithras, that stood on the banks of the Walbrook. Further down the river's course, where the Walbrook split in two, he caught a glimpse of the Thames. A couple of hundred yards directly ahead of him, the huge, imposing colonnaded Basilica and Forum loomed above the densely crowded homes and buildings - like some giant spider sitting at the heart of its web. Reaching an intersection with a side street, Dylis paused and quickly turned to Marcus.

"All right, the plan is to first try and attract the crowds in the Forum," she said in a determined voice. "We need to drum up support and attention for our case. It's market day today and the Forum will be crowded with farmers and their customers. It's going to be busy and noisy with a lot of distractions. That's why I have arranged for us to be given a few barrels, so that we can stand up on them and be seen and heard. We're going to be competing with all the quacks, religious nuts and attention seekers. If anyone asks you anything Marcus, just smile. Give them your best smile and try to look innocent. I will do the talking."

"This is a shit plan," Marcus snapped. "We're wasting our time."

Ignoring her brother, Dylis sighed and turned to look back the way they'd come.

"Once we have done the Forum we will head for the Amphitheatre," she said. "There is always a good crowd there. After that we will visit the baths and the temples, ending today's work outside the governor's palace. An appearance there should get everyone's attention."

"The governor's palace. Is that a wise idea?" Marcus grunted in a sceptical voice.

"Shut up," Dylis hissed furiously. "I am trying to save your life, brother. This is the only way I know how."

Marcus did not immediately reply, as he turned to look away at the crowds milling around them. Then he reached out with his right hand and gripped his sister's shoulder.

"I know. I know," he muttered. "And I am grateful sister for everything you have done. All shall end well."

***

It was after noon and the three of them had just left the busy streets outside the huge and newly completed stone amphitheatre and were heading southwards to the public baths, on the banks of the Thames. Suddenly an old gladiator's net came sailing through the air, crashing down onto Marcus. Instantly, the devious meshing and weight of the net brought him staggering and then tumbling down onto the paving stones. In the narrow street someone screamed, and the pedestrians scattered in panic. Dimly, Marcus was aware of three burly men armed with knives, pushing through the crowd towards him. A fourth had launched himself at Indus. Frantically Marcus tried to free himself from the net, but the thin but strong meshing had snagged and wrapped itself around him, restricting his movement. Desperately he yanked his knife from his belt, as he struggled to free himself. Then the three men were upon him. One of them, a bald man with piercing blue eyes, hit him in the face with his fist - sending Marcus flying onto his back and crying out in pain. As he crashed onto his back, he lost his knife, which went clattering away down the street. Rough hands grasped hold of him and, before he could react he was struck in the face again, by one of the men's fists. Despite the pain, Marcus tried to fight back but the net was making it very hard.

"Get him up onto his feet," a laboured voice hissed. "Get him out of here."

However, before anyone could act, another scream rang out in the street and the man who had attacked Indus, staggered backwards with Indus's knife sticking out of his chest and blood pouring down his tunic. With an explosion of rage and violence, Indus kicked the man backwards, sending him crashing up against a wall. Swiftly the Batavian bodyguard yanked his knife from his assailant's chest and rammed it into the man's throat. On the ground, Marcus was furiously struggling with the men, who were trying to drag him back onto his feet. His assailants were swearing and shouting, and he was close enough to them to smell their foul breath. Then one of the men shrieked, as Dylis came up behind him and hit him in the head with an iron hammer. The force of the blow sent the man crashing sideways into a baker's stall. Loaves of bread went flying in all directions.

"Get away from him," Dylis screamed, in a fearless and outraged voice, as she swung her hammer at the remaining men. "Get away from him. Get away from him."

In the street, Marcus suddenly felt the pressure relax. The two remaining assailants seemed to have had enough. Without a word, they abandoned their efforts to drag him away and fled down the street, vanishing in the chaos and confusion. A moment later, Indus was at Marcus's side and furiously pulling the net off his body. As he staggered to his feet, Marcus, gasping for breath, turned in the direction in which his attackers had fled. Close by, Dylis abruptly wheeled round as the man she'd hit with her hammer came staggering out of the shop entrance with blood pouring down his face. Before he had a chance to see what was going on, she hit him again, striking him full in the face and, as he collapsed onto the ground, she kept on hitting him until his face was a bloody pulp.

"You all right Sir," Indus gasped, as clutching his bloodied knife, he turned to stare around him. In the deserted street, anxious, terrified and silent faces were peering at the scene from windows and doorways, but no one dared set foot outside and take a closer look at the two bloody corpses.

"I think so," Marcus growled, with a painful expression, as he raised his hand to touch the bruises on his face.

In the doorway to the shop, Dylis staggered backwards, clutching her bloodied hammer as she stared at the assailant lying motionless on the ground. Her face was splattered with blood and there was a madness in her eyes.

"Who were they Sir?" Indus gasped, as he turned to form a protective circle around Marcus. "Who would do such a thing Sir?"

"Bounty hunters," Marcus hissed angrily, as he reached down to pick up the discarded net. Examining it for a moment, he contemptuously flung the net into a corner and turned to stare at his sister. "Scum of the earth. Nigrinus has announced a reward for my capture," Marcus snapped. "This is the work of bounty hunters. They know I am here. The streets are no longer safe for us."

***

It was night and across Londinium the city seemed to be asleep. Carefully, Marcus undid the latch, opened the door to Senovarus's house and peered out into the street. He was clad in a dark cloak with a hood drawn over his head and, hidden within his tunic were a knife and a short sword. Outside, in the alley nothing moved. In the darkness all seemed quiet, except for the occasional drunken roar and shout coming from the late-night revellers a block away. For a moment, Marcus strained to listen, allowing his eyes to adjust to the darkness. Then, without further hesitation, he quietly slipped out of the door and into the street and stole away into the night.

Chapter Twenty-Six – The Trial

Senovarus's slaves were standing in a row along the corridor, like an honour guard, as Marcus came down the stairs from his room in the lawyer's town house. At the door leading out into the street, Dylis, Indus and Senovarus were waiting for him, all of them dressed in their finest clothing. The lawyer had a leather satchel slung over his shoulder and Indus was armed with a knife and short sword. Dylis looked tense but managed to flash her brother a quick, encouraging smile.

"Are you ready Marcus?" Senovarus said quickly. "They are waiting for you outside. Do as they say and don't make a fuss. Most of it is for show anyway."

Marcus, looking composed, said nothing as he strode towards the doorway. He was unarmed and clad in a long black cloak with a hood. As Senovarus opened the door and stepped out into the street, Marcus caught sight of a party of legionaries from the governor's personal guard. The soldiers were hanging about in the street, patiently waiting for him to appear. Stepping out into the bright sunlight, Marcus stopped as the centurion in command of the legionaries came up to him.

"I am the captain of the guard," the officer said. "Are you Marcus?"

"I am," Marcus replied.

"I have orders to escort you to the governor's mansion," the centurion snapped. "You are to stand trial. Bind his hands behind his back," the officer called out, turning to his men.

As the legionaries bound Marcus's hands behind his back with a thin rope, Marcus stood still and gazed quietly ahead, his face composed and unreadable. In the doorways and windows of the terraced buildings opposite him, silent and curious faces were peering back at him.

"Ready Sir," one of the legionaries called out.

"All-right, let's go," the centurion cried out, as he started off down the street raising his vine staff in the air. "Close formation," the officer called out. "No one is to harm the prisoner or get close to him."

Abruptly Marcus turned and, followed by Dylis, Indus and Senovarus, began to follow the centurion, as the officer led the way down the narrow street. The squad of legionaries, clad in their body armour and helmets and carrying their spears and large shields, quickly formed up in a protective formation around Marcus. As the party strode on down the road, the tramp of the soldiers hobnailed boots on the paving stones filled the street with an ominous sound. Reaching an intersection, the centurion turned right and, as he followed the officer into the street, Marcus was suddenly conscious of the people pausing to stare at him. As the party marched on the pedestrians in the street ahead hastily moved out of their way.

"Murderer," a lone voice suddenly cried out from the crowd and Marcus caught a glimpse of a red-faced man glaring at him and shaking his fist.

Further down the street, the crowds of onlookers seemed to be growing, lining both sides of the thoroughfare. All were gazing at the small party and its army escort. Then, as the people caught sight of Marcus, a large cheer went up. The cheering, clapping and yelling grew louder as the centurion began to push his way through the mass of people. To Marcus's surprise the people seemed to be on his side.

"Marcus. Marcus. Marcus," the cry went up and, as it was swiftly taken up by hundreds of voices, the legionaries started to force people backwards with their shields.

"He's innocent. He's innocent. Set him free! Long live emperor Hadrian! We want Marcus. We want Marcus. Set him free!"

The yells and shouts grew in volume as the party struggled on through the crowds. Along the edge of the street, dozens of hands and arms reached out, straining to touch Marcus and the noise was deafening. Gazing silently ahead, Marcus kept on walking, forcing his way down the street, his hands bound behind his back, his face composed and unreadable. Not all in the crowds however, seemed to be on his side, and occasionally he heard a man shouting abuse at him. Yet it was clear where the sympathies of most of the onlookers lay. As they approached the Temple of Neptune, the solemn looking priests came out of the temple and gathered together to watch the procession making its way down the street. Quickly, Marcus turned to look back at Dylis, who was following on behind him. He had not been expecting this reaction from the crowds. Had the news of the incident with the bounty hunters spread throughout the city, or had his sister arranged this display of public support? But Dylis avoided his gaze, and instead, kept her cold, hard eyes firmly on the crowds ahead.

The size of the crowds seemed to grow larger the closer to the governor's palace they got. Around him, the legionary escort were grunting and swearing at the populace, as they jostled and struggled to forge a path down the street with their large shields. Along the edge of the street, Marcus suddenly noticed men in familiar looking uniforms and, as he strode on by, here and there in the crowds, a Batavian veteran sprang stiffly to attention and saluted.

"We are with you Sir," a voice cried out, in the Batavian language. "We stand with you Sir! "Thunder and lashing rain, so Wodan commeth. Courage Sir!"

The cries and shouts wore barely audible amidst the noisy tumult. Up ahead the great stone palace suddenly appeared, looming over its neighbouring buildings. A row of iron-faced legionaries clad in their armour were standing in a long line in front of the building, keeping the crowds back with their large shields. As the centurion of his escort reached them, the soldiers quickly moved aside, allowing the party to slip through and into the palace beyond.

***

The windowless-room inside the palace was bare, stuffy and airless. Marcus, with his hands still bound behind his back, stood in a corner, with a silent legionary guard on either side of him. A table had been placed in the centre of the room and, arranged around it were three chairs, two of which were empty whilst the third was occupied by Senovarus. There was no one else in the room. The lawyer looked bored as he sat waiting, calmly drumming his fingers on the wooden surface of the table. From outside the building, Marcus could hear the faint noise of cheering and shouting emanating from the city streets.

At last, after what seemed an age, the door opened, and a man strode into room. Looking up, Marcus recognised Felix, one of the speculatores, law enforcers, who had conveyed the summons to him in Reginorum. For a moment Felix stared at Marcus. Then, carefully he cleared his throat.

"Senator and former Consul of Rome, governor of the province of Britannia, you will stand for Marcus Appius Bradua," Felix announced in a grave voice before stiffly stepping to one side. Moments later, two men came striding into the room. The first was a tall, aristocratic-looking man of around fifty, with a receding hairline and large bulging eyes. He was clad in a fine-looking senator's toga with a thin purple border. On his fingers, a multitude of rings gleamed in the light. As he came into the room, Senovarus rose to his feet and lowered his head in a respectful gesture.

The second man was shorter, younger and fatter than Bradua and there was a slyness about him, as if he was a thief on a reconnaissance mission, eying up what he could steal. As his gaze settled on Marcus, a little contemptuous smile appeared on the man's lips.

"Be seated," the governor said as he gestured at the chairs. Glancing quickly at Marcus, the governor gave no indication that he recognised him, nor did he say anything to him. Instead Bradua turned his attention to Senovarus.

"You are here to defend your client?" the governor snapped.

"I am," the lawyer replied.

"Good," Bradua said, in a business-like voice. "This is a preliminary hearing. The gentlemen beside me," the governor said, indicating the second man. "His name is Otho. He has come all the way from Rome. He is a lawyer and he will lead the prosecution on behalf of the senate and people of Rome."

"It's good to finally see what I am up against," Senovarus said with a bemused smile, as he stretched out his hand in greeting, but Otho declined to take it.

"As this is a preliminary hearing, I would like to get the formula for the trial agreed as soon as possible," the governor said sharply. "First then the *nominatio*. It is agreed between plaintiff and defence council that I, as governor of this province and having jurisdiction, shall be the judge of this case. It is however the right of the defendant, who is a full Roman citizen, to have his trial heard in Rome. Does the defendant wish for his trial to be transferred to Rome?"

"No, he wishes it to be held here in Londinium," Senovarus replied.

"All right, that brings us to the *intentio*," Bradua snapped. "Otho, would you like to make clear the reason for this trial and the charges against the defendant."

"Thank you, Sir," Otho replied, speaking in a crisp clear voice. "The defendant stands accused of treason and the murder of two leading senators. These crimes took place in Rome last summer. I have evidence and a witness that prove the defendant's guilt and, I will be seeking the death penalty."

"All right, I agree to the prosecution," Bradua said with a nod. "Defence council, do you contest these charges? Is there any possibility that we can avoid going to full trial by having your client declare his guilt right now? It would save all of us a lot of hassle and time."

"My client is innocent of all the charges levelled at him," Senovarus replied. "They are politically motivated. He is also willing to swear an oath in front of the gods, that he is innocent. If he is allowed do so, he should go free. Swearing a solemn oath before the gods is a serious matter and proves his innocence. However, if this is not possible he has instructed me to proceed to a full trial, Sir."

"Otho," the governor said, glancing at the prosecutor.

"No," Otho said sharply, as he shook his head. "This case is too serious to be decided on a simple oath. I do not trust the defendant's word and will not agree to it."

"Very well," Bradua said in his business-like voice. "Then we shall proceed to full trial. A jury of twelve leading citizens of this city has been chosen and are waiting for us in the court room. I shall meet you both there in an hour."

As the governor got up and turned to leave the room, without so much as a glance at Marcus, the two lawyers quickly rose to their feet and respectfully lowered their heads. After Bradua had left, followed by Felix, Otho turned and slowly walked over to where Marcus was standing. The prosecutor's face was filled with malice. Pausing in front of Marcus, he took his time examining him.

"I am going to have them decapitate you," Otho hissed suddenly. "And once I have your head, I shall take it back to Rome and put it on a spike for all to see. Nigrinus wanted you to know that this will be your fate, to be remembered as a traitor to Rome and to your colleagues."

"Fuck off you little dog," Marcus growled.

Before anyone could react Otho had spat straight into Marcus' face. Then abruptly, the prosecutor turned away and strode out of the room.

Coming up to Marcus, Senovarus pulled a piece of cloth from his pocket and hastily wiped the spittle from Marcus's face.

"May I have a few moments alone with my client?" Senovarus asked as he turned to the two legionaries. "Don't worry. He is not about to make a run for it."

The soldiers glanced at each other and then, without a word they trooped out of the room and closed the door behind them.

"Stay cool," Senovarus said, lowering his voice. "Don't let that arsehole rattle you. He is just trying to get you angry and flustered. But tell me. Otho mentioned that he had evidence and a witness incriminating you. What could he be referring to?"

"I don't know," Marcus replied.

Senovarus reached up to stroke his chin with a thoughtful expression. Then he turned away and looked down at the floor.

"Don't worry," he said at last. "Whatever they have got against you, I am going to pour darkness over this jury. We are going to win."

***

The large state hall inside the governor's palace was packed. Up in the public gallery, every available inch of space was taken by a crowd of eager spectators and onlookers. Legionaries from the governor's personal guard stood stiffly on guard duty beside the three entrances into the hall and, gazing down at the proceedings from a plinth, was a life-size stone statue of emperor Trajan, clad in military clothing. Close to the main entrance, stood another life-size statue of a veiled and naked woman holding a cornucopia in her hand. As Marcus was led out into the centre of the hall, his hands still bound behind his back, a hush descended on the room, and all eyes turned towards him. Leaving Marcus standing facing the bench where the governor, his advisers and the court officials were seated, the two guards took up a position either side of him, their eyes staring into space. Slowly, Marcus turned to glance to his right, where the twelve men of the jury were seated in comfortable chairs. The men looked solemn and grave, giving nothing away as to what they may be thinking. Hearing someone softly call out his name, he turned to his left and saw Cunomoltus leading Kyna to the spaces reserved for family members. Kyna was clad in a fine white cloak and her face was calm and composed. As she reached the spot where Dylis was standing, the two women quickly embraced and kissed each other on the cheek. Then they both turned to look at Marcus and, as she gazed at her husband Kyna lifted her chin a little in a proud and defiant gesture. At her side Dylis's eyes were hard as stones. Directly in front of the section reserved for family members, the advocates for the prosecution and defence and their teams were sitting at their desks, gazing solemnly at Marcus. Otho it seemed had brought a large team of assistants, but Senovarus was sitting alone.

"This trial is now open," the governor suddenly announced in a loud voice, as he solemnly rose to his feet and turned to gaze around the silent hall. Slowly Bradua extended his hands outwards and turned to face the statue of the emperor. "May we who must pass-down judgement be blessed by the wisdom of Trajan, father of the divine house. May we receive immortal Jupiter's strength and benefit from the insight of the blind goddess of fortune, her most revered Fortuna. May the gods bless us today as we seek their guidance in this trial, so that the affairs of men may once more be well ordered and in balance."

As he finished his solemn prayer to the gods Bradua at last turned to gaze at Marcus as around him, the packed hall remained spellbound. As their eyes locked, Marcus gazed back at the governor, his face unreadable.

"Will the defendant state their name before the court," the governor called out.

Marcus gave his name and, as he did so a spectator suddenly rose to his feet in the public gallery and pointed an accusing finger at Marcus.

"Murderer, murderer," the man screamed at the top of his voice.

"Silence," the governor bellowed angrily as he turned around to stare at the heckler up in the gallery. "The next person who makes a sound will be ejected from my courtroom. We shall have silence unless I give you permission to speak."

As the hall settled down, the governor turned to Otho. "Will the prosecution read out the charges against the defendant in full," Bradua snapped.

With a grave expression Otho, slowly rose to his feet behind his desk, clutching a parchment in his hands. "The charges against the defendant are these," Otho cried out in a loud, confident voice. "That at the start of summer last year, whilst residing at his house in Rome, this former senator, this very same man standing before us, did wilfully and with clear intent betray Rome and murder two of his colleagues in his own home. We, the senate and people of Rome charge this man with treason and murder. We demand the death penalty by beheading for these crimes."

A stir swept through the public gallery, making the governor turn in an annoyed fashion and glare at the spectators.

"How does the defence respond to these charges?" the governor asked as he turned back to look at Senovarus.

Behind his desk, Senovarus rose to his feet and quickly turned to face the governor.

"My client is innocent," Senovarus replied. "This trial is politically motivated. It is a sham. My client should be set free at once. There is no case against him. He is no traitor, nor is he a murderer."

Abruptly, the defence council sat back down and busied himself with his papers, as a quick, little anonymous cheer rose from the public gallery. At the bench, the governor paused for a moment as he ignored the brief interruption, and glanced down at the court clerks, who were recording the minutes of the case.

"Very well," the governor said at last. "Will the prosecution outline their case in detail for the benefit of the jury."

At his desk, Otho nodded and once more he rose to his feet. Turning to the twelve jury members, the prosecutor took a deep breath and a pained expression appeared on his face.

"Gentlemen of the jury," Otho began, in a grave voice. "This man who stands before you accused of these heinous crimes was once a senator of Rome. A respectable man who once wore the same toga as our governor over there. A man with many friends, a man who was appointed as prefect of the grain supply for the city of Rome. He wielded power. He had responsibility. He was respectable. He was trusted by his colleagues. He had everything a man could want." Otho paused, as his sly eyes moved from one jury member to the next. "Except," Otho suddenly cried out. "Except, it was not enough for him. No, this man, he wanted more, more and more. This man was driven by ambition. He wanted unlimited power. He was conspiring and plotting to kill our emperor and the entire divine family and take over the government of Rome. That is treason! That is rebellion! It is most serious, gentlemen. Now, when his senatorial colleagues discovered this man's treasonous plotting, one of them - a senator of good standing, called Nigrinus, decided to confront this man. He could have taken his findings directly to Trajan but, because he was a friend, he wanted to give this man a chance to change his mind and repent. So, Nigrinus sent two senators, including his own cousin, to this man's house. They were there to confront the defendant and put an end to his treasonous plotting. But instead of civilised discussions what did the defendant do? What did he do to these two respectable members of the senate of Rome, who walked unarmed and unsuspecting into his home?"

Otho's eyes raked through the ranks of the jury members.

"He murdered them in cold blood, stabbed them with his own sword," Otho cried out. "That's what he did. He left them lying on the floor in his hall, where we found them several hours later." Otho paused for a moment, as he glared at the jury. "Now if this man were innocent as the defence claims, he and his family would not have fled; but they did. They ran all the way home here to the province of Britannia. If this man was innocent he would have stayed put and explained himself, but the cold facts of this case are that he cannot explain himself. He is guilty of cold-blooded murder and he should be executed for these crimes. That is what I want; that is what the senate in Rome wants; that is what the spirits of the slain want and that is what the gods demand."

"Counsel - proceed with your defence of your client," the governor growled as Otho sat back down behind his desk.

Swiftly Senovarus rose to his feet and came around his desk to face the jury. For a moment he said nothing, as he stared down at the fine mosaic patterns set into the floor.

"Gentlemen of the jury," Senovarus said at last, as he looked up at the jury. "The case presented against my client by the prosecution is a load of bullshit. This trial is not about treason or murder. My client is an honourable man, a decorated soldier, a war hero and one of our most valued veterans. He served for twenty-three years in the 2nd Batavian Auxiliary Cohort. He fought at Mons Graupius in Caledonia. He saved his entire unit at Luguvalium, during the great northern uprising. He served on the Danube where he lost two fingers and later, he served Rome faithfully in the senate personally leading the response to last year's grain riots." Senovarus paused. "This is not the kind of man who would even think about overthrowing our divine imperial family. He is a soldier and he has sworn an oath of allegiance, which he will never break. That is the kind of man my client really is. The accusations of treason are laughable. I could bring forth a hundred witnesses, who know the defendant and have served with him. All of them would back up what I am saying. So, do not listen to that cheap prosecution lawyer over there," Senovarus exclaimed, raising his hand

and pointing at Otho. "It doesn't matter whether the prosecutor cheats on his wife and is cruel to his dog. What matters is that he is lying. This case upon which you are asked to judge is not about treason or murder. It is simply about politics. My client is being persecuted for his politics. The prosecution is trying to dress this case up to look like a murder trial, when it is really about my client's support for Hadrian and the Peace Party, something which they, as members of the War Party, deeply resent. This case should be thrown out. Do not be fooled. I am not fooled. My client is not fooled. The people of this city are not fooled, and neither are the gods."

"Prosecution, you may reply," the governor snapped, as Senovarus returned to his seat.

"If I am trying to fool you all," Otho bellowed, rising to his feet, as he gave Senovarus a quick, furious glance, "and this is all just about politics as the defence suggests; then how do you explain the fact that the two senators were found murdered in the defendant's house? That is not normal, but the facts do not lie. How do you explain the fact that the defendant fled the scene with his whole family? How do you explain the fact that I have a witness, who was there and saw the defendant murder these senators in cold blood?"

"You have witnesses to the crime," Bradua exclaimed.

"I do," Otho growled.

"Then show them in," the governor replied. "I would like to hear what they have to say."

Standing in the middle of the hall, Marcus turned to glance at Kyna, but his wife quickly shook her head.

At Otho's desk one of his assistants got up and hurried away and, as he did, up in the public gallery the onlookers broke into muttering amongst themselves. Sitting on his bench, the governor seemed to have given up trying to silence the public and was instead staring down at his feet, as he waited for the witness to be brought forth. Marcus turned, as he heard one of the doors open. Then his face darkened, as he saw the prosecution assistant returning, leading one of his former household slaves by the arm. The freedman looked nervous and frightened, as he shuffled along towards the prosecution benches, refusing to look in Marcus's direction. As the man approached, Marcus saw that half his face was covered in bruises.

"Who is this man?" the governor called out, glaring at the witness.

"This man," Otho replied in a triumphant voice as he rose to his feet, "this man was a former slave who worked in the defendant's household in Rome. He was present Sir on the day that the two senators were murdered. He saw everything."

"Is this true?" the governor called out, fixing his eyes on the freedman. "You must answer me."

Standing beside Otho, the wretched-looking freedman seemed to be trembling with fear and for a long moment, he did not answer.

"Tell the governor what you saw that day," Otho interrupted, turning to the freedman. "It is important that this court hears what you have to say. You were there. Just tell us what happened and what you saw and what happened afterwards."

"I was a slave in the master's household," the freedman stammered at last, in a miserable sounding voice. "I served them for many years. The master and his wife were kind to me. They treated me well."

"What happened on the day of the murders?" the governor called out.

"The two senators came to the house," the freedman replied, as his hands trembled. "They were shown into the hall where my master met them. They talked. I didn't catch what about, for I do not listen to such conversations. Then my master and his bodyguard killed the two senators. They stabbed them with knives. After that they made me a freedman and fled the city. That's all I know. I swear by all the gods above and below."

An excited stir swept through the hall and, from the public gallery abuse was suddenly hurled at Marcus, who was standing in the middle of the hall with his hands tied behind his back. At the prosecution desk Otho, looked triumphant.

"What does the defence have to say to this," the governor called out turning to look at Senovarus.

"Really Sir," Senovarus said, angrily rising to his feet. "Does the prosecution really think that this man is a reliable and credible witness. Look at his face. Look at how he trembles. They have beaten him black and blue to force him to make these outrageous lies against my client."

"Do you deny then Sir," Otho interrupted. "That this man was a slave in the defendant's home in Rome? Maybe we should ask the defendant himself. Surely he knows what his slaves looked like."

"Well Marcus," the governor said, turning to look at Marcus. "Is this witness who he claims to be? Was he a slave in your household?"

"He was one of my slaves," Marcus replied in a calm and clear voice. "And yes, I did set him free, after the two senators were killed in my house. But he could not possibly have seen or heard what went on in my hallway, for the simple reason that he was out in my garden watering my flowers when the incident took place."

"You see he confesses," Otho cried out in triumph, raising his hand and pointing straight at Marcus. "He confesses to having killed the two senators. You heard him say it. He is guilty."

"Do you or do you not want to know what happened that day," Marcus roared as the courtroom erupted in shouts and cries.

"Silence, silence," the governor bellowed, as he rose to his feet and raised his hand. "Silence in my courtroom."

Then quickly Bradua turned to look at Marcus. "You wish to make a confession? You wish to make a statement?"

"I do Sir," Marcus growled.

"Then proceed," the governor said sharply.

Marcus was suddenly conscious that every eye in the hall had turned to stare at him and, as he paused, the silence in the courtroom grew more and more pregnant with expectation.

"I do not deny that two senators were found dead in my home," Marcus said, lifting his chin and gazing directly at the governor. "I do not deny that I and my family fled Rome shortly afterwards. We had good reason to flee. Our lives were in danger. The two senators did come to my house, but they did not come because of what the prosecution would have you believe. They came to kill me, to force me to kill myself because they believed I had been disloyal to the War Party, to their leader Nigrinus. They came to kill me because they believed that I had exposed their role in the plot to murder Hadrian, three years ago in Athens. They came because my son, Fergus is a close ally of Hadrian, and they suspected me of working with him to the detriment of the War Party's interests. But they and Nigrinus were wrong, for I am still a supporter of the War Party. I never betrayed my colleagues. I gave the War Party my oath of allegiance and I will not break it now for that would be dishonourable. If a loyal man can be convicted because powerful men are not interested in the truth, then Rome truly had lost her way."

Marcus paused, as he gazed at the governor, his face hard as nails.

"Yes, I killed those men, but I did it in self-defence. I did what any of you would have done, faced with the same choice. I do not regret what I did. What should I have done, die for a lie? Nigrinus gave me no choice. It was Nigrinus who sent these senators to my home. It is he who is responsible for their deaths. It is Nigrinus who bears that responsibility. This is all his fault." Marcus paused, and took a deep breath. "Sir," he continued; "if I have been disloyal, then it is only because that man is not fit to lead the War Party. He does not deserve to sit in the senate amongst such distinguished men as yourself Bradua. Nigrinus is a fucking loser and no honourable man will follow him. I was acting purely in self-defence. I never wanted any of this. I am a soldier of Rome, not a politician or a farmer or a lawyer. I am a soldier and I swore an oath of alleglance to our emperor. I have served Rome all my life as my father did before me and my son does right now. Do with me what you please, but if I am guilty of treason and murder, then so is every man who defends himself and his family."

As Marcus fell silent the courtroom too remained silent. Then abruptly, loud cheering broke out across the public gallery and several onlookers rose to their feet, clapping and shaking their fists.

"Marcus. Marcus. Marcus," the chant went up, as the court officials tried in vain to silence the crowd.

In his seat, the governor was slowly shaking his head, as he gazed down at the ground and around him the tumult grew. At the advocates desks, Otho was on his feet shouting and pointing at Marcus, but his words were lost in the uproar. At last Bradua raised his hand, calling for silence and order.

"This trial is closed," the governor bellowed. "The jury will retire, to consider their verdict. We shall reconvene here when they have come to a decision. Take the defendant away."

As the two guards seized Marcus by his arms and led him away, the courtroom erupted once again. From the seats behind the prosecution desks, Cunomoltus suddenly leaned forwards and reached out to slap Otho over the head. In the ensuing chaos, jostling and shouts of outrage, Marcus caught a brief glimpse of Kyna. She was staring in his direction and, as they made the briefest of eye contact she smiled bravely and tears formed in her eyes.

***

As the court reconvened and Marcus, under guard, his hands still tied behind his back, was marched back into the hall, the mood of expectation in the public gallery seemed to have reached fever-pitch. Leaving him standing in the middle of the hall, the two guards stepped backwards and took up position on either side of him. Directly ahead the governor was lounging in his chair, surrounded by his officials and advisers. For a moment Bradua turned to gaze at Marcus, then he looked away with an unhappy, troubled expression. In their seats, the twelve jury members were still talking with each other in urgent, hushed voices. Looking composed, Marcus turned in the direction of the advocates benches and the section of the courtroom reserved for family members. The tension on everyone's faces, as they awaited the verdict, was plain and clear to see. At his desk Senovarus was fiddling nervously with a pen, whilst close by Otho was staring moodily down at the floor.

"Has the jury come to a verdict?" the governor called out at last.

Amongst their seats one of the jury members solemnly rose to his feet and turned to face the governor.

"We have Sir," the jury member replied in a clear and loud voice.

"Will the jury read out the verdict," Bradua snapped, as a hush descended on the great hall.

"Yes Sir," the jury member replied. For a moment the man paused, looking down at his notes. "We the appointed jury members for this trial have not been able to come to a verdict," the man announced, turning to look at the governor. "The jury is split Sir. Six find the defendant guilty. Six find the defendant innocent."

Abruptly the jury member sat back down again, as an excited stir swept through the courtroom.

"Very well," Bradua exclaimed, as he looked down at the floor. "Then it is my prerogative as judge and senior magistrate to cast the deciding vote." For a moment the governor paused. Then slowly he turned to look at Marcus. "I find the defendant not guilty of the charges levelled against him, due to a lack of credible evidence," Bradua snapped. "The case shall be referred back to the senate in Rome, for them to decide what to do now. The defendant is innocent, and he is hereby acquitted. He is to be released. That's the judgement of this court."

As Bradua finished speaking a huge cry and shriek of joy rose from the public gallery. At his desk, Senovarus flung his pen onto the ground, hissing in delight whilst Otho, the prosecutor looked stunned and speechless. Marcus swayed slightly on his feet, as the outburst of noise swirled around him. In his seat, the governor had turned to look at Marcus, his stern face unreadable, but as their eyes locked onto each other, a subtle and silent exchange took place.

Then Senovarus was at Marcus's side, shouting at the guards to cut the ropes that bound his hands behind his back. A moment later, Kyna and Dylis too came rushing up to Marcus, as around them the courtroom descended into chaos. Embracing Marcus, the two women clung on to him, as the uproar grew and grew. Seated at his desk, Otho was staring into space. Then his face exploded into rage, as from behind him, Cunomoltus slapped him playfully over the head again.

"You are free Marcus," Kyna cried out in an ecstatic voice, as she tried to make herself heard above the noise. "You won Marcus. You have won. We can go home. It's over."

As the guards cut him free, Marcus grimaced as he was once more able to move his arms about again. Then before he could do anything else, Senovarus had grabbed hold of his right hand and was shaking it - the lawyer's face sporting a huge triumphant grin. Turning to Dylis, Marcus quickly reached out to embrace his sister in a fierce, silent hug. Then the press of the crowd was sweeping him towards the exit and out of the hall. As the people poured out of the palace and into the streets, the legionaries guarding the building hastily stepped aside. Around Marcus, voices were calling out his name and it seemed as if everyone was speaking at the same time. However, Marcus did not seem to be listening. Twisting round in the mass of people sweeping him out of the governor's palace, he was just in time to see Otho emerge from the building. The prosecutor seemed to be in an urgent conversation with one of his assistants. Then abruptly the assistant nodded and hurried away through the crowds and as he did, Marcus grimly lowered his gaze and turned to look away.

Chapter Twenty-Seven – News from the East

There was no one about on the road leading south towards the coast. In the blue summer sky, the sun beat down on the land, bathing the lush forests and green rolling hills in a shimmering heat. Out on the Roman road, the five riders trotted along, side by side, taking up the whole width of the highway with Marcus riding in the middle. He was clad in a long cloak and his left arm was once more trembling uncontrollably. Riding beside Marcus, Cunomoltus was softly and happily singing one of the Hyperborean songs to himself. Kyna meanwhile had her head turned towards the glorious sun and was bathing her face in its warmth. Indus had retreated into his usual silent self and was stoically gazing at the road. Only Dylis looked puzzled. For a while the five of them rode on without talking, heading southwards towards the coast, homeward bound to the Isle of Vectis that lay across the narrow straights. At last Dylis seemed unable to contain herself any longer and she twisted round in her saddle to look at Marcus.

"How the hell did you manage to get the governor to acquit you?" Dylis asked with a little puzzled shake of her head. "I still don't fully understand what happened in that courtroom?"

Marcus sighed as he reached out to gently rub his shaking left arm. Then he glanced over at his sister.

"Senovarus, your lawyer friend was right," Marcus replied. "The governor was facing a dilemma that could ruin his career and he was looking for a way out. So, before the trial, when you were all asleep, I slipped out at night and went to see him."

"You did what," Dylis exclaimed.

"I went to see Bradua," Marcus growled. "Like I told you. I knew him from my days in the senate in Rome. We are both members of the War Party. The governor was facing a dilemma that could cost him his career and possibly his life. So, I went to his palace on the river to offer him a way in which to save himself. I showed him a way out and he took it. I made a deal with him."

"A deal," Dylis spluttered in confusion.

"That's right," Marcus nodded solemnly. "I told the governor that Hadrian and his right-hand man and enforcer in Rome, Publius Acilius Attianus had put together a proscription list, a death list and that his name was on it. Once Hadrian becomes the new emperor, all the men on this list are going to be executed and their property seized. So, in exchange for acquitting me, I offered to get the governor's name removed from that proscription list, using Fergus' influence with Hadrian. That was the deal I made. I also told him, just to make sure that - if he allowed me to be convicted, a letter would be delivered to Hadrian, detailing the governor's personal complicity in the assassination attempt on Hadrian in Athens."

"How do you know about these proscription lists?" Dylis said with a frown.

Quickly Marcus glanced at Kyna and some silent communication took place between husband and wife.

"I know about the proscription list," Marcus replied, "because Fergus has informed me that my name too is on Hadrian's list. In Rome I met Attianus. He is one ruthless son of a bitch." Marcus turned to glance at his sister. "Once Hadrian assumes power, blood is going to flow in the streets of Rome. There is going to be a reckoning and a settling of scores. Attianus and Hadrian are going to have most of the high-ranking members of the War Party purged."

"So, you see sister," Kyna said, as she glanced carefully at Dylis. "Hadrian is not our friend either. He too is an enemy. He has so far refused to take Marcus from his proscription list because of that assassination business back in Athens - the attack that Fergus helped prevent."

"Only you. Only you, Marcus," Cunomoltus called out in a cheerful voice, turning to Marcus with a broad, happy grin, "could manage to offend the two most powerful men in the world at the same time. You are a stubborn old man. But I don't care about them. I am just glad that this is all over and that we're going home."

"This is not over yet," Marcus growled. "I cannot be legally tried for the same offence twice, but Nigrinus is not going to give up. He wants me dead. I fear now that he will resort to even more drastic measures to bring me down. We must remain on our guard. Nigrinus will not rest until I am dead. He will try again. One of those senators was his cousin or have you all forgotten that."

In their saddles, Marcus's words seemed to have a sobering effect on his companions and for a long moment no one spoke. At last Dylis frowned.

"How did you know that Marcus Appius Bradua's name was on Hadrian's proscription, death list," she blurted out.

"I didn't," Marcus growled as he turned away to look down the road. "I was bluffing but the governor bought it."

***

As Marcus and his four companions came trotting down the rutted track towards his villa on the Isle of Vectis, the slave standing on guard duty in the watch tower, blew his trumpet. The warning rang out across the golden wheat fields and the small vineyard that ran down the south-facing slopes of the nearby ridge. Riding up to the gates of his property, Marcus raised his hand in greeting as he saw Jowan and Petrus coming out of the house towards him. They were followed by a third man, who came limping across the courtyard towards the gates.

"You are back, Marcus," Jowan cried out, unable to hide the joy in his voice. "You won the case. This is great news. I shall have one of the sheep slaughtered and tonight we shall feast. All of us, we shall have a feast."

Dismounting Marcus grinned, as Jowan and Petrus hastened towards him and embraced. The men were laughing with relief.

"It's good to have you back, Marcus," Petrus called out, with a relieved smile. "Every day I have prayed to god for your release and now it seems my prayers have been answered. Thank and praise be to the Lord."

"It's good to be back home," Marcus muttered, as he fondly reached out to grip Petrus's shoulder. "Fucking hell is it good to be back here on the farm."

Then he turned and frowned as the third man came limping towards him. The fit looking stranger was in his early thirties and deeply suntanned.

"Is that you Aledus," Marcus exclaimed in surprise.

"It is Sir," Aledus replied, with a broad, happy smile. "I arrived two weeks ago, but you were away in Londinium. It's good to see you again Sir and you too Lady Kyna."

And before anyone could act, Aledus had smartly stepped forwards, taken hold of Kyna's hand and kissed it.

"We weren't sure who he was at first," Jowan said, glancing at Aledus with a grin. "He claims to be an old army buddy of Fergus and to have served together with him in the Twentieth. He knew so much about Fergus and yourself Marcus, that I decided to give him the benefit of the doubt and allow him to stay."

"Yeah," Petrus interrupted. "But I think he may have got one of the slaves pregnant. The girl you brought back from Rome. She doesn't seem to mind though, but I thought you should know, as she is your property."

Marcus nodded with a content, relaxed look, and for a long moment he said nothing as he grinned at Aledus. Then stepping towards the former legionary, he embraced him.

"It is good to see you again Aledus," Marcus said. "You shall always be welcome here on my farm. I know you and Fergus go way back."

Aledus smiled. "I have news Sir," he began. "News from the east, from Syria, from Fergus."

"News," Marcus repeated as around him he sensed his family tense with sudden expectation and dread. "We haven't heard from Fergus in nearly two years. What has happened to the boy?"

"Yes Sir," Aledus said with a quick nod. "After I left you at Portus I managed to find my way to Antioch in Syria. It wasn't easy but eventually I managed to find Fergus and convey your message to him. He and Galena and their daughters were well and in good health when I left him. This must have been autumn or winter, late last year, Sir."

Aledus paused as up on her horse, Kyna hastily dismounted and handed the reins of her horse to Petrus, before turning to stare intently at Aledus.

"Go on," Marcus said quietly.

"When I saw him Sir in Antioch," Aledus said, turning to Marcus "he had just been promoted to Tribune Laticlavius of the Fourth. It's a big promotion. He is now second in command of the whole legion Sir."

"The boy has done well for himself," Marcus growled approvingly, as he quickly glanced at Kyna.

"I believe the Fourth are involved in the invasion and fighting in Mesopotamia," Aledus continued. "That's what I have heard but I can't be sure. There are troop vexillations all over the fucking place. The picture is confused. A third of the whole army has been concentrated in the east. Maybe you know differently Sir, but the latest that I have heard, is that the war rages on without any sign of a final victory. The Parthians have not surrendered. Nor do they seem to be seeking to make peace. My guess is that Fergus and the Fourth are right in the thick of it, but he's a tough one Sir. Fergus will survive."

"My boy is on the other side of the world," Kyna exclaimed.

Aledus sighed and glanced around at the anxious, tense faces that were staring back at him.

"When I left him in Antioch, he told me to tell you to have hope," Aledus said quickly. "He told me that he would try and enlist Hadrian's help in this quarrel you have Sir with Nigrinus. Fergus however wasn't sure he would be able to do much. He says that Hadrian doesn't always listen. Nor is he always interested. Still he is going to try and use his friendship with Hadrian Sir to help you. That's what he told me."

"Hope," Kyna said. "Fergus told us to have hope?"

"That's right," Aledus replied. Then the former legionary's face brightened. "There is one piece of good news that Fergus told me. He has managed to get Hadrian to take your name off his proscription list. He wanted me to tell you that Hadrian no longer seeks your death. Don't ask me how he managed to do it, something to do with Galena and her friendship with Trajan's wife apparently."

"Well that is something," Marcus nodded approvingly. "That is something. So, we do not need to worry about facing Attianus when the time comes."

"Thank the gods Fergus and Galena and their daughters are all right," Kyna said abruptly, turning to look away. "Thank the gods. Thank the gods. I shall pray for their well-being tonight."

Marcus nodded in agreement.

"I am sorry Sir that it took me so long to get here," Aledus said in an apologetic tone. "Transport was not always easy to find. I was marooned in Crete for a month and the winter storms on the sea didn't help."

"It doesn't matter," Marcus replied, reaching out to pat the former legionary on his shoulder. "You are here now. I would like you to stay with us on the farm. I could use a man with your skills, experience and training. Are you willing to stay, Aledus?"

"I believe he is going to leave behind one very heartbroken girl if he leaves now," Petrus interrupted, raising his eyebrows as he did.

"Yes Sir. I want to stay here," Aledus said, ignoring Petrus. "When we parted company in Antioch, Fergus and I agreed that we would meet again here on Vectis. I have some family in Londinium but I am happy to stay here."

"Good, then it is settled," Marcus said as he turned to gaze at his farm.

"I can help out on the farm Sir," Aledus said. "I may have a limp, but I am not afraid of work. I can work in the fields or with the cattle."

"No," Marcus said sharply. "No, I have something else in mind for you. Something that you are far better qualified for. This business with Nigrinus. It is not over. So, I need you Aledus to do a job for me. I need you to start recruiting a dozen mercenaries; experienced men who know how to fight. I want you to recruit them and bring them here to defend my farm and my family, preferably before the first winter snows. And I am also going to need you to start preparing some fixed defences for me around the farm. Can you do that?"

For a moment, Aledus gazed at Marcus in silence. Then he nodded.

"A dozen trained men? Fixed defences. Shouldn't be a problem if you have the gold," Aledus replied. "Leave it with me Sir."

Chapter Twenty-Eight – An old friend Writes

January 117 AD

The long white rolling waves came crashing and surging up the sandy beach before eventually expending their energy and receding, hissing and foaming as if angry that they'd not been allowed to go any further. Marcus, clad in a thick winter's cloak made of fur, sat alone in his chair on the beach, gazing moodily out to sea. It was a cold, dry and blustery day and the breeze was whipping up the grains of sand and tugging at his long, grey beard. Along the towering cliffs to the west and on the higher ground in the direction of his farm, snow covered the rolling hills, fields and forests of Vectis in an endless blanket of whiteness. The heavily overcast skies seemed to have taken on the same colour as the sea and had merged into the restless waters. Marcus's left arm was shaking, and his face seemed to have shrunk and tightened, revealing his cheek bones. He looked old and worn out. Some way off, near the waterline, the solitary slave who had carried the chair for him, was playing with the three hunting dogs. The animals were barking excitedly and jumping about, as the slave sent them chasing after a piece of wood.

Alone and sitting in his chair out on the beach, Marcus turned to look down at his shaking arm. None of the doctors he'd visited had an explanation for the shaking or had been able to recommend a cure that was not completely stupid. He was just old Marcus thought with a resigned look, as he turned his attention back to the grey sea. Old. Or maybe Indus was right, and the shaking of his arm was a sign that he had been touched by the gods. Moodily, Marcus peered at the waves, as they came racing up the beach towards him but never quite making it. Maybe the gods were reminding him that his time was running out and that they expected him to fulfil the bargain he'd made with them – to do what they commanded in exchange for ensuring Fergus's survival. But what did the gods want him to do? There had been no signs, no omens, nothing except the continuous shaking in his left arm.

As he thought about Fergus, his mood seemed to lighten. The boy had done well, exceptionally well. Tribune Laticlavius, second in command of a legion! It was a worthy achievement. Corbulo, despite a lifetime's worth of service, had never managed to get beyond the rank of company Tesserarius, a lowly watch commander. He himself, Marcus thought, despite commanding the 2nd Batavian Auxiliary Cohort for a short period, had never risen any further up the army hierarchy. But Fergus; Fergus had managed to do what neither he nor Corbulo had managed to do. As he thought about his son, Marcus's cheeks coloured with pride.

With a sigh he reached into his tunic and carefully pulled out a small wooden writing tablet. The letter had arrived the previous day, delivered by a merchant on his way to Isca Dumnoniorum. For a moment, Marcus gazed down at the seal. The letter had come from Paulinus in Rome. Breaking the seal, he carefully opened the tablet and peered at the small and neat words scratched into the soft wood.

Paulinus to his old friend Marcus. Greetings. I heard about your trial in Londinium and that Bradua acquitted you. This is good news. Congratulations. Bradua has shown he is not a complete arse-licker after all, and I am happy for you Marcus. But I fear it is my lot to once again be the bearer of worrying news. Things are not going well for us here in Rome. Morale amongst the War Party is plummeting and the likelihood that Hadrian will be announced as the next emperor grows with every single passing day. We are expecting Trajan to announce it soon. Several of our colleagues have already switched sides and gone over to the Peace Party. I have heard that others are preparing to abandon politics and retire to their country estates. But they shall find no peace and safety there. I suspect Marcus, that some of our colleagues will prefer to kill themselves, before being forced to do so by that awful man Attianus and his band of cutthroats. How Hadrian manages to tolerate that vile creature I do not know. As for myself, I shall stay here in Rome to defend the Treasury. Someone must remain to look after the imperial finances, for they are far too important to be left to any man without an understanding of how to properly manage money. I have vowed to defend the Treasury with my life, for the state finances are my life and I am too old to start anew. I fear though, that in this climate, should they tear my fingers from the Temple's doors, rash men shall be put in charge of the treasury and make a mess of it. Rome may be guarded by the legions, but it is the Imperial Treasury that pays for it all and without that money we shall have only chaos and ruin.

But enough about my own troubles. I write to you, dear friend, to warn you that Nigrinus has taken your court victory rather badly. I have heard it on good authority that he now intends to personally come to Britannia. I do not know when he will go, for at this time of the year the Alpine passes will still be closed by snow. However, he may take a ship to Massalia and travel overland from there. It's hard to say. You should however expect him in the spring. His official purpose in visiting Britannia, I am told, is to try and secure the support of Britannia's three legionary legates and their troops. Nigrinus is hoping that with their support, he may be able to confront Hadrian. I suspect his mission will fail, for Hadrian will not have been so stupid as to have neglected placing his own supporters in high military command. The legates of the Second, Sixth and Twentieth will no doubt, by now all be led by men loyal to Hadrian.

Nigrinus still wishes you dead Marcus. I suspect that in addition to his official travel plans, he will also be coming to personally pay you a visit at your home on Vectis. You should make what preparations you can. Your devoted and loyal friend Paulinus, Chief Magistrate of the Imperial Fiscus.

Chapter Twenty-Nine - Veterans of Rome

The shrill peals of laughter drifted away across the muddy fields. It was noon on a fresh spring day and, out in the courtyard of the villa, Dylis's children were shrieking with laughter as they watched Cunomoltus's and Petrus's puppet show. The two men were standing behind a wagon, hidden by a curtain and were performing an outrageous comedy play, using crude puppets on strings. Close by, surrounded by some of his slaves, Marcus was sitting in a chair in the sunshine and grinning at the performance. At his side, Kyna, her hand resting on her husband's shoulder, was chuckling, as she stood watching the scene.

The winter snows had not entirely melted and, across the fields and in the nearby forest, patches of snow remained but there was no doubt that spring was in the air and with it, the promise of new life and warmer longer days. The mood amongst the spectators was upbeat. Surrounded by buildings on three sides, a long wooden table and dozens of chairs had been brought out and placed in the middle of the courtyard. Upon it lay numerous food dishes and jugs of drink, all in preparation for the feast and party later, to which all, including the slaves, were invited; to celebrate the end of the long, dark winter. Near to the gates and the boundary fence, Jowan had appeared, clutching a fat pheasant in his hands whilst his bow and quiver were slung over his shoulder. He was leading the three excited hunting dogs back to the farm. Carefully he skirted along the edge of the rows of sharpened wooden stakes that had been driven into the ground and were pointing outwards at an angle away from the farm.

Sitting on the ground around Marcus, the slaves suddenly cried out, hollering in approval and started to clap as the puppet show finally came to an end. Marcus grinned and joined the calls of approval before turning to look at Aledus, who was limping towards him from the direction of one of the barns. The former legionary was accompanied by the slave girl, who had come with them from Rome. The heavily pregnant girl was clutching and stroking the black cat, which they had also been brought back from Rome. For a moment Marcus eyed the couple. The slave girl was his property, and, by rights, he could have charged Aledus with damaging his property. But that was a stupid idea. It would be better if he agreed to free the girl and allow her to marry Aledus. The love between those two was clear to everyone. Still toying with the idea, Marcus looked up, as Aledus came up to him,

"We're ready to give you the demonstration now Sir," Aledus said with a grin. "Shall I call out the men?"

"Go ahead," Marcus said, with a curt nod.

In response Aledus turned around and whistled, using his fingers and mouth. A moment later the spectators in the courtyard gasped, as one of the barn doors was flung open and one by one the dozen mercenaries who Aledus had recruited the previous summer, came out. The burly, tough-looking men were clad in a dazzling and exotic assortment of Roman and foreign body armour and were carrying surplus legionary shields, spears, battle-axes, spiked clubs and swords. Silently, in single file, they strode towards the small makeshift arena that had been erected in the courtyard and, as they did, the family and the slaves rushed over to the circular wooden fence that stood in for the Coliseum of Rome. On Aledus's shouted order, the mercenaries came to a halt, smoothly turned to face Marcus and Kyna and bowed.

"Those who are about to get their arses kicked, salute you Sir," Aledus called out, as he turned to look at Marcus with a big grin.

"I look forward to it," Marcus called out.

An excited stir swept through the gathered spectators, as the first pair of mercenaries dumped their weapons onto the ground retaining only their shields, ducked into the arena and picked up the wooden training swords, that had been placed there. With a grin, the two men turned to face each other in a mock gladiatorial combat. Then with surprising speed, the two clashed, striking and lunging at each other with their wooden weapons. A roar of encouragement rose up from the spectators as the two men grunted, moved, jabbed and blocked each other, as if they were fighting for their lives under the gaze of the emperor and fifty thousand spectators. Soon the spectators, standing around the small, marked-off space had broken into two groups, each cheering on their favourite fighter with loud enthusiastic cries.

Marcus was eagerly watching the contest and chuckling at the men's antics, when suddenly from the corner of his eye, he noticed movement beyond the boundary fence and the rows of sharpened wooden spikes, at the edge of one of the fields. A huge, black wolf was standing in the muddy field silently gazing at the mock arena. In its mouth the beast was carrying a dead rabbit. Marcus stiffened, and abruptly the colour drained from his face. Slowly he rose to his feet, as he stared at the animal. Out on the edge of the field, the wolf slowly turned its head and for a moment its yellow eyes seemed to be gazing straight at Marcus. Then, as the three hunting dogs began barking wildly, the wolf turned and calmly ambled away towards the forest, clutching the rabbit in its jaws. Around Marcus the cheering of the spectators faltered, and then died away, as all caught sight of the expression on his face.

"What is it Marcus?" Kyna asked in an urgent voice, as her face turned to alarm.

"It's just a wolf from the forest," Cunomoltus exclaimed, but as he caught sight of Marcus's expression, he too faltered.

On his feet, Marcus said nothing as he watched the beast disappear into the forest. His face was ashen. Then abruptly his features hardened. "I am not afraid of you," Marcus hissed defiantly to himself.

Before anyone could do anything or say anything, a trumpet rang out across the courtyard and the fields beyond. Startled, the spectators turned in the direction of the watchtower beside the gates, where the slave on watch was standing, clutching his trumpet. There was no need to explain the reason for the warning. Galloping towards them down the uneven farm track was a solitary horseman.

Striding towards the gates of his property, Marcus's eyes were suddenly fixed on the horseman, as he recognised the owner of a neighbouring farm.

"Marcus," the man cried out in an urgent voice, as he raised his hand. "Marcus, strangers have been spotted on the island. We counted at least thirty to forty armed-men and some of them have horses. They are heading your way."

**

As the first of the strangers appeared on the track leading to his farm, Marcus, with Indus standing behind him, turned to look down the length of the fence that marked the boundary of his property. The fence itself was not much of a defence and had not been designed to keep people out. It could be broken with one well aimed kick. A few yards beyond it though the rows of dense sharpened wooden stakes extended right around most of the villa and its outhouses, forming a double perimeter. Here and there gaps had been left in the outer defences. In front of the gates however, protecting and blocking the entrance into his property, two heavy but portable wooden anti-cavalry frames had been placed, their rows of sharpened, fire hardened and blackened wooden stakes facing outwards.

Marcus was clad in auxiliary chain mail armour and from his belt hung a sheathed gladius and a pugio, army knife. He was bareheaded, his old, crinkled face was as hard as iron, and his long grey beard fluttered in the breeze. In his hands he was gripping a spear and a small round shield. Gathered around him, Jowan, Cunomoltus, Dylis and Petrus were all armed with an assortment of leather body armour, shields, axes, spears, knives and swords. They looked nervous and tense, as they stared at the approaching horsemen and men on foot who were spreading out across the field, like a dark swarm of insects. Up in the watchtower beside the gates, Kyna, and Dylis's fifteen-year old son were crouching on the platform. In their hands they were holding bows. Calmly Marcus turned to look at his wife. Kyna had raised her bow and was pointing it at the strangers with trembling hands. As he gazed up at her on her platform Kyna seemed to sense him looking at her and turned in his direction and as she did Marcus smiled with sudden fondness. Kyna's hands were not trembling out of fear. It was rage.

At the gates Aledus and his band of mercenaries had gathered together and were stoically peering at the strangers who were slowly advancing towards them. The mercenaries were clad in their body armour, helmets and were gripping their shields and weapons.

On the ground directly below the watchtower, a party of male slaves had gathered together, armed with scythes, pitch-forks, hammers, stones, knives and whatever weapons they could find. Quickly Marcus turned to look back at the villa. Dylis's twins, the female slaves and their children were nowhere to be seen. In the middle of the courtyard, the table full of food and drink, prepared for a party stood, looking forlorn, abandoned and forgotten. In the doorway to one of the barns, one of the slave boys, too young to fight, stood bravely grasping the leads of the three dogs and shouting at them. The dogs were barking, their jaws snapping eagerly as they strained at their leads.

Out on the track and across the fields, the approaching strangers slowly advanced towards the gates and the rows of sharpened stakes. The neighbour had underestimated their numbers Marcus thought. There had to be at least forty armed men, possibly as many as fifty and a third of them seemed to be on horseback. The strangers were clad in dark tunics over which they were wearing coats of chain mail armour. On their heads they were protected by legionary style helmets and they were armed with small, round shields, spears, axes and swords. They looked like they knew what they were doing. Some of the men had hoods drawn across their helmets and all looked well-armed, prepared and confident. Catching sight of Nigrinus riding towards him on a white stallion, Marcus swore softly to himself. Nigrinus was clad in gleaming chainmail armour, sporting a spectacular winged helmet on his head and clutching a spear and, as he spotted Marcus, he calmly veered towards him, surrounded by five mounted bodyguards.

"You should have run, Marcus," Nigrinus bellowed, as he lowered his spear and pointed it straight at Marcus. "You should have run!"

"I am not running from a shit like you," Marcus roared.

"Then you are going to die," Nigrinus bellowed in a furious voice, his eyes gleaming with rage, as spittle flew from his mouth. "I am going to hack you into little pieces right in front of your family's eyes."

"It does not have to be this way," Marcus roared. "You can still turn around and walk away. You do not have to do this. Go home Nigrinus. Go home."

"Home," Nigrinus yelled as he came to a halt a few yards from the fence. "Home! Only ruin and death await me back in Rome. No, I will not go home. If I am going to die, then I am going to take you with me Marcus. You and I are going to hell together, to burn in the flames of Tartarus for all eternity."

"You have lost your mind," Marcus yelled, glaring at Nigrinus. "But if it is my death that you seek, then I challenge you to single combat. I challenge you Nigrinus to try and kill me, man to man. Have you got the balls to do that? Or has fear and terror reduced what manhood you still claim to have?"

On his horse Nigrinus laughed. "I am not so stupid as to fall for your tricks Marcus. You betrayed me, you killed my cousin and for that, you are going to die. I have come to take your head Marcus. I have come to slaughter your family and burn your farm to the ground, so that no trace of your existence shall remain. You are finished. You are going to die today, right here."

Suddenly from atop the watchtower, a woman screamed; a scream of pure fury and hatred and with such vent, that it sent a chill down everyone's spine. From her position Kyna took aim, and sent an arrow flying straight at Nigrinus. The aim however was wide and, instead of striking the man, it hit his horse sending Nigrinus tumbling to the ground with a startled cry. Instantly everything descended into chaos. With a loud outraged bellow, Nigrinus's men charged. As some of the horsemen and men on foot came storming through the gaps in between the rows of sharpened wooden stakes, the ground suddenly gave way beneath them, and with startled, shocked cries, horses, riders and men abruptly went crashing down into the deep camouflaged killing pits and the sharpened wooden stakes that awaited them at the bottom. As beast and man was impaled in the cunningly hidden pits the shrieking and screaming of wounded, dying men and beasts sent flocks of birds rising and fleeing from the nearby trees. Seeing their mounted comrades fate however did not deter the rest of the attackers. Struggling and forcing their way past the sharpened stakes and outer defences Nigrinus's men came surging forwards in small groups of two and three and within seconds the wooden fence marking the edge of the property had splintered and broken beneath their charge.

With a roar of his own, Marcus leaped forwards and drove his spear straight into one of the men charging towards him, nearly impaling him. Yanking his spear out of the dying man he swung it at another's head, knocking him to the ground. At the gates and beside the shattered fence, Aledus and his men seemed to have taken the brunt of the assault. The mercenaries had formed a tight disciplined defensive circle and were standing shoulder to shoulder. There was however no chance of going to their aid. Caught up in fierce hand-to-hand combat, the mercenaries quickly vanished from view, surrounded by a horde of Nigrinus's men. A chaotic, confused mass of screaming, brawling, battling men was swirling around the gates and the anti-cavalry frames as they stabbed, blocked and hacked at each other. At the base of the watchtower the group of slaves was being pressed backwards, as they desperately tried to fend off the attackers.

Flinging his spear at a man running towards him, Marcus yanked his gladius, short sword from his belt. Dimly he was aware of Indus at his side, using his shield and sword to block the blows and deadly spear thrusts that were aimed at himself and Marcus. The savage, unrelenting noise of combat filled the villa's courtyard. Close by, Jowan and Cunomoltus were parrying and fending off three attackers, desperately trying to hold them back but Nigrinus's men outnumbered them and slowly but steadily, Marcus and his five companions were being driven backwards towards the house and away from the slaves, Aledus and his mercenaries. Blocking a man's sword thrust, aimed at his chest, Marcus savagely slashed open his attacker's throat, sending a fine spray of blood shooting through the air. Close by Dylis, with a dead man lying at her feet, was screaming, her face contorted in rage, as she wielded her blood-covered axe with the fury of a mother protecting her children. But, as he blocked another spear thrust at him, Marcus caught sight of Petrus lying on the ground without moving and with blood seeping from a nasty wound to his abdomen.

Next to Marcus, Indus had begun to sing to himself, a Batavian battle song that only he knew, as with fearless concentration and skill, he fended off the attacks directed at Marcus. At the watchtower the slaves had had enough and had broken, fleeing in panic towards the shelter of the barns with some of Nigrinus's men in pursuit. Marcus paused, panting from exertion. With the resistance of the slaves broken, it would not be long before Nigrinus would have them surrounded with their backs against the house. Jowan and Cunomoltus were still on their feet, but they were not trained in hand-to-hand combat like he and Indus. They were not going to hold out much longer. They were going to die and so was Dylis. He had to do something and fast.

Blocking a sword thrust Marcus kicked his attacker backwards. Up on the watchtower he could hear Kyna screaming, but there was no time to see what was going on. His wife and Dylis's teenage son were on their own. Suddenly through the chaos and confused fighting, Marcus caught a glimpse of Nigrinus, wearing his winged helmet. Nigrinus was on his feet, standing back from the fighting, protected by his five bodyguards. Four of the guards had dismounted and Nigrinus was shouting and gesturing at the fighting as if he were in command of a legionary cohort and directing a battle. With a hoarse cry Marcus launched himself at the two men blocking his path, forcing them backwards. Then he was past them and storming towards Nigrinus, his sword stained with blood. Anger lent him strength and courage. Here and there a man leapt into his path to try and intercept him, but he drove them backwards with his shield and sword. A moment later Indus appeared behind him, still singing his savage Batavian battle song, his tunic and arms stained in blood. The faithful Batavian bodyguard had loyally followed him into the very thick of the fighting and the heart of the enemy position.

"You are mine Nigrinus. You are mine," Marcus roared, as he advanced towards him with murderous intent.

Standing back from the fighting beside a section of the ruined and shattered fence, Nigrinus finally spotted him and as he did he raised his spear and pointed it straight at Marcus.

"There he is," Nigrinus bellowed. "Get him. Get him. Kill him."

Ignoring the swirling, screaming battle around them Marcus and Indus stormed deeper into the enemy ranks towards Nigrinus and as they did men peeled away from the fight with Aledus and his mercenaries and came lunging at them. Within seconds Marcus and Indus were surrounded and hopelessly cut off from the others as more and more of Nigrinus's men were drawn away from the mercenaries and into defending their leader. Desperately, Marcus tried to hack his way towards Nigrinus, but there were just too many men blocking his path. Howling and yelling at him, Nigrinus's men pressed around him furiously jabbing and stabbing at him with their weapons. Giving up the attempt to reach Nigrinus, Marcus and Indus instinctively twisted around and, standing back to back, they turned to face and fend off their attackers. Indus was still singing but his voice was growing laboured, as he blocked and parried the growing number of frenzied blows that were coming in at him. Suddenly Marcus cried out in pain, as a knife slashed across his upper leg. Swiftly he was struck again in the shoulder by a blade that pierced him. With a groan he staggered backwards, bumping into Indus as the men around him yelled in triumph. Behind Marcus, Indus seemed to explode in rage. With an ear-shattering bellow, the Batavian dropped his shield, yanked a pugio knife from his belt and, clutching weapons in both hands, he boldly, crazily and fearlessly launched himself head-long at the two men who had knifed Marcus. The momentum of his attack sent all three of them crashing to the ground, but Indus was the only one who tried to stagger back to his feet. The others lay on the ground with Indus's weapons stuck in their throats, blood spurting into the air. But as he staggered to his feet, Indus was swiftly cut down by several swords and knives, collapsing silently onto the bodies of the last two men he'd killed.

Dimly Marcus was aware of triumphant screams and movement around him. Desperately he tried to stay on his feet, as he felt the blood trickling down his chest. Then the breath was knocked out of him, as a sword savagely drove into his back and another stabbed him in his abdomen. Groaning again, Marcus dropped his sword and collapsed onto his knees amongst the corpses. Swiftly someone kicked him in the head and sent him crashing sideways onto the ground.

Time seemed to slow.

Marcus lay on the ground, his eyes glazed and unresponsive. The pain in his body seemed distant and unreal and he couldn't move. The noise of the fighting seemed to dim and grow distant. Was it all over? Marcus's breathing came in weak, ragged gasps. Close by, Indus lay on top of the two men he'd killed, his sightless eyes staring at Marcus. Standing over Marcus, a figure suddenly appeared. It was Nigrinus, his silent face curling in contempt and then triumph. In his hands the man was holding a knife. Then with a terrifying surge of noise and movement reality came rushing back to Marcus and the noise of fighting filled his ears. Something was happening behind him. Close by, one of Nigrinus's bodyguards suddenly staggered forwards and collapsed with a spear sticking out of his back. Another of Nigrinus's bodyguards, still sitting on his horse, was roughly and violently flung from the saddle, as two arrows thudded into his exposed neck. A ragged, defiant roar rose up from somewhere out of sight. Gazing up at Nigrinus, Marcus saw his enemy's face swiftly change from triumph to terror as another of his guards sank to his knees and was cut down by an axe. Abruptly Nigrinus vanished from Marcus's view.

A few moments later Cunomoltus and Aledus hove into view, their faces filled with alarm and shock as they bent over Marcus looking down at him. They were talking but their words were not registering. The remaining mercenaries were storming passed him, screaming in triumph as they seemed to be pursuing someone out of sight. Mustering the last of his strength, Marcus was able to turn his head. The fight seemed to be over. Had he won? Across the barren fields and rutted track, Nigrinus and a few of his surviving men were fleeing, running for their lives whilst a rider-less and terrified horse galloped away towards the forest. As he gazed at the scene without understanding, Marcus saw an arrow bring down one of the fleeing men and another wounded straggler set upon by his three hunting dogs who started to tear him apart. The unfortunate man's terrified shrieks rent the afternoon. Then slowly the light dimmed, and Marcus lost consciousness.

***

Kyna was trembling as she looked down at Marcus, lying in the bed inside one of the villa's rooms. Beside her stood the doctor and Aledus, his forehead covered in a bloody bandage. Cunomoltus were silently gazing down at Marcus whose eyes were closed. He was still unconscious. Marcus's wounds had been bound with fresh white bandages, but his breathing was weak, and he looked in a bad way. At Kyna's side, Cunomoltus, one of his legs covered in a bandage, quietly reached out to steady her.

Then he glanced across the room to where Dylis was leaning against the door. Marcus's sister had an ugly gash across her face, but apart from that, she looked unhurt. She was staring at Marcus with a hard, uncompromising gaze.

"By all laws of medicine," the doctor said, with a weary sigh, "he should not be alive. The wounds he sustained should have killed a lesser man days ago. He is holding onto something, something that is refusing to let him die."

"Is it that bad doctor?" Kyna asked in a voice devoid of all emotion. Her face was ashen.

"The doctor is right," Aledus muttered. "With these wounds, he should have been dead by now, but he is holding on to life. It can't last. He is not going to recover. No man can recover from such wounds. It's just a matter of time until he succumbs."

"I fear he is right," the doctor replied lowering his eyes.

A wretched sob was Kyna's only answer and, leaning against the door, Dylis lowered her gaze to the floor.

"Three fucking days," Cunomoltus exclaimed, shaking his head. "He has been like this for three days. What is he holding out for? How long can he last?"

"I don't know," the doctor replied, with a weary shrug. "He is a strong man and the human body constantly surprises me, but it won't go on forever. If you must still prepare, I suggest that you do so now. The time left him in this world is short. You should prepare. He hasn't got much time left."

"We have made all the preparations," Dylis snapped from the doorway.

"Good," the doctor said, turning to glance quickly at Kyna. "I advise that someone is at his side day and night."

"Someone will be," Cunomoltus said quickly. "Thank you, doctor. We appreciate all that you have been able to do."

At Marcus's bedside, the doctor nodded and then, giving Marcus a final resigned glance, he reached out to shake Cunomoltus's hand, before leaving the room.

Once the doctor was gone, Aledus sighed and slowly turned to glance at Cunomoltus and then Dylis.

"He and Indus turned that battle you know," Aledus said with a little disbelieving shake of his head. "That crazy, foolish charge straight towards Nigrinus drew in Nigrinus's men. It took the pressure from us and allowed us to regroup and hit back. He did that. He bought us that space. Kyna, you and Dylis's son killed three men with those bows of yours and wounded many others. You did well." Aledus lowered his eyes. "I have to admit that I didn't think any of you would put up the fight that you did. You are not trained for this but boy was I wrong. We kicked their arses."

"We did it for him and because this is our home," Cunomoltus said in a serious voice gesturing at Marcus. "All of us. We fought for him for he has a way in bringing the best out in us."

"I know," Aledus muttered. "However, we still have a problem. Nigrinus is still out there. Our situation is dire. We may have beaten him back, but he could return with reinforcements. I don't think that man is going to rest until he has seen that Marcus is dead. We are in no state to fight him a second time. Half my mercenaries are dead, as is Indus and some of the slaves and Petrus is badly wounded. All of us have wounds. We are exhausted. If Nigrinus comes back, we cannot fight him."

"What would you have us do?" Dylis sneered in a contemptuous voice. "Would you have us abandon our home. I am not leaving, and neither are my children. Marcus was right, this is our home."

"We are not leaving this farm," Kyna said suddenly. She was standing gazing down at her husband, her face filled with resolve. "I am not leaving. They will have to kill me before I leave this place."

A tense silence descended on the room.

"The doctor said he is clinging to life," Cunomoltus said at last. "What is he clinging to? What is making him refuse to die?"

"Who knows?" Aledus muttered in a weary voice.

Once more a sombre tense silence descended on the room. Then abruptly the silence was shattered as outside, a trumpet suddenly rang out. In the room all turned to stare at the door in horror. Quickly Cunomoltus pushed his way past Dylis and hobbled through the villa, until he emerged into the courtyard. The late afternoon sunlight bathed the farm in bright light. As Cunomoltus stepped out of the house, he was swiftly followed by Aledus, Jowan and Dylis - all armed.

At the shattered fence, the female slave on watch in the watchtower once more blew on her trumpet and the haunting sound went ringing out across the fields. Moving towards the gates, Dylis suddenly gasped and raised her hand to her mouth. Out on the rutted track leading towards the farm, horsemen had appeared, their armour gleaming in the sunlight. The riders, at least thirty of them, seemed to be in a hurry as they came galloping down the track, sending clumps of mud flying up into the air. Leading them was a red-haired man clad in a fine legate's armour and red cloak, and at his side, rode a soldier holding up the proud square vexillation banner of the Twentieth Legion. As they drew closer, Aledus suddenly cried out, unable to hide his excitement.

"It's Fergus! That's Fergus! It's Fergus!"

"Good gods," Cunomoltus exclaimed, as he went down on his knees in the mud. At his side, Dylis still had her hand clasped to her mouth. Then slowly she shook her head in disbelief.

"Aledus," Fergus shouted, as he peered at the four figures ahead of him. "Aledus is that you?"

"It's me," Aledus roared with delight, as he opened his arms wide in triumph. "Thank fuck you have come Fergus. Thank fuck. You have no idea. You have no idea how good it is to see you."

Slowing his horse, Fergus came trotting towards the gates and, for a moment, he paused and silently turned to gaze at the rows of sharpened wooden stakes, the debris of the ruined, shattered fence and the murder pits still containing the impaled corpses of dead horses and men. At his side, his legionary cavalry escort, came to a halt as the soldiers turned to look at the debris of battle that lay scattered across the fields. Further back coming towards the villa along the track a horse-drawn wagon had appeared in which Galena and her daughters were sitting, gazing anxiously towards the house. The wagon was surrounded by another troop of armed cavalrymen acting as escort.

"Where is my father?" Fergus cried out, as he turned to stare at Dylis, Jowan, Cunomoltus and Aledus. "Where is my father? Where is my mother? What has happened here?"

***

"Father," Fergus said quietly, as he stood in the room looking down at Marcus and holding his hand while Marcus lay in his bed with his eyes closed. "Father. It's me, Fergus. I have come home. I am here with you now."

Standing around the bed, Cunomoltus, Kyna, Jowan, Dylis, Galena and Aledus were gazing down at Marcus, as he lay motionless in his bed.

"He hasn't spoken a word since Nigrinus attacked us," Cunomoltus said at last. "The doctor says he is refusing to die, but that it won't be long now. I am sorry Fergus, but there is nothing more that we can do. His fate is in the hands of the gods."

Fergus remained silent as he gazed down at Marcus. Then with a weary sigh he looked up and glanced at Galena.

"How long has he got?" Fergus asked no one in particular.

"Not long," Kyna replied.

"Good gods how could this have happened," Fergus said, turning away with a little bewildered shake of his head and clutching his father's hand. "How could this have happened? How?"

In the room no one replied and, as the silence lengthened the mood grew more and more oppressive and sombre.

"Fergus," a voice suddenly whispered and, startled, all turned to look down. In his bed, Marcus's eyes had suddenly flickered open and he was gazing up at Fergus. "Fergus," Marcus whispered again in a weak voice that was barely audible.

"I am here father," Fergus replied, gripping Marcus's hand.

"Fergus," Marcus groaned softly. "I am glad. The gods...they want me to join them. They call to me, they summon me, but I would not go. I told them I would not go until I had seen your face one more time."

"I am here father," Fergus said in a reassuring voice. "I am here now."

"You are the father now," Marcus whispered in a faint voice, as his eyes flickered and tried to focus on Fergus. "Look after them. Ensure their survival my boy. Nothing else matters."

"We are all here for you father," Fergus said quietly. "We are all here. Your family is here for you. You have made us who we are. You have been the rallying point around which, we have become who we are; thank you father, thank you."

Around the bed, a mutter of agreement broke out. Then Kyna reached out and gently and lovingly ran her hand across her husband's cheeks and, as she did, Marcus's eyes turned to look up at his wife.

"You are loved Marcus," she said quietly, with a fond smile, "You are loved by all of us. I shall see you again in the next world husband. I shall remain at your side for all eternity, like I promised. You saved all of us. You have won, Marcus. We shall not forget, we shall not forget."

In his bed, Marcus smiled and then closed his eyes and did not answer. Fergus gasped and looked away and, as he did Galena appeared at his side, her eyes filled with concern.

"Let him go to the gods," Galena said quietly, as she reached out to grip Fergus's arm.

***

It was a cold morning, two days, later when around the copse of trees, beside the old moss-covered memorial stone to Corbulo, the small gathering of people stood sombrely looking down at the freshly dug and covered grave. Fergus clad in his legate's uniform, his red cloak nearly touching the grass, stood to one side, his arms linked together with Galena and Kyna, standing beside him. The two women were clad in black mourning clothes and their faces were veiled. Opposite Fergus, an honour guard made up from the troopers from his cavalry escort, stood stiffly to attention, their armour gleaming in the morning light. At the base of the grave, the family and the slaves had gathered together clad in their mourning clothes. The stretcher on which Petrus was lying had been placed on the ground in front of them and on it Petrus lay grasping his wooden cross as he gazed at the grave with tears streaming from his eyes.

No one spoke. At last Fergus took a step forwards and solemnly knelt beside Marcus's grave. For a moment he said nothing as he gazed down at the disturbed soil. Then he reached out with his hand to touch the upturned soil and simultaneously lowered his head, until it rested on his chest. Silently, he said his prayer and, once he was done he rose to his feet and turned to Kyna. In response Kyna, her face obscured by her black veil, took a step forwards and knelt beside the grave. For a moment the copse remained silent, except for the gentle wind rustling in the nearby trees.

"Lords of the underworld, fair gods and spirits, hear my lament," Kyna said quietly, as she slowly closed her eyes, lowered her head and extended her arms over the grave. "Take my husband, my man Marcus into your embrace. Look after him. He goes to you willingly and unafraid. He is a good, honourable man, a soldier who faithfully served Rome, a fine father, brother and husband - the best that nature can produce. Treat him well for he deserves nothing less. Hear also you immortals, guardians of the life beyond this one, I, Kyna, wife of Marcus, give praise to my veterans of Rome, for they are my veterans of Rome. My father-in-law Corbulo, my husband Marcus and my son Fergus. Better men this world has not known, and I look forward, unafraid to the day when I shall see them all again, united once more."

Chapter Thirty – The Legate of the Twentieth Legion

Autumn 118 AD, Deva Victrix, home base of the Twentieth Legion, Britannia

As Fergus in his fine cuirassed body armour and legate's cloak strode into the Principia building at the heart of the legionary fortress of Deva Victrix, the legionaries on guard duty saluted smartly. Inside his personal quarters in the HQ complex, Fergus sighed and wearily took off his helmet, rubbed his red hair with his hand and placed the helmet on a nearby table. Through the open doorway into his family's rooms, he could hear Galena arguing with Briana and Efa, his two eldest daughters. With a little bemused smile, Fergus moved away from the doorway and reached out to pour himself a cup of wine. His girls were growing up so fast. Briana was already thirteen and it would not be long now before he would have to consider her marriage. But the thought of marrying off his daughter filled him with revulsion. It could wait. Taking a sip of wine from his cup, he looked down at the array of official documents that lay on his table. All seemed urgent. In a corner on the table, a stone bust of emperor Hadrian looked down sternly on the room. Sitting down on the edge of the table, Fergus turned to look around his quarters. Through the doorway, Galena's dispute with her daughters continued without remorse.

As his gaze settled on two small clay figurines that stood on his desk, his eyes narrowed. Here he was, Fergus thought, as he took another sip of wine. Here he was at the age of thirty-two, commander and legate of the Twentieth Legion, a legion he had joined as a common soldier; as an eighteen-year old recruit. It was the legion his grandfather Corbulo had first served in sixty years ago and it had a proud history. And now he had made it to the very top. His dream had become reality. He had made something of himself. He had risen from the lowest rank to the highest rank in the legion. It was an astonishing and meteoric rise, but he could not have done it without his father having been a senator or Hadrian's influence and friendship. He could not have done it without the inspiration his grandfather had provided. Would Marcus and Corbulo be proud? With a contented look, Fergus raised his cup in the air, as if saluting an imaginary friend. Then he sighed. He was not only legate of the Twentieth Legion, but also the head of his family and owner of the family farm on Vectis, responsible for all who lived there. One day, when he finally retired, it would be to Vectis, where he would retreat with Galena and where he would grow old with her. But that too could wait. He was still only thirty-two.

On the table, a scroll suddenly caught his eye and reaching out, he plucked it from the pile. It was a letter and, as he peered closer at the seal, he saw that it had come all the way from Rome. With a frown, Fergus broke the seal and unrolled the parchment.

Lady Claudia to Fergus, legate of the Twentieth Legion at Deva Victrix, Britannia. Greetings Fergus. I am writing to you because I have heard about the death of your father Marcus and would like to convey my deepest sympathies. I knew your father well and loved him dearly. He was an honourable man, who served Rome faithfully and it is with great sadness, that I heard about his death. You and Kyna have my condolences and my prayers. I also wish to inform you, in case you are not aware, that emperor Hadrian and his praetorian prefect Attianus have been consolidating their power. Nigrinus, Quietus, Palma and Celsus, the principal leaders of the War Party, have all been executed on Hadrian's orders. The charges were for plotting to assassinate the new emperor, although there were no trials. I must too, add the sad news that my, and your father's old friend, Paulinus, chief magistrate of the Imperial Fiscus has also been murdered. Paulinus was a good man and did not deserve his fate. I am told that they had to drag him kicking and screaming out of the Temple of Saturn in Rome before he was killed. I know you and I come from opposing factions in the senate, but I would like to ask you, out of respect to your father, that we bury these differences, now that we have a new emperor. Your father Marcus was a great man, representing the true heart and nobility of Rome. I recognised that the first time I met him.

I want you to know that I shall soon be leaving Rome and returning to Britannia and I will be bringing Ahern, your half-brother with me. Please let Kyna know for, I know how much she will be missing him. It would give me great pleasure if we could meet when I return to Britannia. Please write as soon as you can and let me know. Your most loyal friend, Claudia.

Lowering the letter Fergus suddenly became aware of Hera, his Mesopotamian slave standing and staring at him from the doorway to his family's quarters.

"You. Look. Sad. Master," the little girl said in broken Latin.

"No," Fergus said as a broad smile appeared on his lips. "No Hera. I am not sad. I am a happy man. Everything is as it should be."

Author's Notes

One of the things that I have tried to reveal throughout the whole Veteran of Rome series is the process of Romanisation that took place in many Roman provinces with Britannia being just one example. In Britannia most people's lives would have at first been relatively unaffected by Roman rule. The people by and large would have gone on living as per before in their small scattered settlements, living off the land, honouring their own gods and maintaining their tribal traditions. Contact with real Romans would have been limited. Taxes would have been imposed on them by a centralised and sophisticated Roman bureaucracy but it's likely the locals already paid some form of tax to their own kings before Roman rule.

As Roman rule endured however the locals would have started to notice changes. Hardened roads would have appeared making it easier to travel. New towns would have appeared - markets would have suddenly been filled with strange new and exotic foreign goods. Long distance travel would suddenly have become more feasible. New techniques of farming, building, new technology and new industries would have appeared creating work and growing wealth. Whereas before the locals would have likely produced only enough food to feed themselves and their community the Romans would have encouraged local farmers to maximise their surplus production of food and sell it in the market to feed the thousands of troops stationed in the province. A similar revolution would have occurred in mining with the Romans pushing production of gold, lead and silver to the limits to pay for the army upkeep. No doubt some smart local entrepreneurs would quickly have become very wealthy under Roman rule as I have tried to show with Dylis and the farm on Vectis.

The phycological impact on the local populace must have been immense. Seeing a bath house and piped running water for the first time must have been an amazing experience on par with eating garum and sweet apples. We can only guess at what the locals really made of it all, but I suspect most would have liked what they saw and would have taken quickly to the new way of life filled with new possibilities and opportunities.

This leads me to Corbulo and his family. Corbulo would have been a full Roman of Italian stock originating from the small town of Falacrinea, near Narnia, seventy-five miles north east of Rome in central Italy (yes, it's mentioned in chapter 15 of Caledonia). Marcus his son however would have been half of Italian stock and half Celt. Fergus, Corbulo's grandson, would have been only a quarter of Italian stock and three quarters Celt and Fergus's daughters only an eighth of Italian stock. Yet it is Fergus, Galena and their daughters who are almost fully Romanised and it is Fergus who rises to one of the highest military positions possible. I have done that because I wanted to show that within a few generations of the start of Roman rule, local men would have been playing a large role in the running and security of the provincial administration. This is highly likely. It shows the success of the Romanisation process and it reveals one of the secrets to the longevity of Roman rule. Over time as they became more integrated the local populations would have tacitly started to support Rome and defend their new way of life. In this period before the rise of the nation state, what the Roman empire did was in effect divide Europe into those who were growing increasingly prosperous and sophisticated and those that were not. The ones on the outside increasingly coveted what the populations in the empire had thus eventually leading to the catastrophe of the fifth century when the Germanic and central Asian tribes mucked it up for all of us.

Veterans of Rome is book nine and the final book in the Veteran of Rome series. **What next?** Well I shall soon be embarking on a brand-new Roman series that will follow Corbulo's paternal ancestors through their long and arduous fight against Hannibal during the epic 2nd Punic War. There is going to be a lot of fighting during this – Rome's finest hour. The link between Corbulo and his ancestors is referred to in chapter twenty of this book. The first book in the new series will hopefully be ready by Christmas 2018. I hope you will read it.

William Kelso, London, June 2018

MAJOR PARTICIPANTS IN "VETERANS OF ROME"

Corbulo, Marcus and Fergus's family

Kyna, wife of Marcus, mother of Fergus

Corbulo, Marcus's father, Fergus's grandfather

Ahern, Kyna's son by another man. Jowan forced to adopt him

Elsa, orphaned daughter of Lucius, but adopted by Marcus and his family

Cassius, Elsa's husband and Marcus's secretary

Armin, orphaned little brother of Elsa

Galena, wife of Fergus

Briana, Fergus and Galena's first daughter

Efa, Fergus and Galena's second daughter

Gitta, Fergus and Galena's third daughter

Aina, Fergus and Galena's fourth daughter

Athena, Fergus and Galena's fifth daughter

Indus, Marcus's Batavian bodyguard in Rome and ex-soldier

Aledus, Friend and army buddy of Fergus

Dylis, Marcus's half-sister, adopted by Corbulo

Cunomoltus, Marcus's half-brother, illegitimate son of Corbulo

Jowan, Dylis's husband

Petrus, Christian boy rescued by Corbulo

Imperial family

Marcus Ulpius Traianus, Emperor of Rome (Trajan) AD 98 - 117

Plotina Pompeia, Empress of Rome, Emperor Trajan's wife

Salonia Matidia, Trajan's niece

Members of the Peace Party

Publius Aelius Hadrianus, (Hadrian) Leader of the peace party

Adalwolf, German amber and slave trader, but also guide, advisor and translator for Hadrian

Vibia Sabina, Hadrian's wife

Publius Acilius Attianus, Hadrian's old childhood guardian (Jointly with Trajan)

Marcus Aemilius Papus, friend of Hadrian

Quintus Sosius Senecio, soldier and supporter of Hadrian

Aulus Platorius Nepos, Roman politician and soldier

Admiral Quintus Marcius Turbo, close friend of Trajan and Hadrian

Members of the War Party

Gaius Avidius Nigrinus, Senator, leading citizen in Rome and close friend of Trajan. Leader of the war party and potential successor to Trajan

Lady Claudia, a high-born aristocrat and old acquaintance of Marcus

Paulinus Picardus Taliare, one of Rome's finance ministers, in charge of the state treasury

Aulus Cornelius Palma, conqueror of Arabia Nabataea and sworn enemy of Hadrian

Lucius Pubilius Celsus, Senator and ex Consul; bitter enemy of Hadrian

Lusius Quietus, Berber prince and Roman citizen from Mauretania in northern Africa, a successful and popular Roman military leader

Marcus, Fergus's father, senator and supporter of the War Party

The Armenians and Parthians

Osroes I, King of Kings of Parthia

Parthamasiris, Nephew of Osroes, who became king of Armenia

Parthamaspates, Parthian vassal king, installed by Trajan

Volagases III, rival Parthian king to Osroes, rules in eastern Parthia

Sanatruces, nephew to the king of kings Osroes

The Fourth "Scythica" Legion

Gellius, legionary legate of the Fourth legion

Britannicus, a young tribune angusticlavii with the Fourth Legion

Dio, a veteran centurion in the Fourth Legion

Other Characters

Cunitius, a private investigator and one-time enemy of Marcus

Heron of Alexandria, a Greek mathematician, engineer and inventor

Similis, ex-prefect of Egypt, placed in charge of all security matters in Rome whilst Trajan is away in the east

Alexandros, Greek captain of the ship Hermes that sailed to Hyperborea with Marcus

Cora, Alexandros's wife

Calista, Alexandros's daughter

Jodoc, Calista's husband

Senovarus, Marcus's defence lawyer in Londinium

Felix, A member of the speculatores, law enforcers

Ninian, Dylis's business agent and grain broker

Hedwig, Batavian officer served with Marcus in the 2nd Batavian auxiliary cohort

Wolfgang, Hedwig's nephew

Marcus Appius Bradua, Roman governor of Britannia

GLOSSARY

Adiabene, region in north-eastern Iraq

Aerarium, State treasury for Senatorial provinces

Aesculapius, The god of healing

Agora, market place and public space

Agrimensore, A land surveyor

Albania, Roman client kingdom at the southern foot hills of the Caucasus

Aila, Red sea port now called Aqaba in Jordan

Alae, Cavalry unit

Alani, A Scythian people living on the steppes to the north of the Caucasus

Armorica, Region of north-west France

Amphorae, a large two-handled storage jar having an oval body

Antioch, Near Antakya, Turkey

Aqua Sulis, Bath, England

Aquila, a sacred gold and silver eagle standard, one for each legion

Aquilifer, a legionary eagle standard bearer

Aquincum, Modern Budapest, Hungary

Arabia Nabataea, modern day Jordan and northern Saudi Arabia

Araxes river, also known as the Aras. Former border between the USSR and Iran

Arcidava, Fort in the Banat region of Dacia

Argiletum, Street of the booksellers in ancient Rome

Artaxata, ancient capital of the kingdom of Armenia

Asses, Roman copper coins, money

Athena, Greek goddess and protector of Athens

Babylon, city 50 miles/80 km south of Bagdad

Babylonia, region around Babylon, Mesopotamia

Balearic isles, Islands of the eastern cost of Spain.

Ballista, Roman artillery catapult

Banat, Region of Dacia, Romania and Serbia

Batavorum Lugdunum. Near Katwijk, the Netherlands

Berzobis, Fort in the Banat region of Dacia

Bonnensis, Bonn, Germany. Full name

Burdigala, Roman city close to modern Bordeaux, France

Bostra, a Roman occupied town in Jordan

Byre houses, crude barbarian dwellings made of wood, thatch and mud

Caledonia, Scotland

Camulodunum, Colchester, England

Capitoline Hill, One of the seven hills of ancient Rome

Carnuntum, Roman settlement just east of Vienna, Austria

Carrobalista, Roman artillery catapults/crossbows mounted on wagons

Castra, Fort

Caltrops, small spiked metal anti cavalry and personnel weapons

Cataphracts heavily armoured shock cavalry

Cappadocia, Roman province in central and eastern Turkey

Caucasian Gates, Darial Gorge Georgia/Russia border

Centurion, Roman officer in charge of a company of about 80 legionaries

Cella, internal space in a temple

Chaboras river, now known as the Khabur river, tributary to the Euphrates

Charax, near modern day Basra

Chatti Confederation, Germanic tribal confederation

Cilicia, Roman province in modern Turkey

Circesium, a town now called Buseira in Syria

Classis Germanica, Roman fleet based on the Rhine

Classis Pannonica, Roman fleet based on the Danube at Carnuntum

Cohort, Roman military unit equivalent to a battalion of around 500 men

Colchis, land around the south-eastern part of the Black sea

Colonia Agrippina, Cologne, Germany

Commagene, Roman province

Consul, Governor of a province.

Contubernium, Eight-man legionary infantry squad. Barrack room/tent group room

Cornucopia, horn

Corona Muralis, Roman military decoration

Cornicen, Trumpeter and signaller

Cuirassed armour, Expensive chest armour that followed the muscles of the chest

Cyrenaica, eastern part of Libya

Currach, Celtic boat

Cataphract, type of heavily armoured cavalry

Ctesiphon, Parthian winter capital, near modern Baghdad

Dacia(n), The area in Romania where the Dacians lived

Decanus, Corporal, squad leader

Decurion, Roman cavalry officer

Demeter, Greek goddess of agriculture

Denarii, Roman money

Derbent, claims to be oldest town in Russia, on the Caspian-sea

Deva Victrix, Chester, UK

Diane, the Goddess of the hunt

Domitian, Emperor from AD 81 – 96

Doura Europus, Near to Salihiye in eastern Syria

Draco banner, Dacian coloured banner made of cloth

Edessa, Sanliurfa, now in southeastern Turkey

Emporium, Marketplace

Elegeia, Armenian town in the region of Erzurum

Eleusinion, Temple of Demeter, Athens

Eponymous Archon of Athens, The city's ruler and mayor

Equestrian Order, The Order of Knights – minor Roman aristocracy

Equites, Individual men of the Equestrian Order

Erebus, the Greek god of darkness and son of Chaos

Euphrates, major river in Iraq, Syria and Turkey

Falx, Curved Dacian sword

Fallujah, Fallujah in Iraq

Fibula, A brooch or pin used by the Romans to fasten clothing

Fiscus, The Roman state treasury controlled by the emperor and not the senate

Focale, Roman army neck scarf

Fortuna, The Goddess of Fortune

Forum Boarium, The ancient cattle market of Rome

Forum Romanum, Political centre of ancient Rome, area of government buildings

Frisii, Tribe of Frisians who lived in the northern Netherlands

Gabala, ancient capital of Caucasian Albania

Gades, Cadiz, southern Spain

Garum, Roman fermented fish sauce

Gladius, Standard Roman army short stabbing sword

Greaves, Armour that protects the legs

Hatra, Hatra in Iraq

Hellenistic, Greek

Hengistbury Head, Ancient Celtic trading post near Christchurch, UK

Hermes - Messenger of the gods

Hibernia, Ireland

Hispania, Spain

Hyrcanian Ocean, Caspian Sea

Hyperborea, Mythical land beyond the north wind

Iberia, Spain but also a small Roman client kingdom south of the Caucasus

Imaginifer, Roman army standard bearer carrying an image of the emperor

Imagine, image of the emperor

Imperator, Latin for commander/emperor, used to hail the Roman emperor

Intentio, the reason for the trial and the charges against the defendant

Invidia/Nemesis, God of envy and vengeance

Insulae, Roman multi-storey apartment buildings

Isca Augusta, Roman legionary base at Caerleon in southern Wales

Isca Dumnoniorum, Exeter, England

Janus, God of boundaries

Jupiter Optimus Maximus, Patron god of Rome

Kaftan, Parthian dress, a long traditional outer garment

Kostolac, City in Serbia

Keffiyeh, Traditional Arabic headdress

Kushan Empire, Afghanistan, Pakistan and parts of India

Lares, Roman guardian deities

Iazyges, Barbarian tribe, roughly in modern Hungary

Legate, Roman officer in command of a Legion

Liburnian, A small Roman ship

Limes, Frontier zone of the Roman Empire

Londinium, London, UK

Lower Pannonia, Roman province in and around Hungary/Serbia and Croatia

Ludus, School

Lugii, Vandals, barbarian tribe in central Europe

Luguvalium, Carlisle, UK

Magusanus, Batavian deity

Mars, Roman god of war

Marcomanni, Barbarian tribe whom lived north of the Danube in modern day Austria

Mardi, Armenian tribe that lived around lake Van

Massalia, Marseille, France

Mausoleum of Augustus, Mausoleum of Augustus in Rome

Mesopotamia, modern Iraq

Mithras, god of a mystery religion in Parthia

Middle Sea, Mediterranean Sea

Minerva, Roman goddess of wisdom and commerce

Mogontiacum, Mainz, Germany

Mons Graupius, Roman/Scottish battlefield in Scotland

Mosul, Mosul northern Iraq

Munifex, Private non-specialist Roman legionary

Neptune, God of the oceans and seas

Nero, Roman emperor 54-68 AD

Nike, Greek god of victory

Nisibis, Known now as Nusaybin in south-eastern Turkey

Noviomagus Batavorum, Nijmegen, The Netherlands

Noviomagus Reginorum, Chichester, UK.

Numerii, Germanic irregular soldiers allied to Rome

Numidians, one of the Berber tribes of northern Africa

Nymphaeum, monument consecrated to the water nymphs

O group meeting, Modern British army slang for group meeting of officers

Onagers, Heavy Roman artillery catapults

Oppidum, tribal capital city

Optio, Roman army officer, second in command of a Company

Ostia, Original seaport of Rome

Osrhoene, a Roman client kingdom around Edessa

Palatine Hill, one of the seven hills of Rome. The Imperial palace there

Palmyra, Palmyra in Syria, ancient city partially destroyed by IS

Panathenaea, Ancient Greek festival in honour of Athena

Parthamaspates, Puppet ruler of Mesopotamia installed by Trajan

Parthian Empire, Iraq, Iran and parts of Saudi, Syria and central Asia

Parthenon, The temple of Athena on top of the Acropolis in Athens

Peplos dress, traditional dress presented to the goddess Athena

Peristyle, open space surrounded by vertical columns

Petra, Petra, Jordan

Pilum/pila, Roman legionary spear(s)

Pistorum, college of bakers

Porolissum, Settlement in northern Dacia/Romania

Portus Augusti, The new seaport of ancient Rome

Portus Tiberinus, Rome's Tiber river port

Posca, watered down wine with added spices

Praefecti Aeranii Saturni, Rome's finance ministers

Praetorium Agrippina, Roman fort in the delta, The Netherlands

Prefect, Roman officer in command of an auxiliary cohort or civil magistrate

Praetorian Guard, Emperor's personal guard units

Principia, HQ building in a Roman army camp/fortress

Propylaia, ancient monumental entrance gate into the Acropolis

Proscription list, a death list

Pugio, Roman army dagger

Quadi, Germanic tribe living along the Danube

Resafa II, Fictitious Roman fort near Sergiopolis

Rosia Montana, Ancient gold and silver mining district in Romania/Dacia

Roxolani, Barbarian tribe in eastern Romania

Rutipiae, Richborough, Kent, UK

Sacred Way, Important road in the ancient city of Rome

Satala, east of Sadak in Turkey on the ancient border with Armenia

Sarmatians, Barbarian allies of the Dacians

Sarmatian cataphracts, Heavily armoured Sarmatian cavalry

Sarmisegetusa Regia, Capital city of ancient Dacia

Saturn, God of wealth

Saturnalia, Roman festival in late December

Scythians, Barbarian tribes, modern Ukraine and Russia

Seleucia, city just west of Ctesiphon

Singidunum, Belgrade

Sirmium, The ancient city of Sirmium on the Danube

Singara, modern Sinjar in northern Iraq

Speculatores - law enforcers on a governor's staff

SPQR, Senate and People of Rome

Stola, Woman's cloak

Stoas, covered walkways

Styx river, Mythical river of the underworld

Stylus, Roman pen

Subura, Slum neighbourhood in central Rome

Sura, ancient city on the Euphrates river in Northern Syria, west of Raqqa and north of Resafa

Tapae, Dacian fort at the entrance to the iron gates pass

Tara, Seat of the High King of Hibernia, north-west of Dublin, Ireland

Tesserarius, Roman army watch/guard officer, third in line of company command

Tessera tile, A small stone carried by the Tesserarius on which the daily password was written down

Testudo formation, Roman army formation, covered by shields, and tactic

Tibiscum, Fort in Dacia

Tigris, major river in Iraq

Tribune (military), A senior Roman army officer

Tribune Laticlavius, second in command of a legion

Trireme, A fast agile galley with three banks of oars

Tubula, trumpet

Turmae, squadron

Tutela, the duties of guardianship

Ulpia Noviomagus Batavorum, Nijmegen, The Netherlands

Urban cohorts, A kind of anti-riot police force in ancient Rome

Island of Vectis, Isle of Wight, UK

Velarium, Retractable canvas roof over the Roman colosseum

Velum, Parched animal skin used as writing paper

Vestal Virgins, Female priestesses of ancient Rome

Vespasian, Roman Emperor 69-79 AD

Vexillatio(n), Temporary Roman army detachment

Viminacium, Roman town on the Danube in modern Serbia

Viriconium, Wroxeter, England

Via Traiana Nova, Roman road between Bostra and the red sea port of Aila (Aqaba)

Zeugma, Roman city located on the Euphrates in Gaziantep province, Turkey

Printed in Great Britain
by Amazon